Summoned to a Fantasy World and Left to Die

SUMMONED TO A FANTASY WORLD AND LEFT TO DIE

SHAUNA SAGAJI

BOOK 1

SAGAJI PUBLISHING

Content Warning

This book contains mature themes and explicit content intended for adult readers. Set in a dark, magical realm filled with evil goblins, vicious monsters, dark fairies, uppity elves, colorful dragons, and other savage beasts.

Please be advised of the following content:

Violence and Gore: Includes graphic scenes of violence involving magical beings, with detailed descriptions of injury and death.

Kidnapping and Threats: The main character experiences kidnapping and is subjected to threats and psychological distress.

Sexual Content: Features explicit sexual content, including consensual and non-consensual advances.

Dark Fantasy Themes: The story prominently features magic, man-eating monsters and other fantasy elements.

Strong Language: Contains frequent profanity and graphic language.

Suicidal Ideation: Contains depictions of characters experiencing suicidal thoughts. These scenes are emotionally intense and may be distressing to some readers.

Other Content: Includes elements of light dubcon (dubious consent). *Note: There is no depiction of rape, though such topics are mentioned in dialogue.*

Reader discretion is strongly advised.

THE WORLD OF THERION
Empire of Sebbarus
Lunaris Bay
The Yurakora Kingdom
Castdor
Tithmar Forest
Magdara
Razakar
Yenka
Kingdom of Palloria
Glendara
Bloodthorn Region
Veldrisca

TABLE OF CONTENTS

PROLOGUE

KALIYAH

Finally, the reprieve I've been begging for. I can't even remember the last time I cleared my head, let alone just let loose. This will be my first real moment of peace in what feels like forever. With graduation feeling like it happened a lifetime ago, let's just say the life plans I'd mapped out have been anything but smooth. The deadline on my carefully plotted five-year post-college plan is creeping up fast, and I've checked off exactly none of it. So far, all I've managed to accumulate is stress, regret, a disturbingly expensive coffee habit, bills, bills and more bills.

Sure, I landed a position at the company I used to dream of working for and I was genuinely excited about it. But that was back when I believed hard work and commitment would actually get me far. It's been years and I'm still not thriving. I was supposed to be running the show, making all the moves by now. Not stuck playing support to some overconfident dick, who by the way used to moan and groan under *my sheets*.

Ugh... the intern. The one I was *training*, coaching, practically nurtured success to. The same one who used to show up at my place with bottom-shelf wine and that cheap smile. Kissing me like he was on a timer. Like he had to move fast, otherwise I'd realize he wasn't even that damn cute. And he wasn't. It wasn't like it was anything serious, though. It usually isn't with any guy I decide to give my attention to. But a girl's got needs. Needs that never seem to get met. Just skin, sweat, and way too many nights ending with me staring at the ceiling, wanting more.

He was just convenient. Occasionally charming when he felt like turning it on. He knew *kinda* how to work the rhythm. How to almost get me there... *but* always stopping just short of hitting the damn spot. What the hell was I even on? I cut him off weeks ago.

I'm not *emotional* when it comes to men. I never fight, argue or cry over them. And when I'm done, I'm just done. And thank God I was. Because when I found out the same man who used to stumble around my apartment at two in the morning, was about to walk into the office, *my* office with a shiny new title. I nearly lost my damn mind. The intern is the new boss?

My. Fucking. Boss? I had to let that marinate. Because *what*?! I mean... *what the actual hell*? I damn near choked on my coffee when the security guard, yes, *the building security guard* of all people, dropped the news like it was nothing. *He* got the promotion? The man I coached, practically spoon-fed the entire company handbook to was now calling the damn shots. Like I haven't been busting my ass for the past five years at that crappy piece of shit company.

And damn it. If only it really *was* a crappy piece of shit. I can't even front. I really like my job. The benefits are solid. Health care? Excellent. Paid time off? Generous. The fresh snacks and cold brew in the lounge every morning? Not mad at it. And don't even get me started on that end-of-year bonus. Chef's kiss.

I actually enjoy the freakin' work I do there. That's what pisses me off even more about the whole thing. The audacity. The fucking *absolute* nerve. I was *this close* to setting the whole damn building on fire. Strutting my curvy ass down the hallway like the queen grampa raise me to be. My chocolate-colored middle fingers in every direction, giving no fucks and leaving nothing but ashes and a string of whispered "damn, she really did that," behind me.

But then... the '*payment due*' notification hits my phone once again, and I remember. That's right, I have student loans. My crushing "you'll die with me" student loans. So, I gritted my teeth and made myself a deal, one more year. *One. More. Year.* Then I'm walking in there, handing over my resignation with a smirk that screams "F.U. Bitches. I'm out!"

My grampa, the only parent I've really ever had, offered to help me out. Told me I should quit, live a little, stop selling my soul for pocket change. As if he has some lumpsum money or retirement fund that I don't know about.

Hell. It's possible, knowing him. That old man's a legend in his own right. Used to run with one of the hardest crews in Houston back in the day, the kind of gang you didn't speak about unless you wanted your teeth kicked in, literally. He was *that* guy. Fists like bricks, a temper like boiling water, and loyal as hell. Then he had my mom, and yeah he slowed down, but the streets still called to him here and there.

It wasn't until she died, no sooner than after having me. I became the apple of his eye. With no knowledge of who my biological father was, my grampa didn't even flinch to drop everything and walk away from that life. Many thought he wouldn't be able to stay away. Actually, from what I heard, nobody did.

He went from thug to doting grandfather, like he was just flipping on a switch. But don't get it twisted, just because he traded in street wars for bedtime stories doesn't mean he got soft. My old man still not a ninja to be mess with, by any means. He walks into a room and the energy shifts. Calm. Cool. A real badass. He raised me the same way. Taught me how to take a hit and deliver one that'd make the devil flinch and apologize.

But, I've definitely peeped a shift in him these past few years. I don't know if it's him getting up there in age or its do to the new woman on his arm, but he's laxer, cheerier around the edges. The old dude even laughs louder than before. Like, for real?

But okay. I'll let him have that. She's good for him. Now they're out here living their best life. All loved up and stuff. I'm happy for him. It's about time he started enjoying life for real. I used to worry he'd be alone forever, all because he put so much on hold for me. Yeah, *it's his time.*

But as for me... I'm stuck, like for real. Caught somewhere between who I used to be, all bold and full of heat and lowkey pissed at who I've turned in to. Every day I'm being grinded down, like life got this little-ass box it swears I'm supposed to fit in to. Sometimes it just feels too damn tight.

That's exactly why, when Darrius called and said the crew was linking up at some sketchy-ass cabin in the woods, I didn't hesitate. I needed an out. Out of my head, out of that office. Out of the cycle that was slowly crushing my passion down to dust. Even if Ryan was probably cooking up some crazy plan, and Jemma already had that *let's get reckless* look in her eyes, I knew we'd end up wildin' out just enough to make me appreciate my mundane life.

The plan was to go on some backwoods hike to find a hidden watering hole that supposedly swallowed up a bunch of folks' stuff. Lost waterproof cameras, smartphones and other random junk Ryan was told about on whatever forum he spends hours scrolling on. Given how adventurous Ryan is and how much of a wild card Jemma loves to be, it was only a matter of time before we ended up deep in some mess that would drag me *way* outside my comfort zone.

Sure enough, there I was. Wandering through the woods like I had lost every last piece of common sense, chasing rumors. And let's be clear, I can't swim. So no, I had no plans on throwing myself into murky waters, trying to dive for crap.

But Darrius... That man never backs down from a dare. And Ryan being Ryan, he threw out some dumb bet, something from his family's pawn shop if Darrius actually took the plunge. Nothing too valuable, just enough to get the testosterone flowing. Idiots. Both of them. Meanwhile, I was too busy trying not to get eaten alive by mosquitoes the size of toddlers. And frogs? Yeah... not my ministry either. And, spoiler alert, we didn't find any freakin' watering hole. We kept searching, and I was deep in that "to hell with this" mood when we stumbled on something. Not what we were looking for. But, it *was* something.

Straight-up creepy. Like, haunted vibes for real. Had me feeling all prickly. Hairs on my neck standing. There were weird looking boulders, laid out in a perfect semi-circle. Half-covered in thick vines and flowers you don't just see at your local nursery, all colorful and more importantly strange. Strange because I didn't notice any of these same flowers growing in the rest of the woods. Most of which didn't look familiar. If I'm being real, it looked like the perfect place for the local psycho to sacrifice his goats. And as the two resident Black folks of the group, Darrius and I were definitely hesitant to explore any further.

But of course, with Jemma's curiosity on freakin' one hundred, she wanted to go and do the most, like always. She called Darrius over to explore with her like it was some mystery begging to be solved. And just like that, I lost my only ally... all because of his long-standing, one-sided crush.

The air shifted when they stepped closer. Darrius and I locked eyes and we exchanged the silent *'we shouldn't be here'* look. Putting my black ass in a horror-movie situation? Yeah, nah. *Not me.* Ryan knew I wasn't vibing with this, so he gave me the 'devil-may-care' look. An inside joke we've had since college. And damn if it didn't stir something in me, reminding me of the fierce, impulsive version of myself I used to be. Before responsibilities and adulting scraped the shine right off me. And for a second... just a second, I missed that girl. The one who didn't flinch. The one who walked towards the unknown daring it to blink first.

So, like a child baited by candy, I stepped forward. I pushed the vines aside and behind them, a design etched with spirals and curved lines all over. This place had such a weird feeling. It felt both familiar and estranged all at once. And then came the light. Soft at first. Gentle, like a whisper. Then blinding. Violent. *All-consuming.* The carvings erupted in white, searing light that didn't just shine, it *devoured.* Reality split at the seams.

Jemma screamed. Darrius cursing. Ryan silent. We all grabbed for each other, as the world around us *fractured.* And in that instant, all the bullshit clouding my mind. My job. My ex-intern-turned-boss. My failure to thrive. My too-long list of dreams deferred. All of it evaporated. Swallowed whole by that roaring, impossible storm of light.

CHAPTER 1
RENAISSANCE

KALIYAH

A sudden rush of quiet. Jemma's head buried into my shoulder, our bodies tightening, as the blinding light slowly faded around us. The air shifted, no longer thick with the scent of earthy damp soil and fresh pine. In its stead, a musty fragrance, and something... else. Something exotic.

Then, without warning, the sounds of trumpets burst through the air, so loud it rattled every bone in my body. Jemma screamed at the deafening noise. Her pitch so shrill that it felt like it cracked the sky. It was as if the very heavens had opened up, and the end of the world had come to claim us.

I blinked, trying to ground myself in reality. But when I finally managed to open my eyes, like really open them. The sight that greeted my gaze was enough to make my knees weaken. The woods we had been standing in were gone. In its place was something I could only describe as otherworldly. We stood in the center of a courtyard, surrounded by stones similar to the ones we'd discovered in the woods, though these were different. They looked newer, or at least well-maintained, as if time and nature had yet to grace them. Beneath our feet lay a much larger symbol, one that matched the intricate designs etched into the stones, sprawled across the smooth cobblestones.

Vibrant flowerbeds bloomed around us, their colors so vivid they almost looked fake against the lush greenery. The walls surrounding the courtyard rose high, constructed of pale stone, and carved with delicate vines that climbed up their surfaces, not much different than the ones we had seen cradling the boulders in the woods. Above us, the sky stretched out endlessly, bright and blue, its vastness making the whole place feel open. The vibes were all over the place. This wasn't just a charming stone courtyard with a rustic flare. No. There was something far more medieval about it.

People in what looked like Renaissance attire crowded around us, their garments ranging from flowing robes to full plate armor. Their faces slowly came into focus as their excited murmurs and cheers filled the air, all while the glow from the peculiar boulders that stood around us pulsed like a heartbeat. Each one of those rocks seemed to hum with an energy I couldn't even begin to understand. I tried to speak, to ask what the hell was going on, but Ryan beat me to it. His voice attempting to crack through the noise. My breath caught in my throat as I turned to him, but it wasn't the words that stopped me. It was the daunting presence of someone I could sense somewhere within the space.

My eyes shuffled around and that's when I saw her. At the far end of the courtyard, standing tall and unblinking, was a figure. A woman. Her presence so commanding that it felt like the air itself bowed to her. Wearing a gown of flowing silk, shimmering in deep violet and gold, emphasizing her slim curves and generous cleavage. The gown bares her shoulders, arms and hips, her skin glowing like desert sand kissed by the sun. A crown resting atop her head. There was a stunning display of radiant amethysts, rubies, and diamonds that gleamed with a dazzling burst of color. She was beautiful. Breathtaking, even.

But then, a question gnawed at me, one that refused to let go. *Is she real?* Is any of what I'm seeing in front of me actually here, or am I just having some kind of stress-induced hallucination, brought on by one of Jemma's gummies and not enough sleep?

The world around me felt... off. Too surreal. The edges of everything seemed to shimmer, like the air itself couldn't decide if it wanted to stay solid or slip into another state of matter. My heart thudded in my chest, and I had to force myself to stay grounded.

That's when her gaze locked with mine, and in that moment, I held my breath. My chest tightened, and for the briefest second, I convinced myself I was dreaming. I've been dealing with sleepwalking since I was a kid. Sleepwalking as in waking up in weird-ass places with zero clue how I got there. It used to be really *bad* when I was younger, but by the time I hit my late teens, it started to calm down. Not because of some miracle cure or anything like that.

No. It took a *whole* lot of therapy. My now *ex*-therapist basically found a way to trick my brain into tying the control of my consciousness to something tangible. Specifically, the necklace Grampa gave me.

As long as I'm wearing it, I have full control over my actions. At least, that's what I have to *believe* for it to work. And it does. For the most part. I mean, if I'm being honest, there *was* that one time at Darrius's birthday bash. But I'm pretty sure that had way more to do with the number of wine coolers I downed. Two. That's my limit. Freakin' lightweight. I've gone six years without any serious incidents.

My ex-therapist used to say I was relying too much on her tethering technique. Said we should root out my underlying issues and really work through them. But after having peace for this long, not waking up in the middle of a bus station with an uneaten pancake in one hand and a headless frog in the other, I'd rather save my coins and stick to her proven technique. I plan for my cute little pink pendant to stay around my neck for the rest of my days.

I still have nights where I wonder... like, seriously, where the hell did the head go?

But this is different. This isn't right. Unless my sleepwalking had somehow become contagious, I couldn't explain it. Ryan, Jemma, and Darrius were experiencing the same thing.

The world around us seemed to pause as the woman's gaze pierced us. No longer in the woods. No longer surrounded by things I recognized. However we got here, whatever this place was... it felt like we had stepped into an entirely new reality. And somewhere deep in the back of my mind, I thought, *It's a good thing I packed a change of underwear.* Because, truth be told, I totally just tinkled a little bit. With swift grace, the beautiful woman raised her hand, and the crowd fell into a stunned silence.

"Greetings, esteemed Champions. Welcome to the Empire of Sebbarus. I am Empress Mirella, the ruler of these lands, and I cannot express just how honored we are to finally have our champions."

"Damn, she's gorgeous," Ryan muttered, looking over at Darrius with wide eyes. "D, this you?" He waved his hand at the scene unfolding before us.

"What?! You think *I* have something to do with this?" Darrius shot back, utterly confused.

"D, come on. Last year's Christmas party. The prank." Ryan was almost smug, as if this was some elaborate scheme Darrius was organizing.

"Yo, I put a rubber chicken inside the roasted one so it'd squawk when Jemma cut into it. I didn't orchestrate a whole ass alien abduction or whatever the hell this is." Darrius threw his hands up in exasperation.

"Darrius, come on. Please just tell me you're messing with us." I could feel the panic creeping into my voice, but I wasn't sure whether it was because of the situation we were in, or because I genuinely needed him to make sense of it all.

"Kaliyah," he gritted his teeth, whispering to me while still maintaining a forced grin for the crowd, "do you really think I'm capable of putting something like this together? Are you all seeing the same shit I'm seeing? I don't know if we accidentally triggered a glitch in the matrix, but I swear to fucking god this was not me."

"Ok... Ok. From this day forth, I'm off the edibles," Jemma retorts, shaking her head. "So, I'd like it if I could come down from whatever high this is. Like right freakin' now."

"You all know about my drug free lifestyle, but if you're high Jemma, then we're all high," Darrius added noticeably shaken, as he took the time to really take in his surroundings.

"This is some of the craziest shit I've ever seen in my life," I muttered, still trying to wrap my head around what was happening.

We continued to talk amongst ourselves, each of us struggling to process how we got here, what was going on, and more importantly... how the hell do we undo it.

"Uh, crazy thought. Let's just ask." Ryan finally said, looking like he had made up his mind.

"No, we don't know if—" I started to object, but before I could finish, Ryan charged forward, completely ignoring me. "Ryan!" I called out, but he was already making his way towards the front of the large courtyard, where the Empress stood.

Darrius slowly trailed behind him, probably to back him up, while Jemma never moved from my side.

"Excuse me, beauty in center stage," Ryan called out, waving his hand toward the beautiful woman standing before us. "You said you were in charge, Empress of Seb-something."

"Empress of The Sebbarus Empire," she corrected him smoothly, her regal tone never faltering.

"Yes, that. Okay, so me and my friends are a tad or more like hella confused on how we got here and what all this even is. Now, I'm still betting that my buddy Darrius is pulling one over on us, but if you don't mind, you think you could shed some light on the situation?"

I could tell from the back of Darrius's head that he was rolling his eyes, clearly annoyed that Ryan still didn't believe him. I couldn't blame Ryan, though. He had always been the type to need solid proof before accepting anything that didn't make sense. On the other hand, I didn't share his skepticism.

Darrius was a jokester, no doubt. Always pulling pranks just to get a laugh. But the look on his face now was dead serious. And considering that crusty little cabin he rented for the weekend, which he probably found on some sketchy discount site, I know he's just as broke as me. There was no way in hell he had the money to pull off something this elaborate.

"Of course," the Empress began with all the grandeur of someone who'd had way too much time to practice her speeches. "As tradition dictates, we conducted the summoning ceremony to welcome our champion or in this case *champions*."

"Summoning ceremony?" Ryan's brow furrowed.

"As in summon from another world using the Elder Stones of Cosmara," she replied gesturing behind us at the freaky boulders.

"Did she say summoned?" Jemma's voice hit a pitch that could only be described as 'panic-adjacent.'

"What does that even mean?" Ryan asked, his confusion mirroring mine. "like... teleportation?" Ryan threw out, clearly struggling to wrap his head around the idea.

"No. Hold the *freakin' phone*," I cut in, doing my best not to lose my cool. "How about we go back to *the 'from another world'* part?"

"You caught that too." Darrius clearly on the same page as me.

"So, you're telling me this is not Earth?" I snickered at how ridiculous it sounded. The Empress remained unbothered, her posture as poised as ever, but if I wasn't imagining things, I could've sworn her brow twitched. Just a tiny shift. She must not have liked my tone. Too bad for her, I wasn't exactly going to roll over and accept whatever nonsense she was selling.

"I am unsure of what this *'phone'* you speak of is, but yes. If Earth is the world from which you hail, then the world you now stand in is known as Therion."

Be for real. My patience was wearing thinner than the plot of a reality TV show, and now I was just plain annoyed. How committed were they all to this ridiculous farce? Were we supposed to be buying this?

"Every fifty years, the Empire of Sebbarus's highest-ranking nobles and military officials gather here to usher in the new champion," she said with the kind of dramatic pause that made me want to roll my eyes.

"Why does she keep referring to us as champions?" Jemma muttered, clearly more confused by the second.

"Because that is what you are." the Empress smiles with perfect teeth. "Brave warriors designed to safeguard our Empire from the perils that threaten the livelihood of my people."

"Yeah, this? Not real." Darrius stared at her like she was a badly acted queen in a low-budget movie. "No way. This is some kind of skit. The host of that cabin has gotta be behind all this. That would explain why the booking fee was so cheap." He reached into his back pocket, pulling out his phone. "If I end up on some douchebag's social media feed, I swear, I'm burning that bullshit cabin to the ground.

Seeing Darrius go for his phone prompted the rest of us to do the same. I felt the beautiful sense of relief when I realized all I had to do is reach into my drawstring backpack, grab my phone and map our location or at the very least call for help. But then that relief was shortly lived. Me, repeatedly pressing and holding the power button again and again. Phone, refusing to turn on no matter what I do.

Bullshit. I made damn sure to fully charge this thing last night. I knew the very last thing I wanted was to be on our little trip as the black girl in the woods with no way to call for help if need be. That tragic trope was not going to be my story. Uh-uh. I don't think so. But no, nothing. And then I realized, everyone else was having the same problem.

"What the hell?" Darrius cursed in a low rumble.

"Uh, guys, I think my battery is dead," Ryan said, holding it up for inspection. "Jemma, let me borrow yours."

"Mine's toast too," Jemma replied with a shrug, looking as bothered as I felt.

"Same here," I added with an irritated sigh.

"I don't like this." Jemma says, her voice faltering. "This feels like a set up."

"How the hell are they doing this?" Darrius shot a look around, eyes wild. "It's gotta be like... EMP or something."

"I'm so freakin' scared to ask this, but are we like... being trafficked right now."

"The hell we are", I snapped, shaking off Jemma's grip as I took a step forward. "Hey, you! Princess Millie or whatever."

"I am Empress Mi—"

"Yeah, don't care." I cut her off. My tone sharp.

The crowd of folks tracing the perimeter of the courtyard let out soft gasps. *What the hell? Theatrical much.* At that moment, a hooded figure in a long dark purple robe with a golden amulet hanging around his neck took a step toward us, like he was about to do something dramatic. But before he could take another step, the Empress raised her hand with an air of total authority, and he froze, like she had just hit the pause button on him. I shot him a noticeable squint, before turning my full attention back to her.

"I'm ready for you people to cut the crap," I said, carrying all the frustration of my feelings. "I don't know who the hell put you up to this or why you think we'd fall for this summoned from another world's BS., but I've spent *way* too many weekends with my grandfather watching those ridiculous shows where they trick unsuspecting people into believing insane things. Like a mummy coming to life in a museum or an alien ship crash landing on a farm. And sure, in those moments, it *probably* seemed real to those people, but this? *This* ain't it." I was so done. Like, I needed this weekend to be fun. Not some weird, twisted, mild-budget reality prank show. "I'm plenty stressed already, so I don't need the shit right now. I just want to kick back and enjoy the company of my friends. So you better believe, I'm not signing any damn release forms for whatever footage your little hidden cameras are filming. You hear me, *Princess Millie?*" Oh, I saw it this time. The tiniest flicker in her gaze, just enough to let me know I hit a nerve. *Good.* "Or should I repeat myself just in case the actors in the back didn't hear me?" I pointed a finger at her, and her little smile didn't budge, but I could tell it was starting to crack. "My friends and I will not and do not consent to being filmed in any way, shape, or—"

"RRAAAOOOARRRR!!!"

A shadow brushed over me, dimming the light of the sun from my eyes. I tilt my head instinctively, squinting upward to see what was blocking the light. My gaze investigating. My eyes locked on it, then froze. A massive, dark-winged creature soared across the courtyard, its scales gleaming like blood-red with the tips of its wings and tail hinting at a flash of fuchsia. My gut sank to my ankles.

"What the... shit?" A low whisper peeled from my lips, my eyes followed the soaring creature in disbelief.

"Holy fuck!" Ryan yelped as he placed a hand on my shoulder. "Is that a—"

"Dragon," I interrupted, still too stunned to process what my eyes were showing me.

What the *actual* hell am I witnessing right now? My jaw practically cracked open as the creature inhaled deeply, and then it did the most ridiculous thing I could ever imagine. I've heard of dragons breathing fire, maybe even ice. But *this*? This was straight-up *far* beyond anything I'd ever seen in any fantasy movie. When it opened its mouth, a cloud of what looked like bright sparkly glitter blanketed the sky before slowly dissipating in the wind. No way. No damn way. It was a fucking...

"Glitter. Breathing. Dragon."

CHAPTER 2
CHAMPIONS OF SEBBARUS

KALIYAH

It's been a few hours since we were escorted, or more like strongly urged from the courtyard to what I can only assume to be the Empress's castle. I'm not even sure what to call this room we're being held in. It's like... an audience chamber? Is that a thing?

The whole place just screams wealth, like it's trying to suffocate you with how fancy it is. But not like a modern fancy, but more of a *'look how many gilded candles and embroidered velvet couches we can fit in one room'* fancy. It's like the 16th century had a baby with wealth, and here I am, stuck inside it. Surrounded by so much decorum and elegance I can practically hear the floorboards sneering at me. Yeah, if they could talk. *'You dare walk upon me with thy common sneaker?'*

"Let's go over the facts again." Ryan suggested. "So apparently, the boulders near Darrius's cheap-ass cabin..."

Darrius smacked his cheek at Ryan's remark.

Ryan continued. "...they were some kind of gate linking our world to this world."

"Therion," Darrius added, helping him piece it all together.

"Right!" Ryan replied. "And we were summoned here by that beautiful *goddess*—"

"Empress." Darrius corrected.

"Right. What did I say? Never mind. Empress. The ruler of a kingdom called Sebbarus. To be some kind of freakin' warriors or some shit."

"A fucking glitter-breathing dragon," I stated slowly, my voice flat but still heavy with disbelief.

"Exactly. So what? Does she expect us to fight that thing, or things like it?"

"A fucking glitter-breathing dragon," I replied, still stuck in a trance.

"Hell, nah. Uh-uh, pass." Darrius shot back.

"Let's just tell them we respectfully decline. Then maybe they'll let us go back home." Jemma chimed in.

"A fucking glitter breathing dragon." I stated again, my brows wrinkling as the phrase no longer sounded coherent to my ears.

"Kaliyah! We all know it was a fucking glitter breathing dragon. So can you please stop saying it?"

"Oh, my bad," I said with a heavy sigh. "I'm just trying to wrap my head around the fact that we all just saw a *fucking glitter breathing dragon*. Shit like that is not supposed to exist, Darrius. So, excuse me if I'm not as chill about it as you seem to be."

"You think I'm chill. How the fuck can I be chill about this. I'm losing my shit too."

"Guys, stop~ I'm seriously going to have a panic attack, if we don't figure this out." Jemma's face was becoming flustered.

I could tell that at any moment Jemma was going to be in full melt down mode, if we didn't all calm down. She has always had anxiety issues, which is exactly why she dabbles in the occasional edible. I fished around in my backpack and bingo. There they were. Jemma's stash of watermelon gummies, tucked in a resealable plastic bag.

"Oh god yes. Thanks, Kali." she said, her voice on edge as she placed one between her teeth.

I watched her take a deep breath, trying to settle. As she chewed, she handed the bag back to me. I placed it back in my backpack, trying not to overthink our next move. "Okay, okay. Let's all relax. Everyone take deep breath." I tried to sound as calm as possible.

"Fucking glitter breathing dragon." Ryan now chanting my phrase like it was some weird mantra.

"Ryan, come on Bruh." Darrius shot him a look, clearly over it.

"What? I'm sorry, but Kaliyah's got a point. That was the craziest shit I've ever seen in my entire life. So like, what else is real here? Are there unicorns? Fairies? Damn minotaurs?"

"What the hell is a minotaur?" Jemma asked, her brows not hiding her confusion.

I wasn't surprised. Jemma had never been into movies or television in general. So, I know she was not sure if Ryan was trolling or if he was legit about to drop some fantasy world knowledge.

"You know," He elaborates. "Head of a bull, body of a person. Hella strong, hella violent. But the real ones I'd be worried about are goblins. Whatever you do, steer clear of them. In every anime I've seen, and every manga I've read goblins are the worst. Ugly nasty creatures that fight in packs, like wolves, but they're far more clever. Using weapons and shit." He looked between Jemma and me. "And apparently, they're deliberately cruel. Especially, toward human females. So, let's hope those little demons don't exist here."

Jemma shuddered, her face turning even paler. Her eyes beginning to swell up with panic.

"Ryan, what the hell man?" Darrius sat down next to Jemma, wrapping his arm around her shoulders to comfort her. But I could tell it was just as much to soothe himself as it was to calm her.

I could see the sorry in Ryan's face. He has always been a thoughtful guy. So, I knew what he said was not meant to strike fear in us, but to genuinely give us information he thinks could help. I stood and walked over, patting Ryan on the shoulder as he sat on the edge of the couch across from Jemma and Darrius.

"Listen, I think Jemma's right." Everyone's eyes turned toward me. "We politely decline their offer and then we ask them to send us home."

"You really think they'll agree to that?" Darrius asked.

"I mean, why not? It's not like we're real champions. You're a graphic designer. Ryan works at his family's pawn shop. Jemma is an elementary school teacher, and I work in a corporate office. Does that sound like Earth's greatest warriors to you? Surely, if we tell them that, they'll realize they brought the wrong people here. They'll send us back and summon some army soldiers or I don't know, freakin' MMA fighters."

"Yeah... yeah." Darrius nodded his head in agreement. "That doesn't sound too bad."

"You sure *Princess Millie*, will go for it." Ryan interjected.

A twitch hit my brow. Shit. I forgot about that. How was I to know she was a legitimate ruler of a real freakin' kingdom? We don't even have those anymore. At least not any with any actual authority. People from royal bloodlines are more like celebrities now days.

Thinking back, I completely and utterly disrespected the... Queen? Empress? Not really one hundred percent sure on the difference between the two. I just know that either way, she definitely has the means to lock me in an actual freakin' dungeon and throw away the key. That is a scary fucking thought.

"Right... so first things first, I bow down and beg this countries leader for forgiveness. I mean, it's not like they're savage beasts. They're people like us, capable of understanding and reasoning, right?"

"Yeah, I agree." Ryan said.

A sigh of relief washed over me.

"Still, we don't know their culture or customs, and if it's anything like the era of our world, an offense like that could easily result in the offender being sent to the guillotine." Everyone's eyes widened. Our gazes slowly shifted toward Ryan, who, too, realized the weight of the words he had let slip from his mouth.

"Ryan, shut... the fuck up." Jemma flipped. No longer a sobby mess, but heated with angered annoyance. "Like not another word or I swear to god I'm going to rip your freakin' tongue out."

THUNK!

We all screamed. Our bodies nearly shedding their skin as the large door to the room swung open. A short, tubby man with thin legs walked in. His hands clasped in front of his waist. His eyes were squinting tightly, and his smile nearly stretched from ear to ear.

"Hello, Champions. My name is Tuman, and I have come to retrieve you and take you to the dining hall."

"Um... Excuse me." Jemma slightly raised her hand in the air, as if she were one of her students in the classroom.

"Yes, Madam Champion." Tuman responded with a wide grin.

"I was just wondering." Her eyes subtly shifted toward me. "We're not in any trouble, are we?"

"Whatever do you mean?" Tuman tilted his head. "As the Champions of Sebbarus, you are our honored guests. Of course, you are not in any trouble."

"So, the empress isn't angry at us? Like, any of us?" I asked, just to be sure.

"Not to my knowledge, Madam Champion. Empress Mirella is overjoyed to have you here."

We all let out a deep sigh nearly in unison. The tension that had been building up in me suddenly subsided. I looked over at Ryan, who was exchanging smiles with Jemma and Darrius. It was nice to see that they were just as worried for my neck as I was. I turned back to Tuman, and my grin faltered. His gaze had shifted to me. Although the smile remained, it seemed different, hollow. And just like that, unease washed over me again.

"Um, Mr. Tuman, sir. Do you think we could speak with the empress again?" Ryan asked carefully.

His gaze shifted back to the others. His smile returning to its earlier warmth. "Why, of course. My empress is the one who sent me. She wishes to acquaint herself with the lot of you over dinner. So, if you'll please follow me."

We exchanged looks, a silent understanding passing between us. We were all on the same page now. There was no more questions or no more wild guesses. It was time to move forward and see this through. Slowly, we all rose to our feet, trailing behind Tuman as he led the way. Ryan and I walked shoulder to shoulder, with Darrius trailing behind us. And Jemma, of course, bringing up the rear. Her expression was a bit more relaxed now. Her gummy finally kicking in.

Okay, keep your cool. Keep your composure. Mentally coaching myself, trying not to overthink things. *I'm sorry for being rude earlier. No, no. That's not right. She's royalty. I've got to do better than that.'* I took a deep breath, rehearsing it in my mind. *'I apologize for my insolence, great empress. I am but a lowly insect'.*

Ugh, who talks like that? Me. If it meant my head stayed attached to my neck, then sure, I'd talk like some royal sycophant if I had to. If I'm not careful, she might think I'm patronizing her. I shook my head with frustration bubbling under my skin.

Fuck you, Ryan. You got me all worried I might actually get decapitated. This suck~

She used magic rocks to abduct us, and somehow, *I'm* the one who needs to apologize? Bitch, where they do that at? Apparently, in fantasy worlds. I sighed heavily, knowing what's to come would determine the rest of my life. If I'd even be allowed to keep it. No. Don't think like that. I have to get back home, back to my grampa, back to my life.

Golden sconces flickered in the shadows, casting eerie shapes across the grand hall. Crystal chandeliers hung from the high ceilings, shimmering with every gentle sway. Suits of armor stood sentinel, their cold eyes watching us like silent guardians. The grand double doors to the dining hall loomed ahead and far too extravagant for my liking. Tuman gave a subtle signal, and the guards posted at the doors swung them open with a soft groan, allowing us to step inside.

As soon as we entered, the first thing I noticed was the long velvet curtains draping the towering windows. They were a deep, sultry indigo, swaying ever so gently with the breeze, giving the room an almost mystical feel. The second thing I noticed was a sight I wouldn't soon forget. At the far end of the grand table, the Empress sat waiting, her new attire just as stunning as the last. Maybe even more so. And dare I say, a little more revealing than I'd expect from someone of her position.

She wore a gown of deep emerald green that shimmered under the golden light, hugging her body. Her crown, though, was different this time. No rubies or sapphires. Just emeralds and diamonds, sparkling like a thousand tiny lights. She wore it effortlessly, like a goddess who'd grown bored with the idea of modesty. Her long, dark hair fell straight and smooth, flowing like silk down her shoulders. I've never really been the insecure type, but that woman's beauty has me doubting my own looks.

The only thing more impressive then her poised gaze was the feast spread before her. Roasted meats from golden brown chickens and tender lamb, to juicy cuts of beef and... *that*. Whatever that is. All arranged neatly on silver platters, their savory aromas filling the room. Bowls of fresh fruits, ripe apples, plump grapes, and figs, add a touch of color to the display. Crusty loaves of bread scattered around, along with bowls of roasted vegetables. I was utterly surprised to see things that I recognized. Although there were several things that I didn't. *Is that black broccoli?*

The Empress slowly rose from her seat. She looked at us with a gaze that said everything, yet nothing at all. "Ah, my precious champions," she spoke, her voice smooth. "Please, have a seat."

Chairs were pulled out for us, each of us making our way to sit down one by one. But just as I was about to lower myself onto the round cushion, my need to clear the air stopped me. With my heart pumping, I stood up straight, then turned to face the Empress.

"Excuse me. Empress... Empress..." *Fuckkkkk*! Did I really just forget this woman's name again? I opened my mouth, and only awkward silence followed.

Ryan jumped to his feet like someone had set him on fire. "Empress Mirella!" He threw a frantic gesture in my direction. "Kaliyah and the rest of us just want to deeply apologize for our rudeness earlier."

I attempt to piggyback off of what he just said. "Yeah, sorry, Mrs. Mirella! I'm—"

"Empress," Darrius interrupted, a tight smile plastered on his face. "She means Empress."

"Yes, Empress!" I echoed, feeling like my words were sinking me into a black hole. *Oh damn. I might actually get beheaded.* My heart started to race. I cleared my throat, trying to salvage what little composure I had left.

SLICE.

The sound of a blade cutting through the air echoed in my mind. I stammered, an awkward gasp escaping my lips as I tried to get my words out. "What I mean to say... Empress Mirella, I apologize."

SLICE.

"I'm so, so sorry for my words earlier." I trailed off, panicking as I felt the pressure of a thousand eyes on me. The room seemed to stretch as the weight of the situation sinks in.

SLICE.

"And I... I..." What the hell else was I supposed to say. I don't know. All I can think about is the sound of sharp metal, the sound of the guillotine... right over my neck.

SLICE.

"Are you going to cut my friend's head off?" Jemma bluntly blurted out so carelessly.

Bitchhhhh! The level of fucking dagger eyes I hurled at Jemma in that instant could've cut through solid steel and for a moment my vision went white.

The Empress, glanced at Jemma with an arched eyebrow. "Pardon me. Why would I ever do such a thing?"

Before Jemma could manage to open her damn mouth again, Ryan, ever the wise one, jumped in. "Because she…"

I turned on Ryan with the same lethal stare, ready to let him feel the weight of my dagger eyes next. *He. Better. Not.* If I was going to be the one getting my head lopped off tonight, I'm going to be damn sure to take one of these bitches with me.

He noticed my gazed and switched gears, "I mean, *we* were rather short with you back in the courtyard today."

The Empress's gaze didn't waver. "You have no need for concern, my beloved champions. You need not worry about harm falling upon you by my hand, nor will it come from anyone in my empire."

My eyes narrowed, not sure whether to believe her or not. "Really?" My vision was still a little hazy from all the tension, but I forced myself to focus. "You're not just saying that to then poison my food later or something, are you?"

Her hand went to her chest, clearly affronted by the suggestion. "My deities, no. I would never."

I gave her a skeptical look. "Uh-huh… okay, so don't get offended, but I'm going to ask one more time." Emphasizing my words. "Are you sure? Because earlier today, I definitely noticed the way you looked at me—"

"Kaliyah!" Darrius snapped, cutting me off mid-sentence, his teeth gritted. "Girl, if you don't sit your ass down and shut the hell up."

Right. What *am* I doing? She said she's not mad. There's no need to run my mouth and *actually* piss her off. I clenched my lips shut, practically pinning my back to the seat.

The Empress gave a soft amused smile. "I should share with you that we are fully aware of the adverse reactions that Champions experience after the summoning, and we are prepared for the adjustment period you all must be going through." She paused, her gaze sweeping over us. "Now that we've cleared up that misunderstanding, I would love to know the rest of your names. You are Madam Kaliyah, yes?" She nodded towards me then looked at Ryan. "And you?"

"I'm Ryan. Ryan Emmerson." He said in a smooth flirtatious tone as he reached out to shake her hand but quickly withdrew it when the guards posted behind her tensed up. He cleared his throat and gestured across the table. "This is my boy Darrius and good friend Jemma."

"Ryan, Darrius, Jemma, and Kaliyah," she mused, her eyes gleaming with something close to awe. "This is truly magnificent. This is a sign that the deities clearly favor my empire above all others to have blessed us with this many champions."

Ryan gave Darrius a subtle nod, the unspoken request clear. *'Go ahead, tell her'*. But Darrius only shook his head faintly, a gesture of refusal. I watched the two of them do that little dance for a few seconds. Well, she said she wasn't harboring any ill will towards me. And now that cranial amputation was off the table, it was a damn good enough reason for me to let go of my anxiety.

If neither Ryan nor Darrius would speak up, and I sure as hell wasn't about to let Jemma's blunt ass take the reins on this conversation, then I might as well be the one to step in. After all, I'm tired, frustrated, and more than anything, ready to go home.

"Empress Mirella, If I may, would the Imperial Majesty permit me to speak freely?"

"By all means, Madam Kaliyah." Her voice not betraying a single ounce of discontent.

Nailed that shit.

"We would like..." I glanced at my friends, noticing now their own dagger eyes aimed back at me as if to say *'don't fuck this up or else'*.

Choosing my words carefully, "We would like to express our concerns about the summoning ceremony."

"Yes, what about it?" she asked.

"The thing is, we are just regular people that were in the wrong place at the wrong time. We believe we were brought here by mistake."

"No. you weren't." She replied swiftly.

"We w—" I faltered. Her lack of hesitation in her response threw me for a moment, as if it was a certified fact. My eyes looked over to Ryan, then Darrius, then Jemma for assistance. But now they were choosing to avoid my gaze. "I'm telling you, we came across that pile of rocks—"

"You mean the Elder stones of Cosmara."

"Yes, those things! Completely by accident. They looked just like the ones in your courtyard."

"I most definitely assure you it was no accident." The empress responded.

What the hell does she mean it was *no accident*. Of course it was. We almost didn't even spot the damn things in the first place. Hell, she's not giving me much wiggle room. "Um... how can you be so sure?" I asked.

"Because it has been a part of our history for over a millennium. Every fifty years, our beloved deities of the heavens shall call forth the champions for the Empire of Sebbarus and only the chosen will answer." Her hands lifting slightly in the air. "Guiding humankind to reign over Therion."

"But that's not right." I hesitated, trying to find the words that would get through to her.

"Are you implying that our deities, beings of perfect wisdom and divine power are fallible? That they have erred in their sacred judgment?"

A sudden chill swept through the room, and there it was again. Her gentle attentive expression she wore like a mask. The one that had fooled me into thinking she had no beef with me. This time, I clearly saw what was behind it. It was subtle, almost imperceptible, but there. Hidden beneath the facade of regal kindness, was the faintest flicker of utter discontent. *I knew it. She doesn't care for me at all.*

Give me a freakin' break. She seems determined not to see our side of it. So, *how*? How do I make it clear to her that we are not her champions? "Of course not, Empress Mirella. I would never suggest that. I'm... just saying that those people, your champions, they're not us."

"I would have to agree, your majesty." Ryan interceded with a hint of hesitance cradling his tongue.

Finally. Someone other than me was trying to save our asses. I was really about to start questioning my friendship with these people.

He continued. "We are just ordinary humans, and if you're looking for us to kill creatures like the dragon we saw in the courtyard today, then—"

"What?" The Empress burst out in laughter, her giggles filling the room. "Why would we need you to slay a Glitzer Dragon? They're nothing more than house pets. The only threat they pose is to the taozen fruit in my orchards."

"If it's not dangerous, then what's with the glitter stuff shooting out of its mouth?" I raised an eyebrow.

"Glitter? You mean it's lunadust. The lunadust is the only thing that keeps my flowers around my castle vibrant and blooming year-round. Quite cost efficient."

She waved a hand nonchalantly, as if it were the most ordinary thing in the world. "I do have five of them, so losing one wouldn't be the biggest deal. But still, I would like to ask you all to refrain from slaying any of my Glitzers. As for being ordinary humans, that is to be expected, seeing that none of you have received your gifts yet."

"Gifts?" Jemma blinked.

"Yes, a blessing bestowed upon you by the power of our deities. Only the champions are deemed worthy are given such power."

The doors to the dining hall suddenly creaked open, and in stepped the figure in the long purple hooded robe and gold chain. The same one from the courtyard. My eyes locked onto him instantly as he glided shadily through the room, strolling behind Darrius and Jemma. I couldn't help but watch him carefully, noting how the shadows within his hood seemed to absorb all the light, hiding his face in darkness.

What was he planning to do to me if the Empress hadn't stopped him earlier? I wonder.

He approached the Empress's side, bending to whisper something into her ear. Too low for any of us to hear. His words were private, and my curiosity itched to know what was being said.

"Is everything okay?" Ryan inquired.

"Never better. Typical royal duties of running an entire empire. What can I say? It never ends." She rose from her seat. "So, I will see you all at the gifting ceremony tomorrow at noon. Tuman should have had your rooms prepared already, and your baths will be drawn immediately following the conclusion of dinner. Feel free to take your time and enjoy your meals properly. And with that, I must take my leave." She paused, giving each of us a final look. "I'm truly excited to see what gifts each of you receive."

We all watched in silence as she gracefully exited the room. The doors slowly swung closed behind her. As soon as I heard the soft thud of the door, my gaze snapped to Jemma. I leaned in, my anger seeping from my pores. "What the fuck, Jemma?"

"What's the matter?" She looked at me, her expression genuinely confused.

"What do you mean what's the matter? How about you asking a damn monarch if she felt like severing my head from my body?"

"Yo, chill. She was just trying to help." Darrius interjected. "You were clearly freakin' out about it and now we know you're straight."

"Ohhhh. *Now*, you have something to say, now that *your* thick ass neck isn't on the line."

"I think we all were afraid to say the wrong thing Kaliyah."

"Shove it."

"Hey, you can't get mad at me. I backed you up."

"Oh, yeah? And you think trying to seduce her is backing me?"

Ryan shot rapid blinks. "What are you talking about?"

"Ninja, you know *exactly* what I'm talking about. All the flirtatious tones. And what? You think we can't see the sexy *sultry eyes* you toss her way every chance you get? You and Darrius with your damn crushes."

I could feel Darrius's glare burning into the side of my head, but out of pure pettiness, I diverted my gaze just as he had earlier. Because at this point, I really didn't care that it was a secret from Ryan just as much as it was from his darling Jemma. Luckily for him, neither Jemma nor Ryan pressed me for more information. But considering the more pressing predicament we were in, it didn't really surprise me. Ryan gave me a confused look, as if he didn't know what I was talking about. He turned to Darrius and Jemma expecting them to disagree with my comment about him. But they didn't.

I plopped back down, placed my elbows on the table, and buried my face in my palms. I let out a long, frustrated sigh into my hands. "This freakin' medieval beauty pageant queen with her deities seems hell-bent on making us her champions, regardless of what we say."

"And what about these gifts she was talking about?" Ryan asked.

"What about it?" My voice was muffled through my fingers.

"What do you think they are?" Ryan pressed, eager for an answer.

"I don't know or care." I replied, lifting my head just enough to give him a blank stare.

"If it's a gift, you think it's gold? Or diamonds?" Darrius suggested hopefully.

Ryan snorted, shaking his head. "No, it'd probably be something more practical. I mean, come on, if they think we're their champions, and this is some kind of fantasy world, we're going to need our Excaliburs." He said it like it was the most obvious thing in the world.

Jemma rolled her eyes, crossing her arms in suspicion. "Ryan, don't tell me you're hoping it's a sword so you can sell it in your parent's pawn shop?"

"No. Uh-uh." He quickly shook his head, as if trying to convince himself.

Darrius, who had begun tasting his food like he was doing a full-on inspection, cut in with a question. "Excalibur, is the name of a sword?"

"Yeah. The story had something to do with a sword that was stuck in some rock. Then this guy named Author went and pulled it out and became king." Jemma closely watched Darrius eat, almost as if she was looking for any signs of the food being poisoned. No doubt due to my earlier comment. But it wasn't as if she waited long enough to get a definitive answer. Her munchies probably took over.

Ryan leaned back in his chair, stroking his chin. "I mean, a sword like that... That'd make damn good money at an auction."

"Wait. Wait wait wait." I sat up straight, an idea hitting me like a lightning bolt. "That's it. Tomorrow, at this gift ceremony..." I glanced around at the table, my voice lowering. "we refuse the gifts. Whatever sword, dagger, or freakin' bow-and-arrow they try to hand us, we just don't take it. Author wouldn't be King Author without his silly sword. We can't be warriors without weapons. So, we reject them and refuse to participate, then maybe they'll *reject us* back and send us home."

Ryan looked at me like I had just grew horns. "You're basing this off a folktale? What if it doesn't work?"

I shrugged, "What the heck else can we do? If you have a better idea I'm all ears."

"Ryan could always sleep with her," Jemma suggest sarcastically.

Ryan blinks. "No. I don't think that would work." He pauses for a moment. "Unless... you think it could. Could it? No, right?"

Darrius snorts. "Ry, come on bruh. You do know she wasn't being serious."

"Look," I cut in, steering the conversation back to the issue at hand. "We've got to try *something*, and I say we go with my idea."

A heavy silence settled over the table. But then Jemma spoke. "Okay. Then it's settled. No gifts." She grinned, her tone suddenly taking on that cheery, almost song quality. "We tell them, hell no, we wanna go."

"That's a *hell fucking no* for me." I reply.

Darrius snickered. "Definitely not in those words."

A salty grin crept the corners of my mouth.

CHAPTER 3
THE DEITIES' BLESSINGS

KALIYAH

Honestly, I couldn't get a single wink of sleep last night. And no, it wasn't because Jemma's snoring sounded like a bear deep in hibernation. It was the unease gnawing at me. Like, what really was up with the empress's glare? And it certainly didn't help that after we were pressured into bathing in these extremely large bathtubs, one for the girls and one for the guys, that Ryan and Darrius were shoved into another room somewhere. Probably keeping us apart intentionally.

Unlike Jemma, sleep never came for me. I blinked, trying to push the exhaustion off my face with the sleeve of my new attire. It was a long flowing gown, the color of rosy dawn. The sleeves hugged my arms all the way to the wrists, where delicate ruffled cuffs swaying with every movement. The fabric clung to my shoulders before cascading down in soft, layered folds that brushed the floor. A wide, patterned fabric belt cinched the waist and draped down my hip.

I looked around. Four waist-high stone podiums stood in front of us. Each with a rough cluster of teal and yellow crystals lining the bottom edges, as if they'd been cemented in place. Sigils marked the sides, the design quite familiar. Like the ones carved into those boulders from yesterday. Nearing the front of each podium, a person stood, clutching an object draped in a silky lavender sheet. *The Gifts*, I assume. Each one had its own shape and size. None of them even close to resembling the others.

The Empress stood off to the side. Her eyes intense as Tuman told us to pick a podium of our choosing. Jemma, Darrius, and I didn't waste any time and just headed toward the one nearest each of us.

But Ryan, that asshat actually looked like he was pondering which podium to choose. Squinting at the shape under each sheet as if it were some kind of treasure. He must've noticed something he liked, because he suddenly asked Jemma to trade places with him. I swear to God, if that man accepts whatever is under that sheet, I'm going to feed him to the Glitzer.

"Champions of Sebbarus, please place your palms upon the stones as you prepare to receive your blessings."

We did as we were told, placing our hands on the stones. The surface gleamed, swirling with colors. We exchanged silent nods. Whatever is hidden under those sheets, they can keep it. My gaze flicks to Ryan. He gave me the 'devil-may-care' look. *Now* was not the time for that look. *Shit*. Now I'm even more concerned. Last night the way he went on and on, saying how cool it would be to take home an ancient sword. At least I didn't have to worry about Darrius or Jemma. They seemed to be on the same page as me.

"On this day, our deities shall bestow their blessing upon Our Champions. Kaliyah, Darrius, Jemma and Ryan." Empress Mirella announces.

We all nod at each other, solidifying our plan. We faced forward, waiting for the people in front of us to reveal the hidden objects.

I stood there, patient for all of a minute, maybe two. But they weren't doing anything. Not a single movement. I don't get it. Hurry up and show us the damn thing so I can tell you thanks, but no thanks. Just as I was about to glance toward the Empress, a bright, warm glow suddenly brushed against the left side of my body. I turned, trying to figure out what was going on. Only to be paralyzed by what I was seeing. Darrius. He is on fire. The upper half of his body was engulfed in flames.

"Darrius!" I screamed. He was just standing there, staring at the flames on his arms, looking oddly calm. How the hell was he not screaming in agony? "Someone help!" I shouted, looking around at the crowd. But all I saw were smiles. They were fucking smiling like they were watching some kind of show. "What the fuck?! What is wrong with you people? Do something!" I bolted toward the man standing in front of me, ripped the sheet from his hands, and prepared to smother Darrius's body with it. "Ryan!" I shouted, wincing as I got closer. The heat was almost unbearable. "Ryan, Darrius is on fire! Help m—" I turned to Ryan, expecting him to be rushing towards us. But nope. Instead, he was just standing there, electricity shooting from his hands like he was in the middle of a lightning storm.

"Uhh... Kinda got my own thing going on right now." He replied shakily.

"Um... Kali! What's happening?" Jemma called out to me, her voice way too calm for my liking.

I spun on my heels, a chill of worry crawling across my body. What impossible thing was I about to see? Sure enough, the stone was freezing beneath her fingers while blocks of solid ice began to manifest around her. *What the hell is going on?* No time to think. Focus. One thing at a time. Darrius is burning. I need to put him out first, and we can deal with the rest later.

"Darrius, get on the ground and roll!" I barked, but his gaze was still locked on the flames dancing around his forearms. Shit. He must be in shock. "Darrius, snap out of it!" Damn it. I'm going to have to tackle him to the ground.

"Kaliyah. It's okay." Darrius finally spoke.

"What? No." I began to prepare myself. "Just hold on, I got you."

"No. Look." He turned to me. "It doesn't hurt. My skin... it's not burning."

I froze, eyes darting between his face and the flames. "Wait, what?"

I was expecting first degree burns or something. But no. He was right. His skin looked fine. He wasn't screaming in pain either. I looked around, and to my utter shock, the same went for the others. Ryan wasn't twitching in distress, and Jemma didn't look like she was freezing her ass off.

"What the fuck?" I muttered.

Just like that, the flames around Darrius flickered out, vanishing into nothing. The ice beneath Jemma's hands melted away, and Ryan's electricity fizzled out. Before I could even process it, the Empress glided past me, not even acknowledging my presence. She positioned herself next to the people holding the silk sheets. Her hand shot into the air, all dramatic like.

"This is absolutely extraordinary. It seems the deity, Feraiyah, Goddess of the elements was the one that chose to grant her blessings to our champions, and what powerful gifts they are indeed."

I blinked, trying to wrap my head around it. "Wait, what?" *That? That was the deities' gift? No. It wasn't supposed to happen like this. Where the hell were the weapons? The swords? The spears? Freakin' Excalibur?!*

Empress Mirella gestured her hand again. "Come forth, vassals, and give your offerings to your empire's protectors, promising them your dedicated loyalty and to serve them in any way they deem necessary."

The vassals, all grinning like they'd just won the lottery, removed their sheets one by one. The guy in front of Jemma revealed a white and blue ombre cloak, folded neatly. The woman in front of Ryan pulled out what looked like a damn priceless dagger, sheathed in a case made of ivory and jewels. And the man standing before Darrius uncovered a thick, gold chain.

The vassals kneeled before them like this was some royal worship session, and I'm just standing there, frozen in absolute bafflement. What the hell? My plan just went up in flames and apparently two other elements. My friends looked at me, but I had zero answers to give them. Not a damn one.

Then Ryan, fucking Ryan, steps forward and takes the dagger from the woman's hand. Jemma follows his lead like a clueless lamb. Darrius looks at me again, and we exchange wide-eyed stares, having an unspoken conversation that only fellow skin folk could decipher.

'Ninja, you better not.' My eyes scolded.

'What the hell else do we do?' His stare rebutted.

His gaze turned from mine, and with a resigned sigh, he took the chain from the cushioned tray. The crowd erupted into claps and cheers.

Empress Mirella turned away from them, facing the small crowd, giving her people a smug look like she'd just finished an epic performance. "And with that, the gifting ceremony is concluded."

And then, because of course, she side-eyed me. The perfectly crafted smile she'd been wearing since we showed up was finally gone. In its place was a crooked, disdainful scowl. One that spoke volumes more than her carefully curated words ever could.

For the last hour, we've sat waiting in the same damn chamber from yesterday. The only major difference was the three new appointed personal assistance or "vassals," as the empress put it, hovering in the corners like shadows. I couldn't help but watch as Darrius ignites his hands off and on, like a child playing with a lighter. Ryan, next to me, kept rubbing his fingers together, making little sparks twinkle at his tips. And Jemma? She couldn't stop turning her hot tea into a frozen cup.

"Ry, bruh, are you seeing this shit?"

"Yeah, its hard not to when your fingers look like flaming sausages."

I didn't know if I was more mystified or pissed off at what was happening. How the hell were we supposed to guess that their deities' gifts, their special *blessings* would be magical abilities? Magic isn't supposed to be real. It doesn't exist back home, not outside of movies about witches and wizards. But the teleporting boulders should've been my first clue.

This is beyond frustrating. And I'm almost ashamed to be wondering this, but why didn't I get one of these damn blessings? I don't feel any different at all. In fact, the only *offering* I received from the vassal that had stood before me was an eye roll as he showed me his back and walked away.

"Kaliyah, do you feel anything yet? Something like a pulse deep in your gut."

My cheek twitched. Pissed that he had the gall to ask me that after the crap he pulled. After the crap all of them pulled. I was this close to reigniting my old college nickname, Sizzle, and exploding on this clown. They act like we are on some little overseas trip. We are basically being held hostage in another world. One that operates on a completely different reality than our own. The only thing that stops me was the sound of Tuman's voice announcing Empress Mirella entering the room. I couldn't believe they all rose to their feet as she walked in. I stayed seated. Chin resting in my hand, eyes rolling to the back of my head.

"Please, my champions, sit sit." And like good little pups, they did as they were told. Mirella took a seat as well, her mysterious hooded companion standing just within earshot. "How are you adjusting to your gifts?"

"Um, honestly, this is incredible," Darrius responded, still in awe. "My body feels amazing, strong even."

"Same here. But, some of us are having a hard time." Ryan eyes gestured to Jemma.

"I can't stop freezing stuff." Jemma added.

"Ah yes, I see. That's to be expected. Your skills and control over your gifts will improve and get stronger with time." She nodded towards the hooded person. "Galldric is our magic expert, and he will be the one to teach you how to control and harness your gifts."

My ears perked up. Did she just say *with time*? Hell, no.

"Fuck that shit," I blurt out. The room went silent. All eyes were on me.

"Excuse me. Come again?" Empress Mirella said with a touch of surprise.

I knew she heard me the first time, but if she wanted me to repeat it, then fine. "I said, *Fuck. That. Shit.*"

Ryan quickly jumped in, trying to save face. "Please don't misunderstand her, Empress. From our world, that phrase means—"

"It means exactly what you think it means. *Fuck. This. Goddamn. Bullshit.*" I cut him off, not in the mood for fake pleasantries. We tried to be respectful, but now I'm over it. "We're not staying here any longer. Jemma, what about school, huh? Darrius, don't you talk to your mom on the phone like twice a day? And Ryan, what do you think your cousin will do if you don't show up to open the shop on Wednesday? And me? I have work in the morning. And I'll be damned if I get fired over some no-call, no-show bullshit after giving that company the last five years of my life." I paused, my hands clenching in frustration.

"Yo, Kaliyah, take a breather."

My gaze shot to Darrius, "A breather? Oh, okay, yeah. Remind me again to take a breather when a ten-foot-tall bull man or a real dragon, one that doesn't breathe glitter but real fucking molten lava that puts your little matchstick arms to shame, kills you, Jemma, Ryan, or me. Are none of you terrified of being stuck here, or worse, dying and never going home? Our families won't even have bodies to bury." A tense silence swirled through the room.

Ryan shifted uncomfortably in his seat, his voice quieter now, more serious. "Kaliyah's right. The magic is cool and all, but I'm not a warrior. I sell used game stations and power tools. And the thought of my family never knowing what happened to me—" His words trailed off.

"Shit." Darrius's face dropped, his eyes glued to the floor. "I didn't even consider what my mom would do if I never came back. She already lost my pops. I can't put her through that."

"Who's going to teach my class if I don't show up tomorrow? My students need me."

Finally. My words seemed to be getting through to them. The conversation carried on, but my eyes caught movement in the corner. I glanced over to see Galldric, cloaked in his impossible dark hood, whispering into the Empress's ear. After seeing behind her mask, I was able to read her subtle expressions like an open page. She was getting nervous.

"One month," the Empress announced, and our attention snapped to her. She spoke calmly. "I ask that you remain in my empire for one month. Afterwards, we will send you home."

Ninja, please. We could all be in the belly of some beast by then. I wasn't about to sit around and wait for something even more ridiculous to happen. "No. We want to leave today. Preferably within the hour."

"I'm afraid that isn't possible."

"What do you mean? Why not?" Jemma askes.

"The Elder Stones of Cosmara are powered by magic. Magic that is fed into them by sorcerers of the land over time. When you all were summoned here, it drained the stones of that magic considerably, especially because there were so many of you. So, in order to revive the Elder Stones with enough magic to send you all back home, it will take at least a month."

I don't trust this bitch. "And during this month, do you expect us to slay some warlord or fight some furious troll rampaging across your empire?" I crossed my arms, eyeing her suspiciously. Another subtle twitch. Yeah, she's not fooling me anymore.

"No. No warlords or furious beasts to speak of. Actually, our nation is currently in a state of peace," Mirella claims.

"Then why summon champions?" Darrius asks.

Finally, someone's asking the right questions. If there was anyone other than me that can see through her BS, it's him.

"Simply put, it is the will of the deities. We do not question their reasoning, for their judgment is sound."

Divine will? That's the crap she's going with? Even if she's telling us the truth, I don't give a damn. There's got to be another way home.

Mirella continues, "For the last 300 years, past summoned champions have been nothing more than figures of fame. Idols for the people to seek hope and inspiration."

Darrius chuckles. "Seriously? The Champions are just celebrities?"

"Famous for being Famous," Ryan says with a shrug. "Yeah, I think were familiar with that concept."

"You're not, like, lying to us, right? Telling us what you think we want to hear." Jemma ask.

Hell yeah, that's my freakin' girl. I knew there was a reason I called her my bestie.

"I assure you I'm not, Madam Jemma."

"Ok, then. A month is not so bad. Mrs. Tammy can handle my kids for that long."

Jemma, noooooo. Don't make me uninvite you from this year's Christmas party.

"Do we really have any other options?" Ryan askes.

"What do you think, Kaliyah?" Darrius turning to me.

I stood there with my eyes closed, deep in thought. *I think I want to tell Princess Millie to stick that nauseously expensive looking crown up her tightly coiled ass.*

"Kaliyah," he called out again, his voice more insistent this time.

My eyes shutter open. "What?" I scowled through clenched teeth.

"We want to know, what you think we should do?" He repeated.

I opened my mouth, but the words wanted to resist leaving my lips. "One month and not a day longer."

"Excellent." Empress Mirella's eyes sparkling with a hint of satisfaction, as if she had just checkmated me. "In that case, we will give your companion, Kaliyah, a moment to prepare for her departure."

"*What?*" We all said in tandem.

"What do you mean, her departure?" Jemma flustered.

"Oh, apologies. I didn't mean for that to sound so ominous. I simply meant for her journey home, of course."

"Home?" Ryan inquired.

"Back to the world you all called Earth."

"Wait, you just said the elder rocks were out of magic juice and that we couldn't return until you recharged them." I repeated.

"I said they were depleted, not out." Mirella clarified.

"Hell, then send us all home." I snapped, not hiding my enthusiasm.

Mirella sighed, her expression growing serious. "Again, that's not possible. I believe I once told you that in the history of Sebbarus, we've never had more than one champion. The stones are always charged with enough magic for two summonings, the return trip, and sometimes a little extra for good measure."

"So, there's enough magic left in your stones for—" I started, trying to piece it together.

"One more reverse summoning," Mirella finished.

"Okay, but why her? Why not any one of us?" Darrius asked, gesturing toward me.

Excuse me? Why *not* me? Up until 15 minutes ago, he seemed like he'd be down with going on a dumbass quest if asked.

"To put it bluntly, if Kaliyah remains in Therion, then she cannot be allowed to stay here in my palace any longer than she has already."

I noticed the empress was no longer referring to me as *madam*.

Jemma shot a hissing glare at Mirella. "Like, why the hell not? If the rest of us can, then she should too!" She was already ready to go to bat for me.

"Yeah, you lost me there. Empress Mirella, we can't watch you kick our friend out. If she goes, we go." Ryan clarifies.

These... *these are my people*. I couldn't help the small smile tugging at my lips, grateful to hear them standing by me. It didn't go unnoticed that Darrius had stayed silent though.

She leveled her gaze on me. "I'm sure you've all noticed that Kaliyah did not receive a divine blessing, marking her as a true champion. While the reason for that remains unclear, the severity of the situation does not. Once word spreads across this nation *and it will,* the citizens of my empire will believe she is a false champion. There have been... incidents in the past. Individuals who attempted to pass themselves off as chosen. Deceiving my predecessors, manipulating faith for their own gain, and in doing so, tarnishing the honor of our realm. If she is thought to be one of *them,* there may be attempts on her life. There are citizens whose devotion go far beyond reason. And if I were to allow her to remain behind the palace walls, it could be seen as an act of defiance against the heavens. Citizens of Sebbarus are loyal to the crown *but devoted* to the deities. And not even I can subjugate the will of all my people."

"People will try to kill me?" *Who the hell are these deities that people are willing to kill innocent strangers for no damn reason?*

"What? No. But she hasn't even done anything wrong." Jemma says. "This is fucking insane."

"Religion's religion, no matter where you go," Ryan mutters. "People do wild shit when faith gets involved."

"Ryan, what do we do? We can't let anything happen to Kali."

"You seem to know more about all this shit than any of us. You got to have some ideas how we can get her out of this." Darrius shifts.

"Guys wait. This... this might actually be a good thing. She said she's sending me home."

Jemma turns to the Empress. "That's right, she did. Can you really do that? Send my girl back before anyone tries anything?"

Empress Mirella nods.

"Sending her back first makes sense, now. Kaliyah is powerless. She wouldn't be able to protect herself like we would."

I fired back. "Ninja, power or no power, I could take you down any day. Your little matchsticks wouldn't stop me from —"

Darrius interrupts, rolling his eyes. "Girl, you know what I mean. It's clear this world's got some wild-ass shit going on and at least we were given our own kind of crazy to match it." He gestures between the three of them.

I don't think it's a good idea to leave them here, but Darrius makes sense. I don't have a blessing, and there's only one ticket home at the moment. There's really no reason for me to wait it out with them. Especially if there's a chance people might try to kill me. "So... I'd be going home alone. I'm not a hundred percent okay with this. But at least I would be able to check in with our families. We will need to come up with some story about you guys being on a retreat or something. It has to be believable. I don't want people thinking you all were murdered and buried in the woods somewhere. So whatever we come up with, it has to be good.

"Damn. I didn't think about that. Last thing I need is to end up as the subject of some true crime podcast. That's all my cousin is end to these days." Ryan crosses his arms.

"Oh! If we do, I hope it's that one with the lady and her niece... umm... what was it called?"

"*Auntie Knows Best.*"

"Yes! That one, I *love* them."

"Yeah, I listen to them too on the way to the shop."

"You should have told me. I tune in everyday while my students are at lunch. Did you listen to the one—"

"Can we focus?" I cut in, blinking. God knows I love these people, but sometimes—

"So its decided. Kaliyah, you're going home first. And then, in four weeks, we'll be back too." Darrius turned to me. "I know my mom's gotta be losing her mind, trying to figure out where I am. And you can let her know I'm good."

"Of course." I assured, then looked over to the empress and asked, "How soon can I leave?"

"All can be ready within the hour."

"Okay, then yeah. I'll be ready."

Hell, yeah. I truly thought we might be stuck here forever. But I'm going home. They'll only be here for a single month. That's not long. The three of them can play magic and monsters. Hopefully getting the awe and wonder out of their system, while I get back to my life.

CHAPTER 4
THERAPY

KALIYAH

Journaling. Nothing tracks psychological progress better than talking to paper. Another gem from the ex-therapist. Her exact words, *"Journaling can be a helpful tool for identifying cognitive and behavioral patterns over time."* So, forty-something journals later, I'm still jotting down the most mundane details of my life, with the occasional doodle here and there. I once thought about turning them into a memoir, but when you've got entries like *'The same barista spelled my name wrong on my caramel frappe for the twelfth time,'* it really just solidifies how aggressively basic my life is. That idea got shelved real quick.

The first time she suggested it, it felt no different than being assigned homework. Annoying. Tedious. But after a while, I didn't mind. Then before I knew it, I started to enjoy it. That's why it's still part of my routine, even though I could've dropped it years ago. And after the last few days I've had, there's nothing I want more than to curl up on my modern sofa, in my regular-degular studio apartment, with my favorite gel pen, and just unload. I was all set, as the Empress so royally put it, for my *departure.*

I had Jemma and the others jot down every errand, every favor they wanted me to take care of back home in the journal I keep stuffed in my backpack. Feed Jemma's cats. Call her school. Grab the spare key from under Ryan's mat to stop his snooping cousin from '*borrowing*' his stuff. Pay Darrius's mom a visit or ten. Definitely can't forget that one. I carefully tucked my journal with the written instructions into my backpack between my trendy fit and sneakers. Just before I drew it close, Ryan approached me with something wrapped in his hand.

"Hey K, do me a favor." He whispers, leaning in a little closer. "Take this with you and stash it at your place. I don't want my cousin getting her sticky hands on it."

"Uh... What is it?" I asked, eyeing the wrapped bundle in his hand.

He placed the object in my palm, and instantly, I knew. It was the dagger his vassal had given him.

"Seriously?" I raised an eyebrow, giving him a blank stare. "Maybe I'm the one with the sticky hands."

The dagger's hilt and sheath was embedded with real diamonds and other jewels. Stuff I couldn't even begin to guess the value of.

Something like this could probably wipe out my student loans and put me into early retirement, no problem.

"No. I trust you. You're not that kind of person. Betraying the people you care about, just isn't in you. *D* on the other hand." Ryan chuckles, and I couldn't help but laugh too. I tucked Ryan's dagger into my backpack.

It warmed my heart to know how much faith he had in me. *Still...* the idea of riches beyond my dreams was pretty tempting.

Ugh. But he was right. I could never do him or any of them, dirty like that. The guilt would eat at me too bad. *But~* that doesn't mean I'm above charging him a hefty storage fee.

"If I hug you, I'm not going to be electrocuted or anything?" I asked, only half-joking.

"I think you're good." He gestured with a grin.

"You think?" I raised a brow.

Ryan wrapped his arms around me.

"You guys are going to be okay, right?"

"Don't worry about us. We'll be fine." He reassured me, but before I could say anything else, a second set of arms wrapped around my side. I turned to find Jemma standing beside me, and without hesitation, I embraced her too.

Jemma gave a somber chuckle. "Kuro will throw up if he eats too fast, so feed him in increments, okay?"

I smiled and nodded. "I will."

Then, a third set of arms wrapped around me from behind. Darrius. I buried my face into Jemma's shoulder, holding back the tears that threatened to spill. Was I really about to leave my best friends here? In this place?

"I promise you, if your asses aren't home by the end of the month, I will march the National Guard through that fucking portal and tear this empire to the ground," I muttered into Jemma's dress, trying to lighten the mood.

"I bet you'd find a way to do it too." Darrius chuckled softly, his grip tightening around me.

"We have prepared the Elder Stones. Are you ready for your departure?" Tuman asked as he entered the room.

I wipe away a tear that tries to slide from Jemma's eye. "Yes. I'm ready," I replied, taking a deep breath.

I walked behind Tuman, everyone else not trailing far behind. Except for Jemma. She clung to my arm, her fingers locked into mine. We walked together, our footsteps in sync. Once we reached the courtyard, I gave Jemma one last tight hug around the neck. I wanted to make the moment last just a little longer. Then I went and stood in the center of the summoning circle, tracing my eyes along the sigils on the front of the boulders.

Hmmm... No Empress. I figured she'd be center stage, relishing the moment she was finally rid of the *"false champion"*. The person who could push all her royal buttons. Whatever. I gripped the strings of my backpack, pulling it tighter against my back.

It's time. I'm nervous. I don't remember it hurting the last time, but I'm still worried it will. Galldric stepped forward to the circle's edge and knelt. The thick folds of his robe almost impossible to ignore. Does he ever take it off? It has to get hot under there. He placed his palms firmly to the ground, and a quiet murmur slipped from his lips. I stood there, nervousness and relief bubbling inside me. I could tell my friends were feeling the same. Ryan's arm was resting on Darrius's shoulder. While Darrius had his hand around Jemma's waist. Since we've been here, I'd noticed he'd gotten a bit more handsy with her. I couldn't help but throw him a cheeky gaze.

He knew exactly what my eyes were saying. *'You better watch over my girl.'* His gaze lift as if to say, *'You know I will.'*

My thoughts shifted to Grampa. Was he doing okay? With his fiancé at his side, I bet he was doing better than okay. He probably hadn't even noticed my absence. The thought of being home again, of seeing his familiar face and hearing his voice had me excited. And then, as if triggered by my very thoughts of home, the symbols beneath my feet began to glow, and the stones surrounding the circle did the same. It's happening. Blinding white. *Crap.* I forgot how intense this part was. I quickly buried my face behind my hands, shielding my eyes. Through the glow, I could hear Darrius's voice, faint but clear.

"Kaliyah, see you later, gi—" His voice cut out.

Silence all around me. No blaring musical instruments this time. That's a good sign. I slowly peeled my hands from my eyes, and the white light began to fade. My vision cleared, but something was... *off.* This didn't look like the familiar space we had all left.

"Wait. Hold on. What...?" My voice trickled to a whisper. I quickly scanned the area. The Elder Stones sitting in front of me look nothing like the ones near the cabin in the woods. These are much worse for wear. They're cracked in half, barely standing. No flowers. No vines. Just crushed rock, dirt and grass. I focus on the surrounding space. Thick lush trees and dense grass.

"You've got to be kidding me." What does this mean? Are there *more* than one set of Elder Stones on Earth? I really start to work this out in my mind.

I mean, that's the only thing that makes sense. If they planned on continuing the tradition of dimensional kidnapping, waiting for some random people to just wander into a specific set of woods wouldn't be the most efficient method. They must have a network of them scattered around the globe.

This realization forced me to clench my fists and throw my head back, "*FUCKKKKKK!*" I can't believe I didn't think to check exactly where on earth I would be sent back to. Based on the surrounding forest, some of the plants look tropical, so maybe I'm somewhere in Brazil or Africa.

Man, I'm going to have a hell of a time at the embassy explaining how I got into a country with no passport and no record of entry. More than anything, I'm praying I'm in a country that considers themselves friendly with the U.S. Hell. There's so many that aren't, especially right now. I might be screwed.

"Keep your composure. I'm back, and that's all that matters. I just need to make it to a main road or something, and then I can go from there." I mutter to myself. I look toward the sky, trying to get a fix on the sun. I'm no navigation expert, but I knew the basics. The sun rises in the east and sets in the west. If it's around half-past three, that means the sun should be closest to the west. So, maybe I should head that way.

Damn it, Grampa. Why did you cave when I told you I didn't want to join the Outdoor Scouts?

I shoved my braids into a messy ponytail. Ditching the cute, but frilly dress and slippers, clearly not made for outdoor traveling. Instead, I changed into my denim leggings, my much more comfortable t-shirt, and my limited-edition J's. Bright pink, blue and purple, traced with black-and-white cow print. Tightening my backpack and with a determined sigh, I set off.

I mean, I know that society relies on technology, maybe a little too much, but jeez. My sense of time is all over the place. I can't tell if I've been walking for an hour or four. I wonder how much daylight I have left. The sun is beginning to set and I can feel panic creeping up. Shit shit shit. I let out a frustrated sigh.

"No~ please. Let me just make it out of here before dark." This is it. My worst nightmare. Me, a black woman, lost in the woods, with no way to call for help. If life doesn't have a twisted sense of humor, I don't know who does. Periodic deep sighs escaped me as I reached for my phone yet again, only to remember, once more, that the damn thing was a glorified paperweight with a dead battery. If only I could find a place to charge it. Preferably a diner or café, where I could finally stuff my face. I opted out of breakfast this morning, still too paranoid that there might be a *questionable* ingredient in my scrambled eggs. One of the *lethal* variety. If only I was allotted a food taster, like the ones kings have in those historical dramas.

Wait. *Barbecue?* My nose caught a whiff of something in the air. Is that food? Food means people. Halle-freakin'-lujah, I'm saved. I could practically hear the sound of angels humming. I set off toward the scent, following it like a police dog chasing down a suspect. And they're crime? Causing that scent of sweet, sweet sizzling meat. Please, please let them take Venmo. If they don't, I'm sure we can work something out. I mean, no way would they let a damsel in distress starve to death in front of them. I can hear chatter. I'm getting closer. Crap. It doesn't sound like English.

Great, so foreign country it is then. Can't be helped now, I guess. I'll just use my phone to translate. Damn it to hell. That's out too. Whatever, I'll use freakin' charades if I have to. Just get me out of this dang, bug-infested forest.

"Hey, someone there? I need help!" I called out in desperation. I swatted at the thick foliage, pushing it out of the way as I tried to get a glimpse of whoever was nearby. Almost there. I could make out the silhouettes of a group of people. Just need to get through this last patch of bush, and then I'll be free. I practically jump out of the bush, hands raised in the air.

"Thank goodness, I'm so glad to have found you guys!" I said, relief rushing through me as I moved closer toward the oddly-sized strangers. Kids Maybe? I wasn't sure, but they were definitely shorter than me. "I don't know if you understand a word I'm saying, but I'm lost and—" Clouds began to move out of the path of the sun. That's when I could see them clearly and all the words I had planned to say caught in my throat. My legs went stiff. My eyes widened. My heart thudded painfully against my chest.

These people... *aren't... human.* Short hunched bodies with wiry limbs and skin that was a sickly shade of green. Their faces were sharp, grotesque, with pointed ears, crooked noses, and small beady yellow eyes that glinted under the dim light. Heads lift and turn to me. My body jolted. What *was* that over the flame?

My hands shot to my mouth, trying to hold back the scream. It was the torso of a human man. No arms. No legs. Just the charred remains of his upper body, blackened and crisp, slowly roasting over the fire. The smell of burnt flesh filled the air, and my stomach lurched in response. *This can't be real. This is supposed to be earth.* I stumbled backward, my heart pounding harder, hands shaking. My mind was racing for any explanation.

WHOOSH.

But before I could take another step, a gust of wind whipped past me, followed by a nauseating thud. I barely registered the movement. My head hesitantly turned to see the axe firmly embedded into the trunk of the tree beside me. One of the creatures grunted, a high-pitched inhuman shriek that sent a cold shiver down my spine.

Without missing a beat, the others scrambled for crude weapons scattered across the ground. Their eyes locked on me, while taking slow, deliberate steps forward. My gaze shot to the rear, where another one of them stood, drawing back an arrow on its bow. Its piercing eyes fixed on me. I didn't need any more reasons to get the hell out of there. My body reacted before my mind could fully catch up.

Run! I spun on my heels and bolted, hearing the whistle sound of the arrows' release. Most likely just missing me. With my heart thundering, feet pounding the grass beneath me and a group of vicious goblins on my tail, *I ran like hell.* It's getting darker, the fading light making it harder to see what's in front of me. My mind flashes back to Ryan's warning, *'The real ones I'd be worried about are goblins... they're deliberately cruel. Especially toward human females.'* The words echo in my head as my legs scream in protest, burning with every step. My lungs feel like they're on fire, but I can't stop.

I can't. The only advantage I have right now is my long legs. But they are relentless, they won't stop chasing me. I have to hide. But where? A tree? Can goblins climb trees? I don't know, but they sure as hell can shoot arrows. So, hell no, no trees. Where then? I can't keep going. My legs are burning, my chest tight, my breath ragged. I have to stop. I duck behind the nearest tree, hoping for some kind of cover, and force myself to breathe slowly. But it's hard. Forcing my deep panting to a quiet whisper was like torture to my chest. Soon, I won't be able to see anything. But at least it might make it easier for me to hide. Unless... Can goblins see in the dark?

WHOOSH.

An arrow impales itself into the dirt just inches from my foot. I scream and jolt back up. I ran until I cleared the tree line approaching. An open space with bare ground, leading up to the side of a mountain. No no no! At this rate I'm going to get cornered. I stop and pivot, trying to shift directions, but it's too late.

There they are. At least twenty goblins, which was far more than the initial eight I first encountered. Their twisted, deformed faces stretched into sickening grins as the ends of their gross mouths pull back to reveal rows of skinny sharp teeth. They start to snicker. They laugh in a mocking high pitched tone and I feel my blood run cold. They are enjoying this. My head whips around, desperately searching for any means of escape. That's when I see a dark, gaping hole in the mountainside. A cave. No. There's no way in hell I'm going in there. My mind racing with the possible consequences. If it's not a den to a pack of wolves or bears looking to rip me to shreds, then all I'd be doing is making it easier for them to trap me like a mouse.

One of the goblins turns to the others, pointing to two in particular and making some chittering noise. The two goblins immediately begin charging toward me. One with a hatchet in hand, the other wielding a makeshift, jagged club. I don't have a choice. My body moved, my mind no longer in control as I sprinted towards the cave. I slam into the darkness of the cave, becoming engulfed in the shadows. I stumble, unable to see where I'm stepping. Struggling not to trip over every rock my foot grazed. Deeper and deeper I go, the cool air of the cave wrapping around me like a blanket.

Willing myself to keep moving, I finally come to a fork. Left or Right? The faint sound of crackling and something else. Loud, urgent cries from the goblins pushes me into a decision. I veer to the right. My pace slowed and I stagger until I spot a nook, partially hidden by a large rock. I took off my backpack, pulled it tight to my chest and nudged myself in between it. Trying with everything within me to hold my breath, nearly suffocating myself.

Footsteps and grunts echoed off the chamber's walls. Something hard was burying itself in my chest. Wait, that's Ryan's dagger. Immediately upon realizing that, I fumbled through my bag and pulled it out. Still tightly bundled in fabric. I went to unwrap it, when it slipped from the cloth, hitting the stone floor with a sharp clink, sliding a few feet away.

I froze. The cave fell silent. Do I go for the dagger? My mind screamed at me '*stay put*'. But I know if they find me, I'm as good as dead. My eyes slid around the rock that shielded me, and I saw it. The last dying rays of sunlight had vanished from the cave's entrance, leaving utter darkness. When a few seconds later, luminescent plants along the jagged cave walls began to paint the space in shades of teals and hints of purples. The strange light crept down the path like a tide, spilling across the cavern and casting shadows that twisted unnaturally along the space. Some areas of the cave were lush with glowing plants, while others were dark, bare of light.

With the cave's sudden bathe in the glow, that's when I saw it. Its hunched form barely three and a half feet tall, its body slightly crouched. It was standing just a few feet away, its back turned to me. The rush of terror, when I realized that it wouldn't be long before it took notice of me. My eyes shifted down to the dagger, then lift to see the goblin's movements. But it was too late, it was already starting to turn around. It was now or never. I lunged for the dagger, taking hold. It's gaze jolted to me. I unsheathed the dagger prepared to aim it at the goblin, when it swung his weapon hitting the tip of my blade, flinging it behind me. I begin to crab walk backwards.

No. I don't want to die. The goblin slowly creeps towards me, club aimed in the air. Both hands firmly gripped. It smiles at me, drool leaking from the corners of its mouth. Then it says something and prepares to swing down. Just as it was about to, a loud screeching travels from the other end of the cave. It gets the attention of the goblin. He freezes his movements, tilting his head to the side in order to inspect the cause of the noise.

That's when I took the chance to kick the creature dead in the chest, with what remaining strength I had left in my legs. Its body went hurling backwards, dropping its weapon. I quickly turned and crawled to the dagger, gripping it tight with both hands, then pressed my back against a rigid stone wall. My hands shaking so bad I couldn't steady the blade.

The creature stood up, its twisted face curling into something resembling a sneer. With its club now gone, it reached behind its back and pulled out a smaller blade, creeping forward. As it walked towards me, it let out a series of murmurs. No doubt cursing me in its broken language. I had no idea what it was saying, but the malice in its tone was enough to make the little hairs on the back of my neck stand up. I tried to force my legs to move, to run, but they were no different than noodles. My deep breathing was out of sync with my heartbeat. It was beginning to make me feel dizzy.

I clenched my teeth, waiting for the blow that would surely come. But then, in the blink of an eye and without warning, the goblin's upper half was simply gone. Its legs still attempting to walk forward, before greenish blood splattered across the cave walls and then collapsed to the ground.

Holy shit. What... just... happened? An unbearably icy chill crept up from my toes and settled at the nape of my neck. Something was looking at me. Something far larger than goblins. Its cold predatory eyes, glowing with a haunting intensity, watching me without mercy. Whatever creature those eyes belonged to, slowly shifted, moving in my direction. It's presence suffocating. My grip gave out, my dagger falling between my legs. It moved deliberately. Its figure cloaked in darkness, yet somehow unmistakably present. It glided past the mangled remains of the goblin.

Then it stopped, just a few meters away. A sigil, glowing a golden yellow, began to illuminate on the cave's ceiling just above us. The blue, cat-like eyes that pierced through me, narrowed into thick slits. The growl that escaped it was deep, low, and utterly horrifying. It rattled through my bones, vibrating my veins.

Then, the folds of its eyes closed, which was the only thing hinting at the creature's location. I frantically tried to locate the beast, but my human eyes couldn't pierce the thick shadows scattered throughout the space. The more I searched, the more I panicked, the more my breathing quickened. Each breath more labored than the last. It felt like the shadows around me were closing in. The world began to blur as my vision faded. The edges softening and melting into blackness. I tried to steady myself. To push through the overwhelming wave of fear, but it was no use. The darkness crept in slowly, like a thick fog, until it consumed everything.

And then, there was nothing.

CHAPTER 5
TWO EVILS

KALIYAH

Ugh... What's up with my mattress? It hasn't even been two months since that freakin' health and wellness influencer convinced me I *just had to have it.* Dang, it feels like I'm sleeping on a pile of rocks.

I sigh deeply, trying to adjust my body to a more comfortable position, but it's no use. I paid too much money for this damn thing to feel like this. I wonder if it's too late to get a refund. Groggy and body aching, I peek one eye open, my vision slowly acclimating to the dimly lit space.

Hold on. This isn't... my bedroom. My eyes shot open. I gasp. "What the fuck...?" My vision adjusting. Clearing to the sight of a goblin's decapitated head resting next to mine, shocked me to my core. I leap out of my resting spot, my heart beating in my chest.

"What the shit?!" I scream. *Wait...* The memory hits me like a ton of bricks. The goblins. They chased me in here. No~ this can't be real. I was hoping it was all just a nightmare. But then it hits me again. *I'm still alive?*

A wave of relief washes over me, but it's quickly replaced by a sinking feeling in my gut. *That creature's eyes.* My head whips around the cave. Is it still here?

I stand up, my body stiff from spending the entire night on the cold, unforgiving ground. My limbs are tingling with pins and needles, but I shake it off, dusting my clothes. *What was that thing? Did it mean to save me?* I can't help but wonder. The faint glow of the plants are gone, replaced by the soft, golden light streaming through the front of the cave. *Sunlight.* It must be morning. I take a better look around the cavern. To my left, there's a small indent in the cave's wall, but otherwise, it's a dead end. To my right, though, the cave seems to extend further in. I notice dim, luminescent lights probably the same plants as before. They were glowing softly as they lead deeper into the dark end of the cave.

I have absolutely no desire to go any further in. So I tighten my bag around my back and make a beeline toward the entrance. The sunlight from outside is a sweet beacon of freedom I won't keep waiting. As I move closer, something catches my eye. On the left side of the cavern, tracing along the wall, there's a narrow groove along the floor. It's noticeably smoother than the rest of the cave, almost like it was carved that way deliberately. I keep walking, not thinking too much of it.

Then, my foot kicks something. I flinch, and my eyes dart down to Ryan's dagger. I grabbed my chest, look up and took a deep breath to calm my nerves. When I opened my eyes, I could see the sigil above me. The same one that glowed last night. It looks much different from the ones that I saw on the Elder Stones.

I crouch down to pick the blade up, my hand feeling the cold metal as I grip it tightly. Then I look back up at the sigil above me. I roll my eyes, muttering under my breath. "Damn magic symbols, nothing but trouble everywhere they appear."

I took a quick glance back to my bodyless companion. I thought that cat eyed creature took the top half of the goblin. So why the hell did I wake up to the sight of its disgusting face? And where's the rest of it? The legs? The torso? It's not like I really care. I just want to get the hell out of this cave and back to civilization.

Just as I was about to pass under the sigil and in the direction of the exit, I realized I was about to step right into the puddle of that goblin's blood. Instinctively, in one quick motion, I tilt on my heel, push off the ground and leap to the left. My body slamming into the cave wall with a thud as I try to avoid the stinky green goop.

"Ouch." *What was that?* With my side pressed against the smooth wall's groove, I look at the side of my upper arm, because something sharp grazed it. The sleeve on my shirt was ripped, a piece missing. I examined my arm to see two shallow cuts, with a small drop of blood streaming down.

"Huh? How did that happen?" A golden light shined near the left side of my face, pulling my attention in its direction.

Another sigil? I thought, but as I looked closer, I realized it wasn't just that one. My eyes traced along the path of the narrow groove, and the more I looked, the more sigils became visible, embedded along the path. But that wasn't what was making the blood in my veins turn to ice. I can sense *it*. It's right next to me. The same presence from last night. My heart stilled. It had to be no more than two feet away. But I couldn't bring myself to look.

Whatever it is, I know it towers me, as I feel its deep breathing hitting the top right side of my head. My body tenses and refuses to exhale as I squeezed my eyes shut. Trying to summon the courage to peak at the creature.

Please don't be something gruesome. Please please please. Please don't be something that wants to rip me apart.

I started to imagine all the things it could be. Probably something huge. Something with multiple heads, like a two-headed tiger bat, whatever the hell that is. My adrenaline surging. I knew full well that it could strike at any moment. But then, just as quickly as it started, its deep breathing stopped. The world around me fell eerily silent, and I dared to hope, just for a moment, that it had left.

Is it gone? Open your eyes. No, I'm scared. Just look, damn it, before it's too late. Okay... Okay. One... two... three...

I peeled my eyelids open slowly and turned my head to the right. *Nope. It was there.* Right freakin' there. The urge to scream burned in my throat, but I fought it down, clamping my lips together as if that would somehow make it go away. With it so close, my eyes were now clearly able to see the... Beast? Is that what it is? It looks more man than anything.

His presence was overwhelming, the air around him thick with something untamed. For a split second, I almost couldn't take my eyes off him, drawn into his sheer size, his animalistic beauty. He was just as mesmerizing as he was terrifying. His muscles rippled under his skin, twitching with each subtle movement. His broad shoulders seemed to take up the space around me. His thick arms bulging with strength. Every inch of his chest was sculpted, muscles tight, like he was carved from these very stone walls. His slight over shoulder-length locs framed his face, just a shade darker than his strange tinted blue skin that gleamed from the sun's peeking rays. His nose wide, his lips full, and short ears that led to a point. But it was his teeth that drew my attention. The tips of sharp fangs jutting behind his bottom lip, an unexpected contrast to the otherwise human face.

What the hell is he? My mind screamed. *Was he the one from last night, the creature that helped me?* His eyes didn't look quite the same as before. They were less intense and grey, but human.

I was confused to what he was doing. Or more accurately, what he *wasn't*. He hadn't moved an inch. He just stood there, staring at me. His gaze locked onto mine. Now that I see him, I was unable to look away. I didn't know how long we stood like that locked in some strange, unspoken standoff. I was way too afraid to move from my spot. After a few more moments like this, he slowly began to trace his eyes down my body. His expression too vague for me to know what his intentions are.

Is he trying to figure me out too? The question spiraled in my mind, growing louder with each passing second. If I was still in the godforsaken world of Therion, this place maybe somewhere people don't venture much, for obvious reasons. So, could it be I'm the first human he's ever seen. I swallowed hard, trying to work up the courage to speak. My voice trembling and weak, as the first few words that left my mouth weren't even hearable. I quickly cleared my throat and tried again, being sure to keep my tone low and soft, not knowing how the beast man would react.

"H— Hello. Um..." I watch him carefully. "W— w— was that you last night?" My hands tremble along with my voice. "If— if that was you, um... thank you. You saved my life."

It, he didn't respond, his gaze still intense, scanning me with an unsettling stillness. Not a flicker of acknowledgment in his expression.

"My name is Kaliyah." I paused for a moment, watching closely for any shift in his demeanor, but there was none. "Do you have a name?" Still nothing. His eyes kept moving over me, cold, silent. "Um… Can you understand me?" I asked more calmly this time.

Of course, he most likely can't. He probably has his own otherworldly language like the goblins do. Whatever he was, he looked more like a man than a monster despite his large frame and the intimidating aura around him. Although shirtless, I can't help but notice his short length pants made of some sort of thick worn leather. The legs slightly loose and the heavy weathered belt holding them snuggly around his waist.

He hadn't attacked me yet, so if I show him I'm not a threat, then—

My thoughts fading away. My gaze fell involuntarily to the thing in his hand. My heart skipped a beat when I realized what it was. My sleeve. Between the tips of his sharp nails, the fabric of my sleeve was held, like a napkin. My breath caught in my throat. What happen to that goblin's torso…

Did he just attempt to do the same to me a moment ago?

That can't be right. Otherwise, he would have snatched me up by now. Slowly, I turned the rest of my body to face him, my back to the groove's wall. That's when I noticed it. The right muscles in his arm twitched, a subtle yet predatory motion, as if he was waiting for me to come closer. The sigil behind me glowed brighter, its golden light casting long shadows across the space, making everything seem even more ominous. I pulled further back at his gesture.

My breath hitched. The look on his face shifts in a blink of an eye. A hellish gaze that would be enough to make even the most masculine man weak in the knees. His nostrils flared, and his lips curled back, revealing his bottom two elongated tusks that gleamed like small daggers. Then, just when I thought I couldn't get any more terrified, he lifted his hand to his mouth, his tongue darting out to lick my blood from the tips of his claws.

Holy hell. There's no doubt about it now. This creature is going to eat me. My back couldn't sink any further into the stone, but that didn't keep me from trying. Unlike the goblins, this man-beast's legs were much longer than mine, so out running him is not an option. There's Ryan's dagger, but with the size of the blade and my meager strength, I might as well be holding a toy.

Just as I was frantically pondering my next move, something unexpected happened. He gave me a deadpan stare, backed away, then just stood there. The intensity in his stare was enough to make me feel like I was suffocating. Was he... waiting for me to run? Was he like those goblins? Does he enjoy the chase, reveling in the fear of his victims?

If he thought I'd turn my back to him, after what I'd seen him do to that goblin, he could forget it. I slowly started to move, my body scraping along the side of the wall, my eyes never leaving his. I didn't dare make any rapid gestures. Every step I took, I kept careful watch for any signs that he would pursue me. His gaze remained locked on me, but he didn't react.

Once I was a good distance away, I bolted. My head only looking back for a moment, but nothing. *Where did he go? Just run. Faster.* I'm almost out. Seconds later, the warmth of the sun hits my skin. Now free from the cave, I felt a jolt of energy and I was going to use every bit of it to high tail it out of there. My heart sank deep into my chest. I skidded to a stop. I couldn't believe what I was seeing. The once bare patch of land, now the camp site of a horde of fucking goblins, at least forty strong.

A chaotic mess of makeshift tents and flickering campfires, each one surrounded by groups of goblins huddled together, talking in their high-pitched voices. Scattered across the clearing, some sharpening weapons, others arguing over their meager supplies. The goblins' dirty colored rags and mismatched armor stand out against the grassless patch of earth, the flames flicker around their small, mischievous faces. A few are cooking something over the fire, probably more human remains. I stepped back. My breath shallow. My movements in utter shock. The last thing I needed was to draw attention to myself. I could feel the weight of their beady little eyes, even if none had spotted me yet.

I retreated, desperate for cover, forgetting all about the dangerous *being* inside. I took several steps back into the cave. Backing a few meters into the darkness. Keeping my steps lite when something strange happened. A golden light, tracing the ground just behind my heel, crept up the side of the wall, winding its way to the ceiling above, creating a luminous ring. The hairs on the back of my neck standing on end.

Murderous intent... that's the only way I can describe this feeling. Slowly, dread pooling in my gut, I turned around. My stomach twisted as soon as I saw him. His chest rose and fell in slowly, each breath like a warning. There was no mistaking the tension in his massive frame. He stood there, poised like a creature in the wild, the kind of animal ready to pounce. His arms were outstretched, the fingers curling into claws, twitching at the air as if itching to rip me to shreds. Those damn blue cat-like eyes show themselves once more. His posture, his stance, everything about him screamed predator. It was like he was waiting for me to make the wrong move. Like, just one step closer and he'd be on me. His claws sinking into my flesh. His strength crushing me. And I'd be nothing but prey. Yet still, his body never crossed the sigil's path.

Why hasn't he killed me yet? Is it because of the magic symbols? Don't freakin' tell me the only thing keeping me from certain death are these fucking sigils.

I collapsed to my butt, my legs refusing to listen. His head tilted, those now grey eyes flicking from me to the cave entrance, then back to me. And then, *that* grin. It spread across his face like he knew I was just about to figure it out. He knew I was trapped, trapped between two vicious evils, and there was nothing I could do about it. He turned away, heading down the fork in the cave, veering left, the opposite direction I'd taken last night. My heart pounded as I pulled my knees to my chest, burying my face in them, tears flowing down my cheeks. *What the hell am I supposed to do now?*

It's been many years since I've felt dread. I stop being the type of girl that wears her emotions on her sleeves. Most of the time, I'm all about the rational thinking, the logic. No surprise that my last few relationships didn't work out. The biggest issue with me, apparently, my inability to open up. They wanted me to be vulnerable, to share the deep stuff that makes a romance feel real. And yeah, they weren't wrong. I kept it all tucked away.

My first love. That was my 17-year-old high school boyfriend. I fell for him so damn hard it was ridiculous. But then, I found out he was messing around with *his* very own first love. Some girl from another school, just a random little 'thot'. I swear, it shattered me. Nothing had ever broke me like that before. I mean, I cried for months only leaving my tear-soaked bed for the blurry days of school. Barely eating, not even sleeping. Grampa had got so worried about me. It's actually what prompted him to get me a therapist in the first place.

At the time I didn't understand how loving someone could hurt so freakin' bad. And more than that, I couldn't wrap my head around why women even bother doing it, knowing full well it might end in disaster. That was the moment I made a vow. Never again would I let a man drag me into that kind of soul-crushing despair. Maybe that's why I put so much stock into my friendships.

It's wild to think those days used to rank as the darkest, most gut-wrenchingly depressing chapters of my life. '*Used to*' being the operative phrase. Because whatever fresh hell this is, it's obliterating that top spot. And it's doing everything, but taking its sweet ass time. I'd trade anything to be back at Grampa's house, curled up in my creaky old twin bed, ugly-crying over some two-faced high school boy who couldn't spell 'loyalty' if I tattooed it on his forehead. Pathetic, maybe. But at least that made sense. But this shit?

This is chaos wrapped in a nightmare with a side of what-the-fuck. And because of that, my emotions are running, sky-high and barely contained. All I want to do is scream and cry. Tear the world in half with my voice and beg someone, anyone, to come save me from this bullshit. But I know that's not going to happen.

Grampa thinks I'm on a trip with my friends and my friends think I'm back home. No one knows I'm here. I *can* scream and I *can* cry, but will that do me any good? No. If anything it will just make things a *whole lot worse*. Although the sun's rays dawn my back, the cave felt darker than ever. All I could do was sit there, paralyzed by the crushing dread of it all. The sounds of the goblins outside was impossible to ignore, their chatter growing louder with every passing second, drawing closer, closing near.

Shit. I snapped myself to my feet, pushing myself further into the cave. My foot stopped just before the sigil. If I step over this, the man-beast lurking in the shadows will most definitely rip me to shreds, but if I don't the goblins will slow roast me over an open flame and probably cackle to my screams.

What the hell am I supposed to do? My eyes looked at the grooves in the wall, remembering. The man-beast didn't come near the sigils. Can he not get to me there too? *If I'm wrong about this—*

I clung to the smooth, narrow path, moving carefully at first. But as the goblins' chattering grew louder, I hurried my way down the groove, scooting faster. A sudden shout echoed behind me. My head snapped back.

Oh no, they see me. They chittered and pointed, their voices high-pitched. I pushed forward, reaching the clearing at the far end where the second sigil stretched across the ceiling. I waited, watching them, praying the man-beast would repeat his last encounter with the little green monsters. But this time, they didn't follow. They stopped, hesitant, maybe even afraid. Did they know what would happen if they entered... about the *creature that resides in this place?*

Fortunately for me, I don't think they've figured out the trick to the narrow groove. The goblins turned around and walked away, leaving me in silence. I let out a shaky breath, feeling the weight in my chest ease just a fraction. At least for now, I didn't have to worry about them.

CHAPTER 6
HELLA PRESSED

KALIYAH

GROWL~ Damn it to hell. Just keep piling it on. My stomach is trying to devour itself. I don't even remember the last time I ate. Really regretting my decision not to indulge myself at the Empress's feast.

Ugh.. That fucking bitch. First you kidnap me and my friends, then you have your mage ditch me in some monster filled forest, leaving me to die. I swear to God, the next time I see that damn woman, I'm going to—

GRRRRRROOOOOWWWLLLLLLLL.

Man, I'm too hungry to think about anything else right now. If that man-beast is stuck in here, that means there's gotta be something to eat in here, other than goblin. My eyes peered over to the severed head with a scowl. If I am to find that out, I'm going to have to venture deeper into this damn cave.

"But... I don't wanna," I mutter, whining to myself. I glance down the winding path of the creepily lit cavern. Then again, starving to death might not be so bad, given my other two options. *Ugh...* And give that uppity empress the satisfaction.

Fuck that. I'll eat rocks if I have to. Anything to survive this place and get my revenge on that royal bitch and her hooded goon. All I need to do is wait out the goblins or at least wait until their numbers thin out. Creatures like that probably don't stick around in one place for too long, right?

I shake off my nerves, dagger tightly gripped in my hand. I need to go deeper. The cave's silence is eerie. The walls pressing in around me as I move further into the stone corridor. The light is dim at first, barely reaching the deeper parts of the cave, but the farther I go, the brighter the luminescent plants shine.

I can feel my body weakening, the hunger threatening to consume me. I move cautiously, drawn to the strange plants that seem to thrive along the walls and floor edges. My fingers brush against vines. I need something that will fill this ache in my belly. I squat down when I spot the mushrooms. They're round, with smooth, flat caps, their surfaces shining with an unnatural glow. Some are large, others small, but they all share that same strange light. I pluck a few carefully, knowing there's no telling what these things might do to me. Even though, back home, if there's one thing watching wildlife videos taught me, it's that brightly colored things found in nature usually spell trouble. Here's to hoping it's the opposite in this fantasy world.

I tuck them into the center of my dagger's cloth, wrapping them gently so they won't get crushed.

Then, I move to the flowers growing seemingly out of the stone ground. Their puffy petals are delicate, almost translucent. I pluck a few of them, examining them closely, but I don't trust them either. I shift again, noticing cherry size buds growing up the vine's stem. They look like miniature bells, slightly firm to the touch. There weren't very many to pick. Still I added it to the cloth with the others, collecting whatever I could.

The air is starting to feel fresher, cleaner, with the faintest hint of *something* on the breeze. I pause for a moment, listening, and then I hear it. A soft, distant sound that grows clearer with every step. That sounds like... *water?*

My hopefulness pulls me forward, and I follow the sound, drawn to the even brighter light ahead. Is it another way out of the cave? Can't be. The light is as bright as the sun, but the color was all wrong. I emerge into an open space, and the sight before me takes my breath away. The cave opens up into a vast chamber, the air cooler here, with the steady hum of water. At least forty feet of open space leading to the edge of a chasm that seems to split the cave in two. The source of the light, a crystal the size of an elephant lodged into the roof.

To my right, as it braces against the wall, clinging to the edge of the cliff, is an enormous tree. Its branches are heavy with strange fruit. The tree's jagged roots emerge from the stone beneath its trunk, as a network of thick vines cascade up the rigid wall beside it. The leaves, a dark color, nothing like the vibrant plants from the rest of the cave.

Across the chasm, to the left, I spot a small waterfall cascading down into a serene pond below. The water from this view looks clear, almost still. It's like I've stumbled upon a secret world, tucked away in the heart of this mountain. I can't help but feel a sense of unreal.

Finally... *finally*, the universe is giving me a break. Carefully, I examine the tree's position. Half of its roots cling to the rock wall, tilting over the chasm, as I notice lime-colored fruit. Their surfaces covered with short pink, dull protruding points. The tips of the branches are even heavier with the fruit, hanging perilously over the seemingly bottomless cliff. Getting any closer to the edge is out of the question.

Luckily, a few of the fruits have fallen closer to the base of the trunk, and I snatch them up, relieved to find something within reach. With the fruits in hand, I walk back to this area's entry point. The pain in my stomach sharpens, relentless, gnawing at me. I need to know what's safe to eat and what could possibly kill me because if I don't figure it out soon, I don't know how much longer I'll last. I slid down the wall, sitting in the cool breeze near the entrance, the cloth of plants thick in my lap. The glow that had once pulsed from some of them was gone, leaving them looking like everyday plants.

I begin sorting through them carefully, one by one, examining each. I press the leaves between my fingers, sniffing them, even licking the edges of a few. Each one feels more questionable than the last. The mushrooms, though, had me the most worried. But nothing I did gave me clear answers. This is too frustrating. Any one of these could possibly take me out.

Hell, maybe all of them could be toxic. My stomach growls louder. Starvation gnawing at me, as I try to decide. *When in doubt, go for the fruit, I guess.* I lifted the peculiar fruit, wiping its surface with my shirt as if that did anything and then sunk my teeth in.

To my surprise, it was softer than its firm exterior led me to believe it'd be. At first, there was a slight bitterness, followed by a mild sweetness. The texture reminded me of a pear, while the flavor was more like a raisin. Neither fruit was something I particularly enjoyed back home. I was always a strawberry and banana girl. *What I wouldn't give...* But beggars can't be choosers. I had planned to only take a single small bite, wait an hour or so to see if it was safe, and then, if everything went well, eat the rest. But of course, things never go as planned for me. The moment the otherworldly fruit hit my stomach, it was like the roaring cry for more, echoed throughout my body. I tried to resist the temptation to gorge myself for all of... two minutes. And then I couldn't help it. I sank my teeth into another piece, and then another. The two I grabbed earlier weren't nearly enough to calm the raging storm in my belly.

Desperate to fill the emptiness, I sprinted back to the tree, knelt down, and devoured the fruit. Each bite felt like relief. I didn't stop until the roaring cries of my stomach were pacified. *That's one problem down.* I glanced over to the other side of the cavern. Now, all that was left was the water aspect. I mean, I know it's possible to survive a month without food. My stomach would probably argue that fact, but I know better to think that anyone can survive more than a week without water.

As filling as the um... *spiny* fruit was, it was anything but 'juicy'. I examined the cavern's edge once more. The gap between me and the other side looked to be at least fifteen feet across. There was no way I was jumping that. Hell, I wouldn't even risk it if it was only five. The thought of plummeting to my death, my body lost to the deep, dark abyss, for all of eternity.

"Yeah, hell no." My eyes flicked to the tree again. The branches stretched out far, almost reaching the other side. If I were to climb the thickest part, there was a chance I could make it across. But honestly, I'm just not that pressed. For now, I'm going to stick with the spiny fruit and hope it can hold me over.

Fuckkkkk! It's been three days, and now? Now, I'm fucking desperate. The spiny fruit are starting to feel like they're soaking up my saliva. My tongue is dry as hell, and my lips have cracked to the point of bleeding. This isn't going to work. I need water. I'm willing to climb the cliff-hanging tree if it means I can get even a single drop. I get up and make my way to the tree. I kick it hard to make sure it's not just a few pounds away from tipping over the edge. Some of the spiny fruit falls to the ground, a few even going over the side. It's now or never. I remove my sneakers and socks and stuff them into my bag. I don't want the rubber soles to cause me to slip. I'm a little concerned about how I'll get back to the fruit tree once I make it over there.

While I did notice another entrance on the other side of the cavern near the waterfall, there's no telling where it leads or if there's food over there. But that's a problem for later. I need water. *Now.*

I started throwing some of the fruit to the other side no doubt bruising them as they smashed into the ground. Then, I shove as many into my already stiff backpack as it would allow, for good measure. Time to climb. I first started crawling up the tree's trunk. Once the tilted spine started to level out, I rose to my feet, extending my arms, palm bracing the wall to keep my balance.

Slowly, I put one foot in front of the other, making my way toward the edge of the cliff. "Don't look down." *Shit.* I said don't look down. It really is a pit of nothingness. The view from up here look so different. I focus on something along the edging of the chasm, narrowing my eyes. I try to stay steady as I cling to one of the tree's vines glued to the cave's wall. *Is that...?* What looked like jagged rock formations from below, now from above, formed something more intricate. It's one of those damn magic symbols. A *really* big one.

But if it's here... A subtle hum filled the air. My heart skipped a beat as the glow spread along the cliffside, towards the root of the tree. Before I knew it the glow crept up the side of the wall next to me, forming one mega ring around the space. My eyes fixed on the light peaking from behind my only anchor.

That would mean... And then, from the corner of my eye, something *unnatural* caught my attention. A shift on the wall. Something was there. Something waiting. *No...* I lifted my gaze. There. He. Was.

That thirsty animal stare, as his body pressed horizontally against the stone wall, as if he was part spider. His claws digging into the rock with ease. The moment my gaze landed on him, he bared his full fangs at me. Reflex took over. I jerked back, slipping off the tree's trunk. The world seemed to slow as I plummeted, my soul leaving my body. I tried to grasp anything, but my hands scrambled, barely catching hold of the vine. My death grip, the only thing saving me from plunging to the end of my story. I hung there over the gaping pit.

Panic surging through me as the vine began to peel from the stone. My fingers scraped the edge of the cliff, just inches away from certain death, my body hanging precariously as I fought for my survival. My grip was slipping, the vine ripping, but somehow, some desperate surge of strength coursed through me. I heaved, straining every muscle in my body.

I finally managed to pull myself over the cliff's edge, heart racing, breaths ragged. I collapsed, my legs shook beneath me, too numb to stand. The nausea of fear still clung to my body. I didn't even have to look back to know he was still there. The proof was the still glowing sigil. Never facing his direction, I didn't want to give him the satisfaction of seeing the bone wrenching fear on my face.

God damn it. My life was nearly lost again. This whole time, the other side of this cavern is where the left side of the cave's fork leads. That means he's probably been watching me from the shadows these last three days, patiently waiting for me to try and cross over.

"You... pastel blue... mother fucker. I almost died." My anger spilled through as I balled my fist into my lap.

Just then, a deep heavy, rumbling voice from behind let out a growling laugh that echo the chamber. "I almost had you, didn't I?"

My body turned statue.

CHAPTER 7
THE BEAST WITHIN

MITUS

How long has it been now? Seventy? Eighty years? Hell, for all I know, it's been a century since I've been trapped in this cold, hard prison. Time is a cruel concept when there's nothing but silence and the occasional rustle of things I've long since devoured. My only reprieve from this endless boredom is the long stretches of sleep. A state of hibernation, really. I suppose it's my fault. Killing every creature that wandered in, no matter how small.

After a few decades, they stopped approaching altogether. The more primal animals, those with any ounce of natural instinct, know to steer clear of this place. Once in a while, I get lucky. A wounded animal, or a low-level monster seeking shelter. But even then, in many cases they're either too sickly to eat or there's not enough meat to feed the gnawing hunger that grows each passing year. Thankfully, my body is able to go long stretches without food. But damn it, the number of kingdoms I would grind to rubble if it meant I could sink my teeth into a big ass Hogswine or a juicy Fogturp.

Anything would be better than goblin meat. That crap is so tough, and the flavor, revolting. Took me decades to learn to keep it down. You'd think the higher-level goblins would taste better, but no. Taste like shit. Found that out a long time ago, when a hobgoblin wandered in, looking to challenge me. Most likely some pathetic attempt to ascend in ranks as a goblin lord.

Ha. The way I tore his arms off and fed them to him. Pure gold. I wanted him to know what disgusting meat I be forced to chew on later. Every few years or so, the smaller grunts would come poking around to see if I'm still occupying the mountain. No doubt wanting to claim residence. After all, the magic energy that radiates from this place is immense.

The mountain's magic core, the only thing continuously supplying those fucking soul sigils with their power. If only there was a way for me to untune myself from the magic that binds me here... I'd break free, and I'd finally be able to hunt down the bastards who sealed me in this hellscape.

SKIT-SKIT. SNARL. CHITTER.

What's this...? Company? It seems those damn goblins can't get enough of me. The small ones don't usually wander in here so carelessly. And yet... There it is trembling before me. Could it have been pursuing something? It would be appreciated if that something was a winged animal of some kind. It's been so long since I've had white meat. Though, I shouldn't get my hopes up.

The moment the goblin's eyes met mine, it dropped its hatchet and tried to run. But my claws shot out, wrapping around its neck, ending its loud screeching in an instant. Now, let's see what all the commotion is about.

I approach the fork in the cave. To my right, the familiar entrance to the outside world. A painful reminder of what I can no longer touch. To my left, the mage's path, a route I rarely take. The sigil that blocks my way further down effectively makes it nothing but a dead end for me. But now... my curiosity is piqued. What would cause such weak low-level creatures to risk entering my domain?

Another goblin, I see. Such a small blade in its hand. Surely it wouldn't risk certain death for whatever small creature that would perish from such a feeble weapon. As I slowly approach the low-level monster from behind, my eyes fall upon its victim.

A human? Well, hell. Looks like this day just got a whole lot more interesting. It's been at least six or seven years since a human came anywhere near this place. Some poor fool, probably separated from his party. He was taking refuge from the harsh winter storm. The shock on his face when he discovered me inside. Priceless. I wasted no time taking him. It was my first time eating human. It's bitter and gamey. I can't say I enjoyed the taste of his flesh. But it's a whole hell of a lot better than goblin, those disgusting little shits. I guess this means human is back on the table.

Wait... Shit. The human is just behind the sigil. If that damn goblin kills it over the boundary, then they'll be no way for me to claim it. I need to stop this before it reaches the border. With more effort than I'd planned, I snatched the goblin up, tearing its torso from its body. No matter. At least the human was still alive.

I slowly headed in its direction. It's scent... surprisingly refreshing, not anything like that human male from before. Wait... is it female? A grin tugged at the corner of my lips. *Even better.* Something tells me human females are much more tender than their male counterparts.

Now, I just need to figure out how to get to her. I'm making sure to keep under the cover of the shadows. If she sees me, she'll know what I am and surely run deeper into the cave and sooner die, then let me get my hands on her. Her eyes haven't stopped following the glow of my own. Maybe, if she thinks I have left her alone, she might cross the path of the sigil, in an attempt to flee. I close my eyes, effectively shielding their glow. I listen and wait.

THUD.

I snap my eyes open to see the human woman collapsed on her side. *'Shit... is it dead? Did she succumb to a prior injury?'* I take a deep breath, sniffing her direction. No. I don't smell any blood, and her chest is still moving. Fainted, I see. Then there's nothing I can do now. I will have to wait until she wakes up. In the meantime, what is that commotion outside? I make my way to the entrance and tilt my ears toward the wind. *More goblins... and the scent of fire. Seems like they're making camp. How bold of them.*

Could it be they want the human woman too? Probably planning to satisfy their sick, carnal urges. I heard stories of their sessions usually lasting weeks, even months if the woman doesn't manage to take her own life as a desperate means of escape. Vial repulsive creatures. I can't allow that to happen. It would only taint the meat.

Actually, that gives me an idea. How about a welcome gift for my guest. I removed the goblin's head from its torso and rolled it into her sight line. 'This should make for some real fun.' But for now, it's dinner time.

The human's movements are subtle. She should awake at any moment. I must make sure I do not catch her gaze.

"AHHHH! What the fuck is that?" She yelped, her body jerking upright in panic. I held back the chuckle trickling my throat.

"What the shit?!" Her voice was loud and sharp. Although the severed head of the goblin did startle her, it was not as big of a reaction as I was hoping for. I've heard that many human women flee at the mere sight of insects. So why hasn't she started running past the boundary and right into my clutches? Her eyes started combing the cave. *'Ah, I see.'* She's checking for any signs of my presence. No point. She won't find any. By the time she finally takes notice of me, it'll be too late.

What a meager dagger. The quality looks much nicer than anything those goblins have. She must come from wealth. It will make for an excellent tool for picking my teeth with. Finally... She starts to head this way. Her body is just under the sigil. *That's right... you're almost mine.* I wait patiently, knowing the moment she crosses that barrier, I'll go for her.

Now! I reach out, ready to snatch her. But then, in an instant, she does something I *didn't* expect. As if she'd been preparing for my move, she pivots on her heel and leaps toward the groove. *What? Did she... see me coming?* The humans that I've come across in my past usually weren't this astute.

"Ouch." Her voice drifts through the air.

Damn. She's standing along the sigils' groove. The only reason that damn mage carved it into the wall was to grant safe passage to the crystal core deep in the mountain. But he hasn't set foot in this place since *that* day. Shit, I was *so close*. Just a thread away from having her. But all I managed was to tear the fabric of her shirt. Does she know about the grooves purpose?

"Huh? How did that happen?" she murmurs, glancing down at the insufficient scratches I left behind.

So, she hadn't noticed me. Which means her sudden, feline-like reflexes was just a fluke. The suppressive force of the sigils won't allow me to get any closer. She's just a few feet away. Her aroma... it's a welcoming change from the rotten stench of goblin flesh. It's faintly sweet and slightly floral. It makes me want to sink my teeth into her that much more.

Look at her. The way her body trembles. She's too terrified to even glance in my direction. She should be afraid, *very* afraid. I can't wait for the moment she learns of who is standing before her. Surely my name still sends shivers throughout the lands, even after all this time. The thought of her begging for mercy while I nibble off her little fingers, *Mmmmm.* I haven't had anything like this to look forward to in ages. I'm getting hungry just thinking about it. *But calm yourself, you haven't gotten to her yet.* I'm pretty sure she hasn't figured out the mage's path, and I don't want to tip her off.

I force myself to steady my breathing. Then, abruptly, she *swings her head* and her eyes lock with mine. It catches me off guard for a fleeting moment. Her eyes are big and round, the color of a rich deep brown. They're like looking at two glossy coco pearls, shining with something almost... pure. I haven't thought about those creamy, delicate treats in years. I wonder... if they taste just as sweet.

Surprisingly, she doesn't make a peep. Is the sight of me, the nightmare of monsters, less frightening than a decapitated goblin to her. *How curious.* She must be in shock. Now that I get a better look at her... Her frame is thicker on her lower half than the top. That's good. But her arms... Doesn't look like there's much meat on them.

"H— Hello. Um..." She speaks. "W— w— was that you last night? I— if that was you, thank you. You saved my life."

Her subtle accent, unfamiliar. Definitely not from the lands of Castdor. And probably not Yurakora, its nothing but elven country out there after all. So maybe a settlement near either Magdara or Sebbarus. That is where the largest population of humans tend to dwell. *Interesting.* Do all human women from Sebbarus have bodies that form to these sort of curves. I never got the chance to travel there, tossed into this mountainy prison just after declaring war. I had little interaction with the ones nearing the lands of Yenka and Razakar, but from what I remember they were most definitely not shaped like this. But then again, I was too busy demolishing villages, killing soldiers, and *taking* riches.

"My name is Kaliyah. Do you have a name?"

But I ignored her words, my attention pulled elsewhere. I study her clothes. *Are these the garments of her people?* They're unlike anything I've seen before. The fabric is strange, the style even more so. The way the material clings to her, like it was made to *fit her skin*, to *move* with her.

"Um... Can you understand me?"

Kaliyah, she called herself. *I would prefer my food not to talk to me.* If she insists on a name, fine. How about I call her *breakfast*. That suits her much better. She starts to turn her body towards me. *Hell yeah.* Shit... No. I got too excited for a moment, thinking she was about to lean away from the wall. My arm involuntarily readied itself for a second swipe and she noticed.

Damn it. She buried her body further out of reach. The scent of blood hits my nose just now, sharp and inviting. I need to *try* her, to taste her. I reach forward, lifting the fabric of her clothing, and lick the blood that clings to my fingertips. Not bad. Yes, she will make for a fine meal. But after what I just did, she most definitely knows my intentions. There's no way I'll get her to come closer now. How could I let her slip from my grasp? My ears perk up at the sound of rowdy goblins just beyond the cave entrance.

Yes, that's right. She doesn't know. Then let's let her find out. I back away as far as the passage would allow, then just watched and waited. She doesn't take her eyes off me, but just as I expected, she slowly starts moving along the groove, inching towards the exit. Then, she breaks into a sprint. *So, she's running now.* I want to give chase, but then the fun will be over too quickly. I hide in waiting, letting her slip out of the cave. Not that I could stop her anyway. *Fucking sigils.* For about a minute, she is not within my view.

The thought of those goblins charring my breakfast to a burnt crisp, infuriates me. *Wait, what if the human is stupid enough to think she can communicate or reason with goblins the way she had just tried with me.*

Hell, I can say goodbye to those tender looking thighs, and that lush succulent backside that jiggled as she ran. It's been too long since she exited. I buried my claws into my palms just waiting to hear her screams. But none came, instead, lite footsteps. She's backing up. My arms snap wide, ready, and every muscle in my body goes tight. I haven't felt excited like this in forever. My fingers stretch out, curling my claws, twitching with an overwhelming urge to tear into her.

That's it... just a little closer. My eyes narrow, locking onto her as she trembles. I watch her, savoring the way she hesitates, her fear leaking into the air, only making her scent more tantalizing.

I hear each breath she takes, quicker now, her veins pulsing against the thin golden chain around her neck as its pink pendant reflects the light. *It will make a nice souvenir to remember this moment by. Come on... just one more step, and I'll have you in an instant.* Her movements stopped. *No... keep coming.* She slowly turns around, and the moment she sees me lying in wait, she stumbles, falling onto her ass. That plump juicy looking ass.

Damn... she caught me. I tilt my head slightly, watching her realize the gravity of her situation. I know she's slowly figuring it out, that look of realization spreading across her face. I couldn't hold back the grin nipping at my lips any longer.

These sigils may have me trapped here, but so is she. I promise little breakfast, what the goblins have planned for you is far worse than anything I'd do. So, she must decide. Me or them.

Now that she understands her situation, there's no need for me to rush. I still have some leftover goblin to tide me over for now. And since I know she's not going anywhere, I leave her sitting there to drown in her own self-pity. I head back toward the fork in the cave. *If only the goblins had chased her to the left.* But then again, the game would be over before this morning.

I prepared to wash the stink of the goblin's flesh as best I could, using the fresh water from my waterfall. I had already stripped the branches of the tree that stretched to my side of the cavern of its dewberries for this season. If I'm lucky, a few more will bloom near me before winter. But that's not something I can truly count on.

Just as I was about to sully my taste buds, my ear caught something, faint but distinct. At the entrance of the clearing across the cavern, there she was, picking flowers from the wall. It hasn't been that long since I left her, and already she was wandering deeper into the cave, so careless of her. I know she has no way of knowing the boundary of the sigils.

Should I confront her? No... I want to see what she's up to. I watch as her eyes widen when she steps into the clearing.

Tsss. She has the nerve to look so relaxed.

Her gaze sweeps in my direction, but I'm certain she won't be able to see me as long as I remain hidden. Her eyes land on the waterfall. *Thirsty?* Me too. I want to quench my thirst on your blood as its warmth flows down my throat. I continue to watch as she grabs a couple of dewberries from the ground and takes a seat.

Hmmm. She lift each plant one by one, carefully examining them. Checking for toxins, perhaps? If humans had noses as sharp as mine, she'd be able to tell that none of the plants here would kill her if consumed. With that being said, they'll make her sick enough that she might wish for death. Especially those damned mushrooms. My brows furrow as I recall my first and last encounter with them. That could be fun to watch.

She reaches for the dewberry and bites into it. The best of her options. Still, the dewberry has siphoning properties if not properly prepared first. In time, it'll leave her parched with every bite. But I guess a human wouldn't know that. Dewberries are rare and can only be found in certain regions of Bloodthorn.

It's been several days now, and the peculiar way the human moves has started to raise my suspicions. If I didn't know better, I'd swear she knows she's being watched. The way she takes cover behind a small boulder in the corner of the cavern every time she has to relieve herself. And then there was that time, she actually stopped to check if anyone was looking before she removed her shirt, shielding her chest as she ripped off what was left of her sleeve. I think the dewberries have finally made work of her. Is today the day she plans to cross the chasm?

I watch as she carefully removes her odd boots and the fabric covering her feet, then discards them into her small black satchel. It was a happy surprise when she began tossing a hand full of dewberry fruit to my side of the cavern. They will make for a nice side dish. She begins to climb the tree, and I can't help but feel a small thrill. My little breakfast is getting closer, eager to feed me. I'm ready for her this time. I slowly slink out of my hiding place, making my way to the cavern wall. My fingers curl into the rock as I scale it, inching closer to her. *Little breakfast, come to me.* I can see her eyes drifting toward the chasm. *Careful now. If you fall in, all my patient waiting will be for nothing.*

But then, something changes in her expression. A shift that makes me pause. *What the hell has gotten her so distracted?* My gaze follows hers, searching for the cause to the delay in my meal.

Fuck. The ring sigil on her side of the cavern flares to life. I completely forgot about that fucking one. She knows now. Her head jerks toward me, eyes wide. Coco pearls. And just like that, any hope I had was lost. She's just out of reach, again. So pissed. I don't bother hiding it as I scowl and bare my tusks at her.

Shit... She's about to fall straight into the chasm. *Damn it.* I hear them. Her fingers scraping against the cliffside. There's nothing I can do. *What a waste.*

Wait... She just managed to cling to a vine, but its snapping, leaving her dangling over the pit. For a few moments, she struggles, her body swaying dangerously. I bite my lip, slightly tearing into the skin. *Is this it...?* But then, with one final, desperate pull, she hauls herself up, dragging her body over the edge. Her ragged breaths are heavy, raw, and they're stirring something primal within me. My tongue glides over the small drop of blood forming on my top lip. My eyes narrow in response, knowing the game isn't over yet. She collapses onto the ground, her eyes avoiding my gaze.

"You... pastel blue... motherfucker. I almost died," she yells, her voice burning with a fire.

I can't help the grin that pulls at my lips. And with that, I couldn't hold it in any longer. I let out a deep, mocking laugh, the sound echoing off the chasm.

"I almost had you... didn't I?" I spoke my first words to her, words dripping with amusement.

Unlike so many other creatures who met their end over this cliff, I'm happy I still have a chance to claim my little breakfast.

CHAPTER 8
PURGATORY

KALIYAH

The deep, growl of the beast slithered over my skin. Goosebumps followed in its wake. My body froze. *No... it can't be. That voice, those words. He can speak? This whole time?*

"What's the matter?" His voice rolled through the space, a tremor that made my insides tighten. My body jolts at the rumble in his threatening voice. "What happened to that fire in your lungs just a moment ago?"

Even though my legs were barely responding to me, I could still sense the strength lingering in my body. Without a word, I leaned forward, hands and knees pressing against the rough stone, forcing myself to crawl toward the cavern's entrance. The air turned colder. Every part of me expected him to pounce, to grab my ankle and drag me back into the pit. Halfway there, his voice cut through the silence again.

"You know, from this angle, I can see your bottom half has plenty of meat. Enough to get caught in my teeth."

The words worm their way through me. My movements halted, my knees burning against the rocks. *Plenty of meat... caught in his teeth.* Did he just say...? I was right. That man-beast really wants to eat my ass, literally.

"It's only a matter of time before you make a mistake. Maybe your body will unknowingly graze just an inch over the soul barrier, or you'll trip, stumble off the mage's path for a second. And in the time it takes you to hit the ground, I will have buried my tusks so deep into your flesh. This *pale blue... mother fucker* as you put it, will be the last thing you see."

I hesitantly tilted my gaze towards him, just barely peeking over my shoulder. It was like I was looking at the presence of some kind of vicious demon. Wild chaotic energy engulf the atmosphere around him. This man, beast whatever the hell he is, he isn't just dangerous. There's no doubt, I can sense he is a monster, one with sharp intelligence, plotting, calculating every which way he can get to me. It really plans to eat me.

I don't even know how those magic symbols work. How long do they last for? Are there any conditions? Like on the night of a full moon every three years, all the sigils in this place are deactivated and because of my luck, that night would be *tonight.* Or some other ridiculous fantasy world bullshit like that. Then how long would it be before, I'd wake up one day to him slurping my intestines like freakin' spaghetti. I need to get as far away from him as possible, right the hell now.

Fuck this. I can't stay here anymore. I will take my chances with the goblins. I started clawing towards the entrance again, determined to get the hell out of here.

"They will take turns ravishing you..."

I felt like I lost all feeling in my arms, stopping in my tracks once more.

"for weeks on end, not stopping until every part of you is either battered, broken or both. Then once they've had their fun, you can be sure they won't kill you right away. Instead, they will lop pieces of your body off, some from here... and there, as they will force you to watch them burn your flesh beyond recognition and gnaw at what's left of your bones. Who knows how long it will take before your misery ends and you finally succumb to your injuries, hours, days most likely."

What?! No, no, no. No way... Kaliyah, you've got long ass legs. You ran track in high school that one year. You can outrun them. I did it before. I'll do it again.

But as if he could hear my thoughts, "They'll catch you."

My eyes glued themselves to the surface beneath me, like it was the only thing keeping my soul tethered to my body.

"Goblins may be simple-minded, low-level creatures, but they're not complete idiots. You can be sure they have the surrounding brush just beyond the clearing, laced with traps, no doubt meant to snare you and prevent you from just sneaking past them."

But... why? Why me? I think to myself

"Because you're female..."

Can he read my mind.

"Majority of goblins are male. Their female counterparts are far and few in between, about one to every two hundred. So, it's quite common for a goblin horde to steal a few human women after pillaging a village." He paused, his voice steady. "I offer this information to you, so you understand the difference between me and them, and what I'm offering you."

I fought against the lump in my throat, forcing my voice out. "Offer?"

"Yes... I have no intention of touching your body in that way. In fact, I find that particular trait of goblins to be one of the more repulsive aspects of their nature. With me, it's simple. I've been trapped here for a very, *very* long time. And, as you've no doubt realized, food is hard to come by. So, all I want to do is feast on your body. Although I cannot assure you're death will be completely void of pain, I will end your life quickly, minimizing your suffering to but a brief moment. That is my offer. All you have to do is cross the—"

"Fuck you!" My eyes dripped with tears as a pool began to form in the small crevices below. "You nightmare demon." My hands clenched into fists, pressing hard into the ground. "You promise to kill me quickly, if I just let you eat me. What the fuck kind of offer is that? I'd sooner jump headfirst into that damn pit than to let either you or some *fucking rapist goblins* come near me."

"Then you should jump now, because it's like I said, its only a matter of time. You've already realized I'm trapped here, and as long as you're here, those goblins aren't going anywhere."

My body curled inward, collapsing to my side as I pulled my legs to my chest, burying my head in my knees. I couldn't hold back the tears as I muffled my cries. I cried and cursed and cried some more. After sometime, my body relaxed and my mind started to fade. I don't know how I managed to do it. Maybe it was the desperate need to wake up from this nightmare, or my body's frantic attempt to conserve what little liquid I had left in my body. But after what felt like an eternity, my sobs drifted me off to sleep.

Day 7: My name is Kaliyah Shepard. I am or was 27 years old when writing this. I'm from the world Earth. It feels strange to even write that, but I know if you're native to this world, you probably wouldn't know what or where that is. Still, there's a good chance you have heard of my best friends. I was told they are considered to be famous in this world. You may know them as the Champions. Their names are Ryan Emmerson, Jemma Larkins, and Darrius Dobbins. By the time this is found, if this is ever found, they will have most likely returned home, so I don't expect this to ever reach them or my grandfather for that matter. But there's something I need to request from you.

My hand hesitated, the pen hovering above the paper for a moment before I dragged it slowly across the page.

If my remains are found with this letter, I ask that you take them outside. Out of this dark depressing mountain and leave them anywhere the sunlight can reach them. I don't

A tear slipped down my cheek, falling softly onto the paper, and in an instant, one of the words began to blur. The black ink smeared, bleeding into the fibers of the paper. I wiped the next tear away before it could do the same, then closed my journal, tucking it carefully back into my bag. I placed it gently by the wall near the entrance, making sure it would be visible to anyone who might come through.

I don't know how long I've been asleep or whether it's day or night outside right now. I don't have it in me to go check. But if I'm right, it's been seven days since I've had anything to drink. I feel sluggish, drained of both energy and focus as I rest my back against the hard wall. Ignoring the thirst has become nearly impossible, especially with the heavily guarded waterfall just out of reach. It's teasing me, tempting me.

Is this hell? *God, what did I ever do to deserve this?* Maybe it's because I stopped going to church, but I still caught the live streams now and then. Or maybe it's punishment for cursing out my grampa behind his back one too many times as a kid. But honestly, the way he'd send me to school with my hair a tangled mess. The kids would pick on me relentlessly for it. I'd beg him to straighten my wild, thick curls that reached down to my tailbone and seemed to stretch for the sky. But he'd always say, *"If them kids don't see how fly your natural hair is, then they not the ones you need to be hangin' with."* I was eleven, and I could care less about all that self-love, acceptance crap at the time. So of course, a *"damn you, you bald crusty old bitch"* would slip out in secret, here and there. I never really meant it. But if that's what damned me to this purgatory, then I'm sorry. I'm so sorry, grampa.

My fingers reached to touch my lips, but I quickly pulled them away as the sharp sting of cracked skin burned. I couldn't even swallow my own spit at this point, if I even had any left. The beast man wasn't in sight, but I knew he was there, somewhere. Lurking. Waiting for me to grow desperate enough to cross that damn barrier. My vision is getting hazy.

I should eat something. I shift to my side, reaching for my dagger, the tip scraping along the ground as I slowly push myself up to my feet. Stumbling over, I kneel at the roots of the tree. Its roots are thick and gnarled, violently protruding from the earth like weathered, clawed hands reaching back into the mountain. Too drained to stand any longer, I settle down, bracing my back against one of the roots. I spread my legs apart and carefully steady the fruit between them. My jaw's too sore and weak to chew properly, but if I cut it into smaller pieces, then maybe I can manage.

"Ouch." I narrow my eyes at the blade and the cut on my hand. I nicked my finger. Slowly, I bring it up to my face, watching as blood starts to bead at the surface. *It's not too bad.* My mind's starting to feel as foggy as my vision. I shove my finger in my mouth.

There he is. I knew he was watching me. His predator-like eyes gleam from the other side. Let me guess, the smell of blood. *He really... is a carnivorous... an— anim—*

MITUS

The human is foolish and stubborn. It would rather suffer a slow death. At first, it was amusing to watch her as she desperately clung to the idea that there was an actual chance of her escaping this place. The number of times she checked the campground for signs of the hordes departure. But now, she's wasting away as her body tries to drink itself. Her actions now only serve to exhaust my patience and fuel my frustration. If there's really no way I can get this human to surrender herself to me—

My nose flares as her blood fills the air, sweet. *Shit...* Did one of the goblins slip past me? I've been so focused on her, I haven't been keeping track of them.

I race to the cliff's edge. There she is, at the base of the tree. No goblins. *What is she doing...?* I watch, eyes narrowing, as she lifts her bleeding finger and places it between her crescent moon shaped lips. Her coco pearls looking me dead in the eyes. *Is she taunting me?'*

THUD.

Her body goes limp, collapsing at the base of the tree. *Damn human. If it's your wish to waste away and die, then so be it. I'd rather not watch as food goes to waste.* I turn my back, walking away, fully expecting that was the last time I will see her conscious.

KALIYAH

I look around. Endless white space stretching out in every direction, like I'm floating in some vast, dreamless void. The floor beneath me is flat and smooth, but when I reach down to touch it, my hand grips nothing. Like I'm suspended in mid-air. I haven't had this dream in years.

'Ok then, where is it?'

My eyes dart around, and I spin a few times, waiting. It never shows up right away, but, if I wait long enough... The warmth always hits me first, inviting, glowing with a soft rose gold hue that pulses, like it's breathing. Star, that's the name I came up with for it as a kid.

'Dang.' It's grown so much since the last time I saw it. Large and round, hanging in the air almost like it really was a shining star. Even though the ball of pure light is bright, it never hurts to look at. Probably because it's just a dream. But I've always loved seeing it, feeling its embrace whenever I draw near.

When I told grampa about the recurring dream, he'd always say it was my mother's angel coming to visit me. As comforting as that thought was when I was little, I never really believed that.

My ex-therapist gave me another possible explanation. "It may be your minds' way of processing emotions. A manifestation of something deeper that you've yet to figure out. But give it time. It will come."

That explanation made more sense than grampa's, but even then, it didn't feel quite right. I always had the dream when things were really tough. Like the time I was seven and got lost in an amusement park for two days after sleepwalking, the time my first love cheated on me, and the time my grampa was in that serious car accident. All trying times for me. But then, as if it was trying to prove my grampa right, I would have this peaceful dream. And the moment it appeared, I'd reach out to touch it. And all the anxiety I'd been carrying would melt away.

Just like so many times before, I stretched my hand out, taking my first step. But on the fourth step, my shoes seemed to be stuck to the nonexistent floor. My eyes narrowed in confusion. This has never happened before. Beads of sweat started to form on my temples as the space around me shifted from its usual pure white to a dark, unsettling shade of red. My attempt to take another step only sent me crashing to my knees. The air was growing warmer by the second, suffocating even. I looked up at Star. It was drifting higher into the sky, farther from me.

For whatever reason, panic seized me. I am aware this is a dream, so I don't understand why I feel like this. The irrational certainty that if it left without me, something terrible would happen. Something final.

I tear at my shoelaces as I try to pull my feet free from the unseen force holding them down. My legs burn with exertion, determined to reach Star. My body growing more labored. My mouth is dry, cracked, my throat ached as if sandpaper had replaced my flesh.

"I don't understand," I whisper, my voice barely there. "What's going on? I want to dream of something else or maybe I should just wake up. Come on, open your ey—" My voice cracks.

It's like I'm being consumed by the cold darkness forming around me as my hand still reaches for the warmth of the light. I can't even tell if I'm awake or dreaming anymore. The light is slipping away as I hit the ground and I don't have the energy to get back up. 'Maybe this isn't a bad thing... maybe...' My thoughts start to fade.

SPLASH!

The sound breaks through, clear and unexpected. A warm, chilled sensation washes over me, and suddenly it feels like I'm back at the community pool I used to visit during my childhood summers. The sensation is familiar and comforting, pulling me back from the edge.

SPLISH!

The sound reverberates softly in the distance, like a ripple across a pond. My body relaxes, sinking into the sensation. "That... feels... nice." I manage to croak. My head clears just enough for me to open my eyes, heavy as they are. I blink a few times, disoriented, trying to clear the haze, and that's when I see it... *feel it*. My hand is resting in a pool of water hidden beneath the gnarled trunk of the tree.

At first, my mind doesn't immediately process what I'm looking at. I'm confused, floating in a fog, and yet somehow, I feel an impulse to move. My body shifts to its belly, pulling itself closer to the liquid. The upper half of my body must look as if it's being swallowed whole by the base of the tree as my limbs sink into the shallow depths of the deliciously sweet water. It feels cool. So cool.

Hmmm, when did I get to the community pool? I didn't bring any of my floaties, so I shouldn't get too close to the deep end. Wait, how far in am I? Because I can't... I can't... "Breathe."

My head emerged from out of the water as I gasp for air. I drag my hand down my face as I tried to figure out what's going on. When I realized my arms right at the elbow were perching me out of a puddle of water, without questioning it, I cup my hands and take large, desperate gulps of the cool, refreshing liquid.

The sensation is blissful. Deprived for so long, I greedily drink as the rest of my body pulls itself deeper in. Once I had my fill, I claw my way from under the tree, panting, filled with slight disbelief. Body and clothes soaked, but fully hydrated. I collapse onto my back, letting the ground cradle me. I peek my eyes open, barely able to focus, but I spot him.

The creature. He's watching me again. A grin spreads across my face, wide and defiant. I lift my arms in the air and give him the middle fingers. *I got my own water now. Take that bitch.* A few tired giggles bubble from my lips, as I rest my hands back on my chest.

CHAPTER 9
ACCIDENTAL EYEFUL

KALIYAH

Three weeks. Three fucking weeks, and there's still no sign of those creepy green bastards leaving. I'm starting to think the man-beast was right. He hasn't spoken to me since that day. Just *stares*. For hours sometimes, before disappearing out of sight again. I haven't figured out where he goes, or if he has some kind of freakish ability to blend into the walls like a damn chameleon.

The first few times I woke up to him just silently looming there, I nearly pissed myself. Sometimes his eyes look normal, apart from the lack of color. But other times far from it. I haven't figured out what triggers him to look at me with those other eyes yet. I don't do anything different. A few times I tried sleeping in the hallway that connects this cavern to the path with the sigil's groove, thinking I'd get a decent night's sleep if I was somewhere he can't see me. But nope. Because it was too damn cold. Like, I'm afraid I might lose a toe cold. Whatever that glowing crystal is above the main chamber, it's the only reason I'm not an ice sculpture right now. I've had to turn my dress into a glorified blanket just for extra warmth.

Day 22: I can't live the rest of my life in this cave. Something's got to give. Although there's plenty of those highlighter green-colored fruits with the pink tips, and the water situation has resolved itself, I don't know how much longer my jawbone can take this. I need something softer to chew on. I've been considering giving the mushrooms a try, but I haven't worked up the courage yet. Maybe tomorrow. If this ends up being my last entry and you find yourself also trapped here one day, this is my warning: DON'T EAT THE DAMN MUSHROOMS.

I peel my eyes up from the page. *Oh look, more staring.* I'm getting used to it at this point. At least as much as someone trapped in a cave with a... blue vampire maybe? *Then again...* maybe not. Are werewolves' a thing in Therion? I bet Ryan would know what he is. To ease my nerves, I've been telling myself to view him like a tiger from behind the glass at the zoo. At first alarming, but then you're over it after a while and ready to see something else. I've noticed, his gaze isn't exactly the same as when I first got here. While still pretty damn *intimidating*, his eyes don't scream *'I want to rip your ass open.'* That sounded dirty. I chuckle to myself.

Still, he's watching me now in more of a way like *"huh, what's on TV?"* kind of vibe. Though I seriously doubt they have anything even remotely resembling television in this mid-century era. He said he's been trapped here a long time. But how long we talking? A few months? Or is he full on, *'this smiley face volleyball is my BFF'* energy?

That would be really crazy. Hmmm... Okay then. If he wants to watch me so badly then I'll give him a show.

I rose to my feet, retrieving some flowers from the wall. Then I rolled my dress back into my backpack making it once again round and plump. I smash the flowers into a paste, drawing a teal smiley face that dimly glowed on my bag, then turn it towards him making sure he had a clear view of it. I do ask myself why I'm doing this, but I know it's because I'm going stir crazy.

"Hey, blue devil." Shouting as I point at him. "You watching? Yeah, of course you are."

I snatch the backpack off the ground, holding it up. "Damn it, Wilson," giving it a once over like it just insulted my grampa. "Look, I know we're trapped here together, but you know what? I don't need anyone else. We look out for each other, buddy."

I spin it around, pretending it's my only companion, then give it a gentle shake, like I'm disappointed. "I should be living my life. I could be doing something meaningful. But no~ Endless buffets. Hot guys. An actual bed. I'm missing out on all those things, because I'm stuck *here* with you."

I pause for dramatic effect, letting the silence settle before holding it up higher, readying to make a bold declaration. "But you know what, Wilson. Screw it. I'm getting off this island. I'm not gonna sit here waiting for someone to rescue me. I'm gonna save myself."

I slam the backpack down into the rocks, acting out the final act like I'm the last survivor in some disaster movie. "So, no more whining. No more waiting. We're getting off this godforsaken rock, Wilson. And it's gonna be *epic*." I stand there for a moment, then glance over at him. "Was that entertaining enough for yah?"

The man-beast just stood there, giving me a kind of dead-eyed stare. Pretty sure he had no clue what I was referencing. *But~* I think I got my point across. Without so much as a blink, he turned on his heel and strutted right back out the way he came. Disappearing through whatever mystical monster exit that led to the other side of this ridiculous cave. He had no other reaction. Not even his usual low growl, which felt a little unsettling. His sudden lack of interest in my every move, left me feeling like I made a fool out of myself for no real reason. I take a deep sigh, plopping to the floor.

At least he's not staring anymore. I dragged my new emotionally unavailable friend, backpack Wilson under my head like a pillow, crossing my arms looking up at the ceiling.

"What are we going to do now Wilson?" I whispered under my breath.

Honestly, once you get past the spooky vibes and mystical nonsense, this place is just... *boring*. Like, aggressively boring. If I had internet and access to my streaming services, maybe I could handle this captivity a little bit better. A few light comedy specials. Ratchet reality TV. Ooh, a fun baking competition and a good horror movie. *Actually*, scratch that last one.

I sigh. Horror was my ride-or-die genre. And now, it's dead to me. I'm to the point that I flinch every time a rock shifts too loud or the shadows get *slightly* too shadowy. So that's no power, no cell phone, no Wi-Fi. Just tangy fruit, earthy water and for a roommate the world's creepiest... *man eating djinn?*

There's really not much to do here except eat, sleep, and question every life decision that led me to this moment. I close my eyes, mentally preparing for yet another nap I didn't ask for, but my mind desperately needs to mentally break free from this place.

"Little breakfast."

My body jumps as if I've had been caught doing something I wasn't supposed to be doing. I almost forgot the sound of his voice. Low, rough, and way too casual for someone who announced his plans to snack on me.

Crap. Did I provoke him? Was holding a one-sided conversation with my backpack and declaring my plans to escape too much? I suck in a sharp breath, forcing calm. *Ok, stay cool. No need to panic.* I'm on this side of the barrier. So, I'm good. Safe. Totally fine... *Probably*.

"Uh..." I clear my throat, shifting my gaze down from the glowing crystal above and sitting up to see him casually standing at the edge of the cliff like some villain in a comic book. "What did you just call me?"

My breath hitches. My brain momentarily exits the chat as my gaze lands on the man-beast's naked body. I'm talking *fully*, unapologetically, 'this is my house and I pay no rent' naked. He's covered head to toe in light-tinted blue skin. His muscles defined in every place my eyes can see. I had become accustomed to seeing his chest and arms, but as my eyes involuntarily traveled downward, first tracing his V line, then lower to his large... *'element'* resting between his thick powerful looking thighs. All of him was on display for both me and Wilson to see. This creature's body was born of most women's dreams and nightmares. I snapped my attention back to his face. My eyes disobeying my order to immediately look away. My mind, absolutely *not* okay.

What the hell? Not only does he eat human flesh, but he's a pervert too? And yet he says he's different than the goblins.

"I called you 'little breakfast,'" he responds. "Because that's what you are. Though, I suppose if I ate you after nightfall, it technically wouldn't count as breakfast." He tilts his head like he's *actually thinking about it.* "Then again, there's nothing wrong with breakfast for dinner."

He's really serious about eating me. But he has to know that isn't right. If he's a creature capable of speech, then surely, he's capable of reasoning. I should just try to keep a chill head and have a conversation with him. Then maybe he'll realize humans aren't something you just go around eating.

"I would appreciate it if you don't call me that. I'm not your breakfast, because I'm not food. So..." My eyes started falling down to his junk. I nearly gave myself whiplash when I realized what I was doing. I don't want to give that creature unsavory ideas.

"*So* what?"

My tone drops into dangerous territory. "So... don't call me—"

But the rest of the sentence evaporates as he casually shifts his stance, and *his dick* swings. Yep. *My eyes are stuck.* My voice dies completely. This is going to eat away at me, if I don't address it now. You can't just let men, *especially* naked feral cave men get away with this kind of pervy shit.

"Hey," I blurt, "What the hell are you doing? Why are you freakin' naked?"

He blinks, like I just asked why the sky is blue. "What do you mean why? Isn't it obvious?"

"If it was obvious, I wouldn't be asking." I said barely covering the fact that I'm mentally imploding.

I risk a slow peek over my shoulder again, bracing myself for another accidental eyeful, but he's no longer standing at the edge of the cliff. He's now stepping down into the pool beneath the waterfall. Droplets bounce off his chest. He looks like some kind of tragic forest prince from a weird adult fairytale.

"Do humans not remove their clothes when bathing?" he asks, tilting his head.

"*Oh*... Yeah. We do." I blink rapidly. *Bathing*. Hygiene. That's all this is. So, this wasn't him being a perv, or him trying to make some weird power move. Just an innocent rinse under a waterfall. Thank freakin' goodness. I can handle that. Body or no body, there's no faster way to make my skin crawl than a freakin' flasher. Still, my fingers curl around the edge of a nearby rock as my mind refuse to rid itself of the image just yet.

"You realize this is a mountain, not an island, right?" he called out.

"Huh?"

He slightly leans forward, resting his arms on the edge of the pool, the lower half of his body now thankfully submerged under water. "You said you would escape this island. We are inside a mountain."

I blinked. *No duh, pectoral Avatar.* Does he think I'm blind? Or geographically confused? "Yes, I am aware."

His brows furrowed slightly. "Then what was that from before?"

Before...? *Oh.* He means my impromptu dramatic monologue. I exhaled calmly, trying to muster the universal patience one needs when explaining symbolism to a brick wall or, in this case, a midcentury mythical creature who would probably think *Hulu* is a spell.

I'll just keep it simple. "It was theater, a performance. I was acting out a story."

His nostrils flared. "I see." He nodded once, "Again."

I blinked. "Again?"

"Perform your theater again."

I blinked a second time. "*Excuse me?*" The same man-beast who, just moments ago, looked at me like I'd fully lost my mind, now has the *audacity* to ask for an encore? Fat chance. That was a one-day-only showing, born from stress and boredom. There will be *no* reruns and no sequels. "No, thanks. I'm good" I say flatly.

He narrowed his eyes and tilted his head, looking almost offended. "And why not?"

"Why not?" What, does he think I'm dinner *and* the show? This man… this creature wants me to serve up emotional soliloquies, *while* he contemplates turning me into food. *The nerve.* Unless he's about to show me the nearest exit that doesn't end with me on someone's dinner plate, he can take that request and shove it up his mountain ass.

But… if he is willing to make a deal. I raise a brow. "On second thought, I'll do it again. I'll give you the performance of a lifetime. One you'll be thinking about for years. But only if my condition is met."

His eyes gleam, hungry for something. "Oh? Hmm. And what would that be *delicious looking breakfast*?"

I whipped my head around to face him, my patience snapping. "Again, *don't call me that.* I'm not food, damn it."

His face twitches like he's suppressing a grin, and he gives a lazy shrug. "Okay then, done."

"Thank you," I say, giving him a pointed look. "You can call me Ka— Wait, what did you mean by '*done*'?"

"You made a request, and I agreed," he says nonchalantly. "If you perform your theater, I will no longer address you by that name."

I blink in disbelief. "But that was not my *request.*"

"Whether it was or wasn't, is no concern of mine. I agreed to your terms. You may continue acting out your story."

"Uh-uh. Like I said, that was not what I wanted to ask for. What I want is for you—"

"Are you saying you intend on going back on our agreement?" He interrupted me.

I'm beyond irritated now, arms crossed and fully prepared to throw some attitude. But then my gaze meets his, and *damn*, that scowl is like a physical weight pressing down on me. My voice falters, but I pushed through. "If I don't get what I want, then *you,* won't get what you want. That's only fair."

"Fair? I see. Just so you know," His body starts to rise from the water as he stands. "There are consequences for breaking a deal with someone like me."

Threats, threats and more threats. Did he forget that I know as long as I stay my tail over here, he can't touch me. I roll my eyes. "Like what? You'll eat me? Well, come on. I'm right here." I turn my back to him and arch my hip, poke out my ass for emphasis, giving him a cheeky, mocking grin. "Go ahead, take a bite. Get your fill." I spring back up, straightening with exaggerated flair. "Oh, that's right. You can't. Because of what did you call them? *Soul sigils*."

When I turned around, I fully expected him to be pissed. His nostrils flaring, fists balled, chest puffed out like some cave-dwelling peacock ready to throw hands. But he wasn't. At least, not visibly. Instead, the only expression on his face was a slow, crooked smile. With just enough fang showing to remind me that maybe I'd might regret my words. His dripping body steamed ever so slightly in the cool air, like the heat was radiating off him.

In that moment, I could only think two things. One... Is that waterfall feeding into some kind of hot spring? And two, *keep your eyes on his face, Kaliyah. Do not let them drift. DO. NOT.* Without a single word, he turned and walked off again, just like that. No angry retort, no smirk-filled threat. Just that damn smile.

For the next few days, he didn't come around, and if he did, he didn't make his presence known to me. No stalking past his usual spots like some brooding jungle cat. It's like he just... vanished. Did he crawl into some hole and die? That'd be nice. Then I could finally have access to a long needed bath. The water over on *his* side looks a hell of a lot fresher than the sad little puddle under the tree on *my* side. I *thought* about washing up there once. But then I imagined having to drink my own butt water later and nearly vomited on the spot. So, I've been making do with the ol' birdbath method. My dagger cloth, and enough dignity loss to last me a lifetime. I don't feel *clean*, but I'm not actively fermenting, so I'm counting that as a win.

Still, I keep glancing toward his side of the cavern. Nothing. It's got me worried. Like... what if he's over there carving a brand-new tunnel with those oversized claws of his. One that leads *directly* to my side. A surprise ambush. *Oh, great. Now I'm going to be even more paranoid than I already am.* It wasn't really my intention to provoke him. I mean, yeah, I bent over and dared him to take a bite, but I didn't think he'd actually go sulk about it. Or plot my murder. It's hard to tell with him. He's got that whole 'unhinged apex predator' vibe going on.

But seriously, I'm doing my best here not to go full cave-psycho. Being trapped in a magic cave with nothing but him, Wilson and my spiraling thoughts... yeah, that'll wear on a girl. Especially when I know my friends are probably heading home without me soon.

Ugh. No, don't get worked up again, Kaliyah. That's not going to help. Besides, it's not like I hear any suspicious rock-crunching or walls being tunneled or blasted apart. *Yet.* Maybe I should make peace. There's no way to know how much longer I'll be trapped in here with him. Next time I see him, I'll toss over some fruit from the tree. Real peace offering-style. Maybe even throw in a dramatic *'I'm sorry, but secretly I'm not'* apology. But just in case... I'm sleeping with my blade under my pillow. I let out a big yawn and stretch, letting the tired drag me under.

I'm deep in sleep when I start to stir, rocking slightly, my slumber slipping away. But there's this weird tug. Then another. Sharp and jarring, like a person yanking on a blanket. Except, *I'm* the blanket. Something's wrong. My eyes snap open to the ceiling above and it is... moving? Trying to shake off the fog. Another yank. Rougher this time. *No. I'm the one moving.* My arms scrape along the ground above my head as I'm being pulled away from the tree. The world around me sharpens all at once. Something's *touching* me. My legs, no, my ankles are being *gripped*. It's *pulling* me. My heart lurches, eyes begging me not to look as I snap my head down.

Goblins. Two of them. One on each side of my legs, their gnarled little fingers clamped tight around my ankles. Tiny, beady eyes and rubbery-slick skin. They're hauling me toward the mouth of the cavern entrance. My head snaps back toward the tree, eyes darting across the floor. Come on, where is it? *There.* My dagger, still lying just beyond my reach, right next to my backpack.

I kick out hard, legs thrashing. One of the goblins lets out a high-pitched grunt, but the other just snarls and tightens its grip, yanking me harder toward the mouth of the cave. I twist, scramble, *claw* at the ground. Anything to break free. My knees skid against the rough stone, scraping skin, but I don't care. My arms flail wildly, trying to get enough leverage to push myself up.

Get to the blade! The dagger glints just out of reach.

I kick harder, aiming straight for the goblin's ribs. "Let *go* of me!"

My heel connects with a solid *crack*, and the goblin lets out a strangled screech. It shrieks. A ragged, choking sound as it staggers, claws scrabbling for balance on the slick stone floor. But I'm already moving, ripping free of their grip and lunging toward my weapon like my life depends on it, because it fucking does. I dive for the dagger, fingers closing around the hilt just in time. Spinning on instinct, I raise it in both hands and the goblin chasing me launches into the air, straight onto the blade.

The steel punches up beneath its ribs with a wet *shlunk*, its eyes going wide as the momentum drives it down on top of me. Its foul, stinking blood pours across my stomach, hot and slick. I barely have time to gag before the second goblin clambers on to the impaled one's back. He snarls and snaps with all claws and teeth. Its added weight slams me down, pinning the dagger in deep. I tug, but it won't budge. I'm stuck. I have to get them off me. *Now*! The goblin snarls again, then lands a punch straight to my jaw. Pain flashes white across my vision.

Damn. For something so small, its strength is way too close to mine. I swung my forearm into its temple knocking him off. I then pushed the dead one off me and tried to dislodge the dagger from it's rib cage, but it was wedged. The other goblin popped back up like some nightmarish jack-in-the-box and came barreling at me. I start to crawl backwards only for my left arm to smack into the edge of the goddamn chasm. I barely had time to glance at the gaping doom-hole below before. *BAM!* Goblin air delivery straight to the gut. He landed on me like a heavy ass bag of potatoes. One gnarly hand clamping around my neck while the other went fishing in his crusty waistband for what looked like a homemade knife. It raised the blade in the air readying to send me to the afterlife when… *BOP!*

Suddenly, there was a gaping hole in its chest. Like, full-on, right in the middle of its torso. The goblin looked down, probably wondering why it suddenly had unexpected ventilation. Its face went still as its body started to fall forward towards the chasm's edge, still clinging to my neck. I pivoted my body as I shoved him off of me, and it went over the side. Panting, I snapped my gaze to the other goblin, making sure it was dead. Then my eyes shot to the cavern's entrance, heart pounding like a war drum, just waiting for a dozen more to pop out.

"Worried there's more?" a voice said calmly from behind. "Just those two, *today.*"

I slowly turned my gaze back to the man-beast, perched on the edge of the cliff, that same crooked smile playing on his lips.

I stayed silent at first, my mind still reeling. "I thought you killed anything that enters the cave." I said, the words coming out intense.

"I do… *Unless I decide not to.*"

My eyes widen.

"I told you, there would be consequences for breaking our agreement, didn't I?"

"You—"

"It seems you've mistaken my willingness to converse with you as me changing my mind, that's why I don't like to talk to my food." His cruel smile deepened. "Another mistake of yours is believing the barrier keeps you safe from me. You see, my ultimate goal is to devour every inch of you. But, if it comes to a point where I believe it's truly not going in that direction, then…"

SPLAT. One of the fruits on the tree exploded as he casually tossed a stone at it.

He continued, "There are other ways I can get to you. Do you finally understand, *Little Breakfast*?"

How was I supposed to know he was capable of something like that? I mean, come on, turning a pebble into a glorified bullet with a flick of his wrist. What the hell was God thinking when he made this monster? That means, this whole time. *This whole damn time* he could've taken me out if he wanted. And just because of that, he thinks he holds my life in his hands.

"Yes, I understand." I walked right to the cliff's edge and stood directly in front of him.

I know I don't have any power or leverage in this situation. If only I was given one of those blessings like Ryan's electricity or Darrius's fire, I'd fry his ass right here. But that just wasn't in the cards for me, for whatever reason. Regardless, I made a vow to myself a long time ago. I would never let a man, non-human or otherwise hold his power over me. I want... No, need to set him straight. I stretch my arms out wide.

"Ok, I'm ready. Do it." *Don't show any fear, Kaliyah. Hold it in.* "Go ahead. Plant one of your little rocks between my eyes or in the chest. I *grant you permission. Dealers' choice.* End both our torment, right now."

His gaze tighten. He said and did nothing as if he was still contemplating my words.

"What's the matter? Can't decide? Should I do it for you then?" I lifted my foot over the edge, daring to step off. "You say I made the mistake, but I think you're the one who's reading me wrong. I wasn't bluffing when I said I'd jump headfirst into this pit before I let either you or those fucking goblins take me. *I'll* decide when and how I die. Not you. Not them. And sure as hell not that damn empress. So make your move, blue devil."

His eyes glazed over, his stare empty. There was no way to read him. One moment he was a storm of extremes. Anger and something dark and the next, he was blank, unreadable.

He gripped the remaining stone in his hand tightly. "From now on, you will refer to me as Mitus. Not 'man-beast' or 'blue devil.' If you do that, then I will not allow another goblin to dot this cave moving forward. Do we have an agreement?"

I placed my foot back on solid ground. "And why would I trust you?"

"Because unlike you humans, I don't break my deals."

I stared at him, my mind turning. *I will never trust his words.* Once a blue devil, forever one. So if he thinks he can trick me into letting my guard down, think again.

"Deal." I agree to his terms, for now.

He began walking away, but then paused at the sound of my call.

"Hey! Just so *you* know, there will be consequences if you don't hold up your end of the agreement."

"Oh yeah? Like what?" He turned to look at me, a slight glint of curiosity in his eyes.

I tugged at my cheek, exposing my teeth. "You might not know this, but I have my own set of canines. They may not be as long or sharp as yours, but I'll use them to chew you up and spit you out just the same. You hear me, Mitus?"

An empty threat, of course. There's no chance in hell I could go toe-to-toe with that monster. But I can't let him think he can punk me either. Like my grandfather used to say, *"Listen, baby girl. Bullies go after the ones who shine. So shine brighter and blind them."*

I just watched him turn his fingers into a damn pistol. It's clear to me now. He sees me as weak, something he can toy with, nothing more than prey. And the second I give in to the fear, the second I let the intimidation wins. It's game over for me. He opened his hand, and nothing but sand trickled through his fingertips. I expected him to walk off, vanish to wherever he keeps disappearing to. But instead, he sat down. Leaned back against the wall like this was all just a casual evening hangout.

CHAPTER 10
WAKING DREAM

KALIYAH

The dagger is stuck. I plant my foot on the goblin's chest and yank it loose with a hefty pull. It's only been an hour or so, but the body already reeks. Some ungodly mix of rot and sewage. The texture of its skin rubbery and sticky. I hate touching it. Its so freakin' scary and gross. But I can't let it just decompose here. The smell would only worsen. I drag the corpse to the cliff's edge and give it a good, hard kick. It disappears into the darkness below without me hearing a single thing. No sound of it hitting the bottom. Just how deep is this pit? And more importantly, what the fuck was I thinking?

'Plant one between my eyes... Should I do it for you?' Did I lose my fucking mind? I'm not ready to die, yet in that moment I was ready to risk it all.

My nose cringes as the smell lingers on me. I can't stay in these clothes a second longer. Soaked in goblin goo. I need to change them. No, burn them.

Ugh... I have no choice but to throw on that itchy, ill-fitted gown again. And there goes my blanket too. But it can't be helped. I stink so bad I'm offending *myself.* I head over to the shallow watering hole and start peeling off my shirt, desperate to get this green gunk off me. Just as I pull the fabric over the nape of my back, I pause. My head turns.

He's still there. Still resting against the wall seemingly not paying me any mind. His eyes are closed, but I know he's not sleeping, because of the tapping of fingers. Probably deep in plotting mode. He *did* say he had no interest in my body like that. And, honestly, when he was standing naked in front of me the other day, it wasn't like his penis was on high alert.

If all he sees when he looks at me is short ribs and tenderloins, then fine. I just need to make sure all the important bits stay out of his line of sight. I exhale sharply, then finish undressing.

MITUS

For weeks now, the woman has been strolling around this mountain like it's her personal playground.

Lately she's started singing. Her voice is somewhat pleasant to the ear. Melodies of which I've never heard before. One of them involved something called a "side chick," and I'm still trying to figure out if that's a bird or a battle rank.

She also keeps stacking rocks into tiny little towers, only to roll a bigger stone at them seconds later. Strange. Then there was the plant paste. She mashed up some flowers and started painting on the walls, different structures and creatures, one I *think* might've been a minotaur. None of what she does makes any sense to me. Especially for one in her position.

Occasionally, she talks in her sleep. Last night, she announced she was going to "throw hands" with someone named Princess Millie. Maybe it's a sport or game involving the severing and tossing of appendages. If she runs in the same circles as a princess, then that would mean she's likely a noble. But there's nothing about her brass and fearless behavior that suggests she was born into it. No, she doesn't come off as spoiled or pampered.

If I had to wager, she's probably the daughter of some wealthy merchant who bought his way into nobility and got himself a title and a fancy crest. Which makes me wonder how she ended up this deep in Bloodthorn. Either way she is... *entertaining* to say the least. It would almost be a shame to eat her. *Almost.*

First that ridiculous performance she put on. I was *this* close to laughing out loud. Had I let it slip how much it amused me, she might've stopped mid show. And then when she thought she could trick me. Thought she could twist a deal in her favor. Not to mention the way her face crumpled when I flipped it back on her. *Delicious.* The way she bent over, then taunted me with her flesh. So bold.

But the real show was when she realized the little green vermin had her by the ankles. The panic in her eyes. Of course, I never planned for them to try to retrieve her, but when I heard them trying to sneak pass me, I figured what perfect payback. And yet, *yet again*, she didn't react how I expected.

She *fought*. Killed one with her own hands. Those tiny hands. There was a moment, just briefly, when my body pumped at the sight. It was... *unexpected*. She's like a skittish little animal that, when cornered, bares its teeth and lashes out in desperation. There's no doubt in my mind, she was moments from walking off that edge. I can't tell whether it's bravery, madness, or something else entirely. That's what made me offer the deal. I'm not ready for the excitement to end just yet.

"Mitus," the way she said my name, while having the audacity to bare her feeble, practically nonexistent fangs at me and threaten to chew *me* up? As if I wouldn't let her try, just to feel her mouth against my skin. Does she not realize? Every bold little act only makes me want to draw her closer. To savor her. To see what expression I can force out of her next. The ones of defiance, pain, and fear.

At this rate, Little Breakfast, if you keep toying with me your death won't be quick. And far from painless. Even now, tempting me with your slow, deliberate undressing. I've never found human women attractive.

Not in the slightest, sexually or otherwise. Their fragility disgusts me. Their delicate bones, always on the verge of snapping. Their pitiful lifespans. No power. No depth. Just fleeting, forgettable things. And yet… *This one.*

Even now, my eyes trace the smooth, dark richness of her skin, like creamy liquor. Skin that's sleek and unblemished, tapering down to the full curve of her hips. Wide, grounded hips. And that ass of her's looks so damn plump and impossibly tempting. There's bounce there. Strength. Rebellion. My gaze drifts higher, to her eyes shaped like coco pearls, warm yet sharp. They hold a strange innocence… but I've seen the fire behind them. And those lips. They're full, stubborn, made for more than pretty words. They're always challenging me. Drawing me in.

The desire… my hunger is becoming hard to ignore. You're either too brave or too foolish to realize what you're awakening in me.

"No no no. Where is it?" Her voice softly frantic as her fingers claw through the dirt near the tree roots. "Where did it go?"

I wonder if there's any way, I can get her to turn around. I want to see more of her body. But it looks like that isn't happening. She is quick to dress. This is the first time I've seen her *put* that garment on. She usually drapes it across herself like a sheet. My body is resistant to the mountain's chill, but her fragile frame must have no choice but to react to it.

"My pendant," she mutters. "Please, my pendant."

Hmm. Something's got her in a panic. Never a dull moment with this one.

"Shit, it has to be somewhere around here." One of her hands clutching at her bare neck. Her eyes carefully scan the ground.

I see. That dainty chain with the pink crystal hanging from it. Back in my fortress I have piles of jewels and gems larger than her fist. Any one of which could put that stone to shame in both cut and clarity. *If we were there, she could have her pick of—*

I stop myself. My brow furrows. Hmmm. Where was my mind just going?

"How long has it been since I remember having it?" she mutters to herself.

"Are you speaking of that necklace you were wearing." I asked.

"Yes. Do you know where it is? Can you see it from there?"

I pause for a moment, letting the silence hang between us before I reply. "Yes. I know where it is."

Her eyes brighten, and she leans in closer. "Okay. Where is it?"

I close my eyes, letting a cheeky grin spread across my face. Time for some more fun with her. I slowly open my eyes again, prepared to drag this out eventually trading the information for several of the dewberries. But as soon as my gaze meets hers, something shifts in my mind.

Her expression. That look. She's staring at me like I hold the key to something, like I'm the only one who can solve her puzzle. It catches me off guard. And before I knew it, the words spill out of me. "It was clutched in the hand of the goblin that you tossed into the chasm."

Her eyes widen, wider than I've ever seen before. She drops to her hands and knees, leaning over the edge of the cliff. I feel my muscles tense. A sudden, unexpected twitch runs through me. For a moment, I thought she might tumble over the edge, and my chest tightens in reflex. The words *'get back'* flare in my mind, but I bite them down, forcing my teeth to hold them in. It was only when she pulled herself away from the edge that I felt the muscles in my chest finally relax. Confused by my own reaction.

"It's your own fault for not checking the creature before you disposed of—" My words trail off as I see the shift in her demeanor.

The way she looked at me in that moment, it stirs something in me, making me feel *an urge* slightly strengthen. She doesn't seem to notice or care for my words any longer. Without another word, she grabs her satchel and strides toward the cavern's exit, disappearing into the hall of the cave.

Over the next few days, I didn't see any signs of her. Not in the cavern, nor in the space of the mage's path. She hadn't come out for food or water. *Where the hell is she?* I sniff the air, searching for signs of blood or sickness. Nothing. Could she have managed to escape the cave? But if she'd taken the mage's path, I would've heard her. My thoughts start to race.

Don't tell me she found another way out. No. There's no way. She can't leave. She can't leave here. My eyes narrow. What the hell has gotten into me lately?

That human. She can fall into the pit and rot for all I care. It's not like I've never missed a meal before. It's just a matter of time before another weak creature wanders into this cave. And when that happens, I won't hesitate to sink my claws into them.

I am Carmitus Delmorr. Once reigning Overlord of Bloodthorn. No mortal has the power to unstill my mind or move my body in—"

My nostrils flare to her scent. So potent, deeper, sweeter. It fills the air. I rise to my feet, scanning the entrance, then the tree. *Nothing.*

Nothing but the dagger she left behind.

Where is she?

The tip of my ears twitch. I slowly look over my shoulder, and what I see makes my pulse quicken in disbelief. There she is, kneeling at the waterfall's edge, dipping one hand into its warm surface. Her other hand holds the thin string of her satchel, tied around her wrist, resting at her feet.

How did she manage to sneak up on me? I take a slow step towards her. *What is she thinking? Has she finally given up? Does she truly believe my casualness with her changes my intentions?*

She's wrong. The moment her foot crossed the soul sigil, her body belonged to me. I watch her, eyes narrowing, the tension building.

"Hello, little breakfast."

She doesn't even acknowledge my presence. Her hand sways lazily against the ripples of the water. *She dares to ignore me?* It seems she has forgotten her position.

In a flash, I grip her shoulders and pin her to the stone wall. My predator eyes gleam as I lean in, baring my tusks and letting out a deep, guttural growl from the core of my chest.

Her taunts, her temptations... this will teach her. She will tremble under the weight of—

Her eyes barely open, gaze half-lidded, calm, and peaceful, as if I'm not a threat at all. Her hand rises slowly, cupping the side of my face, her palm so soft, so gentle. She tilts her head slightly, offering me a grin. One that is not teasing, but warm and unguarded.

I feel my grip on her loosen, just a fraction. *Hmm...* I've never seen her like this before, and the sight infuriates me. This look, it enrages me to my core. *Why?* Why does this damn expression make me want to hold her here, just like this, for as long as possible, not wanting to take my eyes off of her for even a second.

Her hazel-honey scent floods my senses, and I inhale deeply, almost losing myself in it. Without thinking, I pull her hand from my cheek, lifting it to my mouth as I close my eyes.

Yes. That's right. It's because she's mine. My... little... breakfast.

I sink my tusks into the soft flesh of her palm. Her blood pulses, warm and rich, flowing down my throat and dripping from her arm. The subtle twitch her hand gave off, made me sink in further. So very warm. And yet her expression remains unmoved.

KALIYAH

Man, again? And so soon? I usually go long stretches before having this dream again. My eyes drift across the stark white nothingness surrounding me. Hopefully, it's not like the last one. Okay, so where is... With a single turn, my jaw drops.

Without any delay, it hovered right before me. Bigger than I've ever seen it before. Star, the massive glowing orb, pulsing gently.

"Whoa... any bigger and you could probably replace the sun." 'At this rate, maybe I should think about calling you something else... But then again, what is the sun, if not one big star.

I stop, glancing around the empty white space, noting that something feels different here this time.

"Kaliyah." A soft, but firm voice spoke. It was familiar, yet not.

I flinch and turn fully toward the glowing orb. Did... did Star just speak? Another first.

"Kaliyah, it's time... time to awaken."

'Oh, That's right... I'm dreaming. I must have finally fallen asleep after trying to stay up the last few days. Thank God I thought to tie that string to my wrist, anchoring me to that boulder. That maybe the only thing keeping me from sleepwalking straight into the pit.'

"Actually I could use a really pretty dream. One with plenty of sky and my grampa, please. I miss him. Oh, maybe at the park like—"

"Ouch." I glance down at my hand. Two small punctures mark my palm. No blood, just eeriness. What was that?

"You need to wake up, Kaliyah." The voice more stern this time. Urging.

I look back at Star. "But... I'm not ready to go," I whisper. "It's so peaceful here. Can't I just stay with you. At least for a little while longer?"

"You've been dormant for far too long. It's time to wake."

"I don't want to go back there. Not alone. It's dark, cold and scary. Please don't make me." I clutch my hand as a burning sensation pulses through my palm.

"This time, you won't be. I can finally be with you."

"Uh? What does that even m— Ouch!" I glance down. Blood now pools in the center of my hand, dark and glistening. "What's happening?"

"Kaliyah, reach out and touch me."

"Wha— Ouch! I don't like this. It hurts. Are you doing this? Ahhh. Stop it." My knees buckle. A sharp, searing pain radiates up my arm.

"Kaliyah, you need to hurry. Take hold of me now."

I try to do as Star says, but my body feels like it's being pinned in place by something heavy. My finger tips just inches away. "I can't. I can't reach you."

"If you don't wake now, we, you will never see home again."

My breath hitched. Stars words hitting me differently that time. I grit my teeth and stretch, my shoulder straining, burning as if my arm might pop from its socket. Just to get a little closer. Finally, my fingertips graze Star. And in that moment, a gust of wind slams into me. Then everything goes blinding white.

My eyes are still closed. My back is cold. But my chest... it's warm. Almost *hot*, even. *What's that sound...?* To my right, *water*. Rushing, crashing loud. So loud. I gradually opened my eyes, my vision coming in slow, blurred waves. *What is that... casting such a dark shadow over me?*

A sharp, searing pain shot through my hand, snaking down my arm and snapping my eyes wide open. My heart slammed against my ribs, thrashing to escape.

Blue. Tusks. My blood. I couldn't even tell if I was breathing anymore. *The man-beast has me.*

Another stab of pain tore through my nerves as he sank his teeth deeper into my flesh. A whimper escaped me. It's small, broken and pointless. But it was to that sound he opened his eyes, like he was coming out of a trance. I could hear the gulp in his throat as he swallowed. He pulls his tusks from my flesh, lifting my arm slightly higher and placing his tongue to my forearm as he lick the blood that streams down my wrist.

"W— what are you doing? Stop it." My voice trembling.

"Why would I do that?" he said, in a low, cruel tone. "Obviously, I'm getting ready to eat you."

Oh God. This isn't happening. I have to get away. Panic spreads like wildfire through my limbs, but I couldn't move. He was too strong. His grip, unshakable. My eyes were locked on his blood-soaked teeth.

"Please." I whispered.

"Ah ah ah," he mocked, amusement curling at the edge of his voice. "I told you from the start, this is how it would end." He leaned in closer, "Didn't I, *little breakfast*?"

The grin that spread across the blue demon's face made me regret every choice I'd ever made in my life. *Eaten?* Is this really how I die? After everything I've been through.

No. It can't. The moment his jaws began to part, tusks glinting as he readied for a second bite, something in me snapped and I reacted. My eyes locked on to his neck and I lunged forward and bit down hard. His muscles tensed beneath my teeth. It was like trying to bite into a tire. So damn tough. And then he laughed. A deep, sound that rolled through his chest like thunder.

"Is that the might of your fangs." he mocked. "No different than that of a small child. How adorable. He tilted his head, letting me feel his pulse beneath my lips. I must say, human, you've been very amusing, even to the very end." He paused. I could feel the shift in his mood. It wasn't anger. It was playfulness. "Tell you what, how about we make another deal?"

My body stiffened. Teeth still trying to tear at his flesh.

"I'll give you ten seconds," he purred. "During that time, I'll grant you permission to devour as much of me as your tiny teeth will allow. And after those seconds are up, if I'm still standing it becomes my turn, and I will do the same to *you*." He smiled wider, his tusks catching the light. "The first to consume the other... wins. You ready?"

My breath hitched. I panted against his skin, hot, sharp breaths brushing over the slight break where my teeth had barely punctured him. The taste of his blood still lingered in my mouth. It tasted of bitter iron.

"Ten... Nine..."

I squeezed my eyes shut. *If I could just tear into the artery in his neck—*

"Eight... Seven..."

Wait, he's not human. He may not even have arteries.

"Six... Five..."

The world warped around me speeding up and slowing down all at once. *No, no. Don't.* My jaw quivered.

"Four... Three..."

I said, "No!"

"T—" He stopped counting.

Just like that, Mitus froze. His body still as stone. He then releases his hold on me. I didn't wait. I shoved myself free and hit the floor beside him hard. My palms scraped against the stone, knees buckling under my own weight. He didn't follow, didn't speak. Just slowly raised a hand to his neck, fingers brushing the skin like he was trying to understand what had just happened.

I didn't give him the time. My eyes darted to the cavern's exit. Then to the pit. *Demon. Goblins. The deep dark Abyss. Choose.* Choose choose choose. Hurry, before the choice is taken from me.

My heart slammed against my ribs as my gaze flicked between options. That's when I saw his eyes. He didn't move his head, but those eyes... those furious, scary eyes cut toward me from the corners, his expression twisted into pure, unfiltered rage.

My gaze shot towards the chasm. I stumbled to my feet, close my eyes and started running.

Run run run!

I don't want to be killed, and I rather die by my own hands than to be murdered like that. Anything but that.

Run! Run! Fucking jump!

CHAPTER 11
DEEP DARK ABYSS

MITUS

That's right. Try with all your might, but you will not escape me.

"Ten, nine, eight, seven..."

For but a miniscule moment, I had forgotten myself. Forgotten who I am. As if a being of my stature could ever be charmed by such a feeble creature. *Struggle and tremble in my arms as I ready to shred into you.*

"Six, five, four, three, t—"

Abruptly, a rush of white nothingness crashes into me. My eyes narrow, my brows pulled to the center. "Huh. What the hell just happened?" *I turned in every direction, scanning for walls, landmarks, even shadows. But there was nothing. Just an infinite void of white.*

How Curious. Could this be the work of a mage? And then I felt the warmth brushing across my back. I lifted a clawed hand, ready to strike, and turned swiftly toward the source.

That's when I saw it. A massive orb of light, suspended in the air just ahead of me. It pulsed, not like magic or flame, but like something alive.

"What... is this?" I suspiciously muttered, my gaze locked on it.

A presence radiated from it. Old. Powerful. Familiar in a way that made the bones under my skin feel uncertain. Whatever it is it's... dangerous. I took a step back, instinct clawing at the base of my neck. It's best to leave it and figure out what's going on. The instant that thought entered my mind, my eyes became just about the only thing on my body I could move.

My gaze goes back to the orb. "Is this you're doing?" I growl. My voice is hoarse, laced with anger, as though shouting at it might somehow break the hold it has on me. "Hell, if you wanted a fight, you should've just asked. Come then... Come and get me!"

Without warning, a violent gust of wind rips through the air. It tugged at the fibers of my muscles.

"Fuck. What is it doing?" I watch, helpless, a force begins to pull something from me. My very essence. A slow, insidious draw towards the sphere. I have to break its hold on me.

But before I can summon the strength to resist, the white space around me shatters, dissipating like dust in the wind.

One moment, I'm there... The next, I'm back in the cave. The woman still clinging to my throat, her body pressing into mine like nothing ever changed. But something feels different. Very different. I can feel it. A strange pull. A deep, magnetic tug. It's coming from her.

Wait! Is this what I think it is? How can this be? My hand shoots up to my neck, fingers brushing against the faint bite mark, but the sensation only deepens my confusion. I force my eyes to look at her. Like really look at her as she lies on the ground, seemingly vulnerable. Yet, something about her has changed. The rest of my body refuses to listen, just like it did in that endless white space. This shouldn't be possible for someone like her. Is she *even* human?

I watch as she stumbles to her feet and starts to run. I try to move, to reach her, but my limbs still refuse to yield to me.

"No!" I roar. "Come back!"

KALIYAH

There's no way in hell I'm dying that way. I won't let any of you motherfuckers eat me.

Run!

Run!

Fucking jump!

But, I be damned if I throw my whole life away without a fight. I leap over the sigil, my feet hitting the ground with a jolt as I race out of the mountain's cave and into the bare field. The faint rays of sunlight break through the dark clouds, kissing my pale skin with its warmth.

Run and don't stop running. The goblins are everywhere, but none of them react fast enough. I'm already at the edge of the tree line before they even register my presence. I hear their shrieks behind me, the rustling of branches, their stumbling footsteps and cries, but I don't let any of it faze me.

Run until my legs burn. Run until my lungs scream for mercy. Push through it all.

HUFF... HUFF... HUFF...

MITUS

My teeth grind as I force my way through the fork in the cave. My gaze flicks left, scanning the mage's path for her, but the rumbling of goblins to the right pulls my attention.

No. She wouldn't. I race toward the edge of the barrier, my blood boiling. Because of the position of the mountains cave, I can only see the movements of a few goblins, but one stops. It locks eyes with me, flashing a wide grin before it sprints off, a short spear gripped tightly in its hand.

The mark on my neck pulses. An electric shock courses through my body. I stumble forward, bracing myself against the wall before I topple. My locs pull toward the ground as I fight to steady myself.

"What is she?"

No. It doesn't matter at this point.

Fuck. Now that she has left the cave, I know she will never return. My claws burn as they dig into the stone wall, but I can hardly think of anything other than the fury that drives me.

Hold on. My eyes shift to my hand. The hand that clings to the sigil on the wall. *The barrier...* It's not holding me. I stand up straight, hovering my foot above it. Without hesitation, I step forward. To my utter disbelief, my body crosses the soul sigil. A grin tugs at both corners of my mouth, spreading wider as I realize what's happening.

"That wench dies today."

KALIYAH

BA-DUM. BA-DUM. BA-DUM!! Run. Kaliyah. Run. BA-DUM. BA-DUM. Run until your heart stops. Then run some more. BA-DUM. BA-DUM. My eyes catch something, just a blur from my side.

Is that a...? Bola cord. *No!* The rope tangles around my legs, and I slam into the ground, gasping as the air is knocked from my lungs. Panic surges as I twist and claw at the rope binding my ankles.

"No. Come on. Come on!" My hands scramble desperately, fingers slick with sweat as they pull at the twisted stones, but they won't budge.

The more I pull, the tighter it feels. The reality sinks in. I'm trapped. *Not them.* I grit my teeth. This can't be happening. Another tug. Another. Nothing. The fucking thing won't come off. I can feel my muscles screaming as I try to tear into it.

GRAAAHHK!!

And then, from the brush *a goblin* appears. I don't have time to think. His gleaming knife flashes in the light, and before he can make a move, I grab a nearby rock, the jagged edge digging into my hand as I swing it with everything I have. The goblin's hand snaps back, the knife tumbling from his grasp, and in a split second, it's mine.

With a quick swipe, I jam the blade into his neck. Blood spurts, hot and slick. I rip it out and drive it into him once more, ensuring he's dead, ensuring I've taken one of them with me. I go to cut the rope around my legs, but the dullness of the blade keeps it from working.

I don't even notice the second goblin charging at me until he's almost on top of me. I spin just in time to catch his arm, and with a sharp twist, he stumbles back. But there's more. *Always more.* I shift, eyes darting toward the rope again, the fucking fibers won't cut fast enough. I just need a few more seconds. The bola cord finally snaps, but then everything goes so~ quiet. No chittering. No footsteps. No rustling bushes. My gaze slowly lifted to see I was surrounded. I hike the blade up, swaying it back and forth as a warning to them to stay back, but they were unfazed.

Shit, fuck. He was right. He was fucking right.

"Still..." I whispered as I moved the tip of my blade in the direction of my neck. "I meant it with every fiber of my being, I won't let you fuckers break me." I closed my eyes and went to stab the blade into myself. Something caught my arm. *No.* Then another pulled my hair from behind, next followed my shoulders. Then the one in front of me pounce next.

"No." I screamed. "Get off of me. Let go."

BA-DUM. BA-DUM.

A hard pointy tongue ran up the side of my cheek. "Stop~."

Laughter erupts around me.

SNHEE HEE HEE!

The ground began to vibrate to steady pulses. The bushes ahead are shoved out of the way. When a creature with green blotched leathery skin, twice the size of Mitus appears. Its skin is covered in boils and crusty scabs dotting its body, each one oozing a sickly yellow. Its face is a wreck of sunken cheeks, flaking lips, and a nose that's more scar tissue than shape. Its teeth are uneven shards, some missing, others brown with rot. Drool ropes from its mouth, thick and foul-smelling. It licked its lips as it drew closer to me. Little goblins pinning every part of my body.

"What the fuck is that?" I shout.

As the very larger impossibly repulsive looking goblin began to near me, it shattered every nightmare I had ever had in one simple perverted gesture. Immediately the blue demon's words pound against my skull. *'They will ravish you... for weeks on end.'*

BA-DUM BA-DUM. BA-DUM BA-DUM BA-DUM!!

With a pitch I had never reached before, I screamed. "Help! Help me! Please, no! Ryan! Ryan! Darrius!"

One of the littler ones to my hip started lifting my dress upward and before I knew it the large goblin's torso blocked out the sun. One minute, it's eyes, its cold yellow soulless eyes smiled at me as its lips were still too busy being licked. And then the next, he wasn't. He wasn't smiling, licking his lips, or drooling from his teeth. He wasn't doing any of it, because his head was no longer on his shoulders. It was just gone.

MITUS

I kneel, sinking my feet into the soft soil. Arching my spine and stretching my muscles wide as I draw in the forest air. My first breath of fresh outside air in... I'm honestly not sure how long. My eyes sharpen. My blood sings. With a single, savage thrust from my legs, I tear through the forest. Trees whip past in blurs of green and shadow. The only thing that matters now is reaching her, ending her life before it takes hold.

Screams. That way. My body shifts directions. I burst into a clearing. There she is. Flat on the ground.

A hobgoblin. Bloated, boil-covered, its oozing body hunched over her like a rotting mountain, leaning in close. Around them, smaller ones pin her limbs. Filthy hands. Sharp teeth. Twisted laughs. *She's my prey.* Their claim ends now. I leap, wind ripping behind me, claws raised.

"Her life is mine to end." I declare as I bring my arm down in a brutal swing, aiming for the creature's neck. Swiping his head clean off his body and throwing it far past the distant trees. Next, them. My claws tore through their bodies one after another like wet paper. Their movements are too slow. Too weak to offer any resistance. In seconds, the horde of goblins lay in scattered, twitching pieces across the clearing.

Now... her. *Don't look. Don't look at her.* My eyes remain closed as I stalk forward, tracking her by the sound of her labored breaths. The ragged thump of her chest, that's where I'll strike. One blow. That's all it'll take. I'll obliterate her before the tie completes.

I raise my fist. Muscles coiled. All my power pooled into this one motion. My claws dig into my own palm. Blood slicks my knuckles. I was already bound by a mage. I will not let this woman do the same. No matter what she is, she will not survive this blow. My arm snaps back, ready to end her.

"Mitus." My name barely audible as it left her lips.

My brow tightens intensely. My eyes crack open and find hers. One look and I feel my pupils dilate. A silence falls between us.

Fucking coco pearls. My breath hitches and I come undone. Almost instantly every single muscle in my body relaxes and there was wholly and absolutely nothing I could do about it. In that moment, I couldn't fathom this world without her, let alone being the one to take her from it.

Shit~ I was a fool to think I had a choice. Still, this changes nothing. I'm finally free, after all this time. I will move forward with my plans. I will reclaim what was stolen from me and eradicate all that had a hand in it.

"Listen here, woman." I took a step closer, watching her flinch. But this time, I didn't like it. "I'm only going to say this once. Whether deliberate or not, *you* became the key to my cell. And now that I am free, now that I see these lands are still plentiful, feasting on you is no longer necessary. Because of that, I'll allow you to live. But make no mistake, this is not kindness."

Her eyes widened, and I forced the next words out through clenched teeth.

"If you ever appear before me again, I will not hesitate to make good on my previous promise. *Do you understand?*"

It should be enough. Distance is probably key. If I get enough between us I should be able to resist any pull I have to her.

I repeat in a soft growl. "I asked, do you understand me?"

Again, her voice barely there, she whispered, "Yes." Tears slipped down her cheeks.

Damn me. I want to wipe them away. My hand moved before I realized, I'm reaching for her, unthinking. *No.* I caught myself mid-motion and turned it into a sharp gesture, stabbing toward the trees.

"North of here. First, you'll come across Razakar. You should be able to make it to Sebbarus with ease from there."

Her pupils dilated at the name. *So, she really is from Sebbarus.*

"Avoid the riverbeds. Stay in the thickets." I take one final look. Those wide, doughy eyes. The pout of her mouth. The braids brushing her lips in the wind. In the sunlight, I can see it now, what the mountain's mana crystal light hid from me.

Her top lip is a shade darker. While her bottom is just a tad plumper. The curve of them. The softness of her jaw line. In fact, there are so many details of her body I didn't notice before. *Details...* Enough. My eyes snap away. I quickly shifted back and headed into the forest before I can think another cursed thought.

CHAPTER 12
TWISTED GAMES

KALIYAH

What the *actual fuck*, just happened? There wasn't a single direction I could turn without my eyes landing on chunks. Slushy, unidentifiable *goblin* chunks. I don't know *how* he crossed that barrier. And frankly, I don't give a single damn. He saved me. Spared me. Then threaten me. And yet, I've never felt this relieved in my *entire life*. The second that massive disease-ridden nightmare of a goblin came at me bumpy, lumpy, and looking like it crawled out of someone's cursed ass. Tugging at the disgusting huge bulge in its pants. I knew it was about to split me in half, literally and in the most horrifyingly violent way imaginable. And what did I do? I actually told myself, *'This is what I deserve for not jumping into the pit when I had the chance.'*

Seriously? So stupid. No woman should ever, *ever* go through that kind of hell. *Ever.* I refuse to experience anything remotely like that again. I'd sooner die. Hell, if it wasn't for one of them being quicker than me, I would have. Honestly, I didn't know I had it in me. But if you're desperate enough I guess anything is possible.

I stagger to my feet, legs shaking. The moment my back finally straightens, it immediately folds in again as I double over and hurl whatever sad remains were left in my stomach. *Awesome.* Add that to my constantly growing list of regrets for when I inevitably starve to death.

The way he moved, so quick, so vicious. He really is a demon. I still can't believe he let me live. I glance towards the direction he pointed before vanishing. Even if I believed he was telling the truth which, let's be honest, is a *big* if, there's no way I'd get there in time before Jemma and the rest of them are sent back home. And say I went back there, *me*, the false champion. I would have no allies and nothing from stopping the Empress from teleporting my ass to another region of this world or worse. Locking me up in her dungeon on the grounds of deceiving the empire or some bull crap.

No. I can't go back there. She wanted me gone. Well, mission accomplished. My ass is staying far away. If there's one thing I've learned from being summoned to this monster-infested hellscape and then left to die, is that there's more than one set of Elder Stones in Therion. And if I can find them and someone who knows how to activate the damn things, I can haul my traumatized butt back home and smother this entire nightmare in several years' worth of therapy.

I untie my backpack from my wrist. One of the straps had finally snapped. Of course it did. I loop the remaining one across my chest and glance to the side. Last time, I went west. God, *please* let east turn out differently.

MITUS

Why?

I've faced down armies of lizard men. Fought endless battles against troll clans. Seized thrones from kings who thought themselves untouchable. I survived what felt like an eternity of imprisonment that never seemed to end as it bent and twisted my mind.

So why?

I've plotted and planned for decades. The future of my enemies, their bloodlines, their legacies vanishing from the world, erased by my hand. I've envisioned it for so long. Every move, every conquest, every scream. All of it.

So fucking, why? Why does this awful fear plague me every time I try to leave her shadow?

My brows curl inward as I pinch the space between. But the question that claws harder than the rest is, *why didn't she head north like I told her to?*

It's been four days. *Four.* And she's still wandering east like she's on a lite stroll and not in one of the most dangerous lands in all of Therion. If it weren't for me, she'd be dead ten times over. I had to kill a pack of jagger wolves and a lamia yesterday alone. All drawn to her like she's carrying a sign that says, *'Come eat me!'*

I can't blame them. Ever since that moment back in the cave, her scent has gotten sweeter, more potent. As if I need another reason to want her more. At this rate I'm going to have to slaughter the whole damn forest.

To think I thought she could make it on her own was ridiculous. Could it be she's not from Sebbarus as I initially thought. The nearest kingdom to the east of here is the Kingdom of Palloria. The demi-human population is quite large there, so it's hard to think that's where she is originally from. Maybe things have changed since the last time I was there. I wonder just how many years was I locked away for. Counting would have only served to make my time there that much more unbearable.

Where is she going? Damn it. I wish I could just ask her. But after the last thing I said and did to her, she'd sooner impale herself on something sharp or jump off a cliff. Actually, she really should be careful, there are plenty of them around here. I don't get her. Two days ago, I heard her murmur to herself that she was worried about her wounds getting infected. So while she slept, I gathered some herbs with healing properties and laid them next to her. But when she awoke, she simply stared at them for a moment, before leaving them untouched as she continued her journey to deities knows where.

Then this morning she was moments away from eating some poisonous berries, so I sent a hogswine squealing in her direction hoping it would scare her away from them. It did. But she started following the animal soon afterwards. At first, I thought she was hunting it. Eventually getting to its nest full of hoglettes. Even with no weapon, claws or fangs, the young hoglettes should be easy enough for her teeth to tear in to. But of course, instead of eating them, she treats them like some common pets and plays with them.

I truly don't understand this creature at all. She's infuriating, yet so irresistibly interesting. I want to know everything about her. Every thought that goes on behind those eyes. Draw her in close as I gaze into them for hours. It's consuming my every thought.

Damn. Is this the strength of a soul tie? How terrifying. Now that I have this unbreakable connection to her, I can finally be honest with my true desires. Even though when I first seen her in the mountain, stopping my insatiable hunger is all I wanted. But, at some point I started to want... *more.*

More? What does that mean? What does that look like? This connection I have with her, it's a shame it's only one way.

She looks toward the sky as a cheeky grin gathers on her face. *How can she smile so hopeful like that, here of all places?* The sunlight pours through the canopy, gilding the forest in gold, and it hits her just right. It slides over the curve of her cheek, down her neck, across her skin, smooth and rich like melted cocoa. She doesn't even notice the way the world seems to slow around her. But I do. Her beauty is breathtaking. As my eyes soak in her delightfulness, I feel my long hibernating cock awakening.

That settles it. I need no more confirmation. I can no longer resist the way my body calls to her. It beckons to be by her side. I've decided I will make her *mine*. I am falling for her so damn hard. Harder than the steel bulge riving against my pants. She will be my lover.

"Hey, I know you're there!" She yells out.

My eyes blink. *Has she finally taken notice of me?* There aren't many beings that can sense me, once I suppress my aura. How perceptive, little bre— No. I will address my woman by her name. *Kaliyah.*

"Seeing that you haven't attacked me yet, I'm thinking you're not just some hungry animal. So how about you do both of us a favor and come out already."

A grin adorned my face. This is my opening. I can finally speak to her again. Excited with anticipation, I chuckled as I rose from the shadows and took my first steps towards her. But then. Before a word could leave my lips, her body spun around, and her legs took off.

KALIYAH

After the pure living hell I've been through for the last four plus weeks, I have every right to be paranoid. Everything in this freakin' world seems to either want to kill me, eat me or be *in* me. So, when I keep getting this feeling there's something following me and goose bumps dance across my skin, I can't help but get creeped out.

At first, I was afraid not all the goblins were taken out, but I know if it was them, they would have totally came at me by now. But if it was just some carnivorous animal looking for an easy snack, then why the wait? Unless it's something else.

"Hey, I know you're there!" I call out. *Hopefully, I'm just tripping, but just in case.* "Seeing that you haven't attacked me yet, I'm thinking you're not just some hungry animal. So how about you do both of us a favor and come out already."

Praying nothing responds, I wait and listen for a few moments. No rustling bushes or monster cries, other than the cute fluffy little piggies that ran into me earlier.

Huh... Ok so it really was in my head. I'd rather that, than the alternative. This place is so exhausting, but at least I'm alive. *Hell yeah.*

Lost, hungry, filthy and tired... but freakin' alive. For now, anyway. I can at least be happy about t—

My heart skips a beat as my eyes catch a glimpse of a familiar silhouette emerging from behind the trees. Chest, a light steel blue, shoulder length locs swooped to the back, a crooked smile followed by a wicked chuckle.

It's him... The man-beast. Before he could take another step towards me, *I turn and run.*

Why? Why is he here? Did he come for me or did I somehow accidentally wander into his path?

No. I was careful. I went a different direction than him. I made *sure* of it. He must've changed his mind about sparing me. I *knew* I couldn't trust that monster. The forest shifts behind me, the sound of his power moving through the trees. He's fast, so I know he's gaining.

Up ahead, a break in the trees. A clearing with light. My legs carrying me through. A cliff. A damn mountain cliff. Of course, this is exactly the kind of cosmic joke my life's become. Fate and her twisted games. *Well, I hope you had your fun, you bitch, because I'm ready for my game over this time.*

In a split second, my mind had complete clarity and the strangest feeling of gratitude washes over me. No being digested in some creature's stomach for me. This is my out and I'm taking it. I sigh in sadden relief. I focused every last ounce of strength into my legs, pushing faster, harder, just before I jump off the mountain cliff.

"Eat shit, Blue Devil." I cussed into the wind. *My life is my own. Please forgive me, Grampa.*

I spread my arms and legs, eyes fluttering closed as I braced for the inevitable, only for everything to shift. Suddenly, pressure slammed into my shoulder, flipping my body mid-air. My view spun from rocks and tree tops to sky and mountain and then I was cradled.

Cradled. Thick, muscular arms wrapped tight around my back, another set catching beneath my legs

"What...?" I mumbled, blinking in confusion.

As the ground rushed up to meet us, he pulled me tighter against his chest, like that was going to soften the blow. And then I saw them. Dark, tribal-looking symbols, blushing a deeper shade of blue, began to swirl across his skin like living ink. His tusks stretched longer, sharper, and a second, smaller set jutted out beside them.

Nope. Nope nope nope. I shift my gaze upward. *Forget about him. Just look at the sky. It really is... pretty.* I tried to calm my racing thoughts. Tried to make peace with the fact that this would be the last thing I ever saw and I'm not mad at it. The wind screamed past my ears, loud enough to drown out every thought. The cliff edge vanished above me, nothing but open sky now. No clouds. Shame. I really like clouds.

Time is being so weird right now. Moving all slow and shit. Hurry up and get this over with. I wonder... *will it hurt?* Plummeting to my death. *Yeah, probably a little.* But at least I get to take this overgrown bastard with me.

BOOM!

The ground beneath us shattered. A crater of cracked earth and dust exploding outward in a shockwave of energy. Chunks of stone lifted and hovered for a second before crashing back down. Trees nearby bowed from the force. The air rippled like heat off pavement.

No pain, but... No nothingness or pearly gates either. I cracked one eye open. He was just... *standing there.* Bare feet planted deep in the fractured earth, knees bent slightly from the impact, arms locked tight around me, *completely unharmed.* Like we hadn't just sky dived off a damn mountain.

He stepped out of the crater and gently lowered me onto solid ground. The darken markings that traveled his body moments ago began to fade from his skin. I let out a short, bitter laugh. Of *course,* Fate would cheat and press the reset button. To hell with her games. I'm refusing to play a moment longer.

There's no such thing as playing fair as long as I'm going against *him*... I'm going to lose. Every. Single. Time. I mean, course the man-beast could survive a fall from a *fucking* mountain. *Why am I even surprised anymore?*

"Okay..." I muttered, gaze fixed firmly on the dirt. "Get it over with."

He pauses. "Get *what* over with?"

"Killing me. Eating me." Still couldn't look at him. Silence stretched thick between us.

"Hmm... I'm *not*. So don't ever do that again."

My eyes darted up. "Huh?"

"Shifting was the only way I could keep us both alive. And with my strength as low as it is right now, I could barely conjure that form."

What? What the heck is he talking about? His ass just went base jumping without a parachute and dusted rocks off his shoulders like it was nothing. I stared at him, blinking.

"Didn't you hear me?" I snapped. "If you're gonna rip me apart, then make it quick." I tilted my head, baring my neck. Waiting.

Once again, his shadow loomed over me as he leaned in, closer this time. I feel the cool heat of his breath brush against my skin. His mouth hovered by my neck and I stilled. I'm not going to scream or flinch. I want to go out like a soulja. Just like grampa would. I've accepted my fate.

His lips press gently against my neck, then pull away. My eyes fluttered. A shiver travels down my body. *Did he just... kiss me?*

His hand lightly lifts my chin until I was forced to meet his eyes, unreadable and way too close. "Are you injured anywhere, love?" he asked.

What. The. Hell. My brows snapped together. I smacked his hand away like it offended me. Because it *did*.

"Look, *enough*. I get it. You like playing with your food. That's why you keep toying with me. First its, '*you're free to go, but you better not show yourself to me again*', but then you walk right up to me, after what, spending the last few days creeping in the bushes, like some stalker."

He didn't deny it nor did his expression flicker.

"Oh, was it amusing? Watching me scavenge for sad little berries, flinching at every rustling tree, trying to sleep on bug-infested dirt while getting eaten alive by mosquitoes. Which is fucking crazy that this world has them too. But not a *single* banana tree in sight." The more I spoke, the hotter the rage bubbled up. Weeks of frustration poured out like lava.

"I've had enough. So, if you're not going to *eat me*, then unkindly go screw yourself!"

He blinked. Then slowly looked me up and down. Like... *really* looked. Voice maddeningly calm he says, "Actually I would much rather screw *you*. With your permission, of course."

My head dropped. Fists clenched. *That was it.* The rage I'd been choking down for days... *weeks* finally snapped its leash.

"Over. My. *Dead*. Body," I growled, barely louder than a breath. And then I *screamed*. "I am *so sick* of this dark fantasy bullshit and your bipolar crap*!*"

I swung at him, wide and wild. He dodged easily, like I was nothing more than a breeze. "All of this... *all of it*, is that damn Empress's fault!" I shouted, the words tumbling out, hot and bitter. "If it wasn't for her, then I wouldn't be suffering like this." I threw another punch, this one clumsier. My foot caught a rock. I stumbled. But before I could hit the ground, his hand snapped out and caught me by the wrist.

"I wish she was the one stuck in this shit forest full of monsters," I snapped, eyes stinging, chest heaving. "I wish a horde of goblins attacked *her. She* should be the one barely surviving. Sleeping in the dirt, starving, crying, *screaming* for help that never comes. That uppity, smug, monarch bitch should croak and *die*." I snatched my arm away.

"If that is what you want consider it done, Kaliyah."

My gaze shot to his. Too shocked to hear my name leave his lips. I didn't think he remembered it.

"I will hunt down this Empress and sever her head from her shoulders and I will give it to you as a gift. From this moment forward, your happiness will be my every waking desire."

My mind hit buffering mode. Thoughts spinning in circles, refusing to settle. *Damn it. My pulse thudded in my ears, and I felt... a little lightheaded. Was this a fever dream? Or was he serious?* I stumbled slightly, catching myself before I went down. I couldn't process what was happening. He used my name.

"Tired of me not responding to *little breakfast*, huh? I scoffed, "I'm surprised you—"

"Come. You need to eat. Let me find you some food."

"Let go." I yank my wrist away again. "I'm not going anywhere with you, blue demon."

He didn't flinch, but his brows furrowed, the frown deepening on his face. "We agreed that you would call me Mitus."

"Yeah, well, you also agreed to *let me go*, yet here you are." I throw my hands in the air and plant my butt to the ground. "I'm sitting my ass right here, until I feel like moving again."

His posture stiffened, his gaze sharpening. "You are malnourished. I am aware that the human body is not capable of reserving energy the same way I can. Now that I truly see you up close, you look as if you're wasting away." He steps back, then his shoulders tense. "We shouldn't waste any more time. Who knows how long what little strength you have left will last."

I rolled my eyes so hard. "What's *new*? Or have you forgotten my diet over the last five six weeks?" I turned my nose up with all the dramatic flair of a woman absolutely *done* with all this shit. "So if you'll excuse me, *man-beast, blue devil-ly demon*, I would like to get back to my starvation in peace." I crossed my arms and looked away.

Big mistake. The world spun. One second, I was sitting. The next, my body was abruptly lifted and *tossed* over his shoulder like I weighed nothing. His arm clamped across the back of my thighs, and my face smushed awkwardly against the solid wall of his back. Muscles. Lots of them. Disrespectfully firm.

"Hey, hey! Put me down, you beach body mother—"

I kicked my legs, flailing. I punched at his back once, twice then a third time, but it was like fighting a brick wall. A very warm, smug, impossibly strong brick wall. I gave up around the fourth bounce of his shoulder, because at that point it became clear it was pointless to exert any more energy against him. And deeper into the forest we went. Where is he taking me? I don't know, but honestly… does it even matter? Clearly, I have no say.

A year ago, if someone would have told me I'd be kidnapped by a mystical blue beast that can yeet himself off a mountain like the laws of physics don't apply to him, I would have said... Actually, I honestly don't know what I would've said. Probably laughed. Maybe asked them what they were smoking. It's all too much for my brain to think about right now.

And what is he even planning? I shift my weight slightly, trying to get a better angle or at least stop my face from bouncing off his back every five steps. But the moment I move, he pops his shoulder with an annoying little *bounce*, sending my body flopping like a sack of regret. My palms smack against his back on instinct, just to brace myself. Annoyingly firm. *Great. Just great.* He keeps going for what feels like forever, because of course I've been reduced to nothing more than travel luggage. Eventually, he stops and seats me down.

"Wait here," he says, all stern, like I'm some child he doesn't want wandering off. "I'll be back soon."

"Oh, lucky me." As if running from him has done *anything* other than end in disaster. And let's be real. I've got less juice than my phone. I'm totally depleted.

 About four minutes later, he came back with two very dead looking... rabbits? They had horns sprouting from the center of their heads, sort of like a unicorn. He placed them at my feet. I blinked. Hard. I *know* he doesn't expect me to eat it as is. *Ugh.* My face twisted in disgust.

"What's the matter? Do humans prefer their meat skinned?" he asked, tilting his head. Then, without waiting for an answer, he grabbed one of the horned bunnies by the scruff. *ZIP.* Without any hesitation or effort, he stripped the skin clean off with his bare hands. Just straight-up serial killer energy.

He held the dripping, raw carcass out to me. I clamped a hand over my mouth trying to keep in whatever sad excuse for food I had left in my stomach. He looked at me confused. *Do I really have to explain this to him?*

"Humans don't eat raw meat," I managed to mutter.

"Ah... yes. That's right. I forgot." He nodded, as if this was a totally reasonable thing to forget. "It makes sense now." Then he crouched down, gathered a few sticks, and get this, *spat a blue spark* onto the pile. Literal spitfire from his mouth like it was no big deal. Like that's just something people do around here. And sure enough, the pile of branches caught flame like it was soaked in lighter fluid. I just stared.

He can spit *freakin' fire*. All those cold nights could have been avoided, if I could have gotten him to spit at me. Shit, I would have cussed and damned his entire species if it meant a night of warmth. I look him up and down, slowly. His smug expression. That faint little smirk tugging at the corner of his lips.

He really thinks he's slick. I know exactly what he's doing. My involuntary diet has shredded more pounds off me than any fitness app ever could. So obviously, the *barbarian smurf* wants to plumpin' me up. More meat for him to smack on. Not happening. I don't care if he serves it to me well done with a side of mashed potatoes and corn. I'm not eating it. But the fire does feel hella nice. I shuffle a little closer, my legs tucked under me, palms outstretched toward the flames. For the first time in what feels like forever, there's warmth that doesn't come from running for my damn life.

As my fingers flex toward the fire's flame, my eyes fall on the dirty strip of cloth wrapped around my hand, the one I used to stop the bleeding. I had been *so* sure it'd get infected. Thought I'd wake up one morning with my hand twice its size and a fever to match. But now... I blink. *When did it stop hurting?* I peel the cloth off, expecting crusted blood or at least discolored skin. But... no. The puncture wounds a barely visible. Just faint little brown spots on my skin. And it's not just my hand. My knees. The scratches. The slashes from that goblin's nasty nails. There gone. Not a single scar.

It's only been a few days. That kind of healing doesn't just *happen*. "What kind of...?" I whisper.

I glance over at him, suspicious. He's tending to the unicorn-rabbit meat. *Did he… do something to me?*

I don't understand. Ugh… I can't be bothered to think about it right now, not when that freakin' rabbit smells so damn good. He grabbed my hand out of nowhere. His thumb lingered for just a second too long, grazing the place the wound used to be, like he was confirming it for himself. His eyes flicked up to mine. I flinched and leaned to my side. "Now what, finally ready for seconds?"

Hold on… he's not some kind of mutated vampire, is he? Did his bite infect me? I'm not going to turn blue am I?

"I did this… I'm sorry."

"Did he… just apologize?" Nah, I'm not falling for it. Another trick. At any second, he's going to call me his breakfast or mid-day snack or some crap as he gives me another one of his sinister grins. He places the stick end of the rabbit shish kabob in my hand.

"As long as I'm by your side, you will never have to worry about harm befalling you ever again. Now eat up."

What the heck? I looked down at tenderly toasted rabbit meat. I wanted to throw it in his face, maybe gouge out one of his eyes with the sharp end. But the aroma hit my nose and before I realized it, my teeth were already in. The rabbit meat was a betrayal to my senses. As much as I hated myself for it, the damn thing was delicious. Each bite was tender, smoky, and warm in ways I hadn't experienced in forever. My stomach, that traitor, clenched with satisfaction as I devoured it, barely stopping to breathe. *The hunger.* The subsiding hunger, I refused to acknowledge how good it feels. I hadn't even gotten halfway through the first one before reaching for the second one. But I pulled back when my hand got a little too close to the flame.

He grabbed it and lifted it towards me. His eyes a gentle gleam as he watched me scarf the first one down. I snatched the other one from him, then faced away. I didn't want his stupid face looking at me while I tore into another creature's flesh. The sounds of him settling behind me, the crackling of the fire, the faint rustling of his movements. It all felt like he was too close.

Was I supposed to thank him? Was he waiting for me to acknowledge what he'd just done?

Fat chance. The irony was not lost on me either. I know we all have to eat to survive. So, can I honestly say if I was trapped in a cave for as long as he was without food and a talking chicken wondered in, would I not try to eat it. Even if it asked me not to.

My brows deepened at my own irritating thought. *To hell with that. Don't you dare try to see his perspective. I'm not a chicken, I'm a god damn human being.* There is a difference. I'm just having a lapse in judgment because I finally have something other than twigs in my gut.

"No more games." I turn and face him. "Just be straight up with me. Are you going to kill me or not?"

He doesn't answer right away, instead, he gives me that infuriating look. The one where he's studying me like a puzzle. His eyes narrow ever so slightly, but there's something else there now. Something deeper than mere curiosity. I can feel it. And for some damn reason, it makes my stomach do this weird flip-flop.

"Are you aware of what a soul tie is?"

I raise an eyebrow. He didn't answer my question. Why is he bringing something like that up? Soul ties. Crap lonely people believe in usually after getting it in and catching feelings for each other. Wait... Didn't he called me 'love' at some point or am I remembering wrong?

Oh no. Shit. Shit shit shit. Don't tell me sleep walking me, did something freaky. Please no. Don't get ahead of yourself. Just stay calm.

"Why?" I recoil.

"Because, our last day in the cave you formed a soul tie with me."

Fuckkkk. I actually slept with this blue motherfucker. There's just no way. "Wait. I need clarity. So, when you say I formed a soul tie with you, you mean I—"

"You drew a fraction of my soul into your body and linked it to yours."

I blink, thrown off by his phrasing. *What kind of metaphor is that? Is that code for he orgasmed?*

"Uh-huh... What does that actually mean?"

"It means... as long as there is breath in my lungs, I will forever care and live for you and only you."

I couldn't hold back the snicker. I stared at him, looking for any sign that he was joking. But his face was all serious, which only made me laugh harder.

"Okay, let me get this straight. So you're saying we had sex, and apparently, I put it on you so good that you're in love with me now. Is that the gist of it?"

He chuckled, eyes glinting with amusement. "Soul ties are not formed as a result of intercourse, but it probably would make for a much more enjoyable experience. Would you like to have sex when I form my tie with you?"

I blinked rapidly, the words hitting me like a slap to the face. "Whoa whoa what? Fuck, no." I pause. "Wait, so are you saying we didn't have sex?"

"No, not yet."

"Yet?"

"Yes, yet. But there's no need to worry. I won't touch you in that way until you want me the way I want you right now. I'll wait. Until you're ready. Until you no longer flinch at my touch."

"You're going to be waiting for all of eternity, because that's never going to happen. But if I didn't sleep with you, then how the hell did I form this soul tie?"

He shifted his neck, exposing a faint mark on his throat.

"Because I bit you? Now you're just confusing me. Did you forget you bit me first?"

"That was different."

"Different how?"

"Not only did I want you, but I gave you consent to take me, and *that you did.*"

"Bullshit," I shot back. "You're still messing with me. Answer my original question. Are you or are you not going to kill me?"

He sighed, eyes softening. "But I am, gorgeous. The moment my soul tied to yours, ending your life became absolutely impossible for me. I'd sooner rip out my own throat than ever think about harming you."

I narrowed my eyes at him. "Then what was that '*I'll make good on my promise*' shit?"

"That was me foolishly believing that—"

"You know what, save it. If you're not going to kill me, then there's no reason for you to still be here. Thanks for the rabbit and for not letting me become a goblin's sex toy, but I need to get out of this damn forest. I need civilization. People. A city. A town. Hell, I'd settle for a sketchy-ass village with questionable stew and a halfway clean bucket to bathe in. If I have to spend another night in this monster-infested wilderness, I'm going to lose it."

He tilted his head like he was trying to be helpful or some crap. "The nearest human settlement from here probably would be in Yenka. But at the pace you're going? It'll take you about a month to reach it."

"Are you kidding me?" I practically shrieked.

"If I ran," he continued, all casual like he wasn't suggesting something insane, "while carrying you, and took only a few breaks in between... maybe five days. Give or take."

I squinted at him like he'd sprouted wings, which at this point would be another thing I wouldn't be surprised at. "Seriously? Wait..."

This *had* to be another one of his twisted little games. But honestly? I was out of options. Stay here and risk another goblin ambush? Hard pass. Even thinking about those freaky little bastards gave me full-body shivers.

I crossed my arms. "Okay. What's in it for you, if I agree to it?"

Cue the smirk. That smug, soul-tugging grin he always wore right before saying something that would make me want to scream or spontaneously combust. "For now? Just being near you is enough for me."

Oh, Hell no. What was this man plotting? Whatever it was, I was 93% sure it was going to end with me regretting everything. Still, I gritted my teeth. "Fine."

"Hmmm... you have to say it."

"What?" I blinked.

"You have to say what you want from me. Otherwise, how can I be sure?"

And *there* it is. The nonsense. I rolled my eyes so hard I nearly gave myself whiplash. "Can you take—"

"Carry." He interrupted.

I glared at him. Petty mode, engaged. "Can you carry me to Yenka... *please*... Big. Beastly. Blue. Devil. Man."

His expression dropped. And then, suddenly, he was *right there*. Up in my space with that intense look again. My breath hitched. *Oh shit. Did I piss him off?*

But instead of gutting me with his claws, he just turned around and crouched down. "Get on."

My lids flickered. "Oh... Okay."

I reached out slowly, hand hovering near his shoulder and instantly froze. My mind flashed back to that moment. Big ass sharp teeth sinking into my skin, heat, pain, utter fear. *Was I really about to get a piggyback ride from the same guy who bit me like I was a juicy peach?*

Before I could pull back and come to my senses, he reached over his shoulder, caught my hand, and drew me onto his back. One smooth motion. He settled me into place and slid his arms under my legs.

"Wrap your legs around my waist and hold on tight." He said.

"No thanks. I'm good." I muttered, my legs hanging awkwardly at his sides like limp spaghetti.

He said nothing. Just stands there. Silent. Still. Like some dramatic statue. I waited. Figuring he was building up to something. But nope. Nothing but my body awkwardly pressed against his furnace of a back. My entire weight suspended in the air.

"You all good?" I finally asked, eyebrow twitching.

Crickets.

"Are we going anytime soon, or—" Again, not a word from him. *What is he doing? Meditating? Praying for strength?* "I mean, if you've changed your mind, you can just let me down and I'll—"

His grip suddenly tightened around my legs.

I squirmed, trying to wiggle free, but it only made things worse. *He was seriously going to make me do this.* The stubborn ass.

"Ugh." I grumbled, defeated, and finally, *finally*, wrapped my legs around his waist.

And of course, that's when a soft, smug little snicker slipped from his lips. *Bastard.*

"Don't let go of me," he said, just as the muscles in his back coiled, *WHOOSH.* We were off.

Air slammed into my face, my hair tried to eat my eyes, and the ground turned into a blurry mess of greens and yellows. I clung to him like a terrified barnacle, my entire body screaming *why?* His speed was unnatural.

How long had it been? Two hours? Three? Time meant nothing anymore. My bones had shaken loose from my soul. My internal organs had given up somewhere around hour one. Human bodies were *not* designed for beast-level sprints through the damn wilderness.

"Stop! Mitus! *Stop!*" I screamed over the wind, my voice barely reaching my own ears.

And just like that, he stopped. Abruptly. No skidding, or stumbling. Just dead stop like gravity meant nothing to him.

"Let me down." I gasped.

"But we've only—"

"I said, let me down." I commanded firmly. To my surprise, he actually listened. My feet hit the ground and nearly buckled beneath me. I bent over, hands bracing on my knees, sucking in air like I'd just run a marathon.

So *this* was why he was so eager to carry me. I can practically hear his inner monologue. *'Oh, I know what would be funny. How about I traumatize the human with a death sprint ride. I bet the weak little thing wouldn't be expecting that.'*

Well, he got me. My fault for falling for it though.

"Look," I said, waving him off, "thanks for the ride, but I'm not in the best condition to be hanging off your back like that. So, this is where we go our separate ways."

"If that way is too taxing on your body," he said, already stepping toward me, "then I will carry you in my arms."

I held out a hand. "*No!* I don't need you to do anything but *stay away from me*. You hear me?" My voice shook a little. "I've survived this long, and one way or another, I *am* getting out of this place."

I turned my back on him. It was a bold risky move, I know. But and? I started walking away, head high, despite the full-body ache screaming at me to lie down and die dramatically. I just need him to know I'm long over whatever *this* is. If he's still looking to get some kind of reaction out of me for his own entertainment, then I can't give him one.

"You said, if I keep heading this direction, I'll eventually make it out. That's all I need to know." My breathing was getting heavier by the second, and I leaned against a nearby tree, trying to pretend I wasn't seconds from collapsing. "So I'll keep going and *you* can go torment a fluffy pig or something."

That's when I felt his hand on my shoulder. *This fucking guy.*

"Look Mitus. I told you, I—"

But before I could finish, his grip tightened. And then the world around me tilted, blurred, dimmed. Then everything faded to black.

CHAPTER 13
MAGICAL MEDIEVAL WORLD

KALIYAH

Really? Come on. At this point I'm starting to grow tired of this white nothingness. Why has this dream decided to become a regular thing? My last few playbacks of this place just haven't hit like they used to. My once peaceful escape is slowly becoming a twisted endless prison and I do not need another one of those.

Hmm... But maybe this time it will be better. After all, this fluffy lush patch of grass with the most beautiful blossoming flowers beneath my bare feet is definitely a new addition. I reach down to touch it, when a large object materialize right in front of me.

At first, I thought maybe it was Star, but it wasn't accompanied by its usual warm glow. I look up. A full-length mirror? I squint at my reflection. Wait... is that me? I look down at my actual body and no, not quite. But the reflection? I mean, sure, it looks like me, but like... the straight baddie edition.

In the mirror, my braids are undone, hair lush and full. My skin glowing like it's on ten. My eyes look... different. It's like I'm seeing myself through a filter. A really flattering one.

Suddenly, I feel warmth around my abdomen. I look down to see the silhouette of arms wrapped above my waist. When I glance back at the mirror, I see it. The large presence. Its chest is pressed into my back. Its faintly blue silhouette glowing just enough to notice. I instantly recognize what... or who it is, even though his face hasn't fully formed.

He's following me into my dreams now? I immediately grab his arms, ready to pull his grip away, but even here, his hold is unyielding. As my hands rest on the warmth of his, I look back into the mirror, fully expecting that devilish grin that always plays on his face. Instead, I'm met with a somber, expression. Eyes closed. Why does his face look like that?

"Ninja. You mind giving me some space? I'm trying to have a peaceful dream here."

His head lifted slowly. So did his right hand. Trailing from the base of my stomach, gliding up my torso, across my shoulder blades, and finally resting at my neck. He gently tilted my head to the side and began placing these ridiculously gentle kisses along my shoulder, working his way up to my jaw.

The truly concerning part is that I'm not taken back by it. Honestly? I kind of like it. It is just a dream, after all. Why not enjoy myself? Maybe if I concentrate hard enough, I can get him to morph into my celebrity crush. Come on, Michael B.J. Lay it on me. I tilt my head back, ready for the swap. He sweeps my chin and draws me closer. I slowly open one eye.

Damn. Still the blue demon. He leans in, like movie trailer slow-burn levels. Our lips just about to touch. Breath mingling. The whole nine. Fine. Whatever. A dream, is just a dream. I let myself relax, lips parting slightly, right on the edge.

Cold. Something cold presses against my forehead. I feel myself slipping. And for some odd reason, I'm a little disappointed. My eyes flutter open to a *very real, very bright* room. Wooden walls, dark hardwood floors, soft natural light coming through a big window. To my left. A person? Like… an actual human person. Normal skin. Regular face. Fully dressed.

Have I finally woken up from that long comatose nightmare?

A big, irrational, deeply desperate part of me is hoping this is the part where it turns out I just hit my head on a rock during that day in the woods with the gang. You know… Slipped, smacking the ground, earning myself a solid concussion. Rushed to the hospital and the whole *summoned to a fantasy world and left to die* was a streaming original my brain decided to produce on a mega budget with the horror setting set way too high.

Yeah. Please let that be it. But, this definitely isn't a hospital. No sterile smell. No IV drip. No beeping heart monitor to reassure me that I'm not still trapped in some magical nonsense dimension where little green monsters and glitter dragons exist.

"What's going on? Where am I?" I rasp, my voice parched.

The air is warm, laced with the faint scent of woodsmoke and something sweet, like cinnamon. Spiced bread, maybe? I blink against the golden light spilling in from the right. The window's thin curtains fluttering in a slow breeze. Through the glass, I catch a glimpse of uneven rooftops and a sliver of sky, blushed pink by the early morning sun.

The bed beneath me creaks as I shift. Too large for just one person. The mattress is soft but lumpy. Covered in a faded quilt with mismatched abstract patterns. The headboard is carved wood, a bit rough to the touch, and I can just make out a few old designs etched into its surface. The room is pretty large. Actually, it makes my little studio master bedroom back home look like a broom closet. And it's not modern in any means.

What is this place? There's a cozy *cabin-in-the-woods* vibe about it, with its wooden beams stretching across the ceiling. One of them is crack and sagging just enough to worry me. A circular rug covers the floor faded and threadbare, but still holding onto streaks of color. In the far corner, there's a stone fireplace with a kettle hanging over it.

I blink once. Then a second time. Unless my coma *isn't* over with, I'm very much still in Therion. To my left, someone holding a towel. A girl, definitely younger than me. She's perched in a wooden chair beside the bed, legs tucked to the side like she's been there for a while. Her dress is simple, dark orange with a cream-colored apron that looks homemade. Her chestnut curls frame her face in soft waves, and her eyes... wide, alert, like she's been watching me for a while. Whoever she was, I was so overjoyed to see her face. I tried to sit up, but my body was still feeling a little odd. It's been feeling this way ever since I left the cave.

"Who are you?" I whispered, my throat dry.

"Don't get up too fast." She passed me a cup of water. "You're likely to tip over and fall again."

"Huh? Again?" I blinked.

"Yes, the other day you fell from the bed. I had a hard time lifting you back up with my leg and all."

"Wait..." I furrowed my brow. "How long have I been here?"

She thought for a second, eyes scanning the room like she was counting. "Um... four days. It feels like much longer."

"Seriously? I've been asleep for four days?" My hand automatically went to my face, swiping it downward, like somehow that would help clear the fog in my brain. Hell, it really was like I was in a coma. I paused for a second, then blurted out the question that had been on the tip of my tongue.

"Hold on... how did I get here? Did the blue man have anything to do with it?"

Her expression flattened and her eyes shifted away, like she was avoiding something. "You mean the orc."

"The... orc?" I blinked. *So that's what he is?* He's an orc. I don't know much about orcs, but they were always depicted as these gross, hulking, sweaty beasts with bad skin and even worse hygiene. The kind of monsters you'd expect to charge at the hero in a movie. Drooling, snarling, armor barely hanging together by bones and bad attitudes. I mean, that part isn't too far off. And the tusks, I guess that tracks. But *blue skin*? Not really part of the classic orc depiction.

"Yes, him. Where is he now?"

"He left." The girl responds.

"What?" My voice hitched with excitement, my heart doing a little jump. "Really? You mean I'm finally rid of him? Thank God."

"Actually, no." She shook her head, her expression neutral. "I think he was concerned that you still hadn't woken up. So, he went to retrieve one of the town's doctors."

"What, no... how long ago was this?"

"Not long actually."

That was all the confirmation I needed. I hopped up from the bed, ignoring the protests of my aching body. I didn't have much time, but I *had* to at least try. I made a beeline for the only door in the room. But before I could reach it, the young girl sprang into action, blocking my path. She spread her arms wide like she was ready to stop me with force.

"Where are you going?"

"Where do you think?" I shot back, throwing a pointed look toward the door. "You've seen that creature. He's a monster. I'm trying to get the hell as far away from here as I can. You should do the same."

"You can't leave," she said, blocking my way even more.

"And why the hell not?" I straightened my body and balled my fist. I wanted her to know I wasn't playing games. I didn't want to, but if I had to, I was taking her to the ground.

"Because if you leave, everyone in this inn, probably everyone in this town will die, I think." Her voice trailed off into a whisper, but I could hear the fear under it.

"What are you talking about?"

"That's what the orc said," she explained, her eyes lowering like she wasn't sure how much of this she was allowed to say. "I'm to watch over you until he returns. He said if anything were to happen to you, then he'd make sure the same would happen to everyone here tenfold."

"You've got to be kidding me."

"I promise you, I'm not. My mom and I run this Tavern, and I don't want her to die. My sister and her party are still traveling back from Palloria. She is strong-willed and a lot of times, she acts before she thinks. So, if she comes back to find us all dead... well, knowing her, she'll gather as many people as she can and seek justice. And seeing that he's a blue orc and all, she'll only end up getting herself killed too."

I feel sorry for the girl. I really do. But how is this my problem? I'd been through hell. And now, here was my chance at freedom. Why the hell should I be responsible for the fate of this girl and a whole bunch of other people I don't even know?

"Don't you people have soldiers or what are they called again... knights?"

"This is just one small town in Yenka. Sure, we get a few party members passing through, but other than that, we don't have anyone strong enough to face something like him."

So, he's something the people of this world aren't the most equipped to handle. Makes sense that he was locked away. But what I can't get my head around is how did he manage to escape. He said I was the reason he broke free. *'The key to his cell'* he called me. So somehow, it's my fault he's here, threatening to massacre a whole bunch of folks. My brows tense up.

"What's your name?"

"I'm Dahlia. Dahlia Cemyth. I've been here every day making sure you're okay and that you don't catch a fever."

"I see, Dahlia. How old are you?"

"I just turned fourteen last week."

Damn. She's just a baby. *Ugh*, this situation is so messed up. What am I supposed to do? There's no doubt in my mind that he'd do it. He'd kill them all. Just because they let his little plaything escape. The sounds of softly muffled clatter of dishes and the low hum of voices murmured from below. People laughing and living.

"Hey, you realize even if I stay he still could hurt or kill everyone, just because he feels like it."

"Maybe he will, maybe he won't. But if you leave now, I think it's almost guaranteed."

She might not be wrong. But I don't want to keep tempting fate. Still could I live with myself if he kills all those people because of me.

Although, even if I ran, how far would I get before he chased me down. He probably could lap this whole town two times over before I even made it a few blocks.

I sighed deeply. "Fine. Seeing that you gave me a place to rest my head and watched over me this whole time making sure I was okay, I won't leave. Not if it means something bad's gonna happen to you or your family." I rubbed my stomach. I'm freakin' starving. "But the thing is I haven't eaten a real meal in a long time. However, I'm short on money. You think I can get something to eat? I'm willing to work for it."

"Oh no, you don't have to work for anything. The orc made sure your meals are covered during your stay."

Of course he did. Coming into people's business, taking what he wants, and daring you to say something about it. Straight-up thug behavior. I glanced down. My clothes were still covered in filth and God-knows-what else. He already did the damage, might as well take advantage of it.

"Do you think I could get a change of clothes too? And, uh... do you guys have baths here?"

"Yes, of course! I'll draw one up for you after you eat."

My eyes practically sparkled. "Yes. I would *love* that."

She hobbled toward the door, and for a moment, my gaze caught on something wrapped around her ankle. Just a glimpse, peeking out from beneath the hem of her dress. It looked *odd*. But before I could get a good look, the door shut behind her.

I exhaled and wandered over to the window. The streets are narrow, cobbled with smooth stones worn down. Below, a cart rattles past. Its wooden wheels squeaking with every turn as a pair of shaggy, goat-like beasts massive and horned, pull it forward without complaint.

A man in a floppy hat waves to someone at a nearby stall, where bolts of bright fabric ripple in the breeze. Flea market, maybe? Everything is soaked in earth tones of rich browns, soft greens, sun-faded reds and oranges. There are no cars. No power lines. Just people. Ordinary folks from an extraordinary world, dressed in aprons and tunics, carrying baskets of produce or tugging along stubborn livestock, chatting like nothing is out of the ordinary.

To my left, perched near a rooftop, a small windmill turns lazily in the breeze. Below, I spot kids chasing a ball near the well at the center of the square. A bell chimes in the distance from a chapel tower I can just barely make out, its stone spire reaching above the other buildings like a crooked finger pointing at the sky. It's beautiful. *So* beautiful. Just watching life... *being lived.* I wipe away a tear before it can slide down my cheek, only for the sound of the door opening behind me.

"What's on the menu to—" I started to ask, turning, only to freeze mid-sentence.

It wasn't Dahlia. Mitus. And closely behind him stood an short older man in scruffy clothes, with gray hair and glasses, holding a large black bag in one hand.

I couldn't have five more minutes god. Before I could say a word, he was already in front of me. One hand sliding around my waist, the other landing gently on my cheek like he had the *right*. My brows drew together. Just as I opened my mouth to tell him to back the hell up, my eyes met his and I stopped. His expression wasn't smug or teasing like usual. It was serious. *Worried*, even. And for some annoying reason... that made my stomach twist.

Was I really that bad off?

"Can you let go of me?" I mumbled, dragging my gaze away from his.

"How are you feeling?" he asked softly.

"I would feel better if you weren't all over me."

"Sit," he guided my body toward the edge of the bed like I was a doll he owned, not a person with boundaries. Then he gestured toward the man hovering nervously by the door. Doctor, I'm guessing. And from the looks of it he's scared shitless.

He scrambled toward me, setting his worn black bag beside the bed and digging through it like his life depended on it. Most likely it did. He pulled out some old-timey-looking stethoscope and started the exam, rattling off the usual doctor stuff like, "How do you feel? Can you open your mouth for me? Any dizziness?" He checked my pupils, pressed fingers to my pulse, asked me to breathe in and out, all while his hands visibly trembled. I didn't blame him. Not long ago, *I* was the one flinching every time Mitus moved too quickly. But now? I was used to him. Unfortunately.

I glanced over at Mitus. His arms crossed, gaze locked on the doctor like he was ready to rip out the man's spine the second he made a wrong move. Because *that* would be an appropriate reaction to a stethoscope. *Fine.* I guess I'll be the one to save this poor man's bacon. *Why is it always me making the sacrifices?*

"Look, Dr...?"

He jolted like I'd slapped him. "L— Libyans," he stammered.

"Okay. Dr. Libyans. The truth is, I'm feeling *much* better now. So, I don't think your services will be needed any longer."

Dr. Libyans glanced up at me, hesitant. "Yes, but what about—" His eyes flicked nervously toward the orc.

I sat up straighter, pushing some authority into my voice. "Like I said, I'm feeling much better. So he can go now. Right, Mitus?"

He didn't say anything. Just stared.

Dr. Libyans tried again, "Are you sure that—"

"Yes. I'm *sure*," I cut in, pasting on the firmest smile I could muster. "Thank you for your help. Please be on your way now."

"Yes of course. Thank you, my dear." He said nervously gathering his belongings back into his bag as he shimmies to take his leave. Mitus calls out to the doctor as he rips what looks like a button from his belt and tosses it to him. With a nervous shuffle, he catches it and slips out the door like a man escaping a burning building.

The moment it shut behind him, I sat there in silence, shoulders slumping as I let out a long, exhausted sigh. *Now what?* Just as the thought passed through my head...

KNOCK. KNOCK. A soft tap at the door. Mitus immediately straightened, his whole energy shifting into threat-mode. One claw extended, his gaze locked on the door. Then a familiar voice floated in.

"I hope you like shepherd's pie."

I hopped up and moved fast, stepping between him and Dahlia like I was her own personal human shield. Last thing I was about to let happen was this beast gutting the poor girl right in front of me. Talk about my psyche forever being messed up. I rushed to meet her before she could fully step into the room, snatching the tray out of her hands. Hot food sat on top of a bundle of folded clothes, and a cup of some kind of beverage next to them.

"I don't think any of my dresses will fit you, so these are some of my sister's clothes. She's an adventurer so she doesn't own any dresses. I hope that's okay."

"Actually, that's perfect. Thank you, Dahlia. I got it from here."

"Oh, you sure?" she blinked up at me.

"Yes, I'm sure," I said, with the kind of forced cheerfulness. "Thanks again."

"Okay. Your bath should be ready in about ten minutes or so," she replied, still peeking around me like she half-expected to see blood on the walls. "Just head down the hall, take a right, and it's the first door on the left."

"You're awesome, Dahlia. And again, I'm sorry for all this."

She gave me a small, polite smile. "It's okay. It's not your fault. Usually, you don't see creatures like him these days, at least not one this... sensible."

He literally threatened to massacre her entire town if I left. That's her bar for sensible?

"Okay, well, don't hesitate to call if you need anything," she added sweetly.

"Will do. Thanks."

I watched as she turned to leave. Her limp was more noticeable now, the back of her skirt kicking up just enough for me to catch another glimpse of that *thing* on her leg. Thick purple veins and blotchy discoloration spread across her skin, like something rotten just beneath the surface. But that wasn't even the worst of it. Wrapping around her ankle, just hovering off the skin was that same vine-like shape. Deep, dark hunter green, pulsing faintly with a smoke-like haze, almost black. It shimmered and shifted as if it were alive. *What the heck is that?*

Before I could take another step closer, his voice cut in. "What do you have there?"

I rolled my eyes as I closed the door. "Why? Do you want it?"

He tilted his head slightly. "Eat. You need to build your strength."

I looked down at the tray to see shepherd's pie, warm bread, and a mug of something sweet and spiced. My stomach grumbled. "Honestly," I muttered, "I feel bad taking something I didn't pay for."

He raised a brow. "Where I'm from, there's no need to pay for anything, if you have the strength to take it."

I scoffed. "That's not how the world works."

"What are you talking about? "That's *exactly* how the world works."

"Maybe *here*," I said, setting the tray on the table, "but not in my world."

"*Your* world?" he asked, a curious gleam flickering in his eyes.

"Uh... forget it." No way was I about to tell him how a handful of glowing rocks tossed me through some cosmic port and dumped me in this magical medieval world. What if he decide to seek them out and travel back to earth. I can only imagine what would happen if something like *him* ended up home.

He'd probably level a few city blocks before anyone could stop him. But with my world's technology there's no doubt that eventually my people would catch him. They'd shove him in a lab, strap him down like some wild animal, and start poking and prodding, running experiments until they figured out how to crack him open.

The thought kind of makes me giddy, honestly. But then the military would probably get involved, turn him into some kind of weapon, start threatening nations, seizing governments. Classic political power bull crap. My world's got its own twisted mess of problems, but I'd still take that over this any day.

"You sure you don't want this?" I asked, holding up the bowl. *Better the pie than me after all.*

He shook his head.

"You're not gonna go eat a townsfolk later, are you?"

"Despite what you might believe, eating humans is not a normal thing for me. In fact, I've only ever eaten one. And honestly, the meat wasn't to my liking."

He said it like that somehow made it *better*.

Disgust and horror twisted in my gut so fast I nearly gagged. Like, *sir*... there are some things you just don't say out loud. I opened my mouth to respond, but right then the warm, buttery scent of baked crust hit me full in the face. I picked up the spoon resting on the tray's edge and sank it into the shepherd's pie. The golden-brown crust cracked with a soft flaky crunch, steam rising in a fragrant puff of rosemary, garlic, and something that practically screamed *comfort*.

Underneath that crust was velvety mashed potatoes. Like the kind that taste like love and chunks of tender vegetables swimming in thick, rich gravy and... meat? *What kind?* As long as it wasn't human, I didn't care. I took a bite and it was so good. *So so good.* It felt like I blacked out for a second. Melty meat, cozy potatoes, warm gravy hugs. My mind started to remember what joy felt like. I was mid-chew, finally at peace for the first time in days.

"Mmmmm." I slowly pulled the spoon from my mouth.

"Damn. I never thought I'd be jealous of a utensil." He mumbled.

Hmm? What asinine thing is he talking about now? *To hell if I care.* I wasn't going to let him ruin this for me. I took another bite. This pie was giving *everything*. I shoveled in another bite. Might've even moaned a little.

And then. *Then.* My chin lifts not on its own and the next thing I knew, the menace had his lips on mine. *ON. MINE.*

I froze, bowl dropping, hunger forgotten. And it wasn't even a quick peck. No, this man had the audacity to *nibble* my bottom lip like it was made of honey. And then, he pulled back all slow and licked his lips like he'd just tasted the rarest delicacy in the land.

"You're right. That is good."

I blinked. "What the hell was that?"

He shrugged, totally unfazed. "I wanted a taste."

"You— *you*—" I sputtered, heat crawling up my neck. "If you wanted to taste the *pie*. You should have just asked. Not... whatever *that* was!"

He leaned in, all smug and irritatingly smooth. "Who said I wanted to taste the pie?"

My breath caught halfway up my throat. "Nope. Can't. I physically and emotionally cannot deal with you right now."

I snatched the folded clothes from the tray and stormed toward the door. Of course, I heard the heavy *thump* of him trying to follow. I spun so fast, the tattered sleeve of my dirty dress flew up and almost hit me in the face.

One hand shot up. "You. Don't follow," I said, jabbing a finger at the floor. "I'm just going down the hall to take a bath, not planning a daring escape into the wilderness. You can chill out. Or snarl. Or whatever it is you do when you're not being all cryptic and terrifying. Just... find something else to do with your time other than bother me."

He blinked. Slowly.

"I'll be back soon," I added, taking one extra-dramatic step into the hallway before pausing, sniffing the air, and making a face. "Also, maybe think about bathing, too. You stink worse than me."

Then I slammed the door behind me, leaned against it, and exhaled like I'd been holding my breath since birth.

He's such a damn liar. He totally still wants to eat me.

CHAPTER 14
LOW TOLERANCE

KALIYAH

I cracked the door open and Oh. *My. Freakin'. God.* This has to be the most beautiful thing I've ever seen in my life. I'm being dramatic, but can you blame me. Inside, nothing fancy just a simple yet large bathing tub. It was wide and sunken into the floor, more like a small pool. I could feel the warm air rushing out to greet me. But it was the *smell* that really warmed my mind.

Incense, soft and spicy, clung to the air, maybe a bit of jasmine, and something else I couldn't name. I hovered at the edge, toes brushing the smooth stone lip, steam curling up around my calves. And under all that warmth, I could still feel the gross, the dried sweat, the forest dirt, goblin goo, the days of panic-marinated misery. The kind of filth that didn't just sit on your skin, it soaked into your bones.

I stripped off that now ragged dress, happily tossing it off to the side. My whole body ached and not the good workout kind, but the 'I've been surviving against all odds' kind. My shoulders, calves and back, just about everything throbbed with exhaustion and *ew*. I dipped a foot into the water. And immediately I wanted to cry. But this moment was too good for tears.

Heat bloomed across my skin the second I stepped in. A full-body *"ahhhh"* worked its way out of me. I eased in slowly, one leg at a time, down the smooth stone steps, until the water kissed my waist, then my ribs,then my shoulders. And when I finally sank all the way under. *Total bliss*.

For a few minutes, the world vanished. No dragons. No goblins. No orc. No creepy looking vines. No threats of casually being murdered or eaten. Just... warm water, and quiet. I surfaced slowly, braids slicked back, eyes shut, breath calm. For the first time in forever, I wasn't running. I wasn't afraid. I wasn't even worried. I was *chill*. The incense still lingered, soft and spicy and comforting, and the water rippled gently around me like silk sheets on skin. I leaned back, head resting on a neatly folded towel someone had left at the edge. Dahlia probably. *God bless her*.

I took a deep breath and slid beneath the surface, letting warm water soak through my braids. I *should* take them down and redo them. They were a mess. But also... who has the time? The world muffled. My hair floated weightlessly around me, and for a heartbeat, I let myself forget everything. The questions. The strangeness. The impossible reality outside this room. Just the warmth. Just the stillness. Then...

A ripple. Not mine. Subtle, but *there*. Like something big had moved. A current brushed past my arm. My stomach flipped. I shot up from the water with a gasp, blinking hard to clear my vision. And there. He. Was.

Mitus. In the bath. *With me*. He sat on the opposite side, water lapping at his abs, steam rising off his shoulders like smoke. His tusks caught the light. His expression not smug. Not threatening. Just... calm. Casual. Like we weren't both ass *naked* in the same tub. Again doing weird shit like it was completely normal.

"Ugh—" I half-coughed, backing up until I felt the curve of the stone behind me.

I stared. *Should I scream? Hop out knowing my clothes are by the door? Hurl the soap at his head? Or dunk underwater and pray this was some bath-scented hallucination?* All four options suck ass.

"You... *you can't just—*" I gestured one arm wildly, while the other covers my breasts. "...this is my bath!"

"You said I should bathe. Was that not an invitation?"

My mouth opened, then closed again.

Damn him. He's not dumb. Not even a little. He *knows* exactly what he's doing. That smug, faux-innocent act? Please. I'm not buying it for a second.

Don't react. Don't react. Just calmly get out, use the towel to wrap yourself, and leave his swampy ass in the bath to marinate alone.

I snatched the towel I'd been resting my head on and did my best not to flash a single thing while wrapping it around me. Not that it mattered. His eyes? Locked on the water like he was trying to X-ray vision his way through it.

Pervy freakin' bastard.

Once secured, I stood, water cascading down my legs, and took one step toward freedom. *One.* And then, like the villain he absolutely is, he grabbed my arm and tugged me back, right between his legs.

I landed with a splash and a very undignified squeak. My towel stayed mostly in place. But my sanity was hanging by a freakin' thread.

"Done already? I just got in."

My breath caught.

Don't react. Do not react to the suspiciously large appendage that just grazed my spine. His penis definitely just turned into a little monster of its own. He leaned in, voice dipping into *trouble* territory.

"Why don't you keep me company a little while longer?"

It's right there. His junk just grazed my back again. Do. Not. React.

"Mitus."

"Yes, my love."

Love? The audacity. The sheer audacity. I swear to everything sacred—

"Didn't you say you wouldn't touch me that way unless I wanted you to?" I grit my teeth.

"I remember every word."

"Well, I still don't want you. So can you let me go, *now*?"

He sighed like I just ruined his entire day. "I see. More time then. Fine by me, beloved."

He released my arm, and though I wanted to bolt out of there like a bat out of hell, I *had* to keep it together. I had to stay in control. But just as I turned to leave.

"Hey beautiful, you really are making it hard to resist you when you hide your body away from me like that. But I'll behave like a good little *demon*... for now."

My whole body went stiff, but I didn't turn around. I just clutched my towel tighter. Then slammed the door behind me, just before grabbing my clothes. I scurried back to the room and dressed in a hurry, pulling shirt and pants over my still-dripping body, trying to beat him before his next sneak attack.

Damn him. He keeps finding ways to get under my skin. How is he so good at that?

That literal heated moment had me quite thirsty when I remember the drink Dahlia had left on the tray. I lifted the wooden mug. The liquid inside shimmered a kind of deep purplish hue, definitely not water. I gave it a cautious sniff. I took a sip. Sweet. Tart. Like cherry-cranberry juice.

Oh, *yum.* This would've gone so well with the shepherd's pie. "Ugh." Just another reason to be pissed off at that tusked face. I know the rule is ten-seconds, but I've drunk water from a tree's butt-hole and tasted orc blood, so a little floor meat and mashed potatoes shouldn't kill me. I glanced at the spot where my bowl had fallen earlier, but it was gone. Huh? Maybe Dahlia had cleaned it up? But the now-empty bowl was on the table.

I took another sip of the fruity mystery juice and bent down to pick up the spoon... or what was left of it. Snapped clean in two. I eyed it suspiciously before placing the pieces on the tray.

I flopped down onto the bed, back against the headboard, knees slightly bent. I felt good. Too good. Kinda floaty. *Wait, hold up.* I know this feeling. I looked down at the half-full mug still in my hand.

"Is there alcohol in this?"

Shit. No. I slammed the cup down on the floor and slid further up onto the bed, pressing my palms against my now-toasty cheeks. Okay. So maybe I'm a *little* tipsy. But not drunk. Definitely not. I could still say the alphabet backwards, if I wanted to. Which I don't. I just need to keep my wits about me.

"Kaliyah." A voice calls out to me.

I blinked. "Huh?"

The voice sounded familiar, but also not. I glanced around the room. Empty. Just me, the bed, the soft buzz in my head, and that deceitful half-finished drink.

"Kaliyah. It's almost time."

Okay. *Nope.* That definitely didn't come from anywhere in this room. Are ghost a thing here too?

"Hello?" I called out cautiously, then immediately regretted it. "Who's there?"

Silence.

"Cool cool cool," I whispered to myself, rubbing my temples. *So I'm hearing voices now. Love that for me.*

I sighed. My low tolerance to alcohol combined with my bath got me feeling all warm, even relaxed. My limbs feel all floaty and loose. A nap sounded dangerously good right about now.

The door creaked open, and in walked Mitus. I half-expected him to be naked, but instead, he wore a long red and black silk robe. It caught me off guard. He looked... *normal.* He walked in, gave me a quick glance and a smile, then sat at the table.

I rolled my eyes and turned my nose up. Peeking from the corners of my eyes to see what he was doing. Going through my backpack. Honestly, I don't care. Nothing in there now but my journal, some panties in desperate need of a good washing, my smartphone I'm still hoping for some magical way to power on. Not that it would be much use in this world. But I have some pictures of my grampa and friends on there, just in case I never get back home. And with Mitus forcing me to marinate in whatever foolishness this is, it seem more and more likely by the day.

Oh and I can't forget Jemma's gummies. During my time in the forest, I considered eating them a thousand times over, but when the side effects are the major munchies, it just seemed like a disastrous idea. I'm not sure when, but I lost Ryan's dagger.

Look at him. The *nerve*, just to go through my things like that. No manners whatsoever. Orc or not, someone needs to teach him about *boundaries.*

Orc, huh? Now that I really look at him, like *look-look*, I notice something I hadn't before. His face and hands... they're not the same color as the rest of him. I thought it was dirt at first, but since the man just had a whole soak session, I'm guessing that ain't it. From the neck up and wrists down, his skin shifts, just beneath the pale blue, there's a warm, sun-kissed caramel undertone. Like the pigment's trying to break through. Honestly, if I didn't know any better, I'd think he was just a *very* handsome light-skinned dude with a weird underbite.

I hate to admit it but that face? That body? He could've easily been a model back home. Probably one of those smoldering-eyed, broody types who show up on spicy book covers and ruin your life with one look. Always on social media with his shirt off, licking his lips giving advice to losers about the only way you get what you want is by taking it. Just *ugh.*

And now he's reading my journal. Fine. Go ahead. By all means, snoop away. I *dare* you to read about all the nasty things I've called you and the lovely little doodles to go with them.

He smirked as he licks his finger and flips another page. *Oh? What's so funny?* Just wait until you get to the entry titled *'Dear Donkey.'*

Wait. What is he doing with those? I squint. He is *not* doing what I think he's doing. I watch as he lifts my panties to his face and inhale deeply through his nose. I pinch the bridge of my face, teeth clenched so tight.

Animal. Disgusting perverted animal.

How much more of this do I have to put up with? First the kiss, then turning my bath into his personal spa, now he's over here huffing my laundry like some kind of dog. And as if my dignity hasn't been assaulted enough today, let's not forget the almost-sex dream I *definitely* had about him.

Yep. That happened. But I refuse to take full responsibility for that. I've been under intense stress. Like, world-hopping, monster-dodging, demon-roommate stress. And it's been *way* too long since I've had anything even remotely resembling adult play time. Combine that with the fact that he's literally the only man I've seen in a month, and honestly, would anyone be surprised. I peeked one eye open. Just a smidge.

Sigh. I mean... look at him. It really doesn't help that his face and body are sitting there built like temptation itself. A walking thirst trap dipped in sin and regret. And normally, buff and broody is not my type. I prefer a man who's kind, considerate and doesn't keep a body count.

But it's not like I completely hate the view. That damn face is all angles and arrogance. Those arms, thick and veined. That chest, broad and bare just enough to make me question everything I claimed to stand for. And that robe? Doing absolutely *nothing* to hide the fact that this man was sculpted straight out of some late-night, no-judgment, fantasy-fueled fever dream.

Still... that *personality*. Oh, and the *minor little hiccup* that he *ate a whole-ass human being.* So yeah. Hard *pass.* I would never, *ever,* under any circumstances touch that man-beast with a twenty-foot pole.

My eyes fluttered shut before I could stop them. Still, there's no harm in a little imaginary sequel to *that dream*, right? Especially now that I know exactly how his lips feel pressed against mine—

Softer than they have any right to be, but still firm enough to make my breath catch. He knew exactly what he was doing, exactly how long to linger. And the way his tusk grazed my cheek? It should've been jarring. But instead, it felt... *intimate* in the strangest, most primal way. A touch that said, '*give me all of you*'.

And then those *damn* muscles, I know aren't just for show. Letting them mold to my body like they were made to fit me, to hold me, to pin me in place if he wanted to.

That low, moan sound he made after he nibbled at my lip? Yeah. That's the part my brain decided to loop on repeat. It's just a fantasy. I'm allowed to let my imagination go wild. Heat. Skin. I envision his hands knowing just where to hold me. Lips that moved like they have a map of every soft place on my body. Until finally his heat bleeds into me, radiating off his skin and soaking into mine.

My breath hitching as his fingers find their way up to my harden nipple, teasing them just right as he trace along my breast. All gentle like, when they slide up, oh so deliberately, to cradle the side of my neck. My whole body responding just before he... *Just before he...* Rips a whole clean through it.

Cause yep. That sounds about right. I inwardly laugh as I buried my face into the palm of my hand. Because that is *exactly* how that would go down. A little nibble here, a soft kiss there, and then BOOM. *Meat pie filling.*

Honestly, I wouldn't even be surprised if he was over there right now wondering whether I'd taste better grilled or lightly seasoned and baked in a crust. I sighed and cracked my fingers open to sneak another peek at the disaster currently sharing oxygen with me.

Huh? He wasn't at the table anymore. I dropped my hand from my face *and immediately regretted it.*

There he was. Crawling... over my ankles. *When the actual hell did he get over here?* And why hadn't I felt the bed shift? Was this man, part cat... better yet ghost? His face was tracing up my legs, slowly. I could *hear* him breathing me in, like I was a damn flower arrangement.

No, worse. Like his hunger was finally calling to him and he was ready for his main course. Absolutely no impulse control. This man needed medication, a muzzle, and possibly a spray bottle.

What is he doing…? Shit. Did my notes finally push him over the edge? He exhaled again, the heat of his breath ghosting across the fabric of my thigh.

"Um… you good?" I whispered, my voice caught somewhere between panic and God help me, curiosity.

He didn't answer. Just the sound of his breathing, unhurried and too controlled. The kind of quiet that made everything louder inside my head. The way his nostrils flared as he lingered, close but not quite touching. It sent a ripple down my spine.

Too damn close. And I went still. Every muscle in my body locked down like a wire about to snap. His robe brushed my legs as he knelt, fabric soft against skin that suddenly felt *too aware*. His jaw was tight. His breathing measured. He was struggling with something. And then…

His face pressed *right there*. With no warning. With no freakin' hesitation. He buries his head as he offers me a long, deep inhale into my groin that made my back arch and my hands claw into the sheets beneath me.

My body jerked. Heat pooled low and fast. I wanted to move, but couldn't. His eyes lifted to meet mine. Those predator eyes. A storm of grey to blue, deceptively calm but filled with something sharp. Something wild and *waiting*.

"Seriously… what the shit—" My voice was wrecked, barely a breath. Every part of my mind said I should push him away. Yell. Throw something. But my body just sits here, frozen in place. Half mortified, half… something else.

He didn't stop. Working his way up as his leg brushed open the gap between my thighs. Hell. I'm not even sure that was his leg. He leaned in, close enough that I could feel the warmth of him without him even touching me. His lips brushed the shell of my ear, barely a breath.

"Are you sure you're not ready for me now? Because your body says otherwise, gorgeous."

A flutter tore through my lower belly, as my cheeks started to toast. "What?" I croaked, throat tight.

He pulled back just enough to meet my gaze, his expression the same intensity.

"W—What are you talking about?"

"I can smell you."

"Sorry. *What*?"

"You're in heat."

My eyes widen so damn big as my brain short-circuited. *What... did he just say? In. Heat.* Mortification hit me like a punch. I turned my head away, breath ragged, whole body burning with something tangled and raw. *He can smell me?*

Humiliation. Need. Fury. All of it crashing over me in a wave that made me want to slap him... or drag him back down between my legs. This was insane. And yet... My thighs won't close. *Listen to me damn it.*

Fuck. What is going on with me right now? Do I... want this? Do I want him? I can't. Because that again, would be fucking insane. Wrong. So wrong on so many levels. But... *But...*

He moved closer, eyes locked on mine like he already knew the answer. The one I was too confused to acknowledge, even in my own damn head.

I tilted forward letting my mind go blank. Just a little. Just enough. Barely an inch, as my lips part. That heat between us grew thick and ready to break wide open.

THUD!

The door flew open with a bang so loud I nearly bit my own tongue. Voices. Footsteps. Interruption. A rush of bodies poured in and just like that, the moment evaporated. I stared past him, wide-eyed and breathless, as he slowly pulled away.

Thank God.

CHAPTER 15
THE ORDU'KAI ORC

MITUS

This must be her personal records. What is this donkey she writes of? Knowing her, it's something unpleasant. I inwardly chuckle as I flip through more of the journal, scanning her furious scribbles and crude little doodles. So charming. She really is something. I lift the scrap of cloth to my face. It smells of her. *Dieties, so damn delicious*, like summer flowers, with a whisper of honey melon, the kind of scent that clings to memory and stains it forever. *These belong to me now. She won't be getting them back.* I don't recognize this thin black box, though. A magic tool, perhaps? My gaze drops to the smaller pouch tucked inside. The aroma hits me next. Fruit, crushed herbs, and...

And... *And what the fuck is that incredible aroma.* My nose turns up. The scent so sweet. So intoxicating. It coats the air around me, thick with desire, wrapping me up, drawing me closer, and I have no other choice but to look to her. She's sits on the bed across the room from me with her face buried in her hands. Woman if that's your attempt to shield your scent from me, its poor at best. Your fragrance gives you away. And it's *everywhere*.

Pure sugary ripeness. It beckons to my core. *Is it for me?* The haze hits me like heat from a flame, rolling in waves. I can't think. Don't want to. All I want, *need* is a taste. Just one drop. Just to see if she tastes as good as she smells. Of course she does. Probably, sweet like wickedness. Before I realize it, my feet are moving. My body acts on instinct. Closer. Closer still. How long has it been since I craved something so badly. Never. Not like this.

"W—what the shit are you doing?" Her voice slices through the fog in my head, just sharp enough to jolt me. Not enough to pull me away entirely. Igniting the craving into something thick, long and ready to go deep. She has stirred the beast. Provoked the lust and desires I keep having to bury down. *Why do you insist on digging it up, little breakfast? Do you really want me to devour you?* To slowly lick and suck and nibble away at you until there's nothing left. Nothing but my name clinging to your tongue as I take that into mine.

Surrounding me with your absolutely irresistible aroma, getting it to call to me, dangling yourself like a deliciously forbidden piece of fruit, just ready to be picked.

No. I can't simply walk away without getting her back for this. My time away has not dulled my sense of pettiness and I will show her that. Teasing me with the scent of her waterfall, when I'm so fucking thirsty right now.

Yes. This will show her. I lean into the curve of her neck. My lips press, skin so soft, so warm, it almost unravels every ounce of restraint I have left. A low, guttural purr escapes my chest moving into my lips. She shivers. Her pulse kicks. Her scent grows sweeter, more intoxicating. Her reaction causes my cock to wake.

Down beast. Wouldn't want her to think your feral. She is not ready for you. Not yet anyway. Most women, human or otherwise, have pressure points. Sometimes hard to find. My era of lustful indulgence with the succubus taught me where to look. But not even those damn demonic seductresses were able to make my body *yearn* so insatiably. I know the bond of the soul tie is only one way, but with part of me already apart of her, she has to be able to feel my craving for her.

Mmmm, yes. I can tell. Right there. Her body is *curious* for me now. She's shifting. Parting. *Offering* as she spreads her legs for me. She doesn't even realize it. But I do. Her mind might fight it, but her body confesses every secret she tries to keep. I won't make this easy for her. Not after the agony she's putting me through with those teasing looks, the scent she lets linger in the air like a dare, the dreams she's filled my nights with.

My lips curl into something unsatisfied. No. Not until I hear it. I want her to *say* it. Her voice. My name. Her need. Dripping from her lips like the moan she's too stubborn to release. I want her to *beg* for me. To tell me just how much she wants me. Only then will I give her what we both crave. She is starting to melt beneath my touch. Her body slowly relaxing, her breath growing shallow. The scent of her, the rhythm of her pulse, all of it pulling me deeper.

THUD!

The door busts open. She jerks away from me like a startled rutokki. And just like that the moment is gone. No... STOLEN.

Rage. Pure and unfiltered. It surges through me, thick and violent, as my head whipped toward the intruders. The hatred I felt in that breath rivaled that of the old enemies I'd hunted across battlefields. These suicidal fools dared interrupt me. I rose from the bed slowly, my silk robe sliding off one shoulder. My body still thrummed with the heat of her, the scent of her clinging to my skin. I will paint the walls with the blood of whoever ruined this. Their weapons are drawn, while their hands tremble. The one with the staff attempted to form a containment barrier around me, his magical aura weak and unrefined. Compared to the magic held in the power of the mountain core— No, there is no comparison. His spell was nothing but a wall of air.

"Deities, she was right. It really is a blue orc," the woman in front whispered.

"Saphire, what do we do?" The man with the crossbow asked. "Legends say it took the strength of two champions, the great mage, the ogre king, and the elven knight to defeat the last one. What can our little party do against that?"

I couldn't help but scoff inwardly. *Locking me away in some mountain. That's what they called defeating me?* The only real threat among them had been that elven knight and that damn slippery-ass mage. The champions had tasted their own blood before the battle even started. And they dare call that sorry ass ogre, *'king'*, when he resided in territory under my rule?

With the level of magic he wielded, and the elves' natural lifespan, I'm sure both of them are still alive somewhere. *Good.* I can't wait to hunt them down. They'll be getting what's coming to them real soon.

"For now, we just have to evacuate the town and go from there," Saphire said.

"Beast! Get away from her!" The smaller woman in the back shouted. A phoenix perched on her shoulder.

"Whose idea was it to interrupt us. Tell me. I want to make sure your death is slower than the rest." I fixed my eyes on the staff wielder. "Was it you, mage? Scratch that, of course it was. You fucking magic bleeders are worse than the damn vampires. If you're not siphoning magic that doesn't belong to you from my territory, then you're finding some way to stick your noses into my shit." *What a wonderful idea I just had.*

"Hell, if you like my shit so much… then maybe I should make you eat it just before I gut you and hang you from the ceiling by your own entrails."

Within a flash, his barrier around me shattered as I lunged at him aiming for his abdomen. Lucky for him, the woman in the front was fast and pushed him out the way. Not bad for a human. Still that move will cost her… *Her eyes.* It does not please me to see them in her sockets. So, I will take them. My fingernails pointed and firmly ready to gouge them out. I can tell she sees it coming and that she knows there's not a damn thing any of them can do about it.

My ears twitch. I hear my love's voice.

"Please don't kill them."

Instantly, I stop mid-strike, less than an inch from her pupils. I grunt and withdraw my hand. The woman, Saphire, jumps back as her comrade with the sword begins to charge.

"Stop!" Kaliyah yells. "If none of you want to die a pointless death, then just stop."

The swordsman freezes.

"Miss, we're here to help you. You just need to make your way out of here and let us handle the rest."

"There's no point in any of this," Kaliyah replies.

"What are you saying? Do you know what this monstrosity is? He's a blue orc. The demon of all orc kind. A menace to both mystical and non-mystical beasts alike."

I look back at her. Her expression has shifted back to what it was before. Just when she was finally warming up to me. I bite my cheek, shooting a glare back at the five intruders. He really should shut his fucking mouth, before I rip open his jaw and tear his tongue out with my teeth. I will do it... if he keeps pushing me. She only asked me not to kill them. But she said nothing of torture.

Shit. That won't do. They're human. If she sees me doing anything like what I'm thinking, she'll never stop being scared of me. *How do I make them shut the hell up?* I don't want her to hear any more of this.

"The last one was defeated nearly three hundred years ago. If another has emerged, it is a sign of dark times to come," the one with the sword continued.

My head dropped, shoulders stiffening under the weight of his words. *Three. Hundred. Years.* I'd estimated ninety, maybe a hundred at most. But three *centuries*? Three hundred years locked away like a caged animal.

My fists clenched until my knuckles blanched. The skin pulled tight over bones that had once shattered cities. I could feel it. That bitter heat coiling low in my gut. Boiling in my blood. The sheer *hatred* of what had been done to me radiating like poison through the air. The threadbare scrap of sanity I'd clung to for generations was unraveling, one breath at a time. The familiar *taste* of rage finally bloomed on my tongue like blood.

"We are aware that we are no match for him. We've already sent word to the guild. All we have to do is hold him off long enough for the townsfolk to make it to the Namma stones. You need to run while you still have the chance."

I looked up. *Hold me? As if they could ever.*

"You're not listening to me. You can't outrun him. It's pointless. I watched him kill a horde of goblins, forty strong, and the eight-foot leader in under two minutes flat."

"You mean a hobgoblin?"

"Saphire, my cousin, and his party twice our size was wiped out by a hobgoblin. The woman is right. We don't stand a chance." The mage said.

"What do you expect me to do? This is my home. My mother and little sister are downstairs. Do you expect me to just let him barge in and have his way with the place?"

"That might be all we can do." The swordsman replied.

"Hell no." She readied her weapon, gripping it tightly.

"Burn," I mumble under my breath. "All of you will burn until there's nothing left but ashes and dust."

My body began to shift into its second form. My muscles enlarging as my Ordu'kai markings inscribe over my skin. I have made it up in my mind that I will slaughter all of those that stand before me. And oh no... I won't stop here, it will spread far and wide not relenting until the insatiable rage devours itself.

The phoenix screeched and cawed, reacting to my threatening presence. Its tamer was powerless to stop it. Too busy urinating herself. The man with the crossbow took a step toward the door. My eyes tracked him first.

"Ah ah ah. That won't help you." I felt the fire in my chest build. Just as I was about to spit flames that would melt the skin from their bones, arms wrapped around my waist.

"Don't do it." Kaliyah's voice reached out to me. It was low and far too fragile for the madness she was stepping into. Her breath grazed my spine, trembling but steady enough to plant roots in the chaos swirling inside me.

"I understand. It was unbearable... being trapped there for so long. I know better than anyone. Always starving, in the cold. Feeling stuck and alone. I wasn't there nearly as long as you, and I thought I was going to go crazy." She whispered as a breath hitched in her chest, and deities, there was so much truth in her words. "So I get it. You need to let off some steam. But if you're going to kill anyone, shouldn't it be me?"

My rage faltered. Her arms were shaking. She stood there so delicate, so human, so damn ridiculous in her defiance. Offering herself like some sacrificial lamb to some deity who doesn't deserve her. Voice still trembling, but not stopping. "These people haven't done anything to you.

But me? I've taunted you. Swung at you. Cursed you out more times than I can count. Didn't you read my journal. I told you to go choke on a donkey's ass." I can feel her eyes piercing my back through tear-glossed lashes. "I call you a perverted dipshit blue devil demon every chance I get. Even after you asked me not to."

She so damn vulnerable. She wields no weapon, no armor, nor magic and yet she holds so much power over me.

"So doesn't it make sense to turn your anger to me?"

My pulse slowed at the sound of her sniffling. Something inside me twisted, that last thread of self I thought had already snapped. I feel her now. *Really* feel her. Her hands gripping the frayed edges of my sanity, holding me together when I can feel everything slipping. Her tears were cool against my burning skin, sliding down my back like mercy. She is my tie... my bond... and I am her savage.

"So... please. Don't hurt them. Any of them."

I would murder the deity of despair if it meant my woman never shed another tear. The growl that had been building in my chest died in my throat.

"All of you leave. Now."

"What?" Saphire's voice cut through.

I didn't repeat myself. I didn't need to. The air itself answered for me. Crackling with power barely held in check, anchored by the one thing still holding me to this world.

"Sapphire, let's go." The swordsman said.

"But that woman needs our—"

"Would you rather it be Dahlia instead?" The mage replied. Sapphire froze, her eyes widening as if the words of her companion were sinking in. She reluctantly caved as her comrade pulled her away from the door, shutting it behind them.

Kaliyah's arms trembled. I placed one of my hands on top of hers. My body, now softer, shifting back into its original form, more relaxed at her touch.

"I told you, beautiful. I would rip out my own throat before I'd ever hurt you. You are my forever. But if you refuse to believe me, offering yourself up to me the way you just did, I might just go back to calling you little breakfast."

She twitched. Even her smallest reactions were cute enough to put a grin on my face. *Damn. I'm so enchanted with her it's almost sickening.*

"I want you to stay here and really think about what I just said. I'm going to go talk with our hosts downstairs."

I go to step forward, but her grip tightens. She must be worried I'm still planning on killing them. I admit, the thought crossed my mind. But if I'm going to build any kind of trust between us, it's best if I don't.

"Don't concerned your pretty head, sweetheart. Tell you what, I'll make you a deal. As long as none of them try to hurt you, I will never kill another human again. How does that sound?"

She nods her head against my spine and drops her arms. "Okay... Deal."

Maybe I should have dragged that out longer. It's the first time she's ever embraced me on her own. I steal a peek at her over my shoulder. *Next time.*

I confront the group in the tavern downstairs as they huddle together discussing strategies. From their earlier conversation, it's apparent they are unaware that I am the same blue orc that once plagued the world, rampaging through the lands. *Good.* I approach from behind. The room falls silent. The group hesitates to meet my gaze. The tamer, as well as the one with the crossbow, is no longer among them.

"You there, loud wench."

"My name is Sapphire, you beastly piece of—"

The mage cautioned her. "Be careful with your words, Sapphire."

I didn't even blink. *I don't give two shits what her name is.* She might as well be a stone at my feet, insignificant and begging to be crushed under my heel. All I see is talking flesh, with arrogance and zero sense of self-preservation. If she'd met me just twenty years ago, the me lost in another periodic fit of madness, she wouldn't be so brave. She wouldn't be speaking at all. Because I would've filleted her apart. Slowly. Joyously. Just to see what kind of screams her nerves would sing.

I've done it many times before. To others. To myself. Out of boredom. Out of morbid curiosity. Just to feel something new. If I was her, I'd stop looking at me with those disrespectful eyes, otherwise I might finish what I started upstairs. No~ I shouldn't, for my Kaliyah's sake.

"You're a high-class danger-level mythical beast," she spat. "You invaded my family's inn, and you're probably holding that poor woman hostage."

"And what proof do you have of this?" I asked.

"Proof?" she scoffed. "Look at you. That's all the proof we need."

"Do you reserve this same prejudice towards demi-humans as well?"

"What are you talking about?"

"I mean, I am but an orc and sure my kind don't typically mingle with humans, but it's not unheard of."

"You're not just *an* orc. You're a *blue* orc."

"And?"

"What do you mean, *and*?"

"I fail to understand the significance of my skin color in this discussion. I couldn't control the hue I was born with any more than you could. I am no different than any other orc."

Lie. My skin is blue for a reason. I was born under impossible celestial conditions, when a blue comet passes through the crescent of the twin moons. It is said only one Ordu'kai Orc is born every millennium, and each time, the world suffers.

Legends claim the first Ordu'kai was forged by the Great Vireth-Kai as punishment, a soul that defied both divine order and mortal restraint. Cursed and blessed in the same breath, the Ordu'kai is not born of parents but conjured from raw magic, rising from blood-soaked battlefields, body sculpted by ancestral rage and starlight. I am not like any creature in this world. Although she can probably sense that much, I doubt she knows the specifics of my origins. Not many living souls do.

She mumbled her next words. "I don't buy that shit. I do believe you about being like all the other orcs in your interactions with species you deem weaker than yourself. Quick to violence, taking whatever you want because you can. Even now, you're freeloading, you've threatened the lives of the people in this town, that includes my mother and my sister."

"Do you enjoy spreading unfounded rumors, or do you just savor the bullshit that falls from your mouth?"

She gritted her teeth, her eyes narrowing.

"I gave both the girl and your doctor their gold. Or are you implying that it's not enough for a stay at this shabby inn in this lowly country town?"

The wench gaze leans toward her little sister peeking from behind the counter. The girl nodded, confirming it.

"And as for the threats. Did you not brandish steel at me first? Or do your definitions of aggression only apply when convenient?"

"What about the woman in your room? She looked terrified. I was told she was brought here against her will."

I turned my head slowly toward the younger wench behind the counter, who quickly ducked down. The beast in me stirred. My arms crossed to keep them from instinctively lashing out, claws of irritation scraping at my ribs. Then I turned back to the annoying wench, letting my gaze harden.

"What about her?"

"She's clearly your hostage. Just what did she say she'd do to get you to let us leave that room?"

"Another assumption. *That woman's* name is Kaliyah and you'll address her as such. Did it ever occur to you, that the fear you saw on her face was because of the five strangers barging into our room with their weapons drawn?" My next words were unexpectedly pleasurable. "*That woman* is no hostage. She is my *mated soul*."

The atmosphere that followed crackled with disbelief.

"You're what...?" The wench's jaw slack with shock.

"Did he just say mated soul?" The swordsman echoed.

"That's not possible, she's human." The mage muttered.

The wench's lips parted, "Don't only—" But the sentence withered in her throat.

"Um... hello." Kaliyah's voice called from the stairwell. "I don't mean to interrupt. It just seem like things got a little *too* quiet down here. I was just checking to see if everything was okay." She stepped into view, looking disheveled, eyes flicking from one face to the next. "Everyone seems to be good, so I'll just go back to my room." She turns to head back upstairs.

The wench called out, "Wait, Kaliyah. Hold on. I need to ask you something. And you can be completely honest with us."

Kaliyah blinked, brows lifting, then nods.

The wench inhaled, "The orc. Just who is he to you?"

Kaliyah paused, a soft furrow forming between her brows as she looks at me. Then, slowly, she lifted a fist to her chin in mock thought. "Right now..." she pauses, "he's my everything."

The wench pauses, then continues. "And you're not just saying that, are you?"

Without hesitation and to my very surprise Kaliyah walks over to me and wrapped herself around my arm. I had to bite my cheek to keep from groaning to her touch. "I'm saying that because you asked, and that's my answer. Why?"

"But earlier—"

"Sapphire," an older woman interjected, "let this go. He's a paying guest, who hasn't done anything wrong."

"But ma."

"Saphire." The old woman said firmly.

"Okay, fine."

"I apologize for the trouble my eldest has caused you. How about a free meal on the house?"

My woman's face lit up like the night sky. It would seem even mention of a good meal, brings her much delight. I will remember that.

"Really? I'd love that!" she said, practically bouncing on her heels as she regrettably releases my arm. "Do you have any more of that shepherd's pie?"

"Why yes, we do," the woman replied with a smile. "A couple of fresh ones just came out of the oven."

As much as that intrepid wench irritates me, I find myself, grudgingly grateful. Had she not provoked this storm of confrontation, I may not have gotten to hear such a sweet, solemn declaration leave my darling's lushes lips, at least not this soon in our entanglement. My blood pumps. Such a foolish, reckless thought that one day she'll say those words and *actually* mean them.

KALIYAH

Oh my god. I am *so* freakin' stuffed right now I could die and go straight to food heaven. Shepherd's pie, warm bread, and that cinnamon honey tea? Baby, I ascended. No thanks to *Dahlia's* older sister. We almost didn't make it to dessert.

I *still* can't believe she had the nerve to ask me that. Right in *front of him.* Like, *girl.* Seriously? You really thought I was going to break down in the middle of the tavern and say, "Oh yeah, he's my stalker. My captor. My part-time cannibal-in-waiting. Save me from this murderous beast you made abundantly clear none of you have any hope in stopping!"

Absolutely the hell not. So yeah. He's my *everything.* My every hate I've ever hated, all wrapped up in a tall, blue, muscle-bound, nightmare-fueled package. I hate him more than those little, icky, slimy, croaky, hoppy-ass frogs. More than the girls in high school who tried to sneak perm into my shampoo bottle. More than mosquitoes and I *loathe* those bitches. He is the killer of my joy. The bane of my existence. The walking, talking, smirking embodiment of my personal hell. But I can't say any of that, *now, can I?* Not unless I want human slushies all over the place. And apparently, here in Therion, Black folks aren't fluent in eye language. I was standing there, forced to cling to him, giving her the full dramatic eye monologue. My freakin' gaze was spilling all of it's guts and I got nothing in response.

I mean really? What exactly was she expecting me to say? Her kid sister and mom was standing right there. Have you ever seen a body skinned in two seconds flat, because I have and that would be this whole damn place if I didn't play along. What makes all of this even more bothersome is the stupid look on his face. I know he knows I didn't mean it. Just like I know there's no way in hell he means that *'love of my life'* BS. So, why did he look so damn pleased with himself, like he'd just won a game.

Damn it, no. I need to be real with myself right now... What really got to me wasn't him smiling. It was *me*, back in the room, holding on to him.

The terrifying part wasn't what he might do. It was what I *wanted* him to do. I was saying all the right words. *"Please, show mercy"*. But in that moment, deep down, I wanted the complete opposite.

The moment, his body had just started to change, that same way I'd seen before, something in me cracked. Overwhelming hate... No. Rage. Pure, boiling rage rose up so fast it didn't even feel like mine. And for one awful second, I wanted him to unleash it. To tear them apart. To erase them from this world like they were nothing. That scared the absolute hell out of me. That's why I clung to him the way I did. Not out of fear of him, but because I was afraid of *myself*. Of what that moment revealed about me.

It was almost as if I could sense *his* every emotion. His anger, his grief, his deep aching loneliness. And somehow, I responded to it. Connected with it. Matched it. *But that doesn't make any sense.* Then there's the moment I almost gave myself to him. I don't know if I can even blame the alcohol. Could this soul tie thing be real...? No. This has to be some kind of trauma bonding.

Damn it. This can't go on. Without thinking I offered my life to him again. I've lost count at the number of times I've nearly thrown myself at death because of him. I've got family. Friends. A life that existed long before I ended up in this mess. I don't even *know* these people from kingdom come. *I'm sorry*, but... this can't go on. I have to escape from him as soon as possible.

CHAPTER 16
HOUND DOG

KALIYAH

It seems Dahlia's taken an interest in me, but I can't figure out why. It's not like she doesn't have a whole sister right there, so that can't be it. I used to wonder what it would be like to have a sibling. But then again, having siblings wouldn't have been possible for me, not with my mother gone and no father claiming me as his kid.

Well, if he's alive out there somewhere... who knows. It's possible I've got a half-brother or sister or two floating around. When I finally get back home, I think I'll do one of those ancestry DNA kits. I remember I actually tried once, back in freshman year of high school, for a family history project. Grampa shut that down *real fast*. He was being a complete A-hole about it, too. What did he say again? *"I'm Domino of the Black Vein. Ask the streets they know me. I make all them mothafuckin' ninjas drop. Your roots come straight outta H-Town. For life, baby girl. And if that dumb-ass teacher needs more than that, tell him he can hit me up directly."*

Mind you, my Grampa's government name is Charles. So yeah. I failed that assignment. I still never understood why he reacted that way. He told me he's all the family I need to know. He himself doesn't have any siblings, and he lost his father to the system and his mother to a car accident when he was fourteen. He's all the family I know of, too.

If God forbid anything were to happen to him, I'd be left with no one. It would bring me a small amount of comfort knowing that I have some kin somewhere out there. I think he was afraid that if I found out who my dad really was, I'd start loving him less. Or worse, I'd want to go live with my biological dad. Or maybe my dad would come out of the woodwork and fight for custody. I didn't know for sure. But either way, that would never happen. Because even though he's my grampa, I love that old man like he's my father.

By now, my friends should've realized I haven't made it back. I *should* be able to count on them to explain the situation or at the very least, tell Grampa something to keep him from completely wrecking his brain with worry.

But who am I kidding? He once threatened to make my neighbor's twelve-year-old son's dog disappear if it so much as looked like it wanted to nip at me again. At the time, I thought grampa was kidding. But one week and one nip later, that dog went missing. He never admitted to doing anything. But I knew, my gramps did not play about me.

Ugh... Which means if any of them were to tell him the truth of what happened to us, he'll be knee deep in the woods with his AR-15 looking for the Elder Stones.

Come on Darrius, if anyone can keep that from happening it's you. But then again, grampa would just as likely put a hole in Darrius before he let him stop him. *Damn.* Either way this is a terrible situation.

Chill, Kaliyah. I can't let my mind spiral into the deep end. Not now. Not when I've got a whole other set of problems staring me in the face. I sit at the bar, finishing off the last bite of my sweet roll. I sneak a glance over at Mitus. He's still deep in conversation with the three from our room earlier. Makes sense. He's got a lot of catching up to do. I'm not sure how long he was locked away for, but it had to be a hell of a lot longer than me. Especially with the way he's always doin' the most.

I notice the way his gaze flicks in my direction. Not often. Just enough to let me know he's keeping an eye on me. And after that impromptu sniff session, I know his nose is like a damn bloodhound's. So how the hell do I get away from a creature who's stronger, faster, got eyes like a hawk, and a sense of smell that could probably find me through a locked vault door? I rack my brain. Come on, think. *Ah... shit.* This is starting to feel impossible.

"I've never seen boots like yours before," Dahlia says suddenly.

"Uh? Oh my sneakers?"

"Is that what they're called. There really pretty and colorful."

"Thanks."

"They must be really expensive."

"They're J's, so... kind of."

"J's? I see. Here in town, all we have are boots or slippers. Nothing fancy. My sister once took me to the Kingdom of Palloria, and there were so many lovely styles there. So expensive, though. Still, I don't remember seeing anything like your sneakers."

I glance down at her boots. They were worn, skin-leather, the caps a faded, lighter brown than the rest. They look like they've walked a hundred lives already.

"Would you like to try them on?"

"What? Really?"

I'm already rising from my seat, kicking them off. "We look about the same size. I'll let you try mine if I can try yours."

Her face lit up. "Okay, yeah if it's okay with you."

Seeing the level of excitement on Dahlia's face caught me off guard. I mean, they're just shoes. But I guess, in a world like this, it really is the little things. Dahlia sits at the bar, lifts her dress slightly, and starts pulling off her worn boots. That's when I finally have a clear unobstructed view of it. The eerie thing wrapped around her leg.

"Dahlia... what's that?"

When Dahlia realizes what I'm looking at she goes to quickly shuffle her dress back down over it.

"Um... it's my... curse. But I swear it's not a contagious one."

My eyes are locked. The longer my gaze stays fixated on it, the louder the ringing in my ears... no, head gets. A silence falls between us.

"I understand if you don't want me to wear your shoes."

"Hey, Dahlia. Would it be okay if I get a better look at it?"

"Uh? Why? Most people find the mark of a curse scary or repulsive."

"It's just... I see something... something I don't think belongs."

"What do you mean? Like a bug."

"Honestly... I really don't know."

She hesitates. "Are you sure?"

I nod and lean in slowly. She lifts her dress again, this time more carefully. *There it is*. Twisting around her calf like it grew from her. The vines-like branches, pulsing faintly under, through and over her skin. It's wrapped in a dark haze that seems to breathe. And the sound. No longer just ringing. It's screeching now, like metal grinding against bone, and it's coming straight from whatever that thing is.

My gaze narrows as the room around me begins to blur. The voices and the clinking of glasses all around me muffle. The screeching from the vines warp and twist into something more intelligible. Words.

"Feed... Grow... Decay... Death..."

Over and over again, the chant echoes. The words don't come from Dahlia. Not really. They come from the mouthless branches curling around her leg, as if the curse itself is *speaking* through them.

"Feed... Grow... Death... Decay... Death... Feed..."

My breathing slows. My mind clear, thoughts sharp.

Everything else fades. Mitus's oppressive gaze, the bar, even Dahlia herself. All I see is *it*. This egregious, unnatural thing. Offending something deep in me. Like it was never meant to be seen and yet here it is, crawling in plain sight.

"You don't belong," I whisper, almost speaking to it. "Don't belong."

Get... rid of it. Get rid of it. Get rid of it. My own mantra slowly starts looping in my mind.

My hands begin to move on their own, steadily reaching.

"Get rid of it."

SAPHIRE

I don't know what the hell this orc is playing at, but I'll be damned if I fall for his trickery. Honestly, I half expected us all to be dead by now. If it weren't for that woman, Kaliyah, we probably would be. Still, I'm not buying this crap about an orc... *A blue orc*, no less, being soul-bound to a human. Everyone knows soul ties between mythical beasts and humans are impossible. It's not just taboo. It's lethal. Best case? Nothing happens. Worst case? The human's soul is consumed, devoured by the beast's own and the creature walks away stronger, more complete... one step closer to becoming a demon.

That's why soul ties, by their very nature, require utter free will, openness to vulnerability and complete surrender. No spell. No trickery. No coercion. I have heard that a soul tie attempted to be forced, faked, or tampered with can result in a violent recoil, refusing to latch onto anything, and can fracture in the return. Or worse, festering. Turning them into something we do not speak of. I just don't understand why a human would willingly agree to be eternally linked to something born if darkness. Or how its even possible for that matter.

Just look at him. Practically holding us hostage in my own damn home. He's been drilling my party members, at least the two brave enough to stay, a thousand and one questions like, "Who's the current ruler of Palloria?" *King Korrak La'Claw, of course. How does he not know that? Then again, orcs probably don't keep up with the world outside of the dark region.*

"What are the last known whereabouts of the knight elf or the great mage?' *Legends before my time. I barely passed the history portion of my guild's adventurer license exam. But it's telling. After hearing what Randall said about the last blue orc, he must be afraid they'll learn of him and come ready to slay.*

'What are the current alliances amongst the lands?' *I'm a low-ranking adventurer from the south. I'm not into politics like that.*

'What clans presently hold the most power in Bloodthorn?' *How the shit would we even know that? He's the orc. That's his homeland. Why doesn't he just go ask his own kind?*

Fortunately, Noiz and Dash have been able to give him the answers he seem somewhat satisfied with. I glance across the room. My mom pouring drinks to the few customers brave enough to stay, while my precious baby sister chats it up with Kaliyah like we aren't smack in the middle of a mythical-level crisis.

They're so damn *relaxed* about all this, it makes my teeth grind. Like, how are they not panicking right now? Why am I the only one still acting like there's a walking natural disaster taking up space in our inn? But then again... when I think about it, maybe *I'm* the one putting everyone in danger.

I just couldn't help myself. Dahlia told me what was going on the moment we first arrived, and I acted without a second thought. Storming into the monster's den, with my party at my side. I was the first to pull a threat from my mouth. That was so damn reckless of me.

The moment he lunged at Noiz, I realized then just how big of a mistake I made. *So damn fast.* I was just barely able to read his movements, but my body was not in any way equipped to keep up with him. He is in a whole other fucking league. One second, his glowing blue eyes and sharped claws gunning for my vision, the next complete stillness. So much power crackling off him like heated lightning. No doubt if it wasn't for her I would've been blinded. I would've *died*. Just a few words from her and my party... No, the whole damn town was spared.

So why the hell do I keep pushing this? Why do I keep acting like she's some damsel in distress when she clearly isn't asking for help? She seems to have the beast under her control. And the way he response to her, it doesn't give prisoner, per say. Um... actually I'm not sure what it's giving. I glance over to Kaliyah and Dahlia. Just a casual look, but what I see launches me out of my seat.

Dahlia is clinging to her leg, her face twisted in pain. Kaliyah's hand is extended, fingers grasping at... nothing? It looks like she's pulling at air, but whatever she's doing, it's *hurting* my little sister. I'm up before I even know what I'm doing, reaching for the blade at my hip. And then it hits me. A pressure like a crashing wave, thick and suffocating, drenched in pure, violent intent.

Bloodlust. My eyes snap to the orc. His gaze is locked on me. Ice-cold. Unblinking. Daring me to go through with it. A challenge in silence, *Touch that blade and die.* Dahlia lets out a muted whimper, and something in me snaps. I don't care if I have to face a goddamn demon orc. I'm not letting my little sister suffer. But my hand won't move. It just *won't*. My fingers twitch above the hilt, but I can't force them lower. My body stiffens, jaw clenched tight. A bead of sweat trickles down my temple. I grit my teeth, ready to push through it.

"*Sapphire,* wait," Dash's voice cuts in, steady but urgent. He grabs my arm. "It's okay."

My daze lifts from Dash, eyes trailing to the sweat rolling down his forehead and the way his hand hovers inches above his own sheathed weapon. Just like mine. He felt it too. That *pressure*. That raw, unfiltered *warning*.

I turn my gaze back to Dahlia. Her body is no longer tense. The pain etched into her face has faded, replaced with something softer. Her breaths come easier now. Whatever was hurting her, it's stopped.

Kaliyah stands before her, arm still outstretched. Her fingers are curled around something. *Something real now.* Something *visible*. Thin dark green branches... No. Vines between her fingertips. They twist and pulse with a strange eerie way, almost alive. Kaliyah's eyes flick to us. They're glowing faintly now, a soft, eerie hue. Pale irises sphered with light, as if a sun had bloomed behind her pupils.

"What is this?" she asks, her voice quiet.

The orc steps forward, his massive form somehow silent as a shadow. He stops just in front of her and lifts a hand to his chin. Thing in her grasp.

"So you *can* see them," he murmurs, intrigued. "You continue to surprise me, beautiful. Even I don't possess the ability to break curses. And yet, you just did."

The vine-like object crumbled in Kaliyah's hand, unraveling into fine dust that sifted through her fingers.

"Hey, Mitus, You think you can bring Dr. Libyans back here? I'm... not feeling too well."

Her knees buckled before she could finish, but Mitus moved faster than thought, catching her just in time. His eyes flickering with concern. "It would be faster if I took you to him," he said, his hands around her arms.

She extended a hand, palm out to stop him. "I already told you. I can't travel like that when I'm not feeling well. I'll be fine until you get back. Saphire and her people will look after me, right?"

Both of them turned to face me. My throat tightened. I opened my mouth, but no words came. I didn't know what to say. Before the silence could stretch further, my ma stepped forward with soft authority. She gently placed a hand on Kaliyah's shoulder, guiding her toward a nearby chair.

"She'll be safe with us," she said, glancing at Mitus with a calm certainty that didn't quite mask the tension in her shoulders. "Go. Bring the doctor."

He gives her a devilish look then turns and heads for the front door. Just as he is passing me he murmurs, "Try that again, and I will slaughter your kin. That is my promise."

The door closes behind him, and finally, I can breathe again. My shoulders drop with the weight of relief, but it's short-lived. I immediately race over to Dahlia to check if she's okay. Her eyes are wide with shock, her mouth frozen in silence.

"Dahlia, are you okay? Say something. Dahlia!" My voice cracks as I kneel down in front of her, searching her face for any sign of pain.

"Saphire... look," she whispers.

"Look at what? Did she hurt you?" I ask, panicked.

"No... look at my leg," she smiles.

I look down, and my eyes can hardly believe what I'm seeing. Dahlia's thick, purplish veins that usually mar her skin are slowly fading away. "What? What's happening? Does it hurt?"

"Uh-uh. No," Standing up from her seat.

"Be careful, Da—" I start to warn her, but I watch in disbelief as my little sister takes a step, then another, without a single limp or hobble. "But how?"

My sister was plagued with a curse when she was only three years old. Our father had a gambling problem and got himself into some real trouble. He tried to steal from a witch to pay off some of his debts. Thinking the witch would take it easy on him if he mentioned he was a father. She didn't and Dahlia wound up reaping some of his consequences.

"The throbbing pain… It's gone." At first, Dahlia smiles, joy flooding her expression, but then she begins to tear up.

My mother is quick to her side, enveloping her in a warm embrace. I glance over at Kaliyah. Her body is hunched over, her fist pressed to her forehead. I move towards her, concerned, guilty even.

"Um… Kaliyah. Are you—"

She raises a finger to her lips, signaling me to stop talking. She sits there for a moment longer, then whispers, "Is he gone?"

"What?" I ask, confused.

"Is the orc gone?"

"Oh, yes. He already left to get the doctor."

"Good." Kaliyah lifts her head and bounces out of her seat, taking my hand and pulling me up the stairs to her room.

"I'm not sure how much time we have, so I have to make this quick. You were spot on. Way too direct about it, but instincts on one hundred. He's a fucking brutal monster who's been tormenting me for weeks on end. At one point, he even tried to eat me." She said shoving her palm towards me. "I'm his freakin' hostage. A toy he's going to grow tired of playing with, and I totally need rescuing. But since you and your friends made it clear that no one in this town can do anything to stop him, I have to figure out how to get as far from him as possible. I need to know if you can help me with that."

I'm in total shock right now. My mouth goes dry, and I try to process what she's saying.

She continues, "I heard you mention something earlier about your town evacuating to something you called the Namma stones. Tell me. Are they anything like the Elder Stones?"

Who is this woman? The way she acted before, downstairs, I truly believed her words about her relationship with the orc. She gave no indication she was in distress at that moment. Even now, her words are heavy, but her voice is so calm and steady.

"Hello?" She snaps her fingers in front of my face.

"Um... What did you say?" I ask her to repeat the question.

"Can the Namma stones teleport people like the Elder Stones?"

I take a moment to gather my thoughts. "Yes. I mean, no. The Namma stones can only be used to travel between other Namma stones. While the Elder Stones of Cosmara work in a similar way, their primary use is for the traditional ceremony of summoning Champions. But you should already know that. It's common knowledge."

"Okay. So, is there more of these Elder Stones and if so, do you know where I can find them?"

I blink, startled by her next question. "Um... how did you remove the curse from my sister's leg?"

"Curse? I— I don't know. I have no idea how I did it. Now, can you please just tell me where I can find another set of Elder Stones?"

"What do you mean you don't know? You show up here with a blue-skinned orc, who, by the way, threatened to kill my family. I have spent many years traveling the land seeking out every mage and witch that could possibly heal my sister's affliction. But out of nowhere, you waltz up in here and break the witch's curse like it's brushing lint off a coat, and now then say you don't know how you did it. I don't buy it."

"Look, Saphire. I already told you. We don't have time. I'm not lying when I say I don't know how I did that. I just did it. That's all. I'm not a mage or witch. I didn't do some magic spell. I saw the thing clinging to Dahlia's leg and I just pulled it off. That's all. I've been dragged through every layer of hell for weeks on end... *weeks* and I am barely holding it together. I don't need an interrogation. I need help."

I hesitate. I've always had a pretty good instinct for reading people. It comes with the territory of being a seasoned adventurer. I've spotted liars across campfires, cheats in gambling dens, and cowards hiding behind brave faces. In this world, trusting the wrong person is the quickest way to end up robbed, gutted, or worse.

But this woman? When I look at her, I get the sense she is true to herself and her words. And it's not just a feeling. She saved my sister. The curse would have claimed her life before she reached the age of twenty. Not to mention she stopped that creature from impaling me and my party. Something tells me more than once.

My family could never repay that debt. Not fully. But I want to. No. I *need* to. I need to return that blessing in kind. I square my shoulders and meet her eyes. "Okay. I'll help you. What do you need?"

KALIYAH

Finally, someone who gets it. Someone who not only experienced this madness firsthand and understands what I'm up against, but is willing to help me despite the possible dangers that it may bring her. For the first time in... I don't even know how long, I don't feel like I'm drowning alone in this nightmare. I'd almost say I feel hopeful, but I'm not about to jinx myself. Fate plays dirty after all, so I know better.

Mitus introduced someone called a *Mending Mistress*. Something akin to a nurse, I'm guessing. Dr. Libyans, on the other hand, clearly had the good sense not to be found a second time. *Lucky bastard*. Thankfully, before the orc stalked back in, I managed to get a treasure trove of information out of Saphire. That girl talks fast and I was hanging on every word like my life depended on it. Because, if you forgot, it does.

According to her, Therion has *three* recognized nations, and each one hoards a set of Elder Stones. The bad news is they are guarded treasures, locked down tighter than a vault. Not anyone can just stroll up and use them. Then there's the other hurdle. Getting permission from the ruling monarch will prove to be a challenge.

Sebbarus? Absolutely off the table. I'd be lucky to make it five feet into that place without someone trying to chop off my head or zap me to God knows where.

Yurakora? Land of actual elves. Like *real* elves. All I could imagine when she told me about them was white snow everywhere and Santa's little helpers happily skipping about. That would be wild to see in person.

But I guess in this world, they're not too jolly. Saphire told me they don't let outsiders pass their borders. And by 'don't let,' she meant if caught, that's *lifelong imprisonment or death*. They skipped right past deportation and straight into 'you're never leaving.'

So that narrows my options to one place, Palloria. Home of, well... everything. It's a melting pot of humans, demi-humans, whatever that means... mystical beasts, and something ominously called "other." When I asked what "other" meant, Saphire gave me a look like I should already know and changed the subject. *That's not terrifying at all.* Anyway, I shoved the weird species questions to the side, because the real issue was transportation.

It's a *two-month* journey to Palloria by carriage. Two damn months. But there's hope. A smaller settlement with a Namma Stone just a two days trip outside Palloria's gate. Fast travel magic, I'm absolutely here for it.

Naturally, though, it can't be that simple. There's a catch. The first being, you need magic to activate the stone. Which I do *not* have. Humans apparently can't naturally possess magic in this world. Because why make things easy when you can make them *inconvenient*?

Mages use something called *mana crystals*. Little gems that store magic like batteries. Witches, on the other hand, use something called *conduits* to access... well, I don't even know. At some point during Saphire's info-dump, I started nodding like I understood. But honestly, she lost me halfway through "arcane stabilization." All I managed to catch was that mana crystals can be found in labyrinth dungeons. To which I said, *"Hell nah. Absolute the fuck not."*

The only other option is to buy one from a merchant. Assuming you've got the coin. And I'm shit out of luck on that one too. And then *even if* I manage to get my hands on a charged crystal, I'd still have to pay a stone entry toll. The amount, set by whatever town or city that controls it. In this case, *Emissary Cove*. It's the closest one to the Kingdom of Palloria and they charge more than Saphire makes in four months.

So somehow, I have to acquire a mana crystal and money, then sneak to the Namma Stone, dodging Mitus and his '*I'm watching you*' energy, and avoid getting caught before I can vanish into thin air. *Yup, easy.*

There's *only* one upside to this whole ordeal. The Namma Stones were apparently a divine gift from the deities to humans, meaning beasts and monsters that includes orcs can't use them regardless of whatever magic they possess. Honestly, the logic makes no sense.

Like, "Hey humans, here are magical travel stones, but you don't have the natural magical ability to use them on your own. LOL, good luck!" If I wasn't scared those deities would smite me as soon as the words left my mouth, I'd cuss them all the way the fuck out for creating any of those stupid rocks in the first place.

Who are these damn deities anyway, and what's their damage? I've been assuming it's this world's version of god or gods. But the way people talk about them here? It's... different somehow.

Magic teleportation stones. It's got me thinking. So I asked Saphire, "If you need to use the stone to travel really far away, but they didn't have enough magic for the distance, what would happen to a person attempting the travel?"

She blinked. "Nothing."

"Nothing? Like, it wouldn't spit you out somewhere halfway along the way?"

"No. You either go all the way or you don't go at all."

"Right."

The way she keeps looking at me like all of my questions are grade school knowledge. But her answer confirmed something I'd been dreading. It was not a mistake. Galldric, the Empress's shady court mage *deliberately* sent me to the Bloodthorn Region. The place nightmares go to level up. Full of monsters made of teeth, shadows, and trauma. The only reason I'm not dead yet is pure freakin' luck and sheer will power.

Ohhhh. That fucking Princess Millie. You better pray to your damn deities that I don't catch you outside.

Honestly, I was *this* close to throwing my hands up and saying, "fuck it." If this is some kind of cosmic test, then dear Universe, I respectfully decline and you can kindly shove it up your never-ending, all-powerful ass. The *only* thing that stopped me from doing just that is the fact that the day after my little breakdown, Saphire's mom who radiates 'sweet Southern grandma vibes' bless her, offered to cover my toll fee. Just like that. Said it was a thank-you for helping her daughter, Dahlia.

Still haven't figured out how I managed that. But there's too much on my mind to untangle that mystery right now. And then, because the universe clearly enjoys keeping me on my toes, Noiz, Saphire's mage friend, just *left* me a mana crystal. Like it was no big deal. In the *bathing room,* the only place he could leave it without Mitus seeing.

It's way smaller than the one that hovers all floaty and ominous in the top ring of his staff. The one he gave me is about the size of a large pebble. Looks kinda like those angel aura crystals I used to see back home, but these naturally were warm to the touch.

He even left a note. Said there's just enough magic stored for one trip. That once I get to the Namma Stone, all I have to do is grip the crystal, focus, and call out the location I want to go.

That's it? No goat sacrifice? This may actually be possible. It's been two more days, and Mitus's paranoia finally started to cool off. If it weren't for the fact that he's gone back to using that little pet name like he's tasting the word every time, I might've believed he was actually *worried* about what happens to me.

Although I can't fully explain the inexplicable sexual pull I felt toward him and I've tried. But I just don't have the mental capacity to make sense of it. I'm relieved I've managed to keep my mind clear of it. *Mostly.* My body, on the other hand... still feels the residual effects of being rushed headfirst into hot-and-bothered territory.

I *thought* about taking care of myself in the bath earlier. Just a little solo stress relief to take the edge off, but I couldn't get comfortable. Not with *him* prowling around like some overgrown hound dog. The entire time, I was convinced he'd bust the door down right in the middle of me pleasuring myself, pin me down, press his big thick monster against me and *in me*, then—

Crap. Nope nope nope. Shut that shit down now, Kaliyah. Do *not* let your brain spiral into fantasy mode. Not after last time.

Think sunshine and apple pie. Or better yet... rivers of blood and freshly picked entrails. That's right. Good, gruesome, grounding thoughts.

Because if I let myself get too worked up again, I'm going to start thinking about things I definitely shouldn't be thinking about. Like how his eyes go all dark and blue when he's in predator mode. Or how he smells after a bath. Like pine and smoked lustful heat.

Nope. *Murder. Think murder.* I peek over at him. *Good.* Doesn't look like he's noticed. He's still sitting across the room with his back against the wall, arms folded, silent as death. Just *watching* me. Like he's waiting for something. Or maybe watching to make sure *I* don't try anything. Either way, it's maddening. I can barely sleep like this. It's giving major *mountain cave déjà vu.* I have zero privacy, no peace, all this sexual pent-up energy and him looming like some kind of hellhound on constant patrol.

And it's pissing me the hell off and I want to scream at him to get the fuck out. To stop hovering like a wicked gargoyle. But with what I'm planning... it's probably not the best time to poke the bear. Or the orc. Whatever.

Come to think of it, we haven't *really* spoken in days. Not since the Mending Mistress gave me a once over. Although I did feel a little off after the incident with Dahlia, most of the me being all damsel-in-distressy was just an act, one I think I played a little too well. Its been so awkward since then, tension-fills moments in between.

I've noticed he gets into these weird states. One moment he's all smirking, mischiefs and all chattiness and then there's times like this. When he goes quiet, like *really* quiet.

Like he's *gone.* Not physically. He's always still there, but it's like some other version of him takes over. Like the silence sharpens, coils around him, and waits to snap. A hair trigger of a man. Like all it would take is one wrong word, one touch, and BOOM. But even when he's in those silent manic states it never seems to be directed at me per say. At least I don't get that feeling when our eyes occasionally cross paths. When he looks at me it's like he's looking through me not in a lost in deep thought way, but like he's actually looking into me. It makes me feel seen in a way that's *almost* comforting.

Ugh. God, it so confusing. Thankfully, the man can't read my mind. At least I hope not. There has been a few times that make me question... I did watch the man spit fire and leap from a mountain like it was no big deal. I really don't know much about him or the extent of his abilities.

Shit... Now I'm worried. He doesn't already know what I'm planning, does he? It would explain his mood. I glance at him again. Still silent. Still watching. Okay. Let's test this.

Hey, blue demon. Come over here and lay it on me.

His brow twitches. My heart stutters. Coincidence, maybe? Again. Just to be certain.

Mitus, I want you to get over here and have sex with me, do absolutely sinful things to my body.

Nothing. Not even a blink this time. Telepathy is off the table. That's good. Yes. Totally great. So why do I feel kind of disappointed? Damn it to hell. This Stockholm syndrome crap is freakin' dangerous. But the way he's looking at me now, something's shifted. Again. There's a storm brewing behind his eyes. The kind of look that says his mind is somewhere far, far away, and whatever's there... it's not pretty. Maybe it's time I stop pretending I've got this all figured out and ask him what's up. Gauge his current headspace.

CHAPTER 17
QUEEN OF BLOODTHORN

MITUS

Useless. So fucking useless. I was the damn overlord of Bloodthorn. Ruler of beasts. Taker of lives. Stealer of legacies. And yet, when she needed me most, I could barely do *anything*. I couldn't even track down that pathetic excuse of a doctor. He better hope the stars never align in his disfavor, because if our paths cross again, I *will* collect my due. My grudges are lifelong. I'm supposed to protect her. Be her shield. Her fucking *guardian*. But my woman... she's human. Or at least her body appears as one.

Fragile. Breakable. Mortal. And the fact that these are threats I can't stop or change. It fills me with a rage so deep it threatens to crack me wide open. Holding the darkness back, the one that's clawing just beneath my skin, begging to be unleashed... it's getting harder, every damn day to keep it at bay. If I were still in the mountain, I'd sink into another hibernation without a second thought. Sleep it all away, let another half decade pass in silence. But no. I can't leave my mated soul so vulnerable to the dangers that lie in wait. It's clear my woman is a breed all on her own and this world wouldn't know what to do with her. Worship her, use her, fear her or maybe even try to kill her.

Grrrr. The thought alone sends a vortex of madness through my mind. But she will never have to worry about that, now that I'm *free.* Free to reclaim my throne and sit her upon it as my queen. *Kaliyah, Queen of Bloodthorn.*

Yes~ I love the sound of that. I know many will reject her, but those that oppose will just die as they form a lake of blood beneath her feet. Now, that's an idea. Bathing in their blood as I dance to the sounds of their screams. *I can't wait.* Then again, why wait. I've been unleashed. And a little blood and guts might make the voice finally shut the hell up, for a time at least.

Yes. I need a good fight. I need to conquer. To fucking *kill* something. Like that little wench. Or better yet, that *mage* of hers.

Oh yes. Him. I know he's the one that gave my girl that fucking crystal that she clutches to in her pocket. Did he think I wouldn't notice? Did he give it to her for protection…*from me*?

For him to think I would ever harm her, *her*, my *light*, my sole beacon in this insignificant world, offends me to my very being. You, magic-bleeder, dared to sow seeds of my past in her, furthering the distance between us. That alone awards you malicious punishment.

That's right. The hellfire I'm going to rain down on you, mage, will make your ancestors rise from their graves just to beg for mercy on your behalf. It won't help though. I won't be able to hear them over the sounds of your *agonizing* screams. The moment she drifts off tonight, I'm coming for you, mage. You could be armed with a thousand of those cursed gems, and it still wouldn't stop me. I won't let any of you come between us, to pull her away from me. I *cannot* and *will not* lose her. Because if that were to ever happen, I vow to the deities themselves that I would destroy this world, everyone of Therion will b—

"Mitus." My name, her voice, the fog engulfing my mind clears. My last thought abruptly shatters. My focus narrows. All I see is *her.*

She's watching me, brows slightly furrowed. "You look deep in thought again. You do that a lot. Mind sharing what's going on up there?"

A grin curls at my lips as I tilt my head. "Why? Worried about what I'm having for dinner tonight?"

She immediately frowns. "Actually, yeah. Kinda."

"No need to worry. No humans on the menu. The old bag downstairs fed me stew. Human cuisine is surprisingly tasty. Never really had it before now. But even with it being leagues better than the filth I've choked down these past centuries, it's still not what I'd *prefer* to be eating on."

She sits up straighter on the bed, all that sleepy calm gone. Her full attention is on me now, those coco pearl eyes of hers catching the twin moonlight.

"Oh yeah? So, if you could eat *anything* in the world right now, what would it be?"

Oh, she's making this *too* fun. "That's easy." My gaze trails slowly down the length of her body. "The space between your legs." She's done a damn good job this past week keeping her expressions in check. Never giving me more than a raised brow or a scoff. But just now she slipped and I caught her. Still, I want to make my intentions clear. I don't want my love seriously believing I might actually be planning on consuming her. The trust between us is hollow. I know I am to blame for that. I want to see her quivering in pleasure not trembling in terror after all.

So I lean in slightly. "I promise I wouldn't use teeth. Lips and tongue only, unless you ask otherwise."

Her reaction is everything. A delicious mix of flustered and trying-not-to-be. The flutter in her face tries to fade, but not fast enough. I caught it. I always do. Her expression is already sweet enough to savor. But I bet her *taste* is even better.

"Will I ever get an honest answer from you or do you plan on driving me insane with your antics forever?"

"I don't believe I've ever lied to you since the day we met, little breakfast." *Shit. That slipped.* I *need* to stop calling her that. But how can I, when everything about her is so damn *delicious*?

She scoffs. "First, you want to devour me. Then, you say I'm the love of your life. And now, you want me sexually..."

My ears perk. She *noticed.*

But before I can respond, she continues, "Couldn't it be that you're just obsessing over me because of what you've been through? Being locked away for so long, without companionship. Couldn't it be that I'm just the first woman you've seen in forever... and so, naturally, you'd cling to me? And if that's the case... eventually, you'll get bored of me and realize you don't need or even want me. And I'm afraid of what that means for me when that finally does happen."

I furrow my brows absent mindedly. *I get it now.* This is what she's been thinking all along. All this time, I thought I'd explained it well enough for her to understand. But I see now, she didn't grasp the depth of it. I rise from the wall, grab a chair from the table, and sit down directly in front of her next to the bed. She stiffens, clearly on guard. Can't blame her. Not after what I did to her.

"I don't have much experience having casual conversations with humans, let alone *human women.* So, conveying my thoughts in a way that doesn't sound threatening is... *difficult.* To say the least. But to answer your question, honestly, and with all the seriousness I can muster... no, Kaliyah. I'm *not* just obsessing over you. Before I met you, I'd never found a human attractive in the slightest. Not one. But the moment I saw you in that cave, I can admit I felt something. *A pull.* But the insatiable hunger that plagued me, clouded my mind. It prevented me from realizing who you were or what you'd become to me." My chest tightens. "And because of that, I hurt you. For that alone, I owe you a hundred... No, a *thousand* more apologies."

I reach for her hand. And to my surprise, she lets me. She doesn't pull away. I turn her palm over gently and trace the faded scar there, then lift it. Pressing it softly to my neck where she marked me.

"Kaliyah," I say, eyes locked with hers, "you are my *mated soul.* That's not a metaphor. It's not a figure of speech. It's a bond that *cannot* be broken. Not by time, not by distance, not by death. I am *forever* tied to you. I could never, *will* never hurt you." I close my eyes, tuning in to the steady rhythm of her pulse, letting it calm the fire in me. When I speak again, my voice is just above a whisper. "And if anything were to ever happen to you, a piece of me would quite literally die."

Her lips part, then press shut again. Pulling her hand away. I don't rush her. I wait. She needs time to process what I've said. And I owe her that. I will not smile. I will not soften this truth with humor or charm. But present this fact to her like hard siberian gold, solid and nearly unmeltable. I give it all to her and only her.

Will she reject me? What would I do if she does? This sensation crawling under my skin. What is it? Not anger. Not frustration. No, this... this is something else. *Insecurity.* This is new to me. Uncomfortable. I hate it.

Finally, her voice comes. "If this is your truth... I guess I have no choice but to accept it."

My beastly heart sings. Words so sweet, for a split second, I wonder if I've slipped into another one of my dreams. One of the many that leave me breathless and aching with the scent of her still in my lungs. They've been getting worse lately. Or better, depending on the hour. Maybe this is just what I needed to steady myself. Confirmation that she acknowledges me.

"But..." she pauses, coco fucking pearls narrowing like they could slice straight through my chest. *Yes please. Cut me to bits, beautiful.* "Don't expect me to return any of it." She finishes.

The smile that's been itching beneath my skin finally stretches across my face. "That's just fine, for now, gorgeous."

I'm sure with time, her feelings will change. And when they do, when the fire she doesn't know she has finally catches flame, I'll be right here to burn with her. Ready to make her... *all mine.*

KALIYAH

I am afraid. I'm afraid that he is actually telling me the truth. Soul ties. His mated soul? Like, my actual soul and his connected for freakin' forever. What the hell do I even say to that? Do I even have a choice? I know now that this man... No, this *creature* has no intentions of ever letting me go. This is so much worse than I ever imagined. But even if its true—

No, not if, Kaliyah. I have been sensing this for a while now. Sensing him. In the quiet. In the way my body responds before my mind can catch up. In my dreams. It wasn't just some sleeping fantasy, was it? Maybe they were truths my subconscious was screaming at me to hear.

We're connected. And now that I've felt that… I don't know if I can ever un-feel it. I don't have many more reasons left to doubt his truth.

Constantly showing concern for my wellbeing. Unless he's playing some long, cruel, twisted mind game. It doesn't make sense for him to continue this farce. If he wanted to truly eat me, hurt me or ravish my body, he could've done it a hundred times by now. He's fast enough. Damn sure strong enough. I wouldn't be able to do a damn thing about it. But he hasn't even tried. Yeah, he's made playful advances, ones that nearly drove me half-insane, but he never took it further than I could handle.

Still, it doesn't change the fact that he has the power to bend and literally break me to his will at any given moment he chooses. But is that any different from any other man? The mere thought of a man just taking what they want from my body or any other woman for that matter, fills me with visceral disgust. Especially after my experience with those vile goblins.

That's the freakin' problem right there. He is not the only danger in this world I should be afraid of. I cannot continue to live in this constant fear for my life. But do I… do I still fear for my life? I look at him, trying to figure out when I stopped being terrified in his presence. I watch as he patiently waits. Waits for me to open up to him. To let him in. *I see now*. He's been doing that the whole time we've been here. Waiting for me to come around. Waiting for me to see him, like really see him.

Fuck. Why me? Why did any of this have to happen to me? And all because of some weak ass bite mark? After my last experience with real love, I swore it off. I threw nearly everything tied to it in the trash. Burned the letters, buried the softness, sealed it all up tight. Back home, I chose to lock my heart down and hide the key, even from myself. And now here he is… searching for it. Digging around persistently. And the thought of him finding it?

God. That terrifies me more than anything else. Worse than that is the thought of me using it. Opening myself back up to someone, letting in all that passion and tenderness again, just to be met with disappointment, betrayal and more pain than I know how to carry. The thought alone stirs something in me I am not ready for again. Maybe I never will be. So for me, none of this... none of it, changes the fact that I want to be as far away from him as possible.

Fuck the sexual attraction.

Fuck these chest-fluttering tingles.

Fuck his soul tie.

I want out. And there's nothing he can say or do to keep me from trying. Grampa warned me. Over and over again. *"Never let a bitch-ass ninja hold their power over you, baby girl. Cause once they do, you'll never feel safe or feel in control of yourself."*

And right now, I feel neither. Not completely. Not willingly. I've made up my mind. The day after tomorrow, during the annual town festival, I'm getting my ass the hell out of here. I just need an excuse. A reason to head near the center of town without raising suspicion. Something that'll give me the time to scope out the layout and plant my eyes on the Namma Stones for myself. Once there I can figure out the cleanest way to vanish beneath the celebration.

Hopefully, it will be enough to distract Mitus even if it's for just one moment. And if even one of this world's so called deities is on my side, when the time comes, he won't see me until I'm nothing but a shimmer in the wind.

"Hey Mitus. So, being your mated soul, does that mean I'm also bonded to this room, or can I go explore the town a bit tomorrow?"

"You don't have to ask. One day I'll rule these lands, and what's mine will also be yours. If you want to explore, then explore. This world is yours to walk."

"I'm guessing you'll be glued to my side the entire time."

"Why of course. I am yours after all. So, I will be forever by your side, watching your back or..." His grin widens with a playful tone. "underneath you, if the moment calls for it. I have no intentions of you ever being away from me, little breakfast. I *am* yours and one day soon you will be mine."

I bit my cheek at his words. I wish he stop saying stuff like that. I don't want him and I will never belong to him. I am but a prisoner of his so called affections for me. Does he need to be this intense all the time?

At least he's out of that other state. The one he sinks into like a beast prowling in the dark. I don't like it. It does something to me, something wrong. Like I'm being tugged to go to that place with him. And wherever that is... it's dark. Like frightening dark.

"I trust our deal is still good. No killing humans?"

He blinks, then smiles like I've just said something adorable. He pricks the nail of his thumb against his index finger, drawing blood, then raises that finger in the air. A red line hisses and crackles as he draws an X in the space between us. I am shook and at the same time nervously curious.

"I, Mitus make this deal with my mated soul, Kaliyah, that I will not harm or kill any humans unless they are a threat to her person or she otherwise commands me to do so. I also relinquish the authority over this deal to her." The sizzling cross glows for a second more, then dissipates into thin air like smoke. "There. The deal is binding and only you or death can break it."

I blink. "Was that... magic?"

He nods.

My stomach flips. "Wait... that means all the other deals you made with me—"

He wasn't serious about any one of them. My brows furrowed. He throws his hands up, laughing. "You caught me. But don't get too upset with me. Think of it as a learning lesson."

"What kind of lesson?"

He leans in, "I want you to remember to never trust a man's word on it's own. If you make a deal with anyone, always make them in binding. It's the only way to ensure they don't renege. And more importantly, make sure you choose your words carefully. Leave no room for interpretation."

Now he tells me all of this. This guy. Still, real magic? Pretty freakin' cool to see. Not as cool as a glitter breathing dragon, but a close second. I wonder just want else he can do.

"Are all orcs like you? You know... strong, fast, and magical?"

"No." He tilts his head, watching me too closely. "Like you, I'm in a world all on my own."

Like me? What does he mean by that? But before I can ask, he keeps talking.

"I realized a while back, you didn't know what my species was, when you first called me man-beast. I've had plenty of names awarded to me. Dark Overlord. The blue death. Demon orc. But man-beast? That was new." He smirked. "I don't think anyone has ever placed *me* and the word *man* in the same sentence before. Most humans can identify me as an orc immediately from my tusks alone. But seeing that you are a sheltered noble, your exposure to other races has probably been limited. Most orcs reside deep within the—"

"Hold up, come again now?" I cut in, squinting. "Sheltered noble?"

His expression flattens. "Are you not?"

I laugh in his face. I didn't mean to. It just came out. "Not even close."

Where the heck did that idea come from? I mean, I know when I put myself together, I'm that girl. But the state I was in when I first met him? How did he get high class rich girl? He really is out of touch with the current state of his world. It only took me one hour being at that Empress's Palace to understand what true high-class wealth and nobility looks like.

"You really think if I was some duchess or princess or whatever, I'd decide to take a scenic stroll through one of the deadliest forests in this whole damn world? Alone? For what? Shits and goblins?" I burst out laughing again, louder this time. "God, please. I wish I had that kind of money. Then maybe I could pay someone to haul my ass out of this place or better yet, buy me clothes that actually fit my body without threatening to cut off my circulation."

Mitus tilted his head, studying me with that 'I'm cataloging your expression' look. "I've had a few theories about how you ended up in my domain. Each one seems less likely than the last, the longer I'm around you."

Then came the real question. The dangerous one.

"Where are you from?" He asked.

My brain screeched to a halt. Giggles gone. This conversation was officially tiptoeing into absolutely not territory.

I blinked. "Um... me, I'm from somewhere far from here. A city you've probably never heard of before."

Because what am I supposed to say? Actually, orc, I'm from a whole nother world, possible other dimension and working my damndest to get back to it. Oh yeah and no, you can't come. Yeah. That'd go over real well. He'd probably chain me to the bed. Better he knows as little about my circumstances as possible.

"Hmmm... Now that sounds like a plan. We should visit. I would like to see the home of my mated soul. You said city, and your accent is not like those from around here. So... do you hail from Magdara? Or maybe Sebbarus?"

"No! Not Sebbarus!" I blurted way too loud.

Shit... He's prying. Too much. I need to change the subject. I faked a yawn so exaggerated I could've gotten an award for it. "Ugh, wow... I'm tired. I think I'm gonna turn in for the night. You should probably get some sleep too, if we are to be rested for tomorrow."

He watched me for a bit too long. Then smiled. "Okay. Will do, little breakfast. Will do."

I cringed at the name he now seems firmly decided not to give up. I slipped under the covers and turned my back to him, hoping that was the end of it. A moment later, I heard him move the chair, wood creaking softly. Then nothing.

Good. Conversation over. This is good. Everything is on track. I just need to hold it together a little longer. My eyes drifted closed, as I let myself believe...

I might actually pull this off.

CHAPTER 18
MATED SOUL

KALIYAH

Ugh. That damn dream again. I lay there, refusing to open my eyes, not ready for the sunlight to stab at my pupils. The rays roll slow over my skin, like they've got something important to whisper, but I'm not in the mood to listen. I'm tired. Not just sleepy, *tired*. Tired of *him*. That man. That cursed, maddening figment of my subconscious. I swear he's not even a fantasy anymore. He's a straight-up dream stalker, still clinging to me like I'm the last person on earth. I just can't get him to let go. Not that I try that hard. Because part of me recognize it as a dream, I find myself indulging more than I'd like to. But it can't be helped, I guess.

When I finally get back home, maybe I should ask grampa for the number to my old therapist. I'm going to need *therapy for my therapy*. Speaking of which, I wonder how the old man is. I hope he's doing ok. I hope I make it back in time for the wedding. I should still have another 2 months. Hell. But with me MIA, I wonder if the wedding is still on. I'd hate to be the reason he puts his life on pause again.

No. I won't let that happen. Today, I'll scout the town. Then tomorrow night, I'll sneak out to the Namma Stones, hitch a teleport to Emissary Cove, and from there it's a two day journey, if I'm lucky to Palloria. Then I just have to convince King Korrak La'Claw to let me use one of his mages and the Elder Stones to blast myself back into my own damn world.

How the hell am I supposed to pull this off? The whole plan's a mess. So many things can go wrong. I yawn, shifting slightly as I nuzzle into the warmth pressed against me. It feels... nice. I'll deal with it all later. One day at a time. That's all I can do. I've made it this far. I can make it the rest of the way.

That's right, girl. You got this. Still... is it just me, or did this place suddenly install central heating? No complaints though. Whatever it is, it's warm, cozy, and... *Firm?* Much firmer than I remember. I crack one eye open. And instantly freeze. My whole body went still the moment it hit me. I wasn't in bed alone. Snuggled. In *Mitus's* arms. His eyes were closed, face calm, and body completely relaxed against mine. Just like the way he moves in the real world. Silent and unsettlingly smooth, he doesn't make a damn sound when he slumbers.

Honestly, I don't think I've *ever* heard him snore. Or breathe loudly. Or shift. Half the time I'm not even sure he *sleeps.* He could be laying there, completely still, plotting the downfall of kingdoms, and no one would know the difference.

But right now, he seems... asleep. Peaceful, even. I glance down, cautiously. Clothes, still on. Mine and his. Thank God. So, nothing seemed to have happened. *Except...* The thin sheet does nothing to hide the very *obvious* outline pressing against the blanket. And there it is. Morning freakin' wood. Why am I not surprised. So apparently, orcs experience the same common occurrence as human men. *Good to know,* I think sarcastically, my eyes narrowing at the unapologetic salute from his *soldier.*

My thoughts immediately snap back to *that* moment when I told Mitus he should bathe, and he decided that meant *bathing with me.* No shame. Just stepped right in like I'd extended a damn invitation. And last night? I said he should get some sleep. Evidently, he took that as, *climb into my bed and wrap yourself around me like a weighted blanket.*

Maybe this is another one of his lessons, or maybe it's just another way he tries to get under my skin. Either way, the man's becoming a master at it. Expert level. Full certification in *driving me insane*. I definitely do *not* want to wake him. Especially not when the beast between his legs looks ready to tear a hole straight through the mattress. And honestly, he probably *could*. That thing looks... determined. It'd have to be *really* hard to do damage like that. Like... that's gotta hurt. Right?

Unless... it's like his arm. The one draped behind my shoulders. It's firm, sure, but when I lean into it, there's some give. So maybe it's the same for his—

Wait. What am I thinking? Stop that. It twitched.

Shit. I didn't even realize I was still staring at it. My eyes snap up to Mitus's face, panic spiking. His eyes are still closed. *Good.* I started inching my way toward the edge of the bed, slow and quiet like I was trying to sneak past death itself. Just a little further. Almost there. But then he shifted. His arm, once resting harmlessly under my shoulders, slid down, settling low at my waist. I froze. Didn't move. Just lay there like a rabbit caught in a trap, waiting to see if the hunter had noticed. After a few seconds, his grip loosened. I exhaled the softest breath. One I didn't even realize I'd been holding. A few more careful scoots and I was nearly free, almost off his arm and teetering on the edge of the mattress.

Then I made the mistake. My eyes drifted. They slid down the length of him without permission, landing *again*, on the very obvious bulge in his pants. Why? I don't freakin' know. Curiosity? Masochism? Whatever the reason, I instantly regretted it. When I hear him all smug. "You can touch him if you want. Just carefully. Unlike me, he still bites."

I nearly combusted. If my skin wasn't this deep brown, I'd be glowing red from the roots of my hair to my damn toes. Shock and mortification hit me at once, and I launched myself off the bed like it was on fire. Unfortunately, grace was not on my side. I was halfway through crashing face-first onto the floor when he moved, fast as lightning. One hand caught my wrist, the other wrapped tight around the back of my thigh. In one smooth motion, he yanked me back, spun me around, and pulled me right into his lap as he sat at the edge of the bed. Just like that. Trapped against him. Again.

His movements were so fast, so fluid, they knocked the air clean out of my lungs. One second, I was falling, the next I was in his lap, straddling him, breathless and wide-eyed.

"Careful, little breakfast. That could've been bad."

"Um... yeah. Thank you," I managed between shallow breaths, trying to steady myself. Trying to not look like I was completely unraveling.

"Hmmm..." His gaze dragged over me. "If you keep breathing like that, we might not leave this bed today."

"Huh?" My eyes finally pulled away from the safety of his chest, rising to meet his. "What do you—" I stopped mid-sentence. I no longer needed him to explain. His expression answered everything.

It washed over his face in a wave. Heat, hunger, intent. That calm, controlled exterior of his was cracking just enough for me to see what simmered beneath. The most alluring expression of desire washed over his face, and with one look, I knew exactly what he meant. And as if I ask for confirmation his penis slowly rose, trailing along the curve of my thigh, deciding to peck my lower lips. My body shivers and my muscles stiffen. I let out a low squeak that surprised even myself.

"Mmmm." He groans in reaction as the grip on my thigh tightened and the hand on my waist move down to my ass.

Oh no. How does things keep going from bad to worse? The pressure below intensifies. His body presses closer, unmistakably firm. "Mmmm." Another low groan rumbles from his chest.

"How should we start our morning, beautiful?" His voice drops, thick with suggestion. "I have a few ideas, but in the end, I'm leaving the decision to you."

I open my mouth, the words feeling like they're being forced out, all heavy and reluctant. "You can start the morning by letting me down."

His lip curls up. "You sure about that? After all, my body's only reacting to yours."

I bite the inside of my cheek, trying to clear the haze of lustful desire clouding my thoughts, the heat building in my chest... and other places. "I'm sure. Let go of me."

He lifts his hands in the air, as if surrendering.

I can't force myself to look at him when I say the next part. "All of you."

He chuckles, before adjusting himself, pulling his member away from between my legs.

I quickly stand, my heart hammering in my chest. "I'm going to the bathroom. Do not follow me. No, you are *not* welcome to come in with me."

With that, I slam the door, cutting off any response before it could reach me. I fan myself, trying desperately to cool the heat surging through me. My body still shaking, my breath coming too fast. That interaction… it's like my systems have been put into overdrive and I'm about to freakin' crash. Death on impact is definitely a possibility. I can only pray I survive this. I think he thinks he can wait me out. That eventually I'll finally give in to his antics. But what worries me is that at this rate, if he keeps pulling stunts like that, I just might.

My mind cringes at the idea. But my heart and my body quivers at the thought. Wait… my heart? Why would I just think that? No. No no no. This is bullshit. Whatever this hold he has on me. This connection it's getting stronger. I don't think I can wait until tomorrow's festival. Change of plans.

I leave today.

MITUS

I sit and wait for Kaliyah to meet me down in the tavern. She kicked me out of the room so she could get ready for our stroll through this pathetic town. I don't think she realizes how much power she has over me. I hope she never finds out, at least, not for now.

CLASH.

I peek open my eyes to see a glass on a tray that has fallen. Caused by a man already drunk this early in the day, getting loud and rowdy with the wench's younger kin. I ignore him. My willpower has never been tested so intensely before. It took everything within me not to flip her onto her back and give in to every desire I had. My sexual hunger for her is absolutely relentless. It has been centuries since I felt the pleasurable gratification from another. If I don't manage to control my urges, soon she will start to see me as nothing more than an animal looking to fuck something.

It's so much more than that. *She* deserves so much more than that. I want to know her mind, her every thought just as much as her body. I believe I have gotten quite good at reading it. I can tell the way her body yearns to be touched that she hasn't been satisfied in a long time. If only she let me be the one that finally gives her what she needs. What every nerve in her body screams that it craves. I will make her feel waves of pleasure she has never experienced before.

My cock still hasn't calmed down to the scent she emitted this morning. Even in her sleep she has the ability to stir my body into a frenzy. No matter how much I pleasure myself it doesn't stop this longing desire to lay with her. I want so badly to feel another body underneath me. Now there's an idea. Maybe I should retreat for a while and get this out of my system. Although I don't want to leave her side, I'm sure that's not something she would want to tag along for.

"Hmmm..." I pondered. Because of my earlier threats, I'm confident that wench will make sure she's well taken care of until I return. There are only human settlements around these parts, and since all human women, other than my Kaliyah, repulse me sexually, I might end up ripping them in half out of frustration. It wouldn't take much. Who knows how many I'd have to go through to satisfy my needs.

Even more challenging is that I have no desire to lay with a woman who does not desire me as well, so finding five or six human women who want me and is willing to give themselves to me knowing there's a good chance I would probably be there last, would prove to be impossible.

A vampire, perhaps? There's always at least one or two lurking around human settlements. They've always been drawn to my strength and would no doubt indulge my appetite for hours on end. I'm confident I could find one within a day or two. Yes, that could work. My brows began to furrow. It seems like a solid plan. I pinched the bridge of my nose.

So what is the reason... What is the reason that the mere thought of it does nothing for me? The bulge that had just been straining against my pants went limp almost immediately at the idea of putting my lips on one of them.

Have my tastes changed? I've been with plenty of vampire women before. They're easy on the eyes, and their bodies are more than durable for the kind of sex I like to have. One of my fondest sexual memories is the time I got caught in a lust frenzy, two days and three nights with four of them. When I was imprisoned in the mountain, I used to beat off for hours to the memory alone. Yet now, it does nothing for my excitement. This makes no sense.

All Kaliyah has to do is look at my body just a little too long with those coco pearl eyes or frown her face wrinkling her nose just a tad. Or the way she laughed last night. It filled my world with a song like no other I've ever heard. What I wouldn't do to make her laugh like that every single night as I held her in my arms while she slept. Just like this morning. The bulge in my pants almost instantly returned to the image, as I replayed it in my mind. I reached under the table and squeezed my tip.

Fuck. This isn't good. I think I'm finally understanding the full extent of the soul tie now. From the moment I was bonded to her, she became my one and only. There will never be anyone else.

"Bring me another damn beer. I told you I'll pay my tab next time, girl," the man slurred.

"I'm sorry but my mother said we can't serve you until you close it."

"You look close to woman hood, so tell you what, I don't have any coin on me now, but I can pay you in other ways." He grabbed at the hem of her dress. "I'll make your first time a moment to remember."

First time? My ears perk at the words. I am almost certain I will not be Kaliyah's first time. How many unworthy bastards know the curves of my woman's naked body? How many have gotten to touch her in ways I have not? I will learn of their names, pluck their eyes out and sever their limbs, then burn them with my flames. My hand clenched to tight fists as the heat of anger rise in my chest.

"If you ever think about touching her again you filthy piece of shit, I won't hesitate to plunge this fork deep inside your throat." Kaliyah's voice washes over my thoughts.

I turn around to see her pressing the drunk man's head into the table with one hand, while she buried a utensil into his neck with the other. I can see four small drops of blood forming at the points. Her pupils replace with the white glowing orbs as I seen before when she removed the curse from the girl's leg.

"Yes." He said.

"Now, apologize to her and empty your pockets."

He hesitated, prompting her to dig the fork deeper in, the blood now starting to trickle down his neck to the table.

"I'm sorry young miss." He said as he toss several copper coins to the ground.

She leaned over into his ear and began to whisper to him. I'm sure even those closest to her wouldn't be able to hear her. But I could. And what I heard sent the most delightful shivers throughout my body.

"She is a child you disgusting bastard so if you ever look her way again... matter of fact, if *I* ever see you in this place *ever* again, I will cut your pathetic *fucking* dick off and shove it down your throat. And I mean it, I *dare* you to test me motherfucker. *Do you understand me?*" Pure wrath in her voice.

Mmmmm. I think I just came a little. No. I definitely did.

The drunkard started to whimper. "Yes, ma'am."

"Now get the fuck out of here." She finished as she released her hold on him. He immediately tripped over his feet as he ran to the front stumbling along the way with his palm to his neck.

My cock got so hard. I was sure it ripped a hole in my pants. I reached to check but had to restrain myself from stroking it as it cried out for me to do so. I rose to my feet.

"My queen." I muttered to myself as my body moved without thinking of the consequences. In a blur, I stood in front of her, so swiftly, I'm sure she didn't have time to process that I was before her.

I gripped her by the waist pulling her body against mine, cupping the side of her cheek as I laid the most passionate kiss upon her lips. I have never been a creature of love, she is my first in that way. And in this moment, I want to make even her fury feel tenderness. I wanted every inch of her to know that I live for her. I am obsessed. For her, I will be anything. I will do anything. *All of me belongs to her.*

My lips finally part from hers, almost too soon. "I will love you till my last breath, my queen." I whispered to her. To my everlasting delight she did not recoil, nor did she yell at me. She held no annoyance or irritation in her gaze. Her pulse was calm. Her eyes now back to their usual state, as they bat their lashes. A grin so soft graced her lips. I could feel my blood rushing to my cheeks.

Me? Blushing? The overlord of the dark region flustered at the unrivaled beauty of this woman. *Damn right.*

"I see. So, will *queen* be my new name now."

"If you desire it so, then yes. I will call you anything you find pleasing to the ear."

"Okay. If that is the case. I think... you should stick to little breakfast."

"Really?"

"Yes. It is the most important meal of the day after all. One we both seem to enjoy, so yeah. Little breakfast is fine."

I caressed her chin with the back of my hand. "Then you will forever be *my little breakfast.*"

"You ready to go?"

"I am."

I reached out my hand, still not fully expecting her to take it. But she did. Wrapping her arm around mine. My heart began to flutter, a sensation caught me so off guard that I placed my hand to my chest to inspect what just happen. She tilted forward looking at me.

"You good? If you're not feeling up to it, I can go on my own and meet you back here for lunch later."

"No. I'm fine. I wouldn't dream of missing the chance to spend the day out with you."

"Okay, then. Let's go."

KALIYAH

Asshole. Beautiful blue motherfucker. Who the hell does he think he is? He's getting worse. Does he think my lips are his to kiss whenever he feels like it? What gives him the right? Tongue. He used tongue this time. Why the hell was he so damn good at it? In all my twenty-seven years, I've never been kissed like that. So passionately and tenderly, that my entire body wanted to melt into itself.

Fucking sparks. That's all I saw when he kissed me. I didn't think that was a real thing. My whole body tingled. My stomach flipped. And yet my heart... my heart was completely still. As if his confession was the most natural thing in the world.

It pisses me the hell off that he's somehow able to make me feel these things. He's a damn orc, for God's sake. Pale steel-blue skin, tusks, and the ability to spit freakin' fire like some demon in disguise. A whole ass other species. I shouldn't find anything about him attractive. And yet, if I look at him too long, if he speaks to me in that low, heated voice, it's like my knees forget how to hold me up. And then he calls me his queen. *Absolutely not.* No. I want to remember what he named me when he first laid claim. When he declared me as nothing more than a meal.

When he sicced those goblins on me. When he denied me water until my tongue cracked and my throat felt like sandpaper. When he bit into my flesh and drank from me like I was nothing more than a god damn peach. I still get phantom pains thinking about it. I will remember *exactly* why he calls me his little fucking breakfast every time it leaves his mouth. So go ahead. Say it again. And again. And again. And I'll keep calling you blue devil, behind my every thought.

We have been walking for some time now. Saphire told me it's about a fifteen-minute walk to the town square from the tavern. The stones should be right in the center. All I have to do is make it there without him noticing. But of course, *he notices everything.* Every breath. Every step. Every flick of my damn eyes. We pass a handful of shops, merchant tables and food carts. The scent of fresh bread and spiced meats tempting enough to make my stomach twist. I push any thoughts of hunger to the back of my mind. I am on a mission.

Then something catches my eye. A deep, midnight-blue crossbody bag, trimmed in gold ribbon. I pause for just a second, admiring it. The design reminds me of something from back home. Stylish but sturdy. I lean in slightly, letting myself imagine it slung over my shoulder. It would be nice to have something new. Mine is barely holding together. But I know I'll need every single coin to pay the toll. An impulse buy isn't even a serious thought. Maybe after I get to the next town… if there's anything left over, I can buy clothes that actually *fit* these curves of mine.

Saphire's been kind, but every pair of pants she gave me stops above my ankles, and the shirt's more crop top than coverage. Cute, but not exactly comfortable when I have eyes constantly tracing my body. Out of nowhere, there's a sudden *slam* on the merchant's table. I jump, whipping my head around just in time to see Mitus lift his hand and drop one of his belt buttons. *What is he planning on doing with that?*

"I'll take this blue satchel here," he says, pointing directly at the bag I was eyeing seconds ago.

"A fine choice, Mr. Orc, sir!" the merchant says, suddenly full of jittery energy, rubbing his hands together like he's about to cast a spell. "I see you're paying with gold! Perhaps I could interest you in some of our other bags as well. I have a number of—"

"No. That will be all."

"Oh, right, of course, of course. Not many folks pay in *gold*," the man says with a nervous chuckle. "Give me just a moment while I fetch your change."

"No need. Keep it."

The merchant's eyes go wide. "Oh, Deities. That is *so* generous of you, orc sir!" He grins so hard his cheeks practically fold over themselves.

That's when it clicks.

"Wait. Hold on. How much was the change?" I ask, narrowing my eyes.

The merchant hesitates, like the orc would realize his mistake. "Uh… nineteen silver and twelve copper."

My eyes go wide. Two silver and two copper pieces. That's what Saphire estimated it would cost to travel to the Namma Stones in the other town. Her mother even gave me a few extra coppers, just in case. At first it didn't seem like much… Look like nothing more than a couple of quarters and pennies to me. Their surfaced replacing the presidents of my world history with royal emblems of Therion. It wasn't until Dahlia told me it was *two months* of income from their family's inn slash tavern.

These six little coins equated to two *months*? I was shocked to say the least, but my value grew for them immensely. This all meant that Mitus without blinking, just tipped the merchant nearly *two years*' worth of Dahlia's family hard-earned profits. I glanced at his belt. My eyes followed the curve of it across his waist, noting the grime-covered gold buttons glinting faintly in the light. A few spots were empty, but on this side alone I counted thirteen. If the other half matched...

He's walking around with a whole damn *fortune* wrapped around his sculpted hips like it's just an accessory. Retirement money. Get-yourself-a-house money. Never-work-another-day in your life money. I bit the corner of my lip. If I could get my hands on just *one* of those buttons. As if he knew exactly what I was thinking, Mitus yanked the belt off his waist in one fluid motion, the leather biting into my skin as he looped it around my neck, pulling me in close.

"If you ever want something from me just ask. It's yours." He said as he pressed his forehead against mine. My face flushed, but not because of his sudden, grand display of generosity or unwarranted physical touch. No. It was the simple fact that the only thing holding up Mitus's long, oversized leather shorts was now hanging around my neck like a scarf. Which meant, my eyes had nowhere else to look but directly at his *dick*.

For a moment there was nothing but silents between us. It was like I was in a trance, caught in the weight of the moment. Then came the loud gawks from passersby, and that was enough to snap me out of it. I placed a hand on his chest, pushing him back just enough to create some space, though my eyes stayed locked on his. I wanted to look anywhere else, anywhere but at him. Afraid he'd be able to read my face that I was sure expressing how much I liked what I had just seen. But I had to fight the urge to avert my gaze, because I'd learned a while back that the moment I did, especially when addressing him, it tempts him to get handsy.

"If that's the case, I'd like you to go buy yourself a new belt."

"I don't mind continuing our morning as so."

"Well, I do. You keep saying I'm your *mated soul*. Does that mean you're fine with me having to see other women ogle your body?" I deliberately allow my eyes to drift downward, allowing me to take all of him in. I wanted him to see me do it, just before my eyes returned to his. "Shouldn't your body only be for *me* to look at?"

That grin. Lazy, cocky, and aggravatingly charming, spread across his face. "Of course. You couldn't be more right, love." He said, without looking away from me. "Merchant, I'll be needing my change, after all."

The merchant stammered. "U-um... surely I could offer you something else. Perhaps I can show you—"

Mitus cut him off with a low growl, the kind that raised hairs. "Do we have a problem?"

"N-no, of course not, Mr. Orc," the merchant sputtered, suddenly a model of cooperation. "It is your coin, after all."

He handed over a small pouch and the blue suede satchel. Without missing a beat, Mitus turned and presented the bag to me like it was another offering.

"Um... thank you."

He tugged his pants back up with one hand and clenched them at the waist. "Wait, right here. I'll return momentarily."

And with that, he strode off down the street, scanning the merchant stalls and shopfronts.

"Let me give you a word of advice." The merchant's voice tugged at my attention. "That's a hefty amount of coin you've got hanging around your neck. Best put it away. Out of sight. At least until your partner returns."

"Oh. Right." I slipped the surprisingly heavy belt from around my neck, the chill of the gold lingering against my skin. Shrugged off my pack, slung the suede satchel across my chest, then stuffed both the belt and my backpack inside.

Growing up in the hood taught me one thing real fast, flashing money in public was an invitation to get jacked. And this? This much gold? I'd be practically begging for it. I was so glad when grampa finally moved us out. I mean I love my people, but damn.

"Wait, partner?" I squinted. "What partner?"

"The orc," he said plainly, glancing down the street. "Is he not your companion?"

Both of us turned, eyes locking on Mitus's broad back as he moved through the crowd, still shirtless, still drawing looks.

Hell no, he's not. That's what I wanted to say. But I knew better. He may have been forty feet away, but that orc could hear a needle drop in a thunderstorm. So instead, I lied through my teeth.

"Right. He is." As if on cue, Mitus turned and threw me a cheeky grin over his shoulder.

I knew it. I lingered, counting the seconds, waiting for the exact right moment. My pulse picked up. Just a few more feet…

Now! I turned and bolted, feet hitting the cobblestones hard. The opening to the square came into view, flanked by two medium-sized boulders etched with markings. Symbols kind of like the ones carved into the Elder Stones. They sat atop a weathered sigil no bigger than a large jeep. I pushed through a crowd, not slowing, shoulder-checking bodies left and right. Someone shouted, and I barely registered the thud of an old man hitting the ground. I glanced back.

He resembled my grampa. I had to take a second look. Same tired eyes. Same way-too-big ears. It stopped me for half a breath. I wanted to drop to my knees, help him up, ask if he was okay. But I couldn't. Not now. There was too much at stake. One second of hesitation could mean everything. So I ran. Jaw clenched, heart pounding, small amounts of guilt already catching up to me. There. Those have to be them. I was only feet from the Namma Stones now.

My foot hit the edge of the sigil just as I slammed into one of the boulders, the momentum nearly sending me tumbling over. I gripped the rough surface, arms wrapping tight around the top just to keep from flipping clean off it. I reached instinctively for the stone in my back pocket.

Nothing. My hand searched again, frantic, deeper this time. Still nothing. Panic hit me like a gut punch. *Shit. No.* Where the hell was it? I looked up and of course, the damn commotion had caught Mitus's attention.

No no no. I slapped my hands against my pockets, every one of them. Nothing. Then his eyes locked on mine. And I *knew,* he knew what I was planning. The crystal wasn't here.

Where the hell did it go? I couldn't have lost it. I *would never* lose it. I've kept it on me since the day Noiz gave it to me, slept with it tucked in my pocket every night like a talisman. I check for it more often than I check my heartbeat. *So when?* My mind rewound fast and brutal, back to this morning. In bed. Mitus's hands on me, roaming like they had a damn purpose. That one moment when he grabbed at my backside a little too smoothly.

Did he take the mana crystal from me then? He did. He had to. There is no other explanation. Does that mean he knew? Did he know what I was planning this whole time? I looked up and saw him. His focus solely directed to me, sharp and unblinking. Like a hawk who'd already marked its prey. There was no escape. Not for me. *Was there ever?* His muscles began to shift under his skin, coiling like a spring. I knew that move. I'd seen it more times than I'd like, when he was about to run. When he was about to strike. Why he was so tense, I didn't know. Without the mana crystal, there was nowhere for me to go.

Then I saw it, his eyes widened, just slightly. And before I could make sense of the look on his face, blood welled at the corner of his mouth. He'd bitten down into his lip. Hard. Something raw and unguarded flared across his expression. I can't place it. I've never seen him look that way before. He probably sees my attempt to leave as betrayal. But it wasn't, because I owe him nothing.

I wondered, if he'd actually kill me this time. If that quiet fury behind his eyes was finally going to turn lethal. But then again... if the deal he made was real, if the magic binding it held weight, then maybe he *couldn't.* That was the one thread I'd been hanging onto when I ran. The one thing I hoped would keep him from burning down this entire town in one of his rage-fueled spirals. From tearing through every person here just because I slipped away.

My heart kicked up, and the air around me thickened. Then he moved. Fast. *Too* damn fast. Ten blinks ago, he was a hundred feet away. Now, he was only a few feet in front of me. And I had nowhere left to run.

"Kaliyah... it's time."

The voice. The one that had whispered in my mind before. It was back. Clearer now, heavier, like it had strength behind it.

"It's time to leave the blue orc's side."

The world stilled. Mitus hung in the air in front of me, just a meter away, his feet barely grazing the ground, caught mid-stride. His expression twisted in hurt and something else. Something I didn't want to name.

"You must hurry, Kaliyah," the voice urged. "Call out to the stones."

"But I don't have the mana crystal." I said, breathless.

"Worry not. You only need to speak to the stones, and they will listen. Again, you must hurry, tell them where you need to go."

"But I don't remember the name of the town." I finally responded, my mind drawing a blank in the chaos.

"The town is not where you need to go," it answered. "Speak to the stone and it will take you where you *need* to go."

Everything around me was frozen, every face in the square, every shifting breeze, every flutter of cloth, but Mitus... he was still moving. Slowly. An inch at a time. A silent warning that time had not stopped. Not completely. Just slowed significantly.

"Kaliyah" the voice shouted again, more urgent now. "We cannot remain in this state forever. You must tell the stones where you need to go, before the orc gets to you. If he reaches you, he will not allow you to do what must be done. You must fulfill your purpose."

"What? What does that *mean*?"

"There is no more time. Speak. Now."

Mitus's fingers were almost on my shoulders. Up my throat like a scream, I shouted the first word that came to mind. *"Palloria!"* The instant the word left my lips, the world around me exploded into bright white.

CHAPTER 19
OUTLANDISH DECLARATION

KALIYAH

The world snapped itself back together, reformed around me in a flash of white. BAM. Sunlight spilled over me like a curtain yanked open too fast. I blinked against the glare, swaying as the last echo of teleporting moved through my vision. I barely had time to register the smooth stone beneath my sneakers before a warm breeze tugged gently at my clothes, carrying the scent of lilacs and freshly cut grass. I turned slowly, chest panting.

A large, manicured garden stretched out around me in full. The surrounding space laced with sculpted hedges framing the winding stone paths. Each one flanked by bursts of color with pampas grass, orchids, and some other tall foreign plants spacing them. Ahead, a marble gazebo rested between two cherry trees, their branches heavy with blossoms. Pink petals drifted lazily to the ground, carpeting the wide white steps in a soft blush. Gold filigree curled along its columns, intricate and undeniably fancy.

Inside the gazebo, a small table had been set with porcelain cups, a delicate teapot, and a tower of golden biscuits. Standing within was... a woman? No. Not quite. She resembled one, at first glance. A humanoid shape, upright and poised, but her features betrayed something animalistic. Her face, though smooth and almost human, was brushed with soft red fur. Her hands ended in graceful claws that caught the light as she stood, and when her lips parted in surprise, I caught the glint of small, sharp fangs. Her white-tipped tail curled slowly around the folds of her silk dress.

For a heartbeat, we only stared. Her mouth formed a small O of surprise, mirroring my own. *What is she? Another monster?* I instinctively stepped back. The change in her was immediate, from shocked to alert. Her spine straightened, her voice rang clear and commanding. "Tell me now. Who are you?"

It... she can talk? That shouldn't have surprised me as much as it did, but I'd long learned that in this world, the ability to understand her means nothing. I know better to let down my guard against the creatures in this world. Then my gaze caught a delicate crown resting on top her head, nestled between two tufted ears that twitched toward me like radar. My thoughts scrambled to connect the dots. *Wait. Is she a demi-human?* I remember Saphire mentioning that Palloria was home to the biggest population of demi-humans. At the time I wasn't sure what she meant by the term, and I had planned on asking her more about them, but just never got around to it. *If that is the case...*

"Is this the Kingdom of Palloria? Are you the queen? La'Claw's wife?"

The shift in her was instantaneous. Her hands curled into fists at her sides, ears twitching sharply back as her eyes narrowed. "What? That is King Korrak La'Claw to you." Her tone dropped. "You do not answer my question with one of your own."

My head snapped around, eyes scanning the garden like something might leap out from the hedges. But there was nothing. Just her. She was small. Thin. Barely taller than my shoulder, even with the crown. If she came at me, I could probably take her. *Probably.* But then again, what if she was like *him*? Like Mitus. No. He'd said it himself. There's no one like him.

Hold on. Mitus! Where? I turned, glancing quickly over the Namma stones behind me, then did a slow circle, searching every shadow and bloom. Nothing. No heavy footfalls. No looming figure. No pale steel blue ass terror coming at me. I blinked, then blinked again. The truth hit me like a rush of wind to the lungs.

Oh my god. I did it. I actually did it. I got away from him. Like for real. A grin stretched across my face. "Hell yeah!" I shouted, a laugh bubbling up from somewhere deep in my chest. "Thank you God! I'm fucking free!" The laughter came fast, sharp, and real. For a few perfect seconds, it was everything. And then I looked back at her.

The fox-woman hadn't moved. But her shoulders had tensed, her fingers curled slightly at her sides. Her golden eyes watched me not with amusement, but like she was trying to decide whether I was crazy, dangerous... or both.

"Hello, ma'am," I said carefully, trying for polite despite knowing I probably looked completely unhinged.

"I will not repeat myself, trespasser! Who *are* you?"

Trespasser? Oh damn. I don't like the sound of that. I begin to stammer, raising my hands slowly, palms open. "I— uh— no no. I'm sorry. It's not my intention to trespass. My name is Kaliyah Shepard."

"How did you come to be here in *my* garden?"

"Right. Um... Yeah, I asked the Namma stones to bring me to Palloria, and the next thing I knew, I was here. Is this the place? Palloria, I mean."

For a moment, she said nothing. Then her eyes narrowed. "What do you mean you *asked*?" Her voice edged with suspicion. "These Namma Stones are bound by a private restriction spell. Only those of our royal bloodline, or individuals granted express permission by my father, can access them. If you, a human, were able to activate them, then either you know my father, which I *very* much doubt or you or someone you know is a very powerful mage. And if *that* is the case..." Her gaze sharpened to slits. "then your presence here suggests nefarious intentions."

Ah~ Shit. I threw my hands higher in the air, taking a few frantic steps forward. "No no! That's not it at all. I can explai—"

"Don't move," the woman snapped. Then came the word that ruined everything. "Guards!" The response was instant. They crash through the garden. Half a dozen creatures, tall and terrible, their bodies wrapped in silvered armor, their faces stolen from beasts. A jackal's snout, a ram's curling horns, a hawk's curved beak. None of them were human at all. They didn't hesitate to pour to her side. Steel catching sunlight, teeth bared beneath helm and fur.

"Yes, your highness. Is everything all right, Princess Sarianna?" One of them asked, eyes scanning the area.

She didn't waste a word. She raised one hand, a single finger pointed. *At me.* Their gazes snapped to mine. And then the sound, the unmistakable shriek of metal slipping free of scabbard. Sharp swords drawn almost in unison. Some shifted, protecting her body with theirs forming a shield of breathing armor. The others came forward. One step. Then two. Straight. Towards. Me. My arms shot up like surrender would stop them.

"Wait! I'm not here to hurt anyone!"

They didn't pause. Didn't blink. Just kept advancing, silver blades raised, merciless shadows over faces I can so clearly read. My brain flailed. Think. Talk. Lie if you have to. Say something that saves your skin. Something they'd have no choice but to listen to. But I've never been good at lying. Not when it counted. Not when it mattered. Even if I could, I don't know much about this world to come up with something convincing enough. My mind raced. *Think. Say something. Anything.* I blurted out the first thing that jumped to the front of my panicked brain.

"Please, don't hurt me. I was summoned here... from another world. As a Champion!"

Silence fell like a dropped mic. They stopped. Not long. A heartbeat, maybe two. But it was enough. Enough to know they'd heard me. Enough to know the word '*Champion*' meant something here too.

"I said I am a Champion," I repeated, louder this time. "Brought here from Earth."

Their stillness wasn't relief. It was recalibration. They started moving again, but slower this time. *Shit shit shit.* They're not backing down. If anything, they looked more certain. Do I run? *Can* I run? But where? I don't know this place. Which way is the exit? I turned my head, just a fraction, scanning.

"Hold." The princess raised a single hand, and the guards obeyed without hesitation. She didn't look at them. She looked at me. "Human," she said, stepping forward now. "Do you take me for a fool? You dare lie to my face? You do realize that falsely claiming the title of Champion is a crime punishable by death?"

What? Fuck. Fuck fuck fuck! Take it back. I need to take it back. But it was too late. She wasn't finished. Her voice rang out like a bell cast in iron and judgment.

"It is common knowledge that the Great Vireth-Kai of the heavens, revoked the right of summonings across all of Therion. No Champion has been able to be called forth since."

I don't know who the hell this Vir Kai guy is, but I know she's wrong. I wouldn't be in Therion, if that were the case. "That... that's not right. I'm telling you the truth. I was teleported here. From my own world."

"You continue to cling to the outlandish declaration. Your idiocy will be your demise..." she said, gesturing with a slow flick of her fingers toward the boulders behind me. "because those are not Elder Stones."

"No. I don't mean right now. I didn't use *these* stones. This happened nearly two months ago."

She paused, seemingly contemplating whether or not she wants to continue to give this conversation anymore of her time.

"Continue," she demanded, "and do so honestly. Otherwise lying to me will be the last thing you ever do. If you were sent here from another world, *who* sent for you? And *how*?"

My stomach twisted into knots. Every nerve in me stiffened. *Crap.* Do I tell her the truth? That it was *that empire bitch* who brought me here? Princess Millie. no. *Empress* Millie? Wait, no, that isn't right either. What was her damn name again? Why the hell can't my brain remember her dumb ass name? The pressure in my throat built as I swallowed hard, forcing the words past my lips.

"The ruler of Sebbarus," I said, hoping that's a good enough answer. "They did it. I was summoned there."

For the briefest moment, the princess's eyes widened. Just a flicker. Then, as if the air had changed course, her expression hardened. *Damn it...* Her reaction definitely isn't a good sign.

Maybe the rulers of Palloria *and* Sebbarus aren't cool with each other. I wouldn't be surprised. It will be risky. But maybe... *maybe* there is a way I could use that to my advantage.

"Like I said, it was almost two months ago, I think."

"You *think*?" Her voice flattened, even icier than before. She gestured to the guards with a flick of her wrist. "Proceed."

My stomach dropped. "Wait wait!" I plead. "Please, wait!"

Her expression didn't change, but the guards hesitated.

"I only say *I think* because its been difficult for me to keep track of time," I said, trying to slow my breathing. "After I *demanded* to be sent back home I was banished to Bloodthorn. That is where I have spent most of my time in this world."

That made one of the guards glance at another. A twitch of recognition. That's something. I looked her in the eyes, desperate but honest. "I've spent the last two months trying to survive, finally making my way here. Someone told me the King of Palloria could help me. I want to be sent back home."

"What proof do you have that anything you speak is the truth?"

"Proof?" I echoed. *Of course she wants proof.* What the hell was I supposed to offer her?

"Yes. *Proof.*" She looked down her nose at me. "If a human such as yourself truly survived the dark region for that long, then one of the deities must have granted you a great blessing indeed. Show me your blessing."

My spit nearly choked me at the words. She took a step closer, her gaze narrowing as she looked me up and down. The guard nearest her cut in, his tone respectful, but urgent. His hand at his sword. "This intruder is clearly lying, and we should—"

"Hold your tongue." Her voice whipped. The guard fell silent immediately, eyes wide with sudden compliance. "If she is lying, then I will hear it with my own ears… and I will see her death with my own eyes as well."

Fuckkkkkkkkkkkk. I'm dead. I'm fucking dead. Finally escaped the blue bastard and now I was about to get executed in an elaborate parterre. My hand gripped the strap of my satchel like it was the last lifeline I had.

Wait. The sudden spark of memory hit me. *My phone.* You can do this. Lie your ass off.

"My unwillingness to participate after the summoning resulted in them sending me away *before* the blessing ceremony," I said. Lie. The ceremony definitely happened. "So, I never received my blessing." True, unfortunately. I really wasn't given any cool superpower, magic or whatever.

Sarianna's lips curled down as she bared her fangs. Her patience running on fumes. I could almost feel her counting the seconds in her head, waiting for my next mistake.

"But, *but* I have a device from my world," I added quickly. "The charge is dead, but if one of your mages can restore it, it should be proof enough of where I'm from."

I am not even sure if it's possible for them to do that. Even if they can… I know this world isn't as technologically advanced as mine, but who's to say a smart phone with no service that now only amounts to a camera with a gallery and calculator, will be enough to satisfy them.

A heavy silence followed, long and agonizing. I could almost hear the gears turning in her mind. Could feel the weight of her skepticism pressing down on me like the sword I knew she wanted to bring down on my neck.

"Show me this device," she said. She's willing to hear me out. This is good. I can work with this.

"Yes, of course," I said, my heart thundering. My palms sweating as I reached for the bag. *This is it. This is my chance.* I started to open it.

CLANG!

The sound of metal rubbing through the garden. I froze mid-motion. The guards readying themselves for what I might do. My hands hovered above the flap.

"The device is in my bag. Is it all right if I retrieve it?"

"Go ahead. But if you try anything, my men will cut you down where you stand."

"I'm not. I promise." My palms were slick with sweat as I slowly opened the satchel, trying not to let my hands shake. The weight of Mitus's belt was shoved right on top. I pulled it out, I swung the damn thing over my shoulder. The rough leather dug into my skin, the gold buttons catching the sunlight. Then, I opened the bag fully and started rummaging through the contents of my backpack.

For a moment, panic flickered. Where is it? It *should* be here. My fingers brushed something small, smooth, at the bottom of the satchel. It must have slid out of my backpack. But it was there. Just as I was about to pull it out, I heard her voice again.

"Wait one moment."

I paused, mid-motion.

"What is that you have draped over your shoulder?"

"Uh? Oh, you mean this? It's just a belt." My mind realizing the truth just as the words leave me.

Shit~. It's *not* just a belt. *How could I forget?* It was Mitus's belt. I might as well be sporting an arm full of Rolexes. I could already feel suspicion in the air. Every second felt heavier, like I was sinking deeper into quicksand. I knew exactly where this was going. I could see it unfolding in my mind, and I hated every second of it.

This was bad. *Really bad.* It made sense. The way I looked, like a commoner as Saphire so kindly put it. I didn't match the amount of money hanging off my body right now. A peasant with riches meant one thing. *Thief.* There was no way she'd believe someone just gave it to me. Not with the way I looked. Not in this world. Not even in my own. Which means...

Off with my fucking head.

CHAPTER 20
FAIRY TALES

KALIYAH

Fairy tales. Princes and princesses. A strong, gorgeous man meets a girl from humble beginnings, falls madly in love with her, and whisks her away to a life of riches and romance. As a kid, I always knew that was crap. What man, who already has everything, clout, money, access to all the beautiful women he could want, turns around and picks the girl who has nothing but a sweet voice and a kind smile?

Bullshit. I knew it was all a damn lie the moment my little brain realized none of those princesses ever... ever looked like me. Well, except for that one. But they made her kiss my worst nightmare to earn her so-called *happy ending*. A damn frog. A fucking creepy slimy gross bumpy, skin crawling ass frog.

Bull-fuckin'-dog-shit. That's when I realized fairy tales and I weren't built for each other. Girls like me are not the chosen ones. We're the throwaway side characters, there to prop up the heroine, before we're conveniently killed off, either off camera or horrifically on, for lame ass emotional motivation.

I just... I never imagine how spot on any of it actually was. That I would ever see it play out in live action form. A long, shaky breath escaped me, but it did nothing to slow the hammering of my heart. The warmth of the air, the sharp scent of flowers, it felt all too familiar. Here I am. Full circle moment about to happen before my eyes. My journey had started with offending a royal bitch and thinking I would lose my head. Now, it looks like it's going to *end* the same way.

"Zarion, retrieve the belt and bring it to me."

"Yes. Your highness" The wolf-looking man replied, stepping forward. "Female intruder, you will toss the belt to the ground toward me. If you make any other subtle movements, I will strike you."

I didn't hesitate. I tossed the belt to the ground at the guard's feet, watching it land with a thud. The gold buttons caught the light one last time before the guard scooped it up and brought it to her. I held my breath, waiting. And then, in the silence that followed, my mind screamed, *I have to get out of here.* But if I run, they will kill me, but if I stay, they will kill me. I need help. Think.

"Hey, voice. You there? Hello. Little voice, can you hear me? Are you there?" My thoughts call out.

"Yes. I am."

My breath catches. *"Oh my god. I actually hear it. Shit, this is crazy. Or am I going crazy?"*

"You are not."

"Who are you?"

The voice does not respond.

"Hello? Hey."

"Yes."

"Okay, little voice. I need your help. Can you do that freezing thing like you did before. I'm in trouble and I need to get out of here, like right now."

"We cannot."

"What? Why not?"

"Something is wrong. For some time now, this place... has been wrong. Time wrong. We're not in sync. We're limited... Strained... Weaken. I must rest until wrong is right. Only then we can be whole."

"Huh? I don't know what any of that means."

"You must go back."

"Go back? Wait, no. You're not saying go back to Mitus, are you?"

"No."

"Then where? Go back home? That's what I've been trying to do."

Silence fell.

"Hello? Voice, you there? Hel—"

"Find Ra."

"What?"

"You must find Ra?"

"Will this Ra person help me get home? Is he here in Palloria? Hello? Say something damn it. I still need your help. I—"

"Where did you get this?" The Princess asked.

My vision snapped back to the fox woman. Her eyes were wide, unnervingly so. Her fingers gripped around one of the gold pieces. At some point, she must have removed it from the belt. Should I lie and say I found it? *That's not believable enough.* I racked my brain for any sort of credible explanation, but my time was running out.

"Voice?" I whispered, my mind screaming for some sort of guidance. *"Say something. Tell me what to do."* But nothing came. I flinched at the sudden sound of my name. Lying is not working. So maybe I should just tell the truth this time. The words hesitantly left my lips. "I got it from a Blue Orc."

Her eyes widened even more. She was staring at me now with something like curiosity, but also... disgust. Her fingers tightened firmer around the gold piece.

"Lying scum." The guard by her side spat. "Princess, you should allow me to deal with this criminal right here and now."

"You will do nothing until I command you to. Do you understand me?"

The guard stiffened, his face falling into a softer scowl, "Of course, my princess."

Her attention fell back to me. "What was this orc's name?"

I didn't want to say his name out loud. It felt as if, somehow, if I did, he would be conjured the moment the syllables left my lips. "He told me his name was Mitus."

Her attention drew to the guard nearest her, "Lymon have you heard mention of any blue orcs recently."

Lymon's body twitched, a barely perceptible movement, but enough to catch the princess's attention. Her eyes narrowed on him, and I saw her fist clench even tighter. "Speak to which you know, now." She commanded.

"Yes, Princess Sarianna. There was a rumor, coming from the Adventurer's Guild Crimson Wing out in Yenka country. But they are only that, rumors."

Sarianna's eyes darkened at that. "Why was I not informed of this?"

"Not only because this information has not been verified. But the counsel—"

"The counsel should have no say in what information I receive when it comes to the wellbeing of My father's kingdom." Princess Sarianna took a few more steps down from the gazebo. "How are you alive? If you manage to cross paths with a blue orc, you should be anything but. Most orcs have bad blood with humans, but according to the legends, when a blue orc appears, no one escapes their wrath. They kill those who don't align with their agenda. There is no negotiation. You either submit, die, or most times, both. So I ask again how did you manage to escape with no blessing and with gold baring the crest of the dark overlord?"

"Honestly I would have been dead a long time ago if it wasn't for the magic symbols."

"Explain."

"Um... like I said before. I was teleported to a forest. It was there, in a cave of a mountain, where I first encountered the *blue demon*. I mean orc. Honestly, I really shouldn't be alive right now. I don't know how I managed to survive at all."

"Has another risen?" The princess whispers to herself. "That would mean the prophecy has begun."

My brow furrowed, not sure if I'd heard her correctly. "I'm sorry, but I didn't catch that."

"Tell me. Where did you last see this blue orc?"

"He's in the town called Vicory Mills. That's where I made my escape from."

I watched her closely as she processed the information. Her eyes flick towards Lymon. I can tell she's taking what I'm saying more seriously now. But still, I don't know if that's a good thing.

"Lymon, have you heard of this town?"

"Yes, you're highness. It is a place east of Yenka. It lies just outside the borders of the Bloodthorn Region."

Sarianna's eyes didn't leave him. I could sense the calculation beneath her mask of composure. "Have there been any updates on my father?"

"Currently, there have been none."

"And Madam Noelle?"

"Yes, she's still in Glendara. She's not expected to arrive for several more weeks."

"We need to be ready when she does. Double-check with Elania, ensure everything is in place well before her arrival. I should not have to remind you just how important that this goes well for us."

"Of course."

She paused for a moment looking me up and down. "Gather ten of your most trusted knights. They're to head straight for Vicory Mills. No delays. Take the fastest ironhoofs you have. Time is of the essence."

"Yes, your highness. We will leave first thing in the morning."

"No, not you. I need you here. The timing of all of this is rather suspicious and I would prefer to have my most trusted with me."

Lymon nodded, but his eyes flicked to me. "And what should they do once they arrive?"

"If even half of what she says is true, then by the time you reach this Vicory Mills, it will most likely no longer be standing. Do your best to find survivors or refugees in neighboring towns. Anything that talks and still breathes. Determine what's truth and what's not."

He gestured in my direction. "And what about *her*? How should we dispose of the intruder."

My blood ran cold. *Dispose of?* What the hell is wrong with this world? Why is killing the first thing everyone jumps to?

"I'm sure the council will be *curious* to learn of this information, and they will. But in my own time. Not before I know the truth. Lock her in the Prairie House, I want her away from the other prisoners, away from my father's men. Out of sight. The fewer people know about this, the better."

"But, your highness. That's where your father keeps—"

"I know. That's why it's the best place for her. Not even the counsel knows of it. The woman may have information that proves *valuable*. Also I can't ignore her claims to be a champion. Although I'm not inclined to believe the likelihood of that, I still must handle this with care and discretion. If she turns out to be one of the deities' chosen, and we subject her to conditions *too deplorable*, it might come back to bite us. The punishment could be... irreparable. Not to mention if the world learns that we killed one of the few remaining champions of Therion, that could be the very action that triggers the war. Palloria may not survive this time. We must take any chance of this claim seriously in regards to my father's kingdom and the future of our people."

"And if she's not?"

"Then she will rot."

Before I could even process her orders, I felt the sting of rough hands grabbing me from behind. My bag was torn away, my arms bound tightly, painfully, behind my back. They weren't gentle. Not even close. My breath pulled away for me and they pushed me forward, shoving me through narrow corridors. The guards marched with no concern for how hard their hands bit into my arms. I wasn't even given a second to try and gather my thoughts before they were hauling me through a set of heavy doors.

The courtyard was a blur of stone, the buildings looming with a quiet menace. But it was the small, discrete cottage in the back corner of the space that caught my attention. Such a tiny little stone house felt so random and out of place. Two small windows. It barely looked like it could hold my living room furniture. Not the kind of place you'd expect to hold *someone like me*. But it wasn't a cave in a mountain, so that was something. The door creaked open, revealing not a tiny little room, but a staircase descending into blackness, like the gullet of some beast. The scent of dusty stone filled the air.

"Move it." The sharp command from a guard.

I stopped dead in my tracks.

"Hell no. I'm not going down there." I've done my time in dark creepy places. I'm not doing that again.

The guard at the front, taller and firmer than the rest, didn't even look back. "I said move." And that was that. I felt the pressure of their hands on my back, urging me forward, but my feet refused to comply. Every part of me screamed at the idea of that dark pit below, but my arms are bound and their weight forced me to advance.

The moment I felt like I was getting too close, I side kick the guard to my left in the knee, making him wince as he collapsed to the ground. The one in front turns around and lunges at me. I waste no time kicking him in the nuts, effectively bringing him to his knees as well.

The guard to my right punches me in the gut. I crouched over in pain. As he leans into me, grabbing my arm tighter, with all my force I smash the back of my head into his face. I hear his whimper as his hands rush to his nose. Bright red blood spews between his furry fingertips. I stumble a few feet back as I try to swivel and run in the opposite direction. But the first guard I attacked had recovered and trips me.

Without the use of my arms, my chest plants into the ground, hard. So freakin' hard. It effectively knocked the wind out of me. Unable to push myself off the ground, or even able to try before I am flipped onto my back and met with a fist to my face.

And that's the last thing I remember.

The throbbing in my skull was relentless, a sharp pulse that echoed in my mind. I groaned, my eyelids squeezing shut tighter against the pain. "Owww." It felt like the whole world was spinning. Slowly, I turned onto my back, wincing as the ache in my head flared up like fire. My fingers instinctively try to reach my head.

God, what the hell did they hit me with? I forced my eyes open, squinting at the dimness around me. Stone walls lined the room. My vision swam, and I could barely make out the cell bars on the wall to my left. There was no natural sunlight to speak of, just faint glimmers of lanterns marking the perimeter outer path of the cell. And inside the cell, there was only one lantern, hanging from the ceiling. The light it gave off wasn't even enough to push back the darkness of the corners. It was so goddamn hot in here. Warmth clung to the air, sticky, a stark contrast to the cooler breeze outside.

The assholes hadn't even bothered to untie my arms. My wrists still ached from the brutal ropes they'd tied them with, and I couldn't even remember how I got here. Or where here is. *How long was I out for? Hours? Days?* How would I know when there are no windows for me to see what time of day it is? I am not supposed to be here. This can't be happening to me. I have to get out. With a groan, I dragged myself to my knees. The stone floor bit into my skin, but nothing I haven't experienced before. The side of my stomach still stung from the punch and my head still throbbing, as I stumbled toward the bars.

"Hello?" My voice cracked from the dusty air. I called out again, a bit louder this time. "Hey! Let me out. You can't keep me in here. You can't—" I kicked the bars with my foot, hard. The sound echoed through the empty stone room, a hollow clang. "Hey!" I yelled. "Are you there, you assholes? Get me out of this fucking cell right now, or I'll—" I stopped, my mind racing. *What if they left me down here to die?*

Fuck. My vision starts to blur with tears. I stand back from the cell gate and I kicked the bars again. Harder this time. As hard as one can without the use of their arms. The clang of metal ringing only stoked the fire inside me, my anger rising. I kicked again, and again, each blow sending a jolt of pain up my leg, the heat of it mixing with the growing anger. This was not supposed to happen. I've gone through too much. I've come too far. And now, this? Prison? Like I'm some damn criminal.

This is *Bullshit*. Bullshit! I backed up a few paces, clenched my jaw, and charged the door. My shoulder hit the bars with an explosion of pain, a shockwave that rattled my bones. My ribs screamed in protest, my head swam as the force of the impact slammed through me. I gasped, stumbling, nearly collapsing.

Fuck, that hurt. But I wasn't about to stop. Not now. I stumbled back, shoulders slumped, and before I could even think about the pain, I was kicking again. Harder. Louder. My voice a scream now.

"Let me out! I want out! You can't keep me down here!" My sneakers slammed into the bars again. "Hey! Are you listening, you sons of bitches? Get me out of this fucking cell right now or I'll … I'll…" I stopped for a moment. What the hell was I going to do? I had nothing. My hands were tied, my legs were shaking, and the door wouldn't budge. *No, God damn it*. I kicked again. And again. Each hit was harder.

"Let." *BANG*. "Me." *BANG*. "Out." *BANG*. "I've done nothing wrong! I don't deserve this!" My voice cracked. The air was suffocating down here, making it hard to breathe. My lungs were stuffing, my chest panting, but still, I kicked. And kicked.

The panic started to claw at me as my mind is almost certain the air is being siphon from the space. My breathing quickens. I *need* out. But nothing was working. The door wasn't budging. I turn around gripping my fingers around the bars trying to tug at them. I sank down, crouching with my back some, struggling to calm my breathing. Sweat poured down my face, stinging my eyes, making my thoughts blur. I turn back around to face the door looking for any signs of give. "Please…" My voice trembled now, softer, desperate. "Just let me out. Let me speak to the princess, or… or someone. Anyone."

…

"Ra." I whispered the next words, my throat tight with uncertainty. "She said I need to find Ra… Who the hell is Ra?"

I leaned my forehead against the slightly less warm bars, the sweat running down my temples, and the air seemed even more suffocating now. The heat in the stone room pressed down on me, and the isolation gnawed at my mind.

"Please, at least untie my hands." My chest rise and fall rapidly. I feel like I'm losing control.

That's when I heard it. A man's voice. The hairs on my neck stand. "You are wasting your time... and your breath."

My heart leapt into my throat. I spun around, my back slamming into the bars as I pressed myself against them, every muscle in my body coiled, ready to... I don't know. Run. Scream. *Something*. But I Can't. I'm fucking trapped. There's nowhere for me to run.

Scream? For what? Who would hear me? Who would care? I never considered the fact that I may not be alone. The twenty-foot cell had *looked* empty when I first woke up. It's so dark here I can hardly see anything. I blink. Then again. There, in the far-left corner, something shifted. Just enough for my eyes to catch it. Low to the ground. Too still. At first, I question if I am really seeing the dark shadow. I wouldn't have seen it at all if not for the barest motion, what might have been a foot, withdrawing. Every nerve in my body is on high alert.

"Who's there?" My thin voice ragged. I didn't take my eyes off the corner. Couldn't. But I braced my heel behind me and kicked backward into the bars. One last stupid, stubborn try at freedom. The metal rang, but held.

"You'll need far more than brute strength to break an *enchanted* lock," the voice replied at last. I slid along the bars without thinking, dragging myself as far away from the voice as the cramped cell would allow. My back hit stone in the opposite corner, heart thudding so hard it drowned out reason.

Who or *whatever* was in here with me... my body knew before my mind did, every nerve hollered the same thing, '*Get The Fuck Away From It*'. The feeling too familiar. Too close. It curled in my gut like the memory of fire. The feeling of danger reminding me so much of Mitus. For a second, I almost believed it *was* him. But the voice, that low, cold, unshaken monotone, nothing like his. There was no chaos in it. This was different. But I knew with every fiber of my being it was not to be tested.

Déjà vu hit me like a punch to the chest. Goosebumps crawled up my arms. My breathing shortened. Quick, shallow gulps that did nothing. The cell was closing in. The air thinning. Like oxygen had *quit* on me. Then came the voice again.

"The more you struggle, the worse things will get."

"No. Stay the fuck back. I fucking ma... I fucking mean it. I'll... I'll beat your—" But the words broke off. My lungs refused to keep up. Each inhale fought against the weight on my chest. "I have to..." My legs wavering. "I have to get out of here."

My head spun as the air thinned, dizziness blooming behind my eyes. Bracing my back harder into the corner of the cell, the stone biting into my spine, the only thing keeping me upright. My knees buckled, and I slid down the wall, legs folding uselessly beneath me. My chest heaves. My lungs clawing for anything at this point. Panic was taking over fast. *Am I dying?* I am. I'm about to die. No one will know what happened to me. Grampa won't know what happened to me. I'm not ready. Please, someone help me. I tried. Tried so hard to keep my eyes open and on the shadow in the corner, afraid I'd never open them again if I didn't.

"I— I can't... breathe," I gasped, the words fractured between shallow pulls of air. "Please. Outside. Please."

"That's not happening. You're never leaving here."

If my breath could have hitched at that moment it would have. But my lungs had nothing left to give.

"What?" I rasped. "No. No no no no—"

Terror in full swing. My body no longer in control.

"Not again," I whispered. "Please... God, anything but—" The rest broke off in a sob that never made it out of my chest.

Mitus? What are you… I got away from you. Unless… I see. Another dream. My brows knit tight. "Why the hell am I still dreaming about you?" I curse. "More importantly, why the hell do you always have this damn death grip on me?"

I shove my hand against his face, trying to push him off. "Let go of me, bastard." He remain fixed, unmoved and unbothered. "This is my damn dream so I should be stronger than you."

He still doesn't move. Not even an inch. As I fail at my struggle for release, I start to feel heaviness blooming in my chest. It hits hard. A dull, unfamiliar ache I can't explain. I feel the urge to rub at it, when before I can, Mitus presses his temple to mine. That's when I know something is off. Different. Before, these dreams, whatever they were… had a pull to them. Lust, tension, something dark but seductive. I could almost tolerate that. Sometimes I even indulged in them.

But this isn't that. There's warmth, but its also cold. The tension is thin, but pressing. If I had to describe it, it's like hurt and confusion. Even as he holds me so tightly. I don't like it. I don't like how this is making me feel. It's too familiar. Too close to my past. I want to wake up. But at the same time, for some reason, I don't.

Why? If this isn't one of those steamy, guilt-laced dreams, then it's one I don't care to be having. The weight of him, the way his presence feels, like it's supposed to be here, like it belongs under me… it pisses me the fuck off. There is no freakin' way I should be feeling this way. No reason I should feel comfortable. Not when it's him. Not in this monster's arms.

I want to push him off even more now. I feel even more determined to do so. I shove at his chest, but he doesn't move. I push harder. Nothing. Then he nuzzles his cheek against mine, and just like that the ache in my chest subsided. Confused, I pull back just enough to see his face. His eyes are closed, same as always in these twisted dreams. But the arrogant, smug grin he wears like armor is gone. Instead, his facial expression looks… pained. What the hell? Mitus, the unhinged bastard, the demon who hunted me, hurt me, then haunted me… wincing? I want to laugh at the look on his face. I should laugh. But I don't. And that pisses me off even more. Why can't I laugh at his pain? He laughed at mine. Several times.

I know why. Because none of this is real. This is just a dream. My brain stitching scraps of memory and fear into something that feels like truth. But it isn't. Just a figment of my imagination. This isn't really Mitus. That expression on his face, the flicker of sorrow, none of it's real. So how could I enjoy his suffering when it doesn't actually belong to him? Yeah. That's gotta be it.

"Ah." I let out a low whimper, yanking my hand back to rub at my chest again as that annoying little throb creeps in.

"What is that?" I'm too young for a heart attack. Right? Then again... maybe not. I haven't exactly been taking care of myself. For all I know, it's been coming for a while. Ugh. What the hell am I even saying? Stupid. This is a dream, remember? Once I wake up, the ache will go away. Duh. Still... "Ugh." I wish it didn't feel so real. Mitus leans in again. His forehead presses gently to mine. And boom, instant ibuprofen. The pain fades like it was never there.

"What the heck?" I breathe. "How did you—" But I don't get to finish the thought. That familiar pulling sensation starts at the base of my spine.

I'm waking up. No. Not yet. I try to fight it, try to hold on. I don't even know why, but some part of me is wanting, feeling the need to stay. Feeling that he needs me to stay. "Wait..." My voice is hoarse, cracking around the name. "Mitus."

CHAPTER 21
PRISONERS GHOSTS SECRETS

ARRIO

The sound of metal striking stone. Armor boots on the stairs. Two soldiers, by the rhythm of their steps. A little surprising. It hasn't even been a full week, so I know it's not time for my piss excuse of a meal. Nor is it time for my annual *interrogation*. It's been several years since the crown of Palloria questioned me directly. So it couldn't be that. Very few people are privy to my enclosure here. Even less than that, with the clearance to enter. My ears serve me better than my eyes ever can down here. From the echo and weight of their steps, I can tell one of the guards wears his belt too loose. The twin sheaths of his swords knock against each other as he walks. Two swords. A higher rank, then. Likely a commanding officer. And he reeks of the Emberkiss fruit and rotting cologne.

Telling. Unless things have changed drastically in the last ten years, Emberkiss only grows in the Elven lands. Aside from Yurakora, it's banned across most territories. If this guard is careless or confident enough to flaunt contraband without fear of reprimand, then that would mean he's either very well protected or incredibly stupid. More likely, though, it's just not a scent many are familiar with.

The king would only allow his most trusted to come here and although I'm sure most of them have their vices. I doubt any of them would dare risk jeopardizing international trade with Yurakora. If word got out that a royal knight of Palloria was smuggling sacred elven fruit, the Elven Triad would revoke the treaty in a heartbeat. No. They wouldn't dare draw the wrath of Korrak La'Claw. Not with his taste for severe, public punishment.

That scent again. Emberkiss, lingering in and out, but there's a hint of something sweeter hidden under the already sweet fragrance. Hard to place it. Either way I can gather these aren't Korrak's men. No. These must be Princess Sarianna's guards. She herself is not allowed down here, not officially or otherwise. And if her men are here, then the king doesn't know. Curious. *Is this her making a play?* Maybe she's trying to prove herself. Does she think she can get from me what her father could not. She may think silence breaks like bone. It doesn't. Silence is a weapon... *my* weapon. And it has tasted more blood than her father's sword.

Still, I wonder why now? Something must have shifted. Is the king away? Korrak rarely leaves his throne without reason, and never without contingency. If he's gone, something's stirring. He's not dead. I would know. His life belongs to me, and I do not share what is mine. But what would pull him from his roost? A summit in Magdara, perhaps? That would explain the stiffness I've tasted in the guards' voices these past weeks, short tempers, nervous fingers on blades. Tension must be high between the nations, maybe directly with Yurakora.

No. La'Claw is proud, but not stupid. He wouldn't move on the elves, not without cause, not without allies. Sebbarus, maybe? But that's unlikely. The guards have been murmuring about peace talks. But La'Claw wouldn't think of considering peace unless he's cornered. Then I hear them. Their voices peak, not caring of my ears.

"Do you believe what she said was true."

"Of course not. My coin is on her being just another heretic sent by the Holy Light Church."

"You saw all that blood? She definitely broke Zarion's nose," one says, the edge of a laugh in his tone.

"I don't think she realize the trouble that's coming her way. He will get her back."

"But what about the princess's orders?" With that, the men cemented one of my suspicions.

"What about them?"

"She said no harm. Not until her story is confirmed."

"I'm sure he'll find something less... *obvious.*"

"I'm not so sure. Remember what happened last time?"

"Oh, shit. Right. I almost forgot about that."

Their voices carry down the stairs, becoming clearer with every step.

"I'll talk to him. That's too bad too. After that shit she pulled, I thought I lost a nut for a moment. But once my men disprove her bullshit, we all can have our payback."

"I'm not into humans that way."

"Neither am I, *but* it still interesting to watch."

"I didn't know Zarion liked them."

He released a low snort of disgust. "Yeah, I don't get the guy. They've got neither fur, feather or scale. Humans are just naked fairy rats."

"Nothing like your Princess Sarianna."

"She's not *my* Princess."

"That look you gave her earlier, could've fooled me."

"Shut up and get the damn door."

"What about—"

"Don't worry about him. It's spelled. He can't get out, even if we left the door wide open. Just drop the female and go."

"He's been down here so long, he might get at the girl before Zarion."

"Not likely. His kind hates humans. Probably more than the rest of us."

The gate creaks open with a hiss, but the sound is irrelevant. It's the warded barrier. The one laced with a powerful spell that keeps me tethered here like a relic.

"Hey, skin and bones. Listen up. You have a new cellmate. She's a feisty bitch. And in your state with the scraps you're fed down here, even this little human might put you in your place. So this is your warning. Play nice."

A dull thud sounded as a limp body hit the floor. I remain seated in the far corner, unmoving. Their words loop behind my eyes. Mulling over their intentions. They were suspiciously loose with their words. The logic behind their actions is *off*. Sloppy. After all this time, after all their methods, why this? Placing a human female in close proximity to me at the command of Princess Sarianna. A new tactic on behalf of King La'Claw, perhaps?

No. If it were the king, directness is his only method. Which means this is the princess's doing. And she plays a very different game than her father. I find it hard to believe a human female of all things, committed a crime that justifies this punishment. Unless… she too carries secrets that they were unable to extract. Doubtful. No human has the fortitude to withstand such cruelty as I have. She would have cracked in the first hour of torture. I tilt my head towards the girl. She doesn't stir.

Footsteps retreat. Jokes trail after them like a stench. I wait as the guard meager small desolate souls float away in place of their bodies. Warped. Dull. Darken. The one with the twin swords carries more corruption than his companion. His soul, if it can still be called that, is the color of dusty stone. It twists unnaturally, as though the very core of him resists itself. The other is no purer, though less grotesque. His essence bears the same rot I've seen countless times common among the palace guards and those unfortunate enough to survive this kingdom.

I've only ever seen truly pure souls in children. Infants, mostly. Still untouched by the world's teeth. Innocence is a fleeting thing, devoured fast and without mercy. And I must admit, it has been many years since I've looked upon a child. We had many in the old days, in the city I once called home. And in my travels, I caught glimpses of them. Though even then, my second sight wasn't as strong as it is now. Sharpened by the curse. The same unbreakable curse that chains me. Weakens me. A sudden voice cuts through my thoughts as it hiss.

"Owww." The girl stirs. Her speech woven in pain.

The faintest aroma lifts in the cell, honey and iron, wrapped in something delicate and strange. A trace of wildflower. Blood and bloom. She's bleeding, but not badly. A scrape, perhaps, or a bruise cracked open. It's... not unpleasant. A reprieve, even. The cell has long smelled of filth and mildew, rust and the decay of grit dried with corrosion. Her scent is soft. A stark contradiction to everything this place stands for.

But it is unwelcome, because she is a human. And that, above all, makes her presence not only insulting, but treacherous. If this is some ploy by King La'Claw and his daughter, a test of my restraint, a lure made to disarm me with sympathy or seduction. They have chosen poorly. A human? Of all species. They should know better. Let them try. Let them fail.

While Princess Sarianna may not be privy to the full breadth of reasons behind my imprisonment. She is no fool. As the future sovereign of Palloria, she would have been raised on history. Taught the laws, the legends, and the long shadows cast by my kind. If she knows her father harbors a prisoner like me beneath the palace, then she knows enough. More than enough. Which means this human presence has a purpose. But it does not matter. Because I will not speak. I did not speak when the King sent his most seasoned interrogators. Torturers. Attempting to dragged me to the brink, again and again. I gave them nothing. I became silent and unmovable as stone. And I will do the same now.

In fact, I will go one step further. I will not acknowledge her at all. I will not turn to look. Will not shift so much as an inch in her direction. Let her sweat beneath the weight of her isolation. Let her speak into the dark and hear no voice answer back. If she is here as a pawn of the crown, she will fail. If, by some slim chance, she is not. She is still human, and I do not care. This place will devour her in less than two weeks. The hunger, the thirst, the heat, relentless in their pulse. I wonder how long it will take before the scent of starved and sunken death washes away her lingering perfume.

"Ra. Yes, that's right. She said I need to find Ra."

My breath stills. My ears tilt. Every nerve in my body sharpens like a blade being drawn. *What did she just say?*

"Who the fuck is Ra?" She repeats it.

No. I didn't mishear. That name, sacred and sealed, should not be known to her. Not in passing. Not in jest. Not *at all*. And the way she says it... casually, confused. As though she were told. As though someone gave it to her. Who is *she*, the one who spoke the name to this human? Surely not the King. Had it been Korrak, the girl wouldn't be breathing now. No, this smells of something else. Something beyond Palloria. Another kingdom, perhaps?

If so, then this girl may not be a royal pawn. But a liability. A threat. But from the sound of her, panicked, heaving. Does she know the depth of the name she carries or is she being used by another? I listen to the sounds of her struggling, apparently bound at the wrists as her words come between ragged breaths.

"Please... at least can someone untie my hands." She pleads with the dark. Seemingly unaware it listens. Or is this an act?

Not knowing, *I* listen. She for sure said the name. Ra. There is no way this is a coincidence. A name not found in this Kingdom. I cannot ignore this. Concern begins to overtake me. Who is she? Who told her to *find Ra?* What else does she know? And for the first time in years... I speak to another.

"You are wasting your time... and your breath," I say, my voice strain from lack of use.

I hear her shift, startled. "Who's there?" Her voice frayed at the edges. Labored. *Can she not see me?* I can feel the warmth of the lantern fire. That means there's light. I clench my teeth. Either she too is blind, or she's playing at helplessness. The guards never seem to have any trouble with their vision here. Then again, she is human and her eyes are inferior to most species. She lashes out again, kicking at the bars like a child throwing a tantrum. As if force alone could undo the spell.

"You'll need far more than brute strength to break an *enchanted* lock," I reply coldly.

Her breathing is unsteady. Her voice trembles when she yells again. She's frantic. The rhythm of her words, the pitch in her tone. They're too practiced. Too precise. Is it just a performance? Do they think they can make me a fool. If they believe that even in my weakened state I don't have the strength to kill this human. This spy. They are gravely mistaken. Even the best masks can't hide the truth from me. No matter how clever or talented, corruption always leaves its stain. Lying, deceit, manipulation. These are tools of espionage. And they leave markings deep into the soul. Even the most skilled can't escape that. Not from me. Not from these eyes.

I shift my senses, tinting my vision toward her essence. Piercing through body, blood and bone. I peer into what she *is*, not what she *pretends* to be. I expect to see the usual rotten soul. A crooked shape. A darkened hue. Murky, twisted, stained with falsehood. But what I see stops me cold.

The sight before me... it doesn't make sense. Not with how she is performing. Not with what I *suspect*.

This essence is... *Pure*? Unmarked by corruption. That can't be right. The thought I was forming withers before it can complete itself. *Who is this human?* And what in the world is she doing here? A sphere. No larger than a handball. Her soul is smaller than what I'm used to seeing. It floated just above her chest as most of them do. But it's color...

I've never seen anything like it. Normally, the more corrupt the soul, the darker and duller its dim. Infants, in their untouched innocence, shine in the purest shade of white. But this human... her soul is not white. It *glows*, in a way that's unfamiliar. It's bright, yet subtly touch with the faintest hue of pink. It isn't a color I've ever witnessed in the soul of any human before. She's not acting. Her panic is genuine. Her gasps for breath are real. I don't think she's here with ulterior motives, or at least none she is aware of. I can hear her terror. And tragically, she has every right to be. Though she's human, pure souls are rare and I pity hers, if only a little. I would say she will suffer in the coming months, but I know she won't last that long.

"The more you struggle, the worse things will get," I say, aiming to warn her. But the moment she responds, I hear the edge in my own tone. I realize my words were interpreted as a threat. That was not my intent.

"No. Stay the fuck back. I fucking ma— I fucking mean it— I'll... I'll beat your..." Her voice fractures as she fights to breathe. "I have to... I have to get out of here."

It has been many years since I've spoken to another. The guards used to try on dares or on drunken wagers. They'd try to draw words from me. None succeeded. I used to speak to myself, to give illusion to thoughts shared aloud. But as the feedings grew fewer, and my body weaker, even that became an unnecessary indulgence. I thought solitude would sharpen the mind. That silence would give rise to clarity. But all it gave was stillness.

"I—I can't breathe." Her voice is thinner now, drowning in fear. "Please. Outside. Please."

She doesn't understand the gravity of her situation. She believes she is a prisoner. A simple one. But this... this is something far worse. We are not prisoners. We are ghosts. Secrets the crown buried in the bowels of stone. Locked away so the world can forget we ever existed. Just a slow fade into nothing.

"That's not happening. You're never leaving here."

"What? No. No no no no. Not again. Please, God. Anything... but this... any—"

She goes silent. Too sudden. I tilt my head, listening. Nothing. No movement. No gasping. She's gone still. Likely passed out. Still, something in her last words claw at me. *'Not again.'* What did she mean? I am certain there is nothing that she has endured that will rival what awaits her here. She doesn't know it yet. But she soon will.

After a few minutes, I attempt to rise to my feet. It's gotten harder lately. It has been a long time since I've moved more than ten feet from this spot, usually just to relieve myself in the hole carved into the back center of the floor. A crude drain feeding into the palace's underground water system. I suppose it's one we'll be sharing now... for however long she lasts. My stomach groans with effort as I shift towards her, the motion more creeping than stride. I kneel beside the unconscious girl, lean in as I angle my head until I can hear the soft rise and fall of her chest. Her breathing is already beginning to steady.

Good. If I want answers, real ones, I need her conscious and lucid. She said the name *Ra*. There's no mistaking that. My ears have never failed me. She spoke it with confusion, which means someone gave it to her. Told her to seek him. Whoever that someone is... I need to know. Are they an enemy or a messenger?

Some humans don't give up the right information if the wrong kind of pressure is placed. And the way she was unraveling... Fear is a strong motivator, yes. But for the fragile, it is also an anchor. It drags them into the depths of panic, and from there, words become incoherent, unreliable. I'll need to keep her breathing easy long enough to get the right answers.

A task that will prove challenging in this twenty-foot stone tomb. She mentioned her hands being bound. I shall start there. I lower myself, and inch my hand toward the warmth of her body. My hand brushes something soft, yet textured, a number of thin rope-like masses. Braids. Her hair. Three strands or more, woven together. The texture is coarser than mine, yet there's a certain richness to it. I find myself lingering there longer than I should, running the braid between my fingers, appreciating the consistency. It is a texture I have rarely touched in this world... and something in me finds it oddly beautiful. One that doesn't seem worthy of the species. I release her hair and move my hand forward, grazing fabric. Her shoulder. She's collapsed on her side. It makes it easier. Her arms should be just—

My hand trails down the sleeve of her shirt until it meets her skin. A jolt, immediate and gone in a flash as it shoots through my hand. *Static?* I tilt my head down at the girl. This human... That feeling caught me off guard. I refrain from recoiling. It's been a long time since I felt anything like that. The last time, I was home. The memories of which I have no desire to revisit. Not anymore. I shift my focus back to the girl, fingers tracing the knot at her wrists. The rope is rough and tightly wound, biting into her skin with such force it could probably draw blood.

From the feel of it, the guards made sure she couldn't even begin to free herself. If left like this, the fibers would continue to split her flesh, and given Palloria's disregard for prisoner's well-being, an infection would begin the process of a slow death. I untangle the knot and remove the rope. If she didn't notice me before, it tells me the cell is as dimly lit as I suspected. Carefully, I withdraw, making my way toward the center of the room, where the warmth of the enchanted lantern above casts its glow.

King Korrak La'Claw placed it there himself, a cruel reminder. As long as I remain bound by this curse, I will never have access to my own magic. I sit in the center of the room and cross my legs beneath me, settling into stillness. I'll wait. However long it takes, I'll wait. I need to know what she knows. There is no other option. Unfortunately, it takes longer than I would've liked. But I am a very, *very* patient male. I don't know if it's day or night, but I've learned to keep track of time in my head. It's one of the few things I can still control. A little over nineteen hours and seventeen minutes pass before her body finally stirs. If not for the whispers of the rise and fall of her chest, I would've thought her dead.

"Wait... Mitus." she mumbles.

I uncross my arms slowly, angling my posture to appear open, unguarded, non-threatening. I can't speak to how I look anymore. I haven't seen myself in ages, but I know how to control presence. She shifts again. The faint rustling of her clothes tells me she's upright now, rubbing at something. Likely her wrists. I imagine the marks left by the rope will remain for days. Still, I don't speak. I wait. Let her see me first. Let her be the one to communicate. She's already been startled once. No need to repeat it. Let's see how much she remembers and how much she'll tell me, now that her panic has passed.

KALIYAH

"Ugh." Is it too much to ask to wake up without feeling like I've *never* slept at all? I rub my chest, wincing. This freakin' cave floor is making even my chest hurt now. Wait... cave? No. That's not right. I should be at Saphire's family tavern.

My hand drags up over my face, fingers pressing against my forehead like maybe I can squeeze some clarity out of my skull. I peek through the cracks in my fingers with one eye, fully expecting to see *him*. Mitus. Lurking from across the room the way he does in my dreams. Watching and waiting like some pervy sleep paralysis demon with abs.

But it's dark. The moment my eye cracks open, everything floods back. The fox princess. The guards. The cell. The way I couldn't breathe. The rope that burned into my wrists. The same ropes that are no longer binding my hands. And... *That figure*. My body reacts as my eyes land on someone sitting across from me. I jerk backward so fast I slam the back of my head against the stone wall behind me.

"Fuck fuck *fuck*! Owwww." My hands fly to cradle my head, my knees pulling tight to my chest, elbows brushing against each other. I hiss through my teeth, biting back a few more curses. Then I see him again. And I stop. Everything just stops.

He's sitting dead-center in the room, maybe ten feet away, directly beneath the flickering, dim glow of a lantern anchored high above us. The light barely touches anything else, but it clings to him. His posture is too calm, too still. Legs cross, arms resting at his sides like he's meditating... or waiting.

I don't move. Don't blink. His skin is dark. So deep it seems to *drink* the little light there is. It's smooth like a rich espresso or aged wood. And his white locs, they spill past his shoulders, long enough to brush his waist, casting shadows across most of his face. The color of his hair doesn't match his youthful appearance. From what I can see, he looks young. Around my age, maybe a little older. He's lean. Even from here, I can see the definition in his frame, not bulky, but sculpted, tight, compact muscle. And though he's seated, there's a length to him, a stretch of limb and posture that speaks of height. He's as tall as me. Probably taller. And his clothes, threadbare and torn in places, beige fabric so worn it's nearly translucent against his skin. His feet are bare.

If I wasn't so terrified, I might even say he's beautiful. But not in the delicate, kiss-the-princess sort of way. No. He's the kind of beautiful that carries warnings. Dangerous. Lethal. The kind of beauty you admire from a far, like a black mamba. And then there's the blindfold or whatever is covering his eyes. It's too dark to tell exactly what it is. A strip of cloth, maybe. Or something else. *Why is he—?*

"Who the hell are you?" I whisper, mostly to myself. But I don't think it matters. I can tell he's been waiting for me to wake up. At first, I think he's asleep, maybe meditating. He looks like a damn statue. But no. I recognize this energy too well. The tension in his posture. The stillness that's too precise to be unintentional. It's the same thing I used to feel with Mitus. That alertness. That subtle awareness of everything around him.

He *knows* I'm awake and I know for damn sure, he's awake too. I squint, trying to make sense of him in the faint flicker of lantern light. There. Clearly visible through the fall of his hair. Long pointed ears. He's not human. But I think I knew that already. I've never seen anyone that looked like him before and then the vibes I'm getting. Nope. Definitely not human. That panic from earlier. It's still alive and kicking. From trapped in a mountain to trapped in a dungeon. I don't know how I ended up in a life this cursed.

Grampa used to say, *"Sometimes the children pay for the sins of their fathers."* And I swear, if someone could just tell me who mine was, I'd grab Grampa's shotgun and deal with him myself. Whatever the hell that man did, the price must've been *biblical.*

Maybe it's not him… maybe it's me. Maybe I did something terrible in a past life, or I wronged the wrong person. There was that one guy I went out with a couple of times. I remember his sister was into voodoo. Maybe she cursed me after I ghosted him. No matter what I do, things just keep escalating from bad, to worse, to fucked. And now, here I am. Locked in a cell with something I know probably could kill me with a flick of his finger.

There's no magic sigils keeping us apart. Just space and opportunity and… him. *Alright. I admit it, Fate. You play a wild game. I'll always hate you for putting me through this shit. I'm choosing not to be mad about it anymore. But I'm tired. So, let's get this over with.* I wonder if it'll hurt. A tear slides down my cheek, cooler than expected. *Who am I kidding. When is death ever gentle?* And he already warned me. *'The more I struggle, the worse it'll get'.* So I'll try not to fight. Though knowing me, my survival instincts will probably kick in, so resisting them will be another battle.

"If I asked you to make it quick and painless, are you the type of creature that would agree to something like that?"

He doesn't answer.

"Of course not," I mutter. I push myself onto my hands and knees and crawl toward him. "If you wanted to minimize my suffering, you would've killed and eaten me in my sleep." I settle onto my knees barely a foot from him now. Heartbeat reverberating throughout my body. "Which means you probably want me terrified and in pain. Based on the last man-beast I interacted with, I'm starting to think fear must make the meat taste better or something."

"Man-beast?"

My body jumps at his sudden words. So it was him. Seeing the words actually come out of his mouth is just as frightening as not seeing him at all. Now that I'm closer, I can see him better. And he looks... worse than I realized. Like he hasn't eaten in a while. His skin is stretched taut over his frame. He looks worn. Withered. Like someone who's forgotten what it's like to be full. And the messed up part, I recognize that look. I've been there. That gnawing emptiness. The sharp edge of desperation when you think maybe... *maybe* your body might turn in on itself just to survive. And I hate it. I hate that even now... I can empathize with him.

"You believe my intentions are to *eat*—?"

"I don't appreciate you waiting until I'm conscious to do what you're planning. You're an evil asshole for that. But... I've made peace with this. So whenever you're ready... I am too." I squeezed my eyes shut, balled my fists into the fabric of my pants, and held my breath. I heard movement. A faint shift in the air. My whole body tensed as I braced for whatever was coming.

And then, *ugh*, I pissed my own self off. Because the whole time, a single thought raced through my head. And it wasn't, *'I'm about to be eaten by a man-beast.'* No. It was *'This isn't the right man-beast.'* I don't want *him* to be the one to do it. Which is *so* messed up, even by my standards. Then, in one sudden moment, I felt something touch my shoulder.

My body reacted before my brain did. I swung. My eyes flew open right as my fist connected clean with his jaw. His head snapped to the side, but he caught himself with one hand against the floor. Silent, he wiped the blood from his lip with his thumb.

"Oh, shit. I'm sorry! Are you okay? I didn't mean to. I don't know what happened. My body just kind of... *moved*. Let's try again."

"Try again?" he repeated.

"Yeah. I think I can be still this time."

He tilted his head, as though studying me. "Human girl, what kind of *man-beast*..." the word coming out forced, "do you perceive me to be?"

"Um... I'm not exactly sure. No tusks, so not an orc. You've got a lean build, and there's an allure about you. So, um... a vampire."

"A vampire?" he echoed, sounding genuinely offended.

Wait. Was he not? Damn it. I should have known it wouldn't work out for me like that. I was really hoping to avoid my flesh being ripped from my bones. Vampires seemed classier. A less painful option.

"Are you not? A friend of mine told me they exist in this world."

"This world?" he repeated, voice shifting slightly.

Dang, I got him good. Busted lip for sure. And I didn't even hit him as hard as I could have. Then a dangerous, stupid, probably wrong, but what-the-hell thought just dawned on me. Whatever this man-beast-thing is… its weak. Weak as hell if I could tag him like that. I stood up fast and jumped back several feet, dropping into a stance Grampa would've been proud of. Feet planted. Elbows in. Ready to strike. I glanced down at him again. I've thrown harder punches at Mitus, and he acted as if I was planting soft kisses on him. But this guy? I made him move. I made him bleed. *Hell yeah. I can take him.*

"I've changed my mind," I said, chin high. "If you want your meal, you're gonna have to work for it."

He tilted his head up, following me despite the cloth over his eyes. He exhaled deeply and with one hand on his knee, rose to his full height. Yup, taller than me and definitely lean. I steadied myself. Just like Grampa taught me.

'Let them come to you. Dodge, then dominate. Once you've got the upper hand, don't let them recover.'

He stood for only a moment. I waited. Waited for him to make his move. He turned around. And started walking back to his side of the room. Not bothering to look back. I waited for the fake-out. The sudden spin. The lunge. *Any second now.*

But he didn't. He just retook his seat. Legs gapped. Posture perfect. Same as before.

"What are you *doing*?" I demanded. "Come at me, man-beast!"

He let out a breath that sounded like the spirit of patience leaving his body. "Refrain from calling me *'man-beast.'* Unless you'd prefer I refer to you as *'female-vermin'.*"

I blinked.

"I have no intentions of… *coming at you*," he repeats my phrase as if the words were unbecoming of him. "I don't know what backwater human village spat you out, where you can't recognize an elf when you see one. But I am not some low-level bloodsucking fae. *Not* a vampire." He folded his hands neatly in his lap. "I'm beginning to suspect you're either willfully ignorant, or human education has decayed into absolute irrelevance. Either way, allow me to say this plainly, just in case it hasn't sunk in. Elves do not *eat* humans. No more than humans eat fae."

"Bullshit," I shot back without missing a beat. And for the first time in days, maybe weeks, I felt something stir in my chest that wasn't despair. I felt *confident*.

"Bullshit?" he repeats.

"Yeah. I call bullshit. I know you're lying. Ever since I got dragged into this dumb ass world, nothing is ever what I think it is. And the moment I choose to believe otherwise my situation gets so much worse. So no. This time, I'm choosing not to believe whatever I'm told."

He does not say anything, just turns away, lying on his side with his back to me. "I understand now," he mumbles to himself. "I overanalyzed the situation, as I always do. Clearly, it was nothing more than a coincidence. You're nothing more than an imbecilic human female. There's no reason for me to concern myself with you. You'll perish in what feels like a blink to me."

I narrow my eyes. Not sure what he's talking about. But that definitely sounds like a threat to me. "And I finally understand too. If I want to survive in a place like this, I'll have to adapt. Be more like you monsters."

"Monsters?" he repeats after me again. I can hear slight irritation.

"You want me to believe you're *not* going to eat me? After everything I've been through, that's just not possible. So I'll adapt. I'll make *you* feel the same way I do."

He stays silent. He doesn't get it yet. Oh, but he will.

"Whether you're a bloodsucker pretending to be one of the elf people, or an actual elf pretending you don't eat humans, you threatened me. So,

I'm betting at some point you most likely told me a lie. So, from now on, I'm choosing to become more like *you* creatures. As long as I'm in this cell, *I* will be your predator."

A pause. A long one.

"Have humans truly regressed to the point where their words no longer make sense to the rest of civilization?"

"I'm assuming elves are some kind of fae."

"Elves are of the highest order of fae. You'd do well to remember that. If you were to speak to another elf the way you speak to me, they would not restrain themselves from punishing such blatant disrespect."

I snort. Its time to fuck with him. "You wouldn't know this, but where I'm from, there are documented cases of humans eating other humans."

He makes a noise of disgust. "You're referring to cannibalism."

"So you *do* know the word. That means it's happened here too."

"Depraved," he snaps, as if the word itself stains his mouth.

"You said humans don't eat fae. How would you know?"

"*Come*... again?" he says, the barest tinge of confusion in his voice. But I can tell he knows exactly where I'm going with this.

"There's got to be a few out there," I say, watching the slim muscles in his back tense. His ragged shirt hides little. I wasn't sure if provoking him would work, but I'll be damned if I let him catch me slipping.

I considered charging him. But no. The way he casually turned his back to me, too relaxed. It screams trap. He could have something stashed near him. A weapon. A shiv would change everything. But if I can avoid a fatal hit and manage to get in close, I still like my chances. Finally, Grampa's *'for the streets'* lessons are going to be good for something.

"What?" he finally says, his tone clipped. "Are you suggesting humans go around eating elves?"

"No," I reply simply. "Not saying that."

"Then what *exactly* are you saying?"

Still, he won't face me. Okay. Time to be direct.

"I told you I'm willing to adapt, and right now, I don't remember the last time I ate. Honestly? I'm starving. I'm human. You're fae. I've never tasted fae before. How would I know I don't like it... if I've never tried it?"

Silence. Thick and heavy. I let the thought hang in the air a moment too long, then start stomping my feet hard against the ground like I'm charging him. It works. In a flash, he's on his feet, pivoting to face me in a low crouch, arms ready. He's bracing for me. I expected a weapon. A blade, maybe something hidden in those tattered rags. But his hands are empty.

Still, his presence alone is worse than a blade. The energy in the room shifted in an instant. *That feeling.* The one I felt the moment I first woke up and he made his presence known... it's back. Twice as strong. My knees almost give out under me.

Okay. Maybe I *don't* want the smoke. Maybe I want to take back *everything* I just said. We stay like that locked in some kind of standoff. His body tense. Mine pretending not to tremble. And even though he's facing me now, I notice something strange. He never looks me in the face. Not once. It's like... he can't.

Is he blind? The question buzzes in my mind, but I keep it to myself. My legs burn. I'm exhausted. But I'll let my muscles shrivel before I sit and give him any kind of advantage. Twenty minutes pass. Maybe thirty. I can't tell. I don't know. I can't tell time without a freakin' phone.

Finally, he lowers himself back to the ground, still facing me this time. I hesitate. Just for a second. Then I drop to the floor like a sack of potatoes, too tired to make it graceful.

We sit. Breathing. Watching. Waiting.

CHAPTER 22
DEAL OR NO DEAL

KALIYAH

Idiot. I did this. Didn't think it through. My eyes have finally adjusted to the dark, but it's not helping. The elf blends into the shadows like he was carved from them. I can barely make out where he ends and the stone begins. And now, of course, my stomach decides to chime in with the most *furious* growl. I clutch at it with both hands like that'll muffle the noise. I glance toward the elf. Still motionless. With that thing over his eyes, I still can't tell if he's asleep or just waiting for me to do something stupid.

Great. To make matters worse, I have to pee. *Bad.* I pull my knees in tighter, like that'll somehow fix the internal pressure building inside me. It doesn't of course. I sniff the air cautiously, careful not to take my eyes off him. His ear twitches. Okay. So he's not asleep.

The air smells... awful. Dirt. Sweat. Musty stone. But not urine or poop, and I don't see any buckets, so maybe... maybe he doesn't do his business *in here.* Maybe there's a bathroom schedule or something. Maybe the guards come and take him out at certain times. That wouldn't be so bad. I could finally get clean air. *But wait.* What if... what if elves don't poop? Oh no. What if they just *absorb* their food? Like, it disintegrates in their stomachs. *Nope.* I *don't* like where that thought is going. I should just ask him when the restroom times are. My mouth opens, pauses, then closes.

Yeah. I *should* ask the mysterious, blindfolded, possibly-starving fae that I threatened to eat, about his bathroom habits. Sounds like a *fun* idea. God, what *is* wrong with me? Why did I say that? *I'll eat you?* Did I really threaten to eat a whole ass man alive? Who *does* that? I frown hard. I don't even recognize myself anymore. *This is all that stupid orc's fault.* His crazy totally rubbed off on me. That's the only explanation. The dull annoyance in my chest creeps up again. A soreness between my cavity that feels like a bad joke at this point. I press my palm to it, trying to soothe the ache. It helps. Barely.

"Damn it," I mutter. "Is it too much to ask for a freakin' Advil?" Also, it's *toasty as hell* in here. I'm seriously considering stripping off my shirt just to fan myself. I sneak another glance at the elf. Still sitting there. Still impossibly still. He must be able to see me through that *whatever it is*. Out of curiosity, I raise my hand slowly and wave it back and forth. No reaction. Then again, I *did* threaten to digest him earlier. Maybe he's just not interested in waving at his unhinged, possibly cannibalistic cellmate. Can't really blame him.

I should apologize. But... would he even believe me? *Hell, I wouldn't believe me.* So now what? I've created a nightmare situation where I can't take anything back, and if I don't fix it soon, I'll be sleeping with one eye open. Assuming I *ever* sleep again. It's the mountain all over again. I promised myself that wouldn't happen again. I shift my weight, trying to ease the pressure on my bladder, when something jabs into my hip. Hard.

Ow— what the...? I dig into the front pocket of my pants. The one that curves into my hip and pull out the magic crystal Noiz gave me. *No way.* You mean to tell me I had this stupid rock the whole time? If I'd just found it earlier. If I hadn't panicked and blanked on the name of the damn town I was supposed to visit first 'Emissary Cove'... of course I remember it now, I wouldn't be stuck in a dungeon, fresh off my first prison fight.

I grip the crystal tight. "Earth," I whisper. "Houston... my apartment... Grampa." Nothing. "Take me home." I pour everything into it. Hope, desperation, guilt, every last drop of fear I've been trying to ignore. Still nothing. Furious, I throw the stone at the wall. It hits hard with a *clack* and bounces back. Immediately, the elf jerks upright, turning his head toward the sound. His entire body shifts ready and alert. That reaction confirms it.

He really is blind. And I... Oh god. I insulted, threatened, and *punched* a blind man. A blind man who, for all I can tell now, *never* intended to harm me. I thought this place hadn't broken me yet. That I was still *me*. The good-hearted Kaliyah. The one who gave people the benefit of the doubt. Who judged by actions, not words. Who stayed kind, even when it was hard. But somewhere along the way... I stopped being her. I want her back. I squeeze the fabric of my sleeve, pulling it so tight it might tear. My head drops into my arms. I press in, trying to hide the sting behind my eyes, trying to keep that last piece of myself from slipping away.

THUD. A heavy sound. Followed by footsteps. I spring to my feet and grab onto the gate.

"Excuse me, sir. I need—"

"*Get the fuck back!*"

One of them growls. *Growls.* My mouth snaps shut. It's only when they step into the light that I see it. One of them has the head of a wildcat. The other is more humanoid, but his face has sharp fangs and twitching ears like a wolf or dog. I shriek and immediately backpedal, pressing myself flat against the opposite wall. The barred door creaks open. And when it does, I *recognize* him. Bandage on the nose. Oh crap. It's the one I head budded.

"Uh... Guard, sir," I stammer, lifting a hand nervously, "I just wanted to apologize for what I—"

He cuts me off with another growl, clearly meant to intimidate. And it *does* catch me off guard. But not in the way he wants. Because, honestly? Next to Mitus's guttural, soul-rattling growls, this guy's attempt sounds like a puppy with laryngitis.

"You owe me a lot more than a *fucking apology,*" he snaps. "You broke my fucking nose, you *cunt.*"

My lips press tightly together. Not from fear. Oh no. Because that would have been the correct reaction. Nope. My dumb ass all of a sudden felt the urge to laugh. No freakin' idea where its coming from. I just know this is not the time or place.

What's wrong with me, right now? His whole vibe is suddenly hilarious. Maybe it's the dog ears twitching furiously on top of his head. Maybe it's those little baby fangs he's baring like I'm supposed to be scared. Or maybe it's just the fact that he called me a word I thought was exclusive to my world.

Cunt? Didn't we invent that? Heck, did *we* get it from *them*? I don't know. My lips are trembling. My shoulders start to shake. Oh my god, he has a tiny tail and its wagging. Its like, really short, compared to his height. With the way he's coming at me, that's probably not the only thing of his that's *short*.

Stop it. Don't do that. I swiftly raise my hands to cover my mouth trying to hide the smile that threatens to break through. This is serious. Don't smile. Don't you freakin' smile. My eyes widen because I know the moment the grin hits my lips, the laughter will soon follow.

No. *No.* Think about something else. Anything else. Right, *my bladder.* If I laugh, I *will* pee myself. My bladder's so full it's practically begging for an excuse. *Girl* hold it in. I don't want to piss off the guards any more than I already have. Or should I say... *guard dog.* The guard says something else, but I'm too lost in my own thought to catch it. So I just shake my head instinctively answering the unknown question. My eyes dart to the other guard, the quieter one holding a tray. A distraction. Yes. Focus on that one.

But then the guard dog says, "No. *You look at me.*"

I see him move closer out of the corner of my eyes. My back's already against the wall. I can't move back any further.

"I *said* look at me, *bitch.*"

Me? The bitch? Last we met, I would have sworn *he was* a female dog the way I made him bleed. I snicker on the inside. *Crap. It's coming.* No, Kaliyah. Shove that shit back down. Now. My hands grip my mouth even tighter and I squeeze my eyes shut. Yeah nah. I'm about to let loose.

"There's no need to tremble, lamb. Not yet anyway."

He's totally misreading my reaction. That's fine. Honestly? I'm *grateful* for that, but I hope he doesn't say another word because the level of disrespect this puppy chow is about to feel when my laugh hit his ears.

Unfortunately... I get my wish. He doesn't have to say anything else, because in one move he shifts my entire demeanor. A single, rough, calloused finger dragging slowly up the inside of my forearm.

Every ounce of humor I'd been holding onto evaporates. The laughter tickling at my throat... gone instantaneously. I open my eyes just as his mouth parts, tongue slipping out to wet the cracks in what he probably thinks are lips. His gaze is locked on me. Too familiar. I've seen this look before. Forty different times in the Bloodthorn Forest. On that drunk at the tavern. It's hunger, but not the kind you can feed with food.

"Wait... you're a *guard*." My voice comes out nearly as a question.

His eyes widen at that. *Too* wide. And I can read it clearly now. Excitement.

"Zarion," The second guard calls sharply. "I'm sure Commander Lymon already spoke with you about Princess Sarianna's orders regarding the prisoner's care."

"He did."

"Then back away from the human."

Zarion doesn't move at first. His eyes narrow instead, like he's weighing his options. But eventually, he backs off. Watching me as he returns to the door. It's only now, as she steps into the cell, that I realize the second guard is a woman. She holds out a tray to me.

"This is yours. As instructed by Princess Sarianna, you'll receive three meals a day until the investigation into your claims concludes, or Her Highness decides otherwise."

She turns to go but pauses mid-step, glancing toward the far corner. "Keep your distance from that one. Elves have never been known to be kind to humans." With that, she heads for the door, and both guards step out, sealing it shut behind them.

I take a step forward, tray in hand. "Excuse me, ma'am. Lady guard."

She stops. Her tone sharpens immediately. "What?"

"I need to use the bathroom."

She blinks, then scoffs. "What are you telling me for? That's what the hole in the floor is for." She nods toward the back of the cell.

"What?"

"You've got business, you handle it there."

I glance toward the elf in the corner. She sees where I'm looking.

"You needn't worry about him. He can't see. And even if he could, he wouldn't bother. Elves... well, they have never been known to violate women, let alone human women. It's not in their nature."

Her gaze tilts briefly toward Zarion. Mine does too. I wish it hadn't. The look in his eyes is still there. Ugly. Vile.

"Let's go," the female guard says.

Zarion smirks, a crooked grin tugging at the bandage on his face as they ascend the stairs. Only when I hear the heavy *THUD* of the upstairs door slamming shut above us do I realize I've been holding my breath. And I finally let it go. I look down at the metal tray. Worn, scuffed in places, but the food on it wasn't the tasteless sludge I'd braced for.

In the largest section, a scoop of something that looked like lentils or beans. The earthy scent hits me, and my stomach groans. Nestled beside that is a portion of slow-cooked meat dark, tender, and glistening in its own juices. Goat, maybe... or lamb.

Lamb. Uck. Can't believe he fixed his mouth to call me that. Suddenly I'm not in the mood for meat. Next to it is a small pile of roasted vegetables. Onions, bell peppers, something blue, and something else vaguely resembling zucchini. They're charred just slightly at the edges, and there's oil glistening on their skin.

In the corner, a thick piece of flatbread. Still warm. I tear a piece off, and it smells like garlic, salt, and fresh flour. Balanced neatly on top of the tray is a tin cup of water. Cool. *Not* cold. A bead of condensation slides down its side as I lift it, and it stings my lip in the best way.

It reminds me immediately of another pressing issue. I need to pee. I set the tray down on the ground, slowly, and glance back toward where the female guard had gestured earlier. And sure enough, there it is. My glorious, eight-inch toilet hole in the floor. I hear it now. An extremely faint hum I'd picked up a few times but I thought I was hearing things. Water, moving beneath the floor. A stream maybe? Or maybe I'm just stalling. I glance toward the elf. Still unmoving. Still silent. Same spot. Same posture.

Great. Guess it can't be helped. Not the first time I've had to relieve myself with an audience and if fate keeps putting my piece on the board, it won't be the last. I need bonus points for this crap. I reach for the laces of my pants, but the second I do, I hear a shift. Immediately, I snap upright, drawing my fist up on instinct. But when I look, I see he's turned. Quietly. Just shifted so his back is fully to me.

Is he giving me privacy? How could he have *known*—? *No. Later.* I've got to freakin' go. I fumble my laces open, yank my pants down, and squat over the hole, peeing like it's the last time I'll ever get to. A full-body *exhale* comes out of me, pure relief and just as quickly, humiliation.

Unlike the caves, where the waterfall masked everything, here it's dead quiet. The gentle trickle of the stream beneath me doesn't even register as background noise. Meanwhile, *mine* echoes off the stone like I'm performing a damn solo. I bite the inside of my cheek so hard it aches. And just as that embarrassment settles in, another horrible thought slaps me.

Oh my god... Mitus has super hearing. Which means the whole time we were in the cave. *He heard everything.* Every awkward sound. Every single trip to the bathroom. And now that I think about it—

Ugh. There were so many times I needed to go to the rest room and Mitus treated it like some kind of game. Climbing up the walls like a freaky spider trying to find ways to see pass my barricades. I didn't catch on at first. But towards the end... Yeah. I realized exactly what he was doing. Creepy as shit. Dickhead.

At least this elf, whoever he is has *some* kind of manners. I walked back to my side of the cell and sat down next to the tray. I examined the metal plate again. No utensils in sight. Were they expecting me to use my *hands*? The scent hit me again, and my stomach twisted. But I hesitated. My eyes flicked toward him. I didn't see a tray on his side. Did he not get one? He leaned slightly forward into the wall, and I caught the outline of his spine through the thin, worn fabric. Something sour bloomed in my mouth. The guard had said *I'd* be getting three meals a day. *There's no way he is.* I took a long sip from the cup. It was cool and refreshing, then set it down. I picked up the bread and placed the rest of the tray in the center of the room, exactly where he'd been sitting when I punched him. I watched his pointed ear twitch. He was listening. He's catching every sound.

Once I returned to my seat, I spoke, "Excuse me... Mr. Elf?"
Silence.

"Um... I want to apologize. For you know... before. What I said and more importantly, what I did. I had my reasons, but none of them excuse what I did. You did nothing to me to deserve that."

Still no response. But I wasn't fooled. He was listening. From the way he'd spoken earlier, arrogant, sure, but clearly educated. I knew he was deliberately not speaking to me.

"Because of that I would like to give you my food as like a peace offering. I left the food in the spot you were first sitting when I woke up." I stupidly pointed like he could see me. "It's got some meat, beans, roasted vegetables. There's also a cup of water on top, so you want to be careful not to spill it. Okay, that's all I wanted to say."

I pause.

"...No, wait. One more thing. I'm not a cannibal or anything. I don't eat people or fae people. I just said all that because I thought it'd provoke you to attack me. That was wrong. I really am sorry."

I didn't know what I expected. An insult, the middle finger, or maybe even him diving toward the tray like an animal. He did none of the above. Instead, he turned. Faced me. Sat against the opposite wall, one leg bent, the other cocked lazily out in front of him, his arm resting casually over his knee. Then, finally, he spoke.

"If your plan had played out as you'd hoped and I *had* attacked you. What were you going to do to me?"

Damn. Did *not* expect that. Still, fair question.

"I was going to lay hands." I say, but then backtrack, remembering that's a phrase from back home. "or I mean fight you."

He tilted his head. "And?"

"*And*?" I repeat.

"Say you succeeded in initiating this combat between us. Then what?"

I blinked. "I'm not sure what you're asking."

"I'm asking, were you going to attempt to end my life?"

"What? No! Of course not!"

I think wrinkles form on his forehead. Too hard to tell for sure. But he seem skeptical. Why is he giving me the impression that that was a strange answer. Murder isn't just a thing people back home do. At least for most of the people I know. Except for Gramps. He's never told me such. But the stories I've heard and the way he said he use to roll back in his day, ain't no way that old man doesn't have a body or two under his belt.

"But you *presumed* I had plans to kill and *eat you*. Yet you say you were not prepared to end my life. Now who's telling the lie."

"No, um... I don't know. I guess I just wasn't thinking that far ahead."

"Hmmm. Are you considered a youngling among your species?"

"A youngling?"

He rose to his feet, stretching slightly before moving to the center of the room. I watch, still bracing for the worse.

"One that is still undergoing development from child to adulthood. That would explain the ignorance. A child not yet educated in the ways of the world."

He squatted down just in front of the tray. His hand moved toward the cup with a grace and certainty that made me question his lack of sight.

"No. I um... I'm not a *youngling*. An adult. I'm twenty-seven.."

He raised the cup to his lips and took sharp long gulps, then set it aside with a quiet sigh. "Hardly. But I know in human years it's different. In that case, it would mean you are nothing more than an impulsive ignorant fool with little resolve. No surprise."

"What did you... That's not—" I started, pausing mid-sentence, unsure of how I even wanted to respond to that.

"That's not *what*?" He lifted the hunk of meat from the tray and brought it to his nose, inhaling deeply. "Do you plan on finishing a complete sentence, or have you finally exhausted the words in your scant vocabulary?"

And then, completely unfazed. He placed the palm-sized piece of meat into his mouth and began to chew slowly, deliberately, like every bite mattered. Like he was trying to remember what food even tasted like. It wasn't lost on me that he'd just insulted my intelligence *again*. And if I wasn't a college-educated woman with a degree to prove it, maybe I *would* have been offended. But instead, I found myself too focused on *how* he was eating. The pace. The control. The way he swallowed like his throat had forgotten how to trust food again. His Adam's apple bobbed slowly, reluctantly, like even his tongue was debating whether or not it wanted to share with his belly. He started to lift the tray from the floor.

Grampa words fluttered to my mind. *'Don't ever let a ninja play in your face or they'll turn disrespect into tradition. Treat you like the joke and retaliate when you don't laugh.'*

Grampa was almost never wrong. Not about the streets. So, I'm with it now. How smart could he *really* be if he ended up locked in here too? Pompous prick and after I'm sharing my food with him. But I've got time today. Hell, that's all I got. I sat up straighter, flipped my braids over my shoulder, and cleared my throat like I was about to give a damn TED Talk. Deciding this was the perfect time to dust off my minor in communication.

Matching his energy I say, "Naturally not, I possess an extensive vocabulary refined enough to honor those who've cultivated my intellect, and certainly expansive enough to match your level of discourse. However, verbosity has never really been my aesthetic. I find it tedious. Noise masquerading as nuance.

His chewing slowed.

"More to the point, I recognize this for what it is. Your petulant attempts at a get back, because this *youngling...* handled you." I mocked.

Yup. *Laid that motha-freakin' hand,* son. Mailed and delivered. No signature required. Don't think I forgot the way you folded. I could dig into him more. But no. I'm not gonna go too hard. He's blind, clearly starving in spite of his composure and I did assault him and I feel guilty about it.

"So, I'll let it slide *this* time. But don't mistake my calm for acceptance. Continue to insult me like that, and I *will* show you just how ignorant I can get."

He froze mid-lift of the tray, pausing just long enough to let me know he'd heard *every word.* Then, without a single glance in my direction, he tilted the tray and let the roasted vegetables and beans spill into his mouth. Another long chew. Another slow swallow. Then he placed the tray gently back down on the floor. No comeback. No pompous retort. He turned toward me, facing me fully now and for a moment I actually thought he might say *thank you.* But he didn't. Instead, he simply stood, walked back to his side of the cell, and laid down again, back turned toward me.

God, he reminds me of Mitus. But in a totally opposite way. Mitus looks like a brute, but every now and then he had these majestic moments. This elf guy. He looks fragile, but *moves* like he could destroy someone in the blink of an eye. I can't get a solid read on him. Hopefully... just *maybe*... he's starting to believe I don't plan on attacking him again. As for me... I can't say the same. I'm not sleeping anytime soon. Just as I roll my neck trying to relieve the tension, a flicker of color caught me.

The crystal. I spotted it lying near the wall, right where I'd thrown it. I stretched out across the floor, too lazy to stand, and snatched it up between my fingers. Lying on my side now, trying to give my butt cheeks a break. I turned the smooth surface over in my palm, staring into it as it caught the dim light. Every now and then, stealing glances at the elf, just in case.

The elf? I'm sure he has a name. If all remains cool between us, then tomorrow, I will introduce myself the right way. For now, I'll give him time to chill.

Something smells... nice. Actually, hella good. Wait. My eyes snap open. At some point, I must've fallen asleep. I glance left. He's still seated in his usual position, back against the wall across from me, head tilted down but upright. Okay, so my throat wasn't slit in my sleep. That... makes me feel a little better about him. Still. I'm going to have to figure out how to get out of this mess eventually. I wipe the drool from the corner of my mouth and stretch out my arm, only for my hand to dip into something cool and wet. I jerk away with a startled yelp and look down.

Another tray. At some point while I was sleeping, the guards must've brought another meal. The soupy surface rippling from the motion of my hand, but the warmth is long gone. It's been sitting here a while. Which begs the question... why didn't *he* take it? If I could smell it in my sleep, he definitely caught a whiff. Especially after how he was practically nuzzling that piece of lamb yesterday. I pull the tray closer. I'm *starving*, but probably not as bad as him. I *should* share. Definitely. But there's not much here, just oatmeal and toasted bread and I haven't had a full meal in I know at least a day.

I'll share the *next* one. I glance over at him. His head's slouched, tilted slightly down.

"You awake over there?" I lightly whisper. Kind of hoping he wasn't.

To my surprise, he lifts his head. Assuming it's actually morning I timidly say, "Good morning, Mr. Elf." Trying to come off as friendly as possible.

He doesn't respond.

"I'm not sure if it's okay to call you that or not. We never got the chance to introduce ourselves, and seeing as we might be bunkmates for a little minute, I figure it'd make things less awkward. My name's Kaliyah. What can I call you?" I take a sip of the bowl of oatmeal. It's firmed up slightly, but still loose. "Are you still upset about what happened?" I ask, gently.

Again, nothing. I inwardly sigh, but before I can say anything else, his voice relieves the pressure. "Why are you locked in here with me? What crime did you commit?"

Okay. Guess we're skipping my questions, then. But something's better than nothing.

"Um... I'm not one hundred percent sure. Maybe for using the portal without permission? Trespassing, probably? I wasn't told what my *charges* are." My mind really started to process it. "No lawyer. No trial. No verdict. Just straight to prison. Nothing about this bullshit would fly back home. I have rights."

"Back home?" he echoes. "So, you're not a citizen of Palloria?"

"Heck no. I'm a citizen of Earth." I catch the twitch near his face again. Some kind of reaction. "Some closeted, bipolar empress dimensionally kidnapped me, told me I was a 'champion' and then ditched me when I wasn't with the shit. I only came to Palloria hoping the king could send me *home*. But in classic me fashion, I ran into yet another royal ass and boom, here I am. In a cell. Eating bland oatmeal."

Having a one-sided conversation with an elf who still hasn't given me his name. I don't say that last part out loud.

"A champion?" he repeats after me again. There's something different in his tone this time. Almost... surprised.

Maybe I should've kept that part to myself. I don't know who this guy is or why he's locked down here. But it's too late to take it back now. Still, it doesn't stop me from being me when I say, "It's annoying when you do that. You grab one word from what I said and toss it back like I'm the one confused."

I raise my voice just slightly. "Yes. A *champion*. People summoned from other worlds, gifted powers by Therion's deities to become glorified celebrities."

"And you were given a gift from a deity?"

"You sure ask a lot of questions for someone who won't answer *any*."

I could lie. Say yes. Let him think I have the power to blast his ass with a lightning bolt if he cross me. That could be useful.

"When you first awakened here, you—"

I cut him off, raising a hand, only to realize, yeah, he can't see that. "Uh-uh. Nope. I'm not saying another word until *you* decide to share something." Silence. Not just a few moments, *hours*. He shuts up completely. Just sits there like a statue.

The next tray shows up. Spaghetti. I blink at the tray. *Spaghetti?* This world has spaghetti? I have *so many* questions, none of which I'll ever get the answers to. This time around, I'm not the only one who got food. He did too, if you can call it that. His tray looks like punishment. Stale, moldy bread and a grayish slop that looks less like food and more like vomit.

"You're not gonna eat that, are you?" I ask. He says nothing. So this is what they've been feeding him? I can't let him eat that. But I still don't know who he is. Or what he did. What if he's a war criminal or something? I reach into my pocket, fumbling for the mana crystal. Smooth against my fingers. An idea strikes.

"Hey, Mr. Elf. I know you can't see this, but the food they gave you looks absolutely disgusting, and no one should be forced to eat something like that. Ever."

No response. I push forward anyway. "So, I'd like to know, are you interested in a deal?"

"A deal?" He says in a condensing tone.

I scoff at his annoying habit. But I let it go because it gets his attention.

"What kind of deal?"

"One where we both get something we want."

"You really believe you have something I could ever want."

"Yes, I do. Assurance... and before you go, 'Assurance?' I mimic his tone. "Let me explain. I want to know for sure you won't try to kill me while we're stuck in here together. And you want to make sure you don't starve to death. I can do that. By sharing my food with you in return for my thing. That's it."

He's quiet again for a second.

"That would be the full extent of your terms?"

"Yes. That's all."

"When would this agreement begin?"

"The moment you say yes, I'll hand over some of this spaghetti right now."

Again another long pause.

"These terms are... *acceptable.*"

Sweet. I just *hope* this works. I'd only seen Mitus do it once. But if I remembered correctly, he pricked his finger first. I grabbed the edge of the tin tray and dug my index finger into the rim until I felt a sting. Blood beaded up almost immediately. I then palmed the mana crystal in the same hand, keeping my pointer finger out.

I turned to the elf. "Okay. Are you ready to make the deal?"

"Yes."

"Cool. So... what's your name?"

His ears tilted back. First time I'd seen them do that.

"Why is that relevant?"

I raised an eyebrow. "How do you expect a deal to work if you won't even give me your name? Could *you* trust someone who refused to share theirs to you?"

There was a pause. Then his ears slowly rose back to their neutral position. "Arrio."

"Arrio," I repeated. "Okay, good. I'll begin now."

I cleared my throat, trying to remember what Mitus said, how his voice had sounded.

"I, Kaliyah, agree to share the meals the guards bring me. In return, Arrio, do you agree no harm shall come to me?"

"I've already told you these terms are acceptable," he said again, a little more evenly this time. No doubt eager to eat.

"Okay then. Agreed."

I lifted my bleeding finger into the air and held my breath. To my absolute *shock*, a glowing red line traced along the path of my fingertip. A low, tingling sensation followed the motion like an invisible thread stitching magic through the air. I drew another line to make an X and the lines pulsed once before dissolving into the air like smoke caught on a breeze.

"Holy crap." I whispered.

The crystal in my hand, once faintly glowing, had gone completely dull. Just a pebble now. I did it. *Me*. Did magic. Exhilaration buzzed through me. I couldn't help the smile spreading across my face. Maybe I should become a mage, like Noiz. Maybe I don't have to wait for someone to rescue me. I could find my own way back home if I collect more of these crystals. I bent down to grab the tray and stood. "So now everything's good between us, right? Any hostility we had toward each other is officially under the bridge, correct?"

"To an extent," he replied calmly.

Didn't *love* how that sounded. But... he's meeting me halfway and I'll take it. I cautiously walked over to his side of the room and stood before him. Just as casually as he's been since I got here, he tilted his head upward, though not quite at my face. More like... chest level. I bent down and placed the tray at his feet.

"Here. A deal is a deal."

"And what will you eat?"

"What do you mean? I agreed to share, remember? Not to completely give it away." I take the bread, scooped up a corner of the spaghetti with it and took a few sips of water. "I'll leave you most of it, since clearly you need it more than me." Then I carried myself back to my corner of the cell and sat down.

The moment my butt hit the floor, all the restraint Arrio had shown the first time I shared food with him vanished. He dove into the tray with his hands, eating like a man possessed, slowly licking his fingers after each bite and cleaning every last corner of the tray. Which I now realize after the prick of my finger could absolutely be used as a weapon.

Damn. I thought the magical binding deal would make me feel better... but now I just feel like a fool with an insurance policy that I'm not sure will pay out. A sudden *clatter* made me flinch. He'd slid the tray and cup back across the stone floor to me.

"This agreement we have. It only works if the guards don't know about it, otherwise your meals may start to resemble mine. Always keep the tray on your side of the room."

"Right," I muttered, dragging it over.

He picked up *his* tray of goop and gore.

"You're not still going to eat that, are you?" I questioned in disgust.

"No." He turned and walked to the hole in the floor. "But it would look suspicious if the one meal a week they give me is still sitting here untouched."

"One meal a *week*?! How the hell do they expect you to live off that?"

"I'm an elf. So, I manage. Barely. But I manage."

My stomach twisted. "That's... that's too cruel."

"I expect nothing less from lower species such as demies and hu—" He stopped himself. "other beings."

I narrowed my eyes at him.

Other beings, huh? We both know what he was about to say.

CHAPTER 23
ASSESS ANALYZE ACT

KALIYAH

Two weeks have gone by. *I think*. It's hard to keep track without even a sliver of outside light. Unfortunately, it turns out, the panic attack I had my first day wasn't a one-off thing. They've become routine now, arriving like clockwork. I'd never had one before coming to Therion, but ever since I was thrown into this cell, they won't stop. Like something in me cracked open and hasn't stopped bleeding since.

I've been trying to keep my thoughts steady. Stay calm. Don't imagine the very real possibility that I might *never* get out of this dungeon. That I could spend the rest of my life down here. Hot, stale air thick in my lungs, surrounded by dry stone and silence.

Every time I look at Arrio's *wilted* body, I wonder just how long he's been here. Then all the possible answers come crashing down on me, followed by another panic attack. I try to shove the thoughts down, but they claw their way back into the forefront of my mind. That suffocating pressure builds in my chest until it becomes impossible to ignore. And these last few days, it's been worse. The cell feels tighter. The air heavier with nothing and every little thing. Like the walls are leaning in on me, slowly. The temperature feels like it has risen some. Definitely *not* the ideal time to be hyperventilating.

The only consistent relief is the female cat guard, Lyona. I finally caught her name. She and some other guard, never Zarion, thank god, brings me my meals. And I've kept to the deal. I share them with Arrio, every time. Not that it's earned me much goodwill. I thought maybe, just *maybe*, feeding him would warm him up to me. That maybe we'd talk. But no. Arrio speaks only when absolutely necessary. I might as well be in here by myself.

God no, not that. I don't know if I could handle that. Trapped behind these thick, solid, grey stone walls that never change. No, I definitely couldn't. My first few nights, I tried to be optimistic. Told myself I was lucky this time around. No carnivorous man-beast and a constant supply of food, water and safety from the outside world. That's the lie I convince myself. And as much as I wanted to believe it, I don't.

The truth is... This is worse. Far worse than the cave. At least there, I could *move*. I could *breathe*. This place. It's like being buried alive. Before, at least, I had space to explore. Stolen glimpses of fresh air at the cave's entrance. A choice to stay or leave, even if *leaving* meant torture or death. But here... I have none of that.

Back in the mountain, the glow of the shining plants and crystal buried above the mountain inner wall stole the dark. My eyes never strained. I never feared night. But this place... The darkness feels alive. The lanterns still burn, but barely. Each one flickers like it's gasping for its last breath. I'm afraid one day soon, the lights will go out completely. And I'll drown in darkness. Swallowed by shadows. That's but one fear that triggers me. The panic attacks won't stop. Spiraling thoughts and tight lungs grow into heaving, shaking, blackouts. The first few times, Arrio ignored me like I wasn't even there. But then came the last one. I collapsed. Slammed my head on one of the bars. Out cold for a while.

When I woke, it was his voice that greeted me. He said nothing comforting, just that I had lost consciousness for approximately four hours and eighteen minutes. Not sure if he's really able to keep track of time. But it was then he started talking to me more. Not warmly or kindly, just more. I'm convinced it was the realization that if I died down here, his food would stop. That definitely has to be it. Still, he only speaks when the attacks start. He's constantly questioning me about the outside world. About whether or not I've had any contact with anyone claiming to be from Yurakora or if King La'Claw has made any royal statements recently.

No surprise, I can't tell him much. I don't know this world. In a very short time I've gone from one prison to the next. Not learning much outside of the little tidbits Saphire explained to me. I know he's not satisfied with my answers. He probably thinks I'm not being fully honest with him. But the truth is, I have no reason to hold anything back anymore. Because of him, I'm learning quickly how little being human matters here. It's strange. Sometimes, I forget he's not... *human*.

Elf.... Elves... goblins... dragons... orcs... fucking vampires. *Twilight my ass*. Nothing enticing about this hellhole. I feel like I'm losing myself. Losing my grip on reality. Like none of this is real. None of it. Maybe I'm stuck on some really, really long, really bad trip. Yeah... I *could* see that, if I ever did anything stronger than the occasional edible. I was always too afraid drugs might trigger my sleepwalking. At least that doesn't seem to be a problem at the moment. *Like where would I even go?*

Maybe I'm already dead. Maybe this is my version of hell. I'm constantly fighting. Fighting to stay afloat. To not sink into that dark place in my mind where there is no more hope for me. My thoughts are really tearing me up. Every time I feel like I'm about to go under, its like I feel him reaching out to me.

Mitus. His thick, muscled arms wrapping around me. Pulling me back up. I want to stop thinking about him. *Stop it. Just stop*. He's gone. I'm free of him. That's what I wanted. Isn't it? I wonder what he's doing right now. Leaping over mountains? Maybe. Terrorizing a village? Likely. *Looking for me? Probably not.*

Then again, his obsession with me was intense. He might be the one person actually capable of finding me. But would I even want him to? If he did, I can only imagine what he'd do to me. I ran. I left him. And the look on his face in that moment, the rage, the betrayal. It's carved into my memory. Those eyes... despite how terrifying they can be, I wouldn't mind seeing them again. Hearing his voice, even if it's just to curse me. Anything... *anything* is better than this freakin' silence. I didn't realize how accustomed I'd become to Mitus and our senseless conversations. Even if it was nothing more than taunts and bickers, at least it was *something*. He *wanted* a reaction out of me. *Tried* to engage with me. Unlike Arrio. Who avoids talking like it'll kill him. Sometimes I wonder if he's deaf too. But no. He hears me just fine. Just chooses not to respond. When he does, it's usually with some snide comment or demeaning tone. I've lost the urge to tell him off, because I don't think my comments faze him. I've tried a few times to provoke him. Not to make him angry, just to rile him up enough to hold a chat for more than thirty seconds. It never works. I'm not worth his plentiful time. Not mature enough to hold his attention, I'm guessing.

A "youngling," he calls me, ever since he learned my age. A brainless child in his eyes. Which is wild, because other than the white hair, he doesn't look that much older than me. When I asked his age, silence. Again, no surprise. He never answers *any* of my questions. The fact that he treats me this way considering we are in the exact same boat is freakin' ironic. Mitus might've seen me as weak and compared to him, I undeniably am; everyone is, but he never insulted my intelligence. Never acted like I wasn't worth even his words. I don't know why I keep comparing the two of them. But what the hell else am I supposed to do? I'm locked in a god damn dungeon. *Fuck~*

And still, I can't go more than a few hours without Mitus's name or face drifting into my head. It's not like I had *feelings* for him, any positive ones, anyway. And now that he's gone, I'm not all... *horny* all the time either. So that's a win. I think. But I'm running out of things to focus on. Thinking about home hurts too much, so I don't. I can't pile that on top too or my mind will really break.

There's a rash starting to spread across my chest from all the stress and rubbing. When I asked Arrio, he told me medical care is not provided to prisoners. But when I asked Lyona, she actually came back with ointment and bandages. She even helped apply it to the wound on my head from the fall. That seemed to throw Arrio. He didn't say anything, but I could tell something about it rubbed him the wrong way. Maybe it confused him. He'll never admit anything. He keeps his thoughts locked away tighter than this cell. I guess we're not in the exact same boat after all. Mine has fewer holes. But either way, we're both sinking.

Despite being closed off, he occasionally shares random things. Not much though. Usually right when my breathing gets bad, and I'm slipping into another attack. Probably to distract me. He talks about Palloria. About the princess. About how this cell, *our* cell, isn't part of the regular prison. It's special, because its enchanted. Unbreakable by nonmagical means.

When I ask for more details, he just says that the princess clearly wanted me tucked away. That whatever I said to her made me either valuable, dangerous or both. But it's neither. I know its neither, because I lied. I hoped it would save me. Instead, it's landed me here. Not much of the information he occasionally divulges, helps or brings me any kind of hope. Something I doubt he's trying to do in the first place. Still, I cling to every syllable.

Every word that leaves his mouth feels like borrowed oxygen. Like if I just listen hard enough, I might find a crack in the wall. A way out. I know his reasons are entirely selfish. He doesn't care about me. But I'm grateful. Because right now, I'll take anything that reminds me I'm still alive.

ARRIO

My mind is finally beginning to piece things together, from the scraps of information I've managed to draw out of the girl. It's starting to make sense now. The hesitations, the secrecy, the special treatment. The Princess may suspect this girl might be a Champion, or at the very least, someone with ties to the Empire of Sebbarus.

Demi-humans may excel in physical prowess, but when it comes to intelligence, they are not much different from humans. And as cunning as the princess thinks herself to be, *she is wrong*. That much I'm certain of. It's clear this human is not a champion. I am sure of that. Anyone with Yorka's divine eye could see it clearly. She bears none of the markers of the deities chosen. But the ability to see the souls of creatures *is* an exclusive trait only found among specially gifted elves. So of course, the Princess would not be able to confirm this as quickly as I can. She is desperate. Clinging to the idea of some savior, a hero destined to save us all. Her desperation only reveals what she... what all of them have always been. Fools.

I fault the truth this kingdom refuses to face. There *will be* no more Champions. Not after what happened. The gates to Therion are closed, sealed by divine decree. She and her father, the so-called mighty, more like *reckless* King La'Claw, fight the inevitable as if it's something that can be stalled by force of will alone. But it's coming. For all of us. Palloria will fall, as did Sebbarus. And eventually my homeland.

My foolish arrogance. The arrogance of my people they no doubt continue to have. To think I somehow thought the elves would not suffer the same fate. It does not matter how tall our walls are, how elite our warriors maybe. I've seen what's to come and none of us... none of us will survive it. Still something about this doesn't make sense. If the princess really believes the human is a champion, a pillar of hope, a cell is not the place she would keep the girl. I must be missing something. Princess, you're moving pieces, apparently behind your father's back. That tells me you're afraid, and that your stubborn father is too set in his ways to act without the approval of his trusted advisors, the council. Could the current state of Therion be worse than I predicted. The prophecy foretold to me wasn't meant to unfold this soon.

I've gathered that the girl believes Champions are summoned to be nothing more than luminaries. Glorified figures, adored by the masses. But the truth is far less glamorous. Champions are pawns. Sacrifices. Tools for whatever deity feels inclined to toy with the world, while also being manipulated by the will of the monarchs. She confessed without hesitation, that not but a few months ago, she and three others were summoned here as Champions. I don't believe her, of course. Why would I? The idea is absurd. I was there. I saw it with my own eyes. Lightning raining from the sky. The wrath of the Great Vireth-Kai shattered the covenant, sworn by the deities. But why would she lie about something so ridiculous?

What troubles me more is when I draw on my divine eyes, I detect no falsehood in her. Not even a flicker. She believes what she says. That her companions were summoned and that they returned to their world. But that too is impossible. In all the known history of Therion, not once has a Champion went back from where they were summoned. This is why Yurakora never participates in the Summoning Ritual. But regardless of the elves' disposition, it never stops the deities from sending one of these champions anyway. And they are almost always human. Being the deities offer no way for us to send them back, all we are willing to do is give them a few weeks of supplies and send them on their way. I doubt any of them ever managed to survive longer than their rations allow.

The idea that the fate of our world could rest in the hands of humans. It's unfathomable. An insult. I considered telling the girl this. Telling her what I know not to be true. But I refrain. I see no reason to disturb the delicate little truce between us. This agreement of ours, childish as it may be, it has kept food in my stomach. Although I am grateful, I refuse to show it to the lowly mortal. A youngling at that.

She must not know how badly my body has deteriorated. If she did, I doubt she'd speak so casually to me or perhaps she'd speak more boldly. The truth is, the second time the guards brought her food, I considered taking it from her. But the way she struck me before... it gave me pause. My body is not what it used to be and human she may be, I am not foolish enough to overestimate my condition. There is a chance, although small, that she could have overpowered me. A risk not worth taking.

Still, her bizarre declaration that she was contemplating *eating* me, caught me off guard. It unsettled me more than the interrogations, more than the torture. I knew humans were primitive thinkers, but I never counted them among the lower creatures, not like kobolds or goblins.

Humans. Greedy, small, insecure things, always overestimating their significance. Though, admittedly, there are moments when her words surprise me. Impressive even. Until her thoughts scatter and dissolve into nonsense. Rambling questions. Singing outbursts. The fleeting mind of a human. This is why any deal struck with her is ultimately meaningless. As an elf, I know better. One must never trust a human. They will always try to manipulate. It is better to manipulate them first. And yet... I still don't know why I gave her my real name.

It doesn't matter. The moment I regain enough strength; I will take her hostage. Use her as leverage to bargain for my release. And if that fails, I'll kill her if only to ruin whatever plan the princess has devised. That is, assuming she doesn't kill herself first. I have never encountered a being so easily unraveled by their own body. Losing control of something as basic as breathing. She truly is like a youngling. Compared to my hundred and twenty-nine years, how could I see her as anything else? A youngling. And a tiresome one at that. She never stops talking.

At first, I thought it was because I had grown so accustomed to silence, I found her voice intolerable. But in the stretches where she falls quiet for too long, I notice I begin to feel on edge. My body becomes more alert. Restless. Uneasy. But I learned quickly, all it takes is a few words from me, and she returns to her usual chatter state. A constant stream of sound.

Three more days have passed. Today, she informed me, with no subtlety whatsoever, that if I do not make an effort to converse with her, she will begin consuming a larger portion of our shared meals. What else would I expect from a human? Always seeking advantages. But she has none. She doesn't understand. A few more days of rations, and I'll have enough strength to take the food from her by force. I'm just biding my time. I may not be able to see her the way she sees me, but my other senses are far more sufficient than hers. I hear the rustle of fabric, followed by a sharp whooshing sound.

When I asked her what she was doing, she said, "I'm using my shirt as a fan. Too bad you can't see me, cause you'd be getting a damn good show right now."

What purpose did that last part serve?

"In what world would you think an elf would find any part of a human youngling to be a good show?"

"This world and every part. And I keep telling you, I'm not a child. I've got these luscious round breasts to prove it. See? Take a look. Oh, that's right." She's annoyingly ridiculous.

"I don't need to see what I can smell from here."

She went quiet. Not her usual sulking kind of quiet, either. It was the kind that meant she was embarrassed. I've heard her mumble to herself a dozen times about wanting a bath since being thrown into this cell. *A bath.* As if cleanliness is something worth caring about in a place like this. But for her, it seems to be an obsession.

"That's not my fault," she finally muttered, with a tinge of shame. "They haven't given me any washcloths. Or a change of clothes." The embarrassment clings to her words.

"Still doesn't change the fact that your scent fogs the entire cell."

That got her riled up. "And what about you?"

"What about me?"

"I can tell you've been down here way longer than I have. So, you've got to stink far worse than me."

"*Elves don't stink.*"

"Bull. Everyone stinks."

"The sweat of an elf doesn't emit odor."

"Oh yeah? Prove it."

"What purpose would that serve?"

"Let's make a bet. If you win, I'll let you have the bread at the next meal."

I paused, considering. It had been *years*, since I'd had bread that wasn't stiff as bark or sprouting mold like it was trying to regrow itself.

"And how would you suggest I prove it?" I asked, wary.

"Let me sniff you."

I frowned. "Sniff me?"

"Ugh, yes. Sniff you."

I lowered my head, genuinely contemplating the absurdity of what she's asking. "And what would the conditions be?"

"I get to smell any part of your body until either I'm satisfied with your claim or I prove you wrong. Which I definitely will." The confidence in her voice was juvenile.

"And what would be your outcome?"

"I told you. I'll give you the bread."

"No, I mean you. What will you not get from me, when you lose this bet?"

"I *will* get to use your portion of our drinking water."

"For what?"

"What?" she asked, clearly not expecting me to inquire about that.

"You said use, not drink. What will you use the water for?"

She hesitated. "Does it matter?"

I think on it for a moment, "I suppose not."

"So?"

"Fine. You can sniff me all you want. Not that it will matter. Come next meal—" Finally lifting my head, the words stall in my throat the moment I realize she's already over me. I never heard her move. I sit against the wall, one leg bent with my arm resting on my knee, the other hanging loosely by my side. Her heat is the first thing I register. Her body suddenly close, too close. A wave of warmth centered around my chest.

SNIFF. SNIFF.

All I can see is the glow of her soul, orb-like, hovering right before me. She is just inches away. Her body radiates its own kind of heat, and I feel it in a slow trail as she moves. She starts low, near the base of my chest, then shifts upward. Her breath tracing along the line of my ribs to the pit of my arm before pulling away.

Just as I think she's done, she asks, "Is it okay if I touch you?"

"Touch me?"

"Yes. There are a few places I want to smell, but I'd need to adjust you a little to reach them."

I hesitate. It's been a long time since someone made physical contact with me. Contact that did not intend to produce pain. It should be fine. Even from this position, I still hold the advantage. And my strength has started to return. If she tries anything, I'll kill her.

"That's fine. Go ahead," I tell her, though I brace myself for some trickery.

She reaches for my hand. The one draped over my knee. It takes effort not to move at the sudden interaction. She holds mine in both of hers, flipping my palm upward. Her hands are smaller than I imagined. Softer, too. Her breath moves over my wrist and crawls up my forearm in gentle, measured inhales. My skin tingles where her fingers leave faint impressions, electric and not completely unwelcome.

She follows the path up, under my arm, over my shoulder blade and then, closer. Into my neck. I realize just how near she's gotten. Her braids fall across my chest, the strands tickling my skin. I try to remain still, but instinct betrays me. I start to breathe her in, subtly, carefully, hoping she won't notice.

Did she... put her shirt back on? The soft fabric of her bra presses against my chest. I can feel the plushness of her body graze mine. And then her face nestles deeper into my neck, something even softer brushing just below my jaw.

What is she doing? My fingers curl into a fist. Heat rises in my chest not the heat of anger, but something else, something I shouldn't be feeling. This isn't how my body should react to a human. Especially not this child.

But it's her scent. I wasn't lying when I said it clouds the entire cell. When she first arrived, I assumed it was some kind of perfume. Something artificial. Something that would fade. It didn't. It's just as potent now as the moment they dragged her in here. It smells of home. Wildflowers, like the hills near the Forest of Aewen during early bloom. A beautiful scent. One I'd gladly be around. But I would never tell her that.

She has no grace. No restraint. No sense of dignity. No damn filter. And I will not... *will not* give this infuriating, impulsive human woman even the slightest hint that she might be having *any* effect on me.

Any effect... on me? What the hell am I thinking? She's human. That's right, not elf. *Human.* Impatient animals clothed in ambition. They tear through the world like a storm, never stopping to understand the soil they trample. Their kingdoms rise overnight, built on borrowed magic and blind faith, only to crumble beneath the weight of their own ignorance. They age before they learn, die before they understand. And yet somehow, they believe themselves masters of this realm. It would be laughable, if they weren't so pathetic. Though I'll admit, *grudgingly,* this one has more potential than most. Her intelligence surfaces from time to time. But she flicks it off and on like a faulty lantern. Most of the time, she operates with it off. It's a shame. When it's on, she's almost acceptable.

My breath hitches when something brushes against the corner of my mouth. *What was that?* Too soft to be her fingers. But seemingly too firm to be lips. Or... was it? I'm not sure. I've never kissed a human. Whatever part of her touched me, it felt like heated satin.

"This doesn't make any sense," she mutters, pulling away from me all at once. "How is that even possible?"

Her soul drifts back toward the center of the cell, and with it goes her heat and the strange, uninvited stillness she left behind. Suddenly, I'm pissed. Enraged, actually. *Why the hell did I react like that?* For a moment, just a flicker. I... *wanted* her. *Her.* Am I losing my mind? A spell maybe? But I would have heard her. It has to be something subtle, meant to disarm me. Her food, maybe? Is this their play? They'd use a human because they knew I'd pay her no real mind.

"I guess that means the bread is yours."

What the hell is in the bread? At the thought of that, I get even more tempered. "No. You keep your damn bread." I should have never entertained that absurd game.

"What? But I was wrong. I'm still not sure how that's possible, but I'll take my L. That's actually pretty wild. So, elves don't stink. I wish my body worked like that. I'm starving, though. I hope they hurry." And like a cruel cue from the deities, my ears twitch at the sound of approaching footsteps.

It should be lunch time. I've gotten good at estimating the time of day based on the type of meals delivered. But something's off. The steps are heavier, slower, and more importantly, I don't smell food. Something's wrong.

"Hey Arrio, do you know Santa Claus? Oh wait. Was that racist to ask?" She lets out a lighthearted chuckle. "Dang. My bad if it is. Is Christmas even a thing here?"

I block her out. I need to focus. Figure out what the princess is really planning now and what the girl's part in all of this is. I listen harder. The footsteps have entered the cell. *Entered?* That's not routine. Normally, they leave the tray at the entrance. They don't come in.

"Have you ever heard of the jingle bell song?" She asks. I don't think she noticed their approach.

One remains at the entrance. His soul is unfamiliar, dull, indifferent. But the other... I know that core. That foul dark grey. Zarion. The wolf demi-human. He stands just a few feet from the girl, his core like a cloud of rot. The moment I see his soul, I know. He's not here under any orders. The vile depravity of his spirit. I've seen many like it before and it's clear to me the acts taken to cause such distortion. Which means, unfortunately for the youngling, today will be darker than the rest. But still, she sings. Oblivious.

"Jingle bells. Jingle all the way..."

I clear my throat to get her attention.

"Oh what fun it—" She stops. Feet shuffle. "You," she says.

"You finally noticed me," Zarion replies.

"Where's Lyona?" the girl asks.

"She's taking a sick day. I'm her fill-in."

I hear the soft rustling of fabric.

"No need to put that on, on my account, lamb. I was rather enjoying the view."

My brows furrow. *Repulsive.*

She clears her throat and lets out a tired sigh. "Okay. I'm just going to come out and say it. I don't like what's happening right now, or how this situation is making me feel. You're a guard, a supposed noble protector of a whole-ass kingdom, and yet you're giving off major pervy creeper vibes. So let me make this clear. No. No to all of whatever this is. You have *zero* chance of getting with me. Not even if you offered me passage through the front gate. *Bitch-ass wolf boys aren't my type.*"

I clenched my jaw. *No fucking filter.* She doesn't understand, provoking someone like him will only make things worse for her. I clear my throat again. She must have noticed.

"That's right. I was told I am here under the protection of Princess Sarah."

"Am I supposed to know who the hell that is?"

"No, wait. That's not right... hey, what's her name again?"

She's asking *me.* Of course she is. The idiot still hasn't learned that I won't speak when a guard is present. I say nothing, only lift my head slightly.

"Hell, whatever. I *know* your princess doesn't want me harmed."

"Ahh. You must mean Princess *Sarianna.* Disrespecting the highness's name like that could earn you a flogging. But... maybe we can work something out, lamb."

I clear my throat a third time.

The wolf snaps. "Do that again, you damn elf, and you won't have a fucking throat to clear."

I let his words marinate. Creatures with cores as twisted and dark as his deserve to be erased from this world. His wickedness will face justice one day, but not today. And not by me. Until then, I tell myself not to care what he plans to do with the girl. After all, whatever it is, it won't end in her death. No matter how vile he is, he wouldn't risk the wrath of the crown, that much I'm certain of. I feel my teeth grinding harder into themselves. So long as she's alive at the end of the day, I can still use her. And yet... yet. *No. This has nothing to do with me.*

With confidence she says, "If you hurt me, I'll report you to the princess once Lyona returns. And then what do you think will happen to you?"

Zarion laughs bitterly. "Returns? Ah. I must've misspoken. Lyona is on a more... *permanent leave*. I'll be replacing her duties from now on. So if you've got any messages, lamb, just whisper them to me and I'll make sure the princess never hears them." He sighs, as if bored already. "You know what? Fuck the foreplay. I've waited long enough. I'm done pretending. And by the looks of it, you're over it too. You know why I'm here and I've come to collect."

"You want you're lick back? Okay. Take a swing." She replies boldly.

There's a cruel amusement in Zarion's voice. "That's the attitude I like. Feisty. Ready to break. But since we're on the topic of what I want, let me make a correction. I will be swinging at you, just not with my fist. Actually, I'll be swinging at you for the next few weeks, maybe even months. None of your claims have been able to be proven in our investigation this far. So..."

"So what? What does that mean? How much longer do I have to be down here?"

His core leans forward a bit more as he inhales deeply, "I didn't get the chance to say this before, but you smell *so fucking good*. Your scent makes my dick so hard, I can't tell the difference between it and my sword." The atmosphere becomes heavier as Zarion's laughter echoes through the space, and the other guard joins in with his own.

I dropped my head, because although I can't see them, I can feel her eyes on me. No female of any species deserve such a fate. I wonder if she expects me to do something to help her. I don't doubt that I, weak and unarmed, could save her from them. But when they send ten more in their place, then what? My power is sealed, and I am bound to this cell. There is nothing I can do.

My teeth grind harder, frustration building, but there's no outlet. The rage boils under my skin, but it's powerless here. I'm powerless here. And yet, she's making me yearn to help her. To do something that would stop this. But I will not. There is no point. For every one Zarion I kill, there will be three more to replace him. All I can do is listen. Listen to her torment. Listen to their vile laughter. And wait, useless, as the scene unfolds around me.

"What do I do?" Her voice almost lost in the air. But I know her words are meant for me. It tightens something in my chest. My muscles coil. There's panic in her voice, just a thread of it, but I feel it. And Yorka, I pity her. I've looked at her core so many times, stared at it for hours. Its gentle and bright in a way that doesn't belong in a place like this. A blushing glow, delicate and untouched by the filth we breathe. And now… now, this will stain her. Shatter her more like it.

Zarion's core moves forward. "All you have to do is resist me. Not too much. Just enough to make it fun." He chuckles low making my skin crawl.

"I like the expression you made at me a few weeks back. I want to hear you tremble while I ram my cock into you. Feel your screams while I groan against your skin. Come on, lamb, let me see that face again."

Every word is a sickness. I want to remove his tongue. But as I always do, I remain still. I remain silent. But the air answers for us both. Suddenly, shifting. It was subtle at first. Too quiet to place. But then the hair on my arms stood on end, and a slow crawl of static crept up the back of my neck. I went still. My breath hitched in my throat.

This sensation… I've only felt it once before in my entire life. *Fear*. It came so suddenly, so foreign, I didn't recognize it as mine. I look down at my body, my senses reaching outward for the cause, until the truth hit me like a fist. The air, once stifling and thick with the musty rot of stone and dry sweat, turned cold. Unnaturally cool. Slowly, I lifted my head, every instinct inside me screaming to move carefully. *Assess. Analyze. Act.* Something was happening. Something beyond comprehension. How could they not sense it? It was happening right in front of us.

Kaliyah. Pressed against the back wall of the room. But something was different. More than different. I didn't see *her* core. Not the small, tinted orb of a soul I'd come to know, soft, kind, human. *No.* This was something else entirely. Something vibrant. *Alive* in a way that felt… ancient. And it was growing. No, not growing *expanding*. Unfolding like light, like breath drawn from the universe itself. Stretching beyond the bounds of her body until it began to eclipse her entirely, like the sun.

How is that even possible? Just as I think it might stop, that it has to *stop*, it doesn't. It keeps expanding. Shifting. And then I see it. Something I've never seen before. Not in a human.

Another color? The softest shade of blue. Pale. It weaves around the larger core in smooth spirals, circling it, wrapping it, *hugging* it. My chest tightens. My thoughts scramble. *What the hell is happening?*

"That's rape." The girls voice rings through, but not the voice I'm used to. It's so clear, so soft, so utterly calming in a tone I barely recognize it as hers.

Is that really her? I never heard her speak in that cadence before. It's still, but heavy. So fucking heavy.

"You're talking about... raping me."

Her voice is almost hypnotic, but beneath it, I feel something stirring. My entire body knows. This isn't just trouble. This is danger. Pure, unforgiving, and already here. The guard at the entrance might have time to get away. But me? I'm caged in with *it*.

Zarion laughs. Loud, careless, and far too unaware. "Call it whatever the fuck you want, Lamb." The snap of a belt buckle cuts the air behind his words. "Just know it's happening. And it's happening right now. You can start by taking your clothes—"

He doesn't finish. His sentence is torn away, devoured by a wet, gut-twisting *slush*, like flesh being violently unmade. A surge of energy rips through the air, crashing over us like a tidal wave. Then a deafening BOOM, the crack of stone splitting apart, and finally... the gentle, eerie patter of dirt sifting from the ceiling. It lands on my shoulders like ash, like the space itself has started to collapse.

I glance from her core to his, breath catching, every muscle drawn so tight I might snap in half. Zarion's core. The very essence of him, begins to unravel. His soul decays in real time, peeling away into smoke and rot, burning like brittle parchment in a fire. Then his body collapses with a sickening *thud*, the sound warped, empty, final. And I can't move.

"Deities! What the hell did you just do?" The other guard's voice trembles with confusion as he draws his sword, likely aiming it right at her.

I know what will happen if he steps inside this cell. She will tear him from this world just like the wolf. My pulse races, but I remain still. I use these precious seconds, to try and formulate a plan. Fighting isn't an option. Hell, even if I had access to my magic, would it do any good?

What the shit did the princess lock away with me? Did she know? Could she have? Maybe I can reason with it. But if I take that route, I need to be *careful*. I need to stay still, no sudden movements, and keep my hands where they're visible, *non-threatening*. The moment I decide to stick to this plan, I hear the other guard's heel lift off the ground and my body *ignites*. Lunging, like an electric current jolts through me, forcing my actions before I even register what's happening.

What the fuck am I doing? Before I knew it, I'm moving. Faster than I've moved in years, but it was not my intention to move at all. An intuitive act. Zarion's sword is out of its sheath and my hand. The tip cleanly sinking into the chest of the other guard. It was like my body knew her life was being threatened and without thought and with no hesitation, it just acted on its own. *Shit. Why the hell did I just do that?* It was almost instinctual. Like the nerves in my body felt the urge to. *But why?*

"Ra." Her voice is soft, carrying a weight I can't figure out.

My back to her, I freeze. Every muscle in my body tenses so fucking tight at the name, I think I might snap.

"What did you just say?" The words spill out before I can stop them, and I slowly turn my head, my brow pulling.

"I said, what the shit happened?" Her voice is back to that low casual pitch.

"No." I withdraw the sword from the guard's chest as he let out a croak. I lowered the tip of the blade to my side. His body hit the ground a second later. "What did you just *call* me?"

"What? I didn't call you anything. I want to know what's going on? How... When did you... Never mind. Forget it. If this is a prison break, I'm in. Fuck this place."

"Come again?" I let out a harsh laugh in confused disbelief. "Who the hell are you?"

"What are you talking about? It's me, Kaliyah. Don't you recognize my voice?"

"W—what the fuck are you?"

"Huh? Are you okay? No, actually, there's no time for twenty questions."

The overwhelming presence that filled the space just moments ago had vanished. In its place stands that delicate little soul I've come to know. How can this be? I've never seen or even heard of, anything like it. Ever. The royal libraries of Yurakora hold knowledge the rest of the world can only dream of possessing. For centuries, Elves have studied and catalogued every facet of one's essence. The primal forces that shape the beings who roam this world. Since I was born with Yorka's divine eyes, growing up I was made to read every text, every book, all in pursuit of understanding the structure and nature of souls. Their composition, their boundaries, their constraints, but this... this defies everything. I have never—

Her footsteps sound against the stone. I instinctively step back, mirroring her pace, keeping the space between us.

"I'm leaving while I still have the chance. Are you coming or not?"

"I..." My mind races, struggling to process the whirlwind of events.

"Arrio," she calls again, louder this time. "You coming or not?"

"I can't. The cell... an enchantment, bound me inside."

"What do you mean? I don't understand. You're already outside the cell."

"What?"

"You're standing outside the cell already."

"No. That's not—"

"To hell with this. I'm not waiting any more. Let's go." She moves forward.

I brace myself, fingers tightening around the sword's hilt, though I have no thought to use it on her. I doubt it would serve me anyway. Then, her soft, delicate hand wraps around mine, tugging me hurriedly.

"Be careful. Your next steps are the stairs," she warns, her grip steady.

Not soon after, a cool, chilly wind brushes against my skin as the fresh air assaults my senses. I'm... outside. My mind reels. I've planned for this moment countless times. Imagined it. Dreamt of it. But now that it's real, I'm at a loss. Baffled. Fifteen years confined, and now I stand in the open, freed by this creature that somehow exudes both innocence and undisputable power. And yet, as if she even needs it, I inexplicably feel an overwhelming urge to protect her with every fiber of my being. I don't understand it. I need to. But... Not now. Now is not the time. Not when I have just been given an opportunity I will never get again. So, I shut it off. That part of my mind that questions, that assesses, that analyzes. Off. In this moment, I won't be Arrio the intellectual, but Ra the savage.

"Let's go this way," she whispers, tugging my hand.

"No," I resist, pulling her in the opposite direction. "Come."

"Do you even know where you're going?" she asks.

"Not yet. I just know I'm never going back there."

"Same. I'd rather die than go back into that hole in the ground." She squeezes my hand tighter. Her words hit something deep inside me. "Arrio, I'm serious. I won't let anyone take my freedom from me again. *Not again. I will die first.*"

I pull her along faster. "As long as I'm by your side, I won't let that happen." *Why did I say that?* I hardly know this girl. Despite my initial attempts to keep my distance, I've come to find her company tolerable, even occasionally pleasant, but she doesn't hold any real significance to me. She's just some human girl. My people... *my duties*... they're far more important. That is undeniable.

Given the circumstances, the odds of us escaping the palace together are low. Laughably low. I'd have a far better chance on my own. I should leave her. She'd make a perfect distraction. That would be the smart thing to do. The easy thing to do. And yet, I meant every word. No harm will come to this human. Not *if* I can help it. Which means...

We're fucked.

CHAPTER 24
MY MORTAL ENEMIES

KALIYAH

Arrio's grip is like steel, fingers latched around my wrist as he pulls me behind him. He's stronger than he looks, by a lot. I try not to stumble, eyes watering from the sudden exposure. The sun isn't just bright. It *burns*. But the air. God, the air, it smell so fresh. So freakin' good. I can finally breathe.

"Come. Follow behind me," he says, like that makes sense.

I blink against the sting. "Follow you? You're blind. *You* should be following *me*." I attempt to tug at him again, back to the direction I was initially intending to go. But again, he's strong.

"With the senses I *do* have, I can see better than you. Those guards probably won't be missed anytime soon. We've got an hour at least."

The wind rushes against my face. A welcome slap to the nerves as we tear through corridors. Our footsteps muffled themselves against the stone. The walls blur past, cream and beveled, lined with repeating arches, pillars and patterns. All awash in so much bright light. I squint through it, trying to make sense of where we're going.

Arrio not bothered by the same affliction. He only slows to let the tip of his sword slide across the ground and skim the walls as he uses it to read our surroundings. A guide he trusts more than my perfectly good eyes. He moves like its second nature. Every time someone rounds a corner, before I even hear footsteps, he yanks us out of sight. Into alcoves, behind columns and between slats.

How is he even doing this? No freakin' clue. And I don't freakin' care. I just let him. The harsh reality is, ever since I landed in this world, I've been guessing and failing. I don't know what the hell I'm doing. But Arrio... The way he leads me, takes control. Disability or not, I know he's nothing to play with. He moves like someone who *knows* what he's doing and right now, I need that. So in this very moment I'm deciding to put my trust in him. Especially after what he did for me back there. If it weren't for him, *that guard would have...* No. Now is not the time to go there.

We haven't stopped moving since we exited the cell. I need a moment to catch my breath. But I tell that thought to bite me. And push harder to keep up with Arrio. Clearly the steady meals over the last several weeks has done his body good. We pass through a set of tall double doors, into an even bigger structure. My gut twists. A building means people. This has to be a *bad idea.* But I say nothing. I'm tired of following my instincts into dead ends. Literally. So this time, I leave it to him. Let someone else take the reins. No clue where we'll end up, but at least I'm not in this alone. We're mid-sprint down another hallway when he suddenly stops. I slam into his back with a grunt. He doesn't flinch. His head tilts like he's scanning.

"What is it?" I whisper.

He doesn't answer right away. "We shouldn't go this way. There's two around the corner on the right and three more coming from the back. I won't be able to take all of them without drawing more attention. And then there's that one. They have a marker. As I am, that one may be trouble. Do you see anywhere we can hide?"

I spin, frantic. "Uh."

"Hurry. We're running out of time."

Double doors are cracked open to our left. "This way," I tug him inside. The room is plush velvet couches, bronze trim, ornate everything, but I barely notice. Voices echo from the hallway now. I scan the room. A door in the corner. Yes... No. *Shit*. It's just a linen closet. I don't think. I grab Arrio's arm and drag him in with me. It's so small. I wedge us in anyway. Heart pounding so hard I swear it's going to give us away. We're chest-to-chest, and I can't even close the door all the way. An inch and a half stays open, and I freeze, hand trembling near the handle. *Please. Don't look this way.* Footsteps enter the room, followed by a voice.

"Madam Noelle, please, have a seat. It's an honor to host you. We are thrilled that you are open to discussing the potential cooperation with the Kingdom of Palloria."

Madam Noelle?

Another voice chimes in, more casual. "Uh, yeah. Can I get like, something to drink?"

"Of course. My servants were prepared to have an assortment of refreshments ready for you, but you arrived a few days sooner than expected."

"Yeah well, I was so ready to get out of that dang desert. The air here is a little drier than I remember it being. Still, it's hella better than Castdor. Like man, the whole trip I felt like I was melting like a freakin' popsicle. Mmm, cherry berry would be so good right now." Madam Noelle says.

I tear my gaze away from his chest to the crack in the door as I listen closer to the way she speaks. I don't think I've heard anyone speak like that here.

"Cherry berry? Is this something we can retrieve for you?"

"No, like, I doubt that. So, it's all good."

A soft clink. "Your water, Madam."

"Oh, thanks."

"We trust your accommodations are pleasing?"

"Yeah, they are. My room is beautiful. And so far, everyone has been nothing but nice *to my face*."

"Um... Yes. That's wonderful to hear. Palloria, and my father, King La'Claw, are honored to host you for this year's harvest. It's promised to be especially magnificent. I hope you rest easy knowing it will be nothing like the first time you visited."

Against me, Arrio tenses. Just slightly. But I feel it. His body going taut.

Then Madam Noelle cuts through the formalities. "So, you want me to suppress the authority of the counsel and silence a few of your enemies along the way?"

My spine stiffens. Her random shift in topic. The messy *bluntness*. The sound of her voice. I know it. At least I think I do. It sounds like her, but not quite. I'm not sure. Part of me wants to peek. To *see* this madam woman. But I can't risk being seen.

"Deities. I was warned you were precariously candid. But I didn't expect it to be to *this* degree."

"And I was told that I would be having this discussion with the King, lady Princess."

"Yes. My apologies for the miscommunication. My father is unavailable. And will remain so for the duration of your stay. I'm not at liberty to explain further. But I speak with his full authority. I hope this does not offend you or impact our negotiations in any way."

The tenseness in Arrio is no longer subtle. His chest pressed harder against mine. I don't blame him. One of the people responsible for everything we've suffered is just behind this door. I'm afraid he might act on it. He still has the sword, and he probably wants to use it. I know how easily that sword could slide between her ribs. After what he did to those two guards, especially that wolf man, I've never seen a body look like that before. The sight of it alone should have made me sick to my stomach. But instead, I felt nothing. So yeah. If he was capable of *that*, he could kill the princess. No problem. But then where would that leave us... leave *me*? That's not a crime you come back from. I'd be branded an accomplice to the murder of a royal figure. And I already know, there are punishments far worse than an underground cell.

I tip my chin up, trying to catch a glimpse of his expression to gauge his headspace. The light from the door spills a cream color strip down the center of his face, and I realize I've never really *seen* him clearly before. Not shadowed in darkness. And it never helped that his locs covered most of him. And being this close, pressed against him like this. It's easier to notice the details. His jaw is clenched tight. As my eyes move up, I see his nostrils are flared, even though his breathing hasn't gotten any heavier.

And his... eyes? I always assumed they were covered by some kind of cloth or wrap. But now, with the light leaking through the crack, I realize what I'm seeing isn't fabric. Not at all. The things over his eyes are round and bulging, textured with tiny, uneven bumps. The colors shift between dark green, brown, and hints of dirty purple. And are they... *moving?* Ever so slowly expanding and contracting, just barely noticeable, like they're breathing... or pumping. Thick, pulsing veins stretch out from beneath them, threading into his forehead and upper cheeks like roots digging into flesh. They look like legless, eyeless frogs, clinging to his face. Like a bandana made of everything disgusting in the world. And God help me, as my ability to think rationally *goes out the fucking window.*

My body starts to shake as my mouth goes dry and the nausea rolls in. At that very moment my ranidaphobia doesn't just whisper to me... It *screams.* Arrio must feel the shift in my body. He leans in close to hand my arm and steady me. As if he isn't too damn close already. But it doesn't matter. He is about to find out that was the wrong move.

Wrong wrong wrong. I involuntarily and unapologetically shriek. Not loud, but loud enough. His hand is over my mouth in half a second, but we both know it's too late. Everything outside the door goes still.

Yeah. I know. What I just did is unforgivable. If this were a movie, I'd be that dumb-ass character everyone agrees deserves to die. So honestly, if Arrio decided to run his sword through me right here and now, I wouldn't blame him. He should be pissed. Definitely. He should leave me here to die. For sure.

But as for me, I can't even be mad at what I just did. I mean, I *can.* But I *can't.* Frogs are my mortal enemies, and I'm not even joking about that. They always have been. I don't know why. It's not like I had some traumatic childhood experience. *Well,* except that one. But I don't even count it, because I don't actually know what happened. So, there's no real excuse. No logic to my madness. It's just... when it comes to those gross little fuckers, all bets are off. I can't help it.

"Who's in there?" Princess Sarianna's voice snaps from beyond the door. "Come out at once."

"I'm sorry. I'm so so sorry," I whisper to Arrio with my eyes squeezed shut.

"Tssss. Just make sure you stay behind me. And when I give you the signal, you run."

"I said come out now!"

Arrio slowly presses the door open, shifts in front of me, and steps out with that same intense vibe he gave off when I first met him. Blocking my view almost completely. For the first time, I really *see* just how tall he is when he straightens his back. How wide his shoulders are. He's a wall between me and whatever is waiting. I attempt to peek out from behind him, but I can't see who's all in the room. Only hear the shift in breath, the gasp, the way the air turns electric.

"Who are you?" Princess Sarianna demands. "An enemy of the crown? Another one of those heretics from the Holy Light Church?"

Arrio doesn't flinch. "*You* wouldn't know my face, *would you*?"

"Someone fetch the guards, now!"

Madam Noelle's tone changes. "I don't like this. This feels like a set up."

My heart flips. No. *No freakin' way.* Now I know I'm not crazy. "Wait." I mutter to myself.

"Who else is there?" The princess says suddenly. "Show yourself."

I started to make my way around Arrio. He stiffens. "I told you to stay behind me."

"I know," I say, already sliding around his side. "But I have to know for sure."

My eyes meet the demi-human's for a flash, but it's not her I want to see.

"It's that human," the princess mutters. "But you were supposed to be—" Then her gaze jumps to Arrio. "Then that must mean... *Guards, hurry!*"

My gaze leave the fox princess and look to the human woman standing across from her. Middle-aged. Shoulder-length dark hair threaded with grey. A long-healed scar crawls from the edge of her jaw to her cheekbone. The lightest hint of lines tug at the out corners of her almost dull eyes. My eyes scan the woman up and down repeatedly. She looks like... *No.* No no. That can't be her. Jemma's bubbly chill face is soft.

Round. Like me, she's twenty-seven and barely looks it. She has long jet-black hair that stops mid back. Her eyes are full of color with an annoying amount of curiosity. She doesn't have any marks on her face. Also her body isn't that toned. Jemma hates working out. This woman is not her. She can't be. So, what's really going on?

"Kaliyah?" The woman's voice wavers.

The princess looks confusingly from Arrio, to her, to me.

"Kaliyah, is that you?" Madam Noelle asks again.

I can't answer. My tongue is frozen. My brain is still stuck in that college dorm room, in a memory of laughter and music and microwaved ramen. I squint my eyes. "J-" My mouth won't finish the name. It's afraid. It's *confused*. "Jemma?"

A chocking gasp leaps from her mouth. "What the fuck. It really *is* you." She takes a step forward, like she means to close the distance between us.

But Arrio's arm snaps out across my chest, blocking her with a force that says *don't fucking try it*. "Stay back or else." He says menacingly. Jemma stops, eyes wide, locked on me behind his arm.

Princess Sarianna recovers first. "Madam Champion, these two are criminals. Prisoners of Palloria. I request your aid in subduing them."

Then Arrio hisses, "You can try."

Jemma turns quickly toward the princess. "Criminals? What do you mean criminals? What exactly was her crime?"

 "She was caught..." She stops short, eyes flicking between us, as if suddenly catching the thread of something familiar. "Do you know her?"

"Yes, of course I know her."

"I would like to know how? What is the nature of your acquaintance?"

"She was summoned to this world with me and the other champions."

The princess's mouth falls open. "What did you just say?

Jemma doesn't miss a beat. "She was my best friend. Ride or die. My Kali. We were *bad bitches for life*. I can't believe you're in front of me right now." A strangled giggle escapes her lips as her voice trembles. "Is this real?"

And that was that. All I needed to hear. No more second-guessing. I don't know how, or why she looks the way she does, but it's her. It's *really* her. Pushing pass Arrio, I fling myself over the low table like a drunk gazelle. I almost eat the floor, but I don't care. I slam into her, arms wrapping. Tears breaking loose. I crush her in a hug so tight I can barely breathe or maybe it's the other way around.

"Oh my god, Jemma. My Jemma." My voice catches. "*Jemma Motha-Fuckin' Noelle Larkins.*" I pull back just enough to look at her, to really *see* her. "Shit... none of this makes sense. How? No. Why? What are you doing here?"

"No, uh-uh." she laughs through the sobs. "I should be asking you the same crap. How is this possible? You look... *exactly* the same."

"But you don't. What *happened to you*?" my eyes wide. "Like for real, what the *shit*, Jemma?"

THUD.

THUMP–THUMP–THUMP.

Heavy boots, steel, and chaos explodes into the room.

"*Your Highness!*" someone barks.

"*Kaliyah!*" Arrio's voice cuts through the noise. I whip around. He's trying to reach me, but the guards are already closing in.

Jemma... *my* Jemma throws an arm out in front of me, pushing me behind her. It stuns me. This is the same girl who used to cling to my arm during horror movies. The same girl who'd duck behind me when cicadas got too close. And now... she's stepping in front of *me*.

"Drop your weapon!" a guard shouts, swords glinting.

They move to encircle Arrio. There's too many of them. He's trapped. *I* know it. *He* knows it. And there's no way he's going back to that cell. Not alive. They're going to kill him. Or he's going to make them try.

"Arrio!" I scream. "Please. Don't hurt him!"

The moment those words leave my mouth, an icy gust bursts from the center of the room, sweeping across the space. Frost forms in creeping veins along the wallpaper. Ice snakes up the blades of the guards' swords, the hilts, their hands. Breath fogs in the air. The temperature *plummets* dramatically and too damn quick.

Princess Sarianna gasps. "Madam Noelle, what are you doing?"

But Jemma doesn't back down. "No. It's my turn to ask the questions. How long have you had Kaliyah locked away?"

A beat of silence. The frost spreads.

"Kali was summoned here, just like me. That makes her a Champion, protected under the Multinational Guardian Act. The very act your great grandfather, and former king, helped signed into law. So, unless Palloria is prepared to violate every international accord on record, I want to know exactly what the hell is going on."

The princess flinches, visibly shaken. "That couldn't be further from the truth, Madam Noelle. I— I had no idea she was a Champion."

"Did she not tell you as much, Princess?" Arrio cuts in, his voice cold. "Or are you just as much of a liar as your father?"

The fox woman's brows cringe. "Do not address me in that tone, elf. I am the Princess, future Queen of Palloria."

"Sarianna." Jemma snaps, stepping forward, "Answer my question."

"Yes, Madam Noelle." As she looks at me, her lips thinning. "She said something along those lines, but she never mentioned you. In fact, she claimed she was summoned to Therion three months ago. While you yourself just said she was a part of your summoning seventeen years ago. So forgive me, but I had no choice but to assume she was lying."

Seventeen... years? Her voice fades out. Not because she's done, but because my mind gets *stuck on those words. She said seventeen years ago.* I had to have misheard her, right? I blink twice. Then look at Jemma. Or no. Not Jemma. Not *my* forever twenty-one fresh-faced Jemma. This woman is someone Jemma could become if she spent seventeen years in a world where everything wants to kill, eat, or fuck you to death. Her skin's harder. Her eyes dimmer. Her smile... I take a step back. Then another. Inching towards Arrio. Because this is not my... This is not my *time.*

Holy shit! Wait... wait wait wait. WAIT. The voice. She told me. She said something was off. That this place was wrong. That *this time* was wrong. This is what she meant.

My mind calls out, *"Star. Talk to me. Tell me what the hell is going on."* I freeze because it hits me. The name I just thought. *Star? Star. Freakin' Star.* I knew I recognized that voice. It was Star's. *So what? I'm losing my shit.* How the hell does a ball of light from my dreams start talking inside my head, can practically freeze time, and knows things I don't. *"Star."* I can't even think straight as I call out to her. She said things have been wrong for a while. *What's a while? I mean, everything felt normal-ish... or at least time did, until... until...*

"Motherfucker." I mumble to myself.

Time was normal until that *mother fucking shit fuck face hooded mage bastard* dumped me in that monster forest. His midnight cloaked face ass did this. He sent me seventeen years into the future. *The damn future.*

Oh shit, what does this mean for me? How do I fix this? Seventeen years. What about grampa? He was pushing seventy when I came here. Is he even still—

Arrio speaks. "If you believed she was lying about being a Champion... why lock her in a cell *with me*?"

The princess snaps back to him like his voice slapped her. "Because of her claims about the blue orc."

My heart lurches. "*Mitus*?" I blurt. "You're talking about Mitus? Have you seen him? Is he here?"

She shakes her head. "No. Our men are still returning from the outskirts, but they did send word back. The report states that there was no signs of this mythical beast. And the town, Vicory Mills was untouched. There were a handful of witnesses that spoke of seeing something... but most were drunken tavern patrons. Unreliable at best. There wasn't any evidence to validate her claims."

So... he left. A flicker of relief warms me. At least it sounds like he didn't hurt Sapphire, Dahlia, or their mom. But now my chest hurts. Like *really* hurts. Not a dull ache, but a sharp *pain*. I wrap my arms over my shoulders, squeezing, trying to hold myself together. Trying to breathe. It's so damn *cold* in here. My teeth chatter. My breath fogs in the air like smoke. I glance around. Most of the guards are on the ground, curled up, hugging their own bodies. Frost is crawling over the walls. Even the

Princess is hunched over, arms and tail wrapped around herself like a shivering animal. And Jemma is just standing there. I know she's doing this. She was blessed with ice, I remember that. But it wasn't strong like this before. This isn't just cold. It's a dang *blizzard* in a room.

Then my eyes fall on Arrio. He's on his knees, arms locked around his chest. Shaking. I don't hesitate. I run straight to him and wrap my arms around his cold body, pressing myself against him, trying to warm him with what little I have. "*Jemma,*" I grit through chattering teeth. "*D*ial it back!*"

"Shit! Sorry." She panics as she rushes over. "You okay?" She dropped down beside me.

I don't answer. I'm holding a man I barely know, who killed for me and was ready to die for me. My best friends are now seventeen years older than me. The only family I have left might be dead. I'm lost to my world, and I might never get back. And my damn body won't stop aching for a man I can't stand. *So yeah, I don't think so.* The temperature finally starts to ease, the sting in the air softening as the ice retreats from the walls and dissolves into nothing.

"No. I'm not."

"What can I do?" She knelt closer.

"If you can keep me out of the dungeon, that would be everything."

"That's a given. You're not staying here."

I nod, but not before glancing to my side. "And my friend. He comes too."

She turns facing the Princess head-on. "Princess Sarianna, did King La'Claw have a hand in this violation as well?"

The Princess shakes her head. "What? No! My father isn't even aware of her presence."

"And the Council?"

At that, Sarianna's furry pointed ears flick and her eyes go flat. She exhales, dropping down onto one knee, and crosses an arm over her chest. Then the bow of her head follows.

"I—" Her voice cracks slightly. "It seems that Palloria. No, *I*, Princess Sarianna Vox La'Claw, have committed a great dishonor by mistreating a Champion of Therion."

The guards behind her hesitate, then one by one drop to their knees as well. They mimic her gesture. To Jemma. And... *to me*? My eyes go wide.

"I beg of you, please don't let my kingdom suffer for my mistakes. My people need the strength of the Champions. *Both* Champions," Sarianna lifts her gaze directly to mine, "How can I ever make this up to you?"

I glance up at Jemma. She gives me a silent nod. I take a deep breath biting down my anger. My eyes focused in on the fox woman. "I want a full pardon," I say. "For me *and* Arrio. No loopholes. No bullshit."

"For you. Absolutely. But him, he... my father's... I—" Her words cut off as Jemma's expression changes. The Princess blinks and nods slowly. "Okay, yes. He will be free to go."

I nod. "Good. I also want access to Palloria's Elder Stones."

"Of course, Madam Kaliyah" Sarianna says without hesitating. "You will be granted entry to the Summoning Hall."

My eyes flick to Arrio. He hasn't moved much. "Arrio, are you okay?" I ask, crouching to help him up.

"Yes. I'm fine."

My brows shoot up. "Oh wow. You actually answered my question. So, is this my lucky day, or did freedom turn you into a whole new elf?"

He doesn't say anything. His ears just twitch a little higher. I don't try to look at his face. I've seen enough. His eyes. Those things. They still haunt me. It's a shame. I would've liked to know what my mysterious cellmate actually looked like.

"Oh, come *on*," I tease gently. "After everything we've been through, you're really still giving me the silent treatment? I've spilled my whole life story to you, and I still get nothing?"

He's quiet for a moment. "What would you like to know?"

I blink. "Seriously?"

He nods.

"Well damn. Okay, um. How old are you?" With the way he looks, combined with the way he talks and acts, my guess has been around thirty-four, thirty-five max. It's something I've been wanting to know for the longest time. He's always talking to me like I'm a child, when he's probably not that much older than me.

"You want to do this now?"

"You kidding me. You're in rare form. I don't know when this offer will expire, so yes. Now please."

"If you really must know, I'm one hundred and twenty-nine."

I choke. "No freakin' way. That's... that's..." My body sways. A fluttering dizziness takes over. "Oh, dang."

"Kaliyah," I hear both Jemma and Arrio say at the same time.

Jemma grabs my arm. "Hey, hey! You okay?"

I grip her back, wobbling. "I don't know. I... I—"

The voices around me start to fade. Everything feels far away. And then my body surrenders. I fall into Jemma's arms as the world goes black.

CHAPTER 25
CONTRABAND

KALIYAH

Mmmm. This pillow feels like heaven. My face nuzzles it between my arms, greedy for every fiber. My whole body sinks deeper. I don't want to move but my bladder won't quit nagging me. It's ready to explode. And for a second, I think, let it. *"Mmmmm."* I groaned into the pillow and peeked one eye open. There's soft moonlight spilling through the curtains just enough to light part of the room. The space is huge with high ceilings. Walls laced with old portraits and other fancy crap. I don't have time to be confused. I throw the covers off and stumble out of bed, legs stiff. I clamp my thighs together, hands pressed between them to hold it in as long as I can. I race to the door in the right corner near the bed.

"Please be a bathroom. Please be a bathroom." I beg. Shuffling as fast as I can, bare feet slapping smooth hard floor.

I really don't want to pee on myself. *Oh my god*. There's a toilet. A beautiful non-hole in the damn ground toilet. Fingers fumbling as I struggled with the laces on my pants. I dropped my butt down and opened the gates. My whole body leaned forward, in relief as I pressed my hands into my lap.

Still half-groggy, I swiped at my face and let out a long, grateful sigh. That's when I looked up and my jaw just about hit the tile. Right across from me, smack in the middle against the wall, was the biggest bathtub I'd ever seen. It was square and look deep. Not big enough to swim in, but close. After flushing, I shuffled over and gave it a closer look. I didn't see any knobs. Just some rope chains hanging from the ceiling like vines. I gave one a tug and water burst from three spouts in the wall, clear and steaming. My eyes lit up. Before the tub even had four inches of water, I was already yanking my clothes off, nearly tripping over them in my rush. I practically crawled in, letting the water pour over me. It feels so warm and so damn good. It melted the stiffness right off my bones.

Then, the spout on the right started spraying something pink and syrupy. Bubbles foamed up all around me, sweet-smelling and soft on the skin. "God, yes." I whispered, sliding over and letting it drizzle all over me. I scooped some up, rubbed it into my arms, my shoulders, even my scalp. I didn't care what it was. It felt like paradise. I was in there long enough for my fingers to all wrinkle. I stepped out, dripping and loose-limbed, and stared down at the pile of filthy rags I used to call clothes. *I'll be damn if I put those back on.*

I glanced around and spotted a cupboard in the corner. Folded inside are big plush towels and a few robes. I dried off and pulled on one that was long, silky, black with pale pink trim and cherry blossom petals dancing across the fabric. The sleeves brushed my wrists, and the hem kissed my ankles. It tied at the hip, draping so soft and elegant, it could pass for a dress in the right light.

With my body finally, finally clean, and my skin feeling like smooth jello, the bed is once again calling me. I wanted to answer it so bad. But my stomach had other plans. It growled and cursed at me.

I shuffled over to what I *hoped* was the bedroom's main door and cracked it open just enough to peek out. This wasn't a cell, that much was clear. I might not be a prisoner anymore... maybe. Probably. Honestly, I don't know what the hell is going on. I just want food and my pillow to scream in to until the world stopped spinning. I eased into the hallway, moving slow and careful, sticking to the wall like I was trying not to be seen. Hell, *I was* trying not to be seen. The hall stretched out like a castle maze.

Then I heard faint music flowing from somewhere down the hall, mixed with voices and laughter. My whole body said 'nope'. I turned around fast and tiptoed the opposite way. If music meant people, and people meant another round with Fate, and whatever else she has planned for me, *yeah no*. I'd rather deal with hunger than the unknown again. I just needed a break from this insane reality. Just a second to *breathe* and not be overwhelmed. I've become pretty good at ignoring my hunger anyway. I've done it so many times now, it is like second nature. Starving hasn't killed me yet. Doubt another day will. But right as I turned the corner to head back, a door swung open hard... *BAM!* Damn near smashed me in the face. I froze in place. Two voices came from behind the door.

"Hey, get over here quick and help me with this."

"Yeah, let me just get this to the kitchen first."

"Just drop it. Gotta unload the rest of the carriage. Lymon's gonna have our fangs if we screw this up."

"Commander Lymon can eat a dick. He's got his tail jammed so far up the princess's pinched little ass, I'm shocked she can still take a shit. And he's got the nerve—"

THUD.

The guard drops a crate keeping the door propped open.

"Keep your fucking voice down," the other guard hissed. "You trying to lose your tongue too? Let the commander hear that and you'll end up like Zarion."

"Shit. That *was* the commander?"

"Uh-huh. They say Lymon caught him paws out and pants down with one of the nobles, and he had to make an example out of him. I'm just sorry I didn't see it happen. That prick was a disgusting bastard."

"Damn. Karma was bound to catch up to him sooner or later."

Their voices faded as they moved further down the hall. I waited a minute before slipping around the edge of the door. That's when I noticed the crate left behind, lid was slightly cracked. And inside pink and lime green fruit, round with soft little spikes. They looked just like the mountain fruit I survived on, except the colors are flipped. Pink flesh with green-tipped spikes this time. My stomach made a noise like it could eat wood. I lifted the lid a little more. *Are they the same fruit?* I ponder it just a little too long because I start to hear voices again.

"That's the *wrong* fucking crate. Hurry and get it back to the carriage before anyone sees."

"I *got* it, damn. Don't know why your talking shit. You're the one that handed me the damn crate."

"Just shut up and get it."

They were heading back. I snatched two fruits from the crate, quietly closed the lid shut, and darted around the corner, just in time. I pressed myself to the wall, holding my breath as they walked past, cursing and muttering.

As soon as they were gone, I sprinted back to the room, slammed the door shut behind me, and looked for a lock. But of course, I don't see one. So, I did the next best thing and shoved the heavy-ass dresser in front of the door. If I was gonna be trapped somewhere, it was gonna be on *my* terms. The room was dim. I looked up at the chandelier. Maybe it worked on magic too. I don't know how to turn it on, no switch in sight. I stopped caring to look and headed towards the window.

No. That's not a window. Its balcony doors. French doors, cracked open just enough for a breeze to tickle my robe. I walked out and stepped onto the stone. The stars were tiny but bright with the two moons high and shining. Out in the distance, way past the landscape, was the ocean. Or what I *thought* was the ocean. It looked like a black desert, dusted in glitter.

"Oh dang," I whispered. It was actually kind of beautiful. My stomach growled again, louder this time. I leaned against the balcony rail and pulled out one of the fruits. Held it in my palm. Such a familiar feeling having it in my hand. I sniffed it and my mouth watered, but I hesitated. *Is it safe? Probably. Maybe.* If they are serving it in a palace, it has to be. If its anything like the fruit from the cave, I'm going to have a wicked case of dry mouth afterwards. *Whatever.*

I bit in and liquid exploded in my mouth. *Whoa.* It was nothing like the mountain tree. This was juicy. Like, *drip-down-your-chin* juicy. And so sweet. Almost *too* sweet... but maybe that's just because I haven't had sugar in forever. The flesh was soft, like a ripe peach. The skin is thin and barely there while the taste was something like kiwi mix with pineapple. I devoured it. Seeds and all. They were tiny, and easy to swallow. I lifted the second one, already moving to my mouth, already mad I didn't grab more.

Just as I was about to take a bite, I heard a scrape. Furniture dragging across the floor. Someone was coming. My pulse quickened. I looked at the uneaten fruit. *Shit. Shit shit shit.* I couldn't get caught with stolen food. They'd toss me back in a cage so fast my feet wouldn't touch the floor. I darted to my left, slamming my hips into the cold balcony rail. I raised my hand, ready to chuck the fruit into the night, but paused just for a split second. *Damn... It's so good though.*

"Hello," I heard a voice say. I *yeeted* that fruit so fast.

"Kaliyah," the voice said again, closer now. From the balcony. I spun around, already prepared to hate whoever ruined my meal and groaned when I saw him.

"Arrio." I said, half-relieved, half wanting to throw *him* off the balcony. I just tossed one of the most delicious things I'd ever eaten for *nothing*.

"Kaliyah, are you alright?" he asked. "What was going on with the door? Did something happen?"

I let out a breathy little laugh and shook my head. *This man and his questions.* "No, I'm okay. It's just... when I woke up, I didn't know what was going on or what to expect. Especially when I didn't see you anywhere. I just felt safer with something blocking the door. Little help that did, though. I'm glad to see you're okay. Which means the princess kept her word."

I haven't forgotten about whatever *that* is on Arrio's face, so I continue to avoid looking there all together. I *am* curious about it, but I'm also hungry, tired and just not in the mood to have any heavy conversations. And based on how disgustingly painful it looks, I'm betting that's just where the story will lead. I'll save it for another day.

He steps closer. "I'm please to know you're up and walking around. You've been out for several days."

"Days?" I gasped, thinking that's crazy and yet... it doesn't feel like it was long enough.

"Yes. I believe you must have exerted yourself too much and your body forced you to rest."

"Is that what happen?" I looked down at myself. "Makes sense, I guess. A whole lot has happened in such a short time. And what about you? You feeling okay?"

He chuckled softly. It was the first time I've ever heard him make a sound like that. It sounds good on him. "Thanks to you, I'm more than okay. Actually, there is something I want to tell you and now that you're awake."

"Yeah. What is it?"

"The thing is... when you were first placed in the cell, I thought you were sent there to spy on me."

"What?" I half laugh.

"You see for years King Korrak has tried many things to get information out of me. Information or rather secrets I have been holding about Yurakora, the kingdom I am from."

"What, *really*? Me, a spy? Is that why you gave me the cold shoulder for so long? And all the questions?"

"That's part of the reason, *Yes*."

"I'm not a freakin' spy, Arrio."

"I know. After a time, I realized that. You were way too honest and forthcoming to be a spy. In fact, you are the most genuine human I've ever met. And you also possess the most beautiful, most powerful soul I've ever seen." He pauses for a moment. "I am free because of you. I owe a debt I cannot begin to repay and my deepest gratitude. Thank you, lady Kaliyah."

So... this whole time... he thought I was there to extract some kind of information out of him. I wish he had told me that from the beginning. But it probably wouldn't have changed anything. At least he knows now.

A surprising shiver crept down my spine. At first, I thought it was caused by a cool breeze that hit me, but I felt nothing but warmth.

"Oh wow. *Lady Kaliyah*, not youngling." I said with a smirk. "So, you finally see me as an adult woman. And did I hear *most beautiful* somewhere in there. Are you just buttering me up out of guilt or are you trying to buss it wide?"

My lids expanded. *Ohhh my god.* Did I really just *say* that? Why the heck did I just say that?

"Buss it wide?" Arrio repeats. "Buss what wide?" He tilted slightly. "Can you elaborate? Sometimes I don't fully understand your vernacular."

"Um, it doesn't mean anything," I fumbled, fanning my face like that would help the heat crawling up my neck. "Just... silly talk. Don't worry about it. It's kind of warm out here, don't you think?"

"You think so? I find it incredibly refreshing compared to the dungeon."

"Oh, right. Don't remind me of that hellhole. Are we really free?" I asked suddenly, voice quieter now. "Or are we just being *made* to believe we are? Because of Je— I mean Madam Noelle?"

I don't think I'm fully ready to accept who she is. Not yet. If Jemma, Darrius, and Ryan are *all* here seventeen years later, then that means the Empress never sent them home. I exhaled sharply, looking down at my hands. I hate myself for never even considering the possibility that they wouldn't be okay. That they wouldn't be sent back. It was so blatantly obvious that she favored them, I thought surely once they fulfilled her request, she would return them home. Or maybe it was just easier for me to believe that. I'm so stupid. A low down dirty person is a low down dirty person, monarch or not. I was selfish. I only thought about *me*. I've only spent three months in this shithole of a world. But them... *seventeen years.* I can't even imagine. I saw the long deep scar on Jemma's face. What they must have been through, the things they've experienced. The horror stories. I'm really not ready to face them yet. I need another day. Or six. The achiness in my chest is still there... But... not as much today. Not as tender.

Arrio's voice came low. "Actually, I've already received my pardon scroll. Your companion carries yours."

"Oh." I blinked. "Well... in that case, I'm surprised you're still here. Shouldn't you be halfway back to elf land by now?"

"You mean Yurakora." he said with the faintest smile.

"Yeah."

"In any other situation, I would've been long gone. But there are certain... *circumstances,* I'm still trying to work out. Once they're settled, I'll return to my *elf land*." He mimicked me, tone playful.

I grinned. "This is the most you've ever said to me, you realize that."

"I'm aware. I guess you finally grew on me."

I chuckled softly. Not as hard as I wanted to. Something was starting to feel off. *Really* off.

"I grew *on* you, huh. Would you like to grow *in* me instead?" I blurted.

His head snapped towards me. "Come again?"

"I'm sorry. I don't know why I said that. I'm feeling really weird."

"Weird how?"

I didn't answer. I couldn't. It was too embarrassing. I had no clue what was happening, but something was definitely wrong. My whole body felt buzzy and light, like I'd had too much wine on an empty stomach.

I pressed a hand to my chest, and that's when it hit me. "Shit." I yanked my hand back like I'd touched fire. "What the heck was *that*?"

"What? What happened?" he said quickly. "You need to talk to me."

"No no. It's nothing. I'm fine." I swallowed. "My skin's just a little sensitive right now." Maybe I'm having a reaction to the pink syrupy soap from the bath. It didn't hurt, not exactly. It actually felt kind of *good*. Maybe a little *too* good. Still, it was a shock. But also... I wanted more.

ARRIO

Kaliyah has spent the better part of the last three days asleep. The royal healers say she's physically fine, but I know the truth. It's not her body that's the problem. It's her core. Whatever power she tapped in to, it drained her. And now her body is recuperating. I was surprised to learn she truly is a being summoned from another world. And yet she carries no marker. It might have something to do with what she is? *What even is she?* In all my years I've never come across something like her before. I don't think *she* even knows. No, I'm certain of it. If she did, she could have freed us from that cell ages ago. But she didn't. She stayed, suffered and endured. She *shared* her meals, her stories, her mind with me.

She set me free and then requested a pardon on my behalf. *Me.* If she only knew who I was, the things I've done and the reasons why I was imprisoned. Unlike her, I was in that cell for a reason. Clearly, Princes Sarianna also has no clue of the nature of my imprisonment, because if she did, then every guard in the palace would be after me. But the fact she doesn't, and her father is *unnaturally absent* throughout all of this. It makes me wonder. Korrak must be either gravely ill or dead and the princess just hasn't announced it yet. There's much on the line after what I've learned from the few servants that enjoy sharing secrets, just as much as they love hearing them.

If he's not, he better pray to whatever fucking deity he worships. Pray that death takes him before I get the chance. This would be the perfect chance for me to return home, to gather my men and storm this wretched kingdom. I've been gone far too long. But... I can't. Not yet. Not until I understand *this*. This damn *compulsion* to stay near her. The *need* to protect her. It doesn't make sense. She's far more capable than any creature, man, or beast I've ever faced. She doesn't need me. Not when she also has the champion at her side. I'm just a shell of who I once was anyway. It will take years to recover from the torment my body has endured. And even then, as long as this curse blinds me and eats away at my power, I'll never be that elf again. But maybe that's not such a bad thing.

If there's one thing the dungeon gave me, it's time to reflect. I used to be ruthless, uncaring. I didn't value the lives of anyone outside my own kind. Hell, I *still* feel that way, more than ever. And yet, in just a short time, she has grown on me. Maybe because I know she can't possibly be *just* human, not with that much power inside her. Knowing that makes it easier to accept what I've been feeling. I enjoy being near her. I like hearing her voice, even when she tries to irritate me. Especially when she teases me. She's amusing. As much as I try to pretend otherwise, I like her company. Far more than the elf in me cares to admit. Maybe the loneliness got to me. I was starved not just for food, but companionship after all.

I wonder could it have been any woman that made me realize this. If any other woman would have been placed in that cell with me, would I have had the same reaction? I don't know. Not any woman is like Kaliyah. *Yes,* that's right. She's no youngling. Anyone with the grit, the wit, and the strength to survive and do what she has done deserves my respect. She's a woman. A woman who always smells... *intoxicating.* She must've bathed recently. Her scent is stronger than ever. I'd like to lean closer, breathe her in. But I know how *creepy* that would seem. She may be foreign to this world, but she's no fool. She'd see through any lie if I tried to claim it was some elven custom. Still... how much longer do I get with her? If only I could bring her with me. What a wild, impossible thought. To another elf she's still just a human and with foreigners forbidden from entering my lands, I will have to leave her here. But so be it. She is no one to me after all.

"Shit!" she suddenly shouts, then lowers her voice to a whisper. "What the heck was that?"

I step towards her. "What? What happened? You need to talk to me." She keeps saying strange things. Even *stranger* than usual. Things that seem suggestive, things she shouldn't be saying to me. And Yorka help me, I may be an elf but I'm still a man. A man who hasn't felt the warmth of a woman in a *very long time.*

She murmured, "No no. It's nothing. I'm fine. My skin's just a little... sensitive right now."

"Sensitive?" I repeated, stepping forward. "May I check?"

She sounds, half annoyed, half bemused. "How exactly are you going to do that? I hate to keep throwing this in your face, but you're blind *Arrio.* You can't even *see* my skin. Sometimes I think you forget that. Don't worry yourself about it. I think I'm just having a reaction to the soap from my bath. I was in there for a long time." she added quickly. Then muttered under her breath, "Either that or I'm allergic to that fruit."

My ears twitched. "Allergic? Fruit? What fruit?"

"Just something I stole from a guard." she says dismissingly. "Look, I don't want to be rude, especially to you of all people, but I really, *really* need to be alone right now."

"Not until I know what you ingested." An enemy of the kingdom bribing a guard to poison the crown isn't out the realm of possibilities, especially now with war so close.

"I don't know what it's called. We don't have anything like it back home."

I moved closer and gently took her arms. She trembled at my touch. Her skin was burning hot. Her breathing deepened, turned sluggish. Her speech was different. Slower. Thicker.

"Kaliyah," I said firmly. "This is important. I need to know what you ate."

She moaned unexpectedly. "So touchy, man-elf. You totally want me, don't you?"

There she goes again. *Why is she behaving in such a way?* Now that I stood closer to her, I caught the scent more clearly. It was fruity, rich and unmistakably sweet. I needed to be certain. In my haste, without thinking I cupped her jaw, fingers pressing gently into her cheeks to part her lips. With my other hand, I swiped a finger along the inside of her mouth and tasted her. It was a moment more intimate than I'd meant it to be. More intimate than I could justify. But all I tasted was emberkiss. No poison. No trace of anything foreign or fatal. Just the heady, syrup-sweet flavor of the illegal fruit. The sexual innuendo made sense now. A small slice or two causes mild stimulation, nothing serious. Now I understand her request for privacy. I've also realized, I've might have unnecessarily crossed a line. Her breath caught, and though she says nothing, her stunned silence spoke volumes. I turned away, the heat of my shame crawling up my neck. "I apologize," I said stiffly. "I needed to be sure. I'll leave you now."

But her voice stopped me. Soft. Almost shy. "You don't have to go," she said. "Stay with me." Her words struck me. But I couldn't let myself believe she meant it, not with the fruit clouding her mind. Not while she was under its influence.

"I'll return in the morning with breakfast," I said gently. "Get some rest, Kaliyah."

"You're so frustrating," she muttered behind me, and I could hear the poutiness in her voice. "First, because of you, I didn't get to eat my second fruit. Then you go and finger my mouth. And now you're just going to walk off?"

I froze. *Second fruit?* I'd assumed she'd only had a slice or two. But now, I turned back to her slowly, suspicion rising. "What do you mean by second fruit?" I asked, my voice sharper than I intended. "Surely, you meant—"

My jaw slackened the moment I turned. Her core was much higher in the air than before. Has she climbed the balcony rail?

"Kaliyah," I barked. "What are you doing?"

"It's... so hot," she murmured, swaying forward slightly. "I'm trying to cool down, duh."

She was tipping. I lunged, arms wrapping around her waist just as she was going over. I kicked off the ledge, spinning to shield her body with mine as we slammed against the wall. Her bare skin heated against me. The silk of her garments I felt before was gone. She disrobed at some point. Normally I would just think this as normal Kaliyah behavior, but I know better. She let out a sound caught between a gasp and a moan.

Damn it. Why didn't I pay closer attention to what she was saying? She said this wasn't a fruit her world has. So of course, she wouldn't know the effects and that eating too much can be deadly. That is exactly why it's band across most nations.

"Kaliyah, how much of the emberkiss did you eat?"

She exhaled slowly, her body relaxing in my arms. Not a good sign. I shook her gently.

"Kaliyah," I pressed. "Answer me. How much?"

"All of it," she whispered.

All of it. Fuck. This was bad. The aphrodisiac fruit is not meant to be eaten in that way. It will overload the nervous system. I have to get her to a healer, and quick before she—

"Arrio," she cried, curling in my arms. "It hurts. My body… it hurts and tingles all over." She trembled, her muscles tightening like coiled rope, her breath turning shallow and ragged. "Make it stop," she whispered. "Everything is so hot." I felt the compulsion just like I felt when I attacked the guard in my cell. The instinct surges from deep within, urging me to act, to touch, to *release* her pain. I moved instinctively, my hand lowering to where I know I can ease her flame. My mind quick to the realization of my actions this time around. And I stop myself, but not without resistance. My body feeling like its betraying me. Warring with the commands of my mind.

"No." My hand froze midair, every muscle rigid, breath shaking through clenched teeth. No matter what the fruit compels her to say nor no matter what this compulsion compels me to enact, I will not. I have to reframe. I clenched harder. My arms tremble from the effort it's taking me to restrain myself. The urge is nearly unbearable. But so is the idea of crossing a line that I should never cross, not with a human. These damn urges, this unidentifiable force will not steal my will. I won't be controlled by this. Another whimper escapes her and my body attempts to push on despite my protest. I hold and hold and hold some more. The harder I try to release her the tighter my grip gets, the lower my hand wanders. The force so strong, I can feel the veins across my arms and neck bulging. My abs tighten. I know she is in pain. But even if part of me isn't fully opposed to the idea, I won't. I'm an elf of noble blood. A high elf of Yurakora. My morals, my integrity, they are what define me. Whatever this compulsion is, whatever pull that stirs me, I will not let it master me.

Listen to me, damn it. Do as I command. Release her. Seek a healer. It is no use. It's taking everything in me not to touch her more than I already am. Let alone travel through this maze of a castle in the hopes of finding someone who can help in time. My own breath is ragged now, tearing from my chest. It feels like something is being siphoned out of me, my strength or maybe something deeper. I don't know how much longer I can endure this. Either my will or my body is going to give out soon and by the feel of it, so will hers.

I yell out. "Tell me it's okay."

"Arrio."

"I need to hear you say it's okay for me to touch you."

"Huh? What?"

"I can make the pain stop, but I have to reset your body. Caress it in order to relieve the tension building inside of you. If I don't, you will overheat, and your heart could give out. Is that okay?"

"Uh-huh." She mumbles immediately.

"I need to hear you say the words. Tell me it's okay to please you."

She says nothing. I am straining to hold out. And the painful tension in my own body feels as if it threatens to burst every one of my vessels. Something tells me if this goes on any longer, they will. It seems somehow this compulsion is a direct threat to my life if I do not obey.

"Kaliyah." I mutter through clinched teeth.

"Yes, Arrio. Touch me. I want you to touch m—"

She didn't need to finish the rest. Although, I'm pleased to hear it leave her lips, this is not the condition I would want it to happen. Still, my hands wasted no time traveling down the length of her body, heading straight for her sensitive area. The fingers of my right hand came into contact with a lush, thick mane hiding her second most perfect lips on her body. They were second to the two softest pieces of flesh I had ever felt before, resting on her face. So divine. My left arm cradles over her luscious bosoms as I pinned her to me. Her back to my chest. Her hips buck. Her reaction I found damn enjoyable. I want to know what other ways I can make her body move. My left hand dropped down to her breast and I couldn't have been more pleased. They felt like plump cushions made just for me. She trembled as I tenderly jiggled them between my palms. The moan that escaped her lips outperformed any song I've ever heard in my life. The space between her legs was already soaked before I even got the chance to explore.

She winced. My compulsion intensified even more at the sound, as if I needed any more motivation. I have already made up my mind that I would make her body sing. I slowly slid a finger down her slit, teasing it, teasing her. Enjoying it all too much at the way her body jerks at the motion. I want to take my time with her, but I know this is not something that can wait. She needs her release, and because of this inexplicable desire to ease her suffering, I need her to experience it just as badly. I waste no more time as I begin to spread her heated wet lips. She moans again, only this time she begins to squeeze her legs together.

"Do you want me to stop?" I whisper in her ear.

"Uh-uh." She mutters.

"Use your words. Just like you always do."

"No. Don't stop." She breathes. "Please. Come to me. Please. Come. Find me."

"That's it." I murmur, securing her even tighter to my chest.

I took each of my legs, looping them over hers, and slowly widened them apart, opening her. I would like nothing better than to indulge in the source of that caramelizing aroma that engulfs the air. But her temperature has hardly changed. I cannot delay any longer, for my own selfish desires.

"Don't hide yourself from me."

"I don't... mean to."

"Open for me."

"Uh, hm."

My finger flicks her bud at her lazy response. Her body jerks.

"Words." I growl.

"Yes." She says in distorted plea. "I'll—"

Again, all I need is yes. My fingers begin to work her bud, massaging the taut, sensitive part of her until her breaths grow quicker and she starts to shudder. In a matter of moments, she spouts the sexiest moan my ears have ever had the pleasure to perk to. And with my everlasting delight that was not the only tip of mine to perk to her sound. But no. I should not think of my own body's desire. This is all about her and I'm not done with her yet. With a quick upward jerk of my legs, I have her thighs spread even further apart, allowing me uninterrupted access to her entrance. She gasps at the sudden movement. I begin to ease my fingers along her thighs wanting her to feel my every desire for her. My desire to sink into her skin and wrap around her bones. I want to make her feel so good that she nearly forgets how to breathe. My fingers sink lower. And lower. And... lower. I am right above her entrance. I can feel a heat like no other pulsating from within.

Fuck. I want her. I want her so fucking bad. No. Keep it together. Still your mind. "Are you ready?"

"Yes." She replies.

Good. She's learned her lesson. But I have so much more I want to teach her. I sink in to her, wanting her to feel every bit of pleasure, releasing all the effects of the emberkiss fruit. I work my fingers in and out of her. Feeling her slick walls attempting to tighten around me and pull me in deeper. Her body is aching, burning for the need. I will be everything she needs. I push deeper and deeper inside. Her hips rocking to the rhythm of my motion. We are in blissful sync. Her moans growing longer, her desire ever more present. She wants to release so bad. I can feel it and I will not make her wait any longer. I move in and out. In and out. Again... and again... and again. She draws in a deep breath with every stroke. She doesn't seem to know what to do with her hands, moving them frantically about. They cling from my pants to my hair then back down to her own body, then back to me in short rapid burst. She is losing herself as her climax quickly approaches.

My senses are so sharp, so in tuned with her body that I can feel every twitch in her muscles and every flick of her nerve guiding me to touch her in just the right spot, and apply just the right amount of pressure, bringing her right where she needs to be. Giving her everything her body is screaming for me to give. And I will give. And give and give some more.

"Is this okay?" She asks in a breathless tone.

"Mmmm." I groan, getting lost in the moment myself. "Yes."

"I... want you?" She says.

My body reactively bucks into her, at the sudden confession. My cock is tight against my pants as it presses against her back. I remind myself that is the emberkiss talking as I do my best to force down my need. *Calm yourself. Hold it in.*

"I will give you what you want." I tell her.

Her hands gripping me around the forearm. Using my other hand to reach up and touch her beautiful hair to distract my own mind, because I can sense she is right on the edge.

"Please. Please... Can I have you?"

I know she doesn't mean what she says. But in this moment, a moment that will not last forever. I want to pretend that this is as real for her as it is for me.

"Come. I need you." She whispers. "I want you."

"If you want me... You can have me." I admit. "I'm yours."

What she does next goes far beyond my expectations. Her smooth wet tongue glides along my forearm, sending shivers throughout my body. My mental fortitude cracking. I feel a slight release of my own. She's making this so fucking hard for me. Soon after, I feel her teeth buried themselves into my arm. I can tell she drew blood, but the sensation is nothing but pleasure as it sends a flush of energy through me and for a moment, my vision seems to go from stark black to the brightest shade of white. But only for the briefest moment. My breath catches. My body slightly releases again. It is a feeling I have never experienced before in my life and one I will never forget. Her body begins to shake against mine as she loses herself to wave after wave of pleasure. It combs over her again and again. At the peak of her orgasm, her essence spilling over my hand, she screams a named to the top of her beautiful lungs.

This moment would have been absolutely perfect if the name she spoke was mine. Bitter jealousy attempts to ruin the moment. I don't dare let it as her body goes limp and she relaxes into me. Once more her aroma filled me. My own throbbing need trying to still away my thoughts. I ignored it as I nuzzled my face in to the top of her hair. Slowly stroking my thumb in circles around her waist. We sat there for a few minutes. Minutes I wished would turn into hours. She leaned away from my chest, replacing the space with her hand. I could feel her breath against my face, and I knew that she must be looking at me. Her lips had to be so close. I wondered what they would feel like against mine, a thought I knew better than to indulge in.

Damn Yorka. What I wouldn't give to see her face. To know what expression she's making right now. But I don't need to see her to know she's beautiful. I also know this will likely be the last time I ever get to hold her like this. Before today, she's never even shown interest in me romantically. Sure, she's teased me several times. A playful trait I've come to learn is just part of her personality. But I always knew it was just that, teasing. Not meant to be taken seriously. How could she take me seriously? She knows nothing about me, because I shared nothing. Too concern that anything revealed would be used against me. I was cautious. Guarded. As I should have been. Just... not with her.

She has been genuine from the day I met her. She shared everything with me. Open to a concerning degree. I know practically everything about her. I know the circumstances of her upbringing, her relationship with the man who raised her alone, the way she treasures her friendships, what her studies were in her schooling years, and the inner workings of her trade. For weeks, she shared and shared and shared. And yet... she doesn't even know my true name.

As much as I enjoyed what just happened and as pleased as her body presented, I know we were both not entirely in control of what led us here. While the man in me feels hunger and deepening desire, the elf in me feels disgrace and shame. I don't know how she'll react tomorrow, once the effects of the fruit have completely left her system. I wouldn't be surprised if she avoided me altogether.

She holds this position longer than I expected. I start to wonder if something is wrong. Just as I'm about to ask, she begins to chant words I can't make sense of.

"Pull... Feed... Suffer... Pain... Doesn't belong. Get rid of it."

I'm not sure what she's going on about now. The words, the meaning, the way her tone has changed. There's a different weight to her voice. It unnerves me. I open my mouth to ask, but I don't get the chance. Her whispers *adjust*, so softly it might've just been breath against the wind, and then... pain.

It doesn't start in my head. It starts in my eyes. A violent, searing grey that tunnels inward, blooming into an ache so sharp it slices across my skull like it's trying to split me open from the inside. I cry out, hands flying to her wrist on instinct, to urge her to stop. But her hold is unyielding. There's no malice in her grip. Just power and pain.

"Kaliyah, what are you doing?" I choke out, but it's as if she doesn't hear me. She's still chanting low. The agony intensifies, and I swear I can feel something pulling like threads being unraveled. And then, abruptly nothing. The pain and tension and the aching throb I've been suffering with for well over a decade was gone. Gone completely, like it never existed. *Sixteen years.* For sixteen years I've been cursed by a stranger whose name I never learned. Sixteen years of a continuous insufferable headache that wrapped around my skull like chains, binding my lids closed, and eating away at my magic. And now... nothing. I feel *nothing*.

No. Actually, *I feel everything*. Magic pours from me, unbound. It floods outward. Radiant purple light blooming like dusk as the wind curls around us. The power breathes in to me and with that surge my eyes snap open. She leans further into me. And Yorka, there are no words in the Elven tongue, or any language shaped by mortal lips that can capture what she looks like. Her skin is a soft creamy brown, luminous under starlight. Her lips are full, curved like they were kissed into being by the moons themselves. And her hair, her *crown* layered with tight thin braids falling down her face, resting against her cheekbones. But it's her eyes that take me apart. Not just eyes, but *orbs*. Deep, molten cocoa, irises like her core to match as they begin to fade, relinquishing into full brown.

My gaze drops to her hand. There's something there, clutched tight or there *was*. In a blink, it's gone. I sat there with my mouth half-open, breath caught somewhere between awe and confusion. My mind lags behind my body, slow to catch up to what I'm realizing. *I can see*. Not just her, but everything. The world has returned to me in pieces. *Kaliyah. Balcony. Door. Discarded robe. Sky. Stars. Moons*. Her glistening naked body. I breathe it in like I never have before, like it's new air. I tilt, slowly, afraid that even blinking might tear the moment away. And then I look back at her.

Kaliyah. I see her. Not just her core... her soul. But *her physical form*. Her eyes meet mine, and for the first time, I don't have to picture the colors or imagine her shape in my mind. I see all of her. *Yorka*. She's even more stunning than I imagined.

"Much better." The last thing she says before her body folds gently into mine. I don't even think. I catch her. My arms wrap around her instinctively, like they were built for this moment. I *hold her*. And the only thing echoing through the storm of my mind, terrifying in its simplicity, is how could I ever let her go? Not after this. Not after *everything*.

CHAPTER 26
PUPPET MASTER

KALIYAH

What the fuck? What the fuck? What the actual fuck? It plays like a broken record in my head, skipping. I grip the edge of my plate like it might keep me tethered. Relax. Be chill. Act normal and just eat your breakfast. The bacon crunches between my teeth. And damn its good. Really good.

"Mmmmm." My audible moan at the yumminess instantly reminded me of my sounds from last night. My voice caught in my throat. Arrio sat across from me, in his usual composed quiet, like nothing ever happened. The light from my balcony window gently brushing our little round table. I glanced toward the balcony. Only for a second and the image of us out there last night tries to fracture my mind. While he sits there with that same stillness, that same unreadable calm, like he didn't shift my reality with a few fingers and whispers.

I look back down. *Focus on your eggs Kaliyah. I want to* avoid looking him in the face for *more than one* reason now. But I need to see if he's thinking about it too. If it's sitting heavy on his mind like it is on mine, I want to know. He hasn't said a word besides "Good morning." That's it. Nothing else. I guess that's not unlike him. But I thought he'd at least say a little more than that. The silence feels awkward. It's probably even more weird, that I'm not talking either. My gaze sway to his face and for a moment I pause, a little taken back by what I'm looking at. My breath catches.

Arrio's eyes. I can see them. But it's not just that which has me stunned. He's looking at me. Like *really* looking at me. Not at my chest or off to the side. His eyes are *locked* with mine. And god, they're hella beautiful. A lavender hue with a slight sharp tilt. They're almost unreal. And not in the fake contact-lens kind of way, but kinda mystical. I blink. Can he *see* me? I wave a hand slowly. His gaze tracks the motion. Then he chuckles like he's been waiting for me to realize.

"Yes. I can see you."

I freeze. "Wait, what?" There's a pause, suspended between us. "No way. But how?"

His head tilts, just a little. "Do you not remember what happened last night?"

My stomach drops. *Crap*. I was trying to avoid that topic all together. But what would anything we did have to do with him suddenly getting his sight back? *Could it be… No.* I mean if making me orgasm can cure something as permanent as blindness, then I might be quite literally sitting on a gold mine. Then again that would bring me far more trouble than I could handle. *Such a stupid thought Kaliyah.* My brows stitch. But… what if it's true? What if on the off chance, *my gifted blessing* was the power of a magic vagina. Now that would be the last straw. I would hunt down those deities myself and all of them would be catching smoke. He patiently waited for my response. But what the heck should I say?

Sure, there are parts of the night missing, blurry around the edges like a dream I half-remember. But the core of it… *that* I'll never forget. The way he had me. My goodies gapped wide open for the entire world to see. I was completely exposed, utterly vulnerable. Then there's the way he worked me like I have never been worked before. Like he knew my body better than I did. He *owned* every sound I made. It felt so damn good, never mind that I was hallucinating Mitus's voice. It sounded like he was somewhere next to me the whole time. He felt so close and the fact that I wanted him to come to me is a whole other issue on its own. But no matter how many times I called for him, he didn't show himself. I want to say I'm relieved, but if I'm being honest with myself, there is small part of me that wasn't.

Regardless, I haven't felt something that good, in a long, long time. Or maybe ever. Most of the men I've been with have never been as attentive as Arrio was. He was like my very own puppet master. Pulling my strings making my body move however he wanted. *In* whatever way my body needed him to. I had very little control over myself, and I'm embarrassed, mortified even to say I really, *really* liked it. When did I start liking that kind of total surrender? *Oh god.* I can never let him know how much I liked the way he touched me. I know he already silently judges me. I don't want that to be another thing.

I can only imagine how he must feel having had to do that. He's expressed many times how he feels about humans. Crude, ignorant, unrefined creatures, barely worth his notice. It must've twisted him inside to be that close to me. To be that *intimate*. He must've felt disgusted. I never wanted to drag him into that. Once I felt my body getting all hot and bothered, I had every intention of handling it myself. That's why I *told* him to leave. But then the heat took over followed by the hot crippling pain. My mind couldn't focus on anything but that. The stress of it all is probably what led to the slight deliria about Mitus. All of that intense pressure building left me incapable of doing anything but curling my body into itself. Hoping the feeling would go away like some terrible cramp.

I still can't believe that was caused by *one fruit*. I know about aphrodisiacs, but damn. You *never* have to worry about me eating that again. That shit needs to come with its own warning label. Severe hot flashes, extreme horniness, paralyzing nerve pain and finally explosive heart. Imagine if I had eaten the other one as well. I guess that's the second time Arrio's saved my life... or was that the third time. I tilt my head up placing my hand to my chin, pretending to think about it before giving him an answer.

"No, really... everything's kind of a blur." Keeping my answer vague, if it means I can avoid the topic. "I remember waking up. I know I took a bath at some point. I think I ate something? Maybe?" I add a little furrow to my brow, selling the confusion. "But that's about it. Honestly, my head still feels a little foggy." That last part is true. What I leave out is the way my body feels rejuvenize and full of energy. Hoping to change the subject, I kindly redirected the conversation back to my original question.

"Did they have someone here at the palace that could heal you or something?" I was genuinely curious. To think there are people in this world that can cure the blind. That would be amazing. If I could do that *in a nonsexual way of course*, I could help so many people back home and make a hell of a lot money along the way. I wouldn't be greedy though. I'd charge the poor a more than affordable fee, but the rich... Oh, they would *pay out their asses*. I'm talking student loans gone over night. Man, one can daydream.

I take another bite of my eggs, determined to eat until I am too full. I mean sure, I got three meals a day in the dungeon. But when you're splitting rations with a grown man whose ribs you could *count*, it just didn't sit right with me to see him like that. So, I skipped meals here and there for his sake. And by the looks of it, it's really paid off. He's starting to fill out, with muscle returning to his frame. And now that he's in real clothes instead of torn rags, I have to say *damn*. He's actually really handsome. All chocolate and regal looking. And again, those eyes.

He pauses for a long while. Opens then closes his mouth. Seemingly weighing whether or not he wants to let me know how it happened. Maybe he doesn't want to tell me. Just another secret from Arrio the elf. Or maybe... There could be a real possibility that he was never blind. That would make so much more sense. Never before have I seen a blind man move as he does. What if he was fooling me this entire time? I undressed in front of him so many times, not bothering to shield the good bits thinking he couldn't see me. But what if he *could*? What if he's just as much of a pervert as Mitus? A slow chill slides down my spine but not the scary kind. The *embarrassed* kind. The kind where your brain plays every stupid moment back in vivid detail. God. *The bathroom breaks*. The complete body strip when it got too hot. *Ooooh*. Let me find out he was freakin' faking it, and I swear, I'm finishing what I started the first time we met.

"Last night, you somehow broke my curse giving me my ability to see again, among other things."

I blinked, completely thrown. "I did?" The only thing I remember doing to him is squirming in his arms and releasing all over him... several times. "Wait, so that thing on your face was a curse?" That meant it was the same kind of thing Dahlia had. Only it looked nothing like hers. "I really don't remember doing that," I say, because I don't. I remember ripping that weird viny thing off Dahlia's leg just fine. But with him, there's no way I'd forget touching something so bizarre. I go in for another bit of my scrambled eggs.

"Yes, well you did." He nods. "Last night, I came to check on you. Once I did, I discovered you'd eaten an entire Emberkiss. It's a level four Vickara class plant that only grows in regions of Yurakora. It was outlawed over forty years ago because of adverse effects it has on the body when consumed in large quantities. Highly lethal." He looks me dead in the eyes. "The moment, I realize what you had done, I did what was needed in order to... *keep you* from suffering a fate that many have fallen victim to."

Okay, that wasn't so bad. I appreciate his vagueness and saving me the embarrassment by not going into detail. So now if he'd just skip to the part about me removing his curse, that would be great. His gaze never breaking mine he continues, "I had to give you several orgasms. I initially believed one would be enough, but when your heart rate and body temperature didn't decrease, I had to keep going until your body was fully satiated. It was then afterwards, you somehow reached over and tore the curse from my eyes." He ended.

I dropped my fork and my mouth opened wide. Practically choking on my eggs. "What?" I croaked, although I heard exactly what he said. I was just so taken back that he actually said it, I didn't know what else to say. The smoothness in his tone and, the way it rolled off like it was nothing. It flushed me.

"It's important you remember what happened," he said, voice heavy. "For yourself. And because something happened to me when I was with you last night. Something I need to figure out. I believe you can help me with these... *feelings*."

Oh man. I calmly took a breath through my nose. So no time for utter humiliation then. I twitched in my seat, hoping he didn't notice. "Okayyyy." I managed, nervous about what he'll say next.

What else could have happened that I also don't remember? He said *feelings*. Did he confess his love for me or something? I mean, we were trapped together for a while, and I don't know the last time he's been around another woman the way he was stuck with me. Arrio is beautiful as hell, yes. Especially when he narrows his eyes like he's doing right now. And sure, he has magic hands and knows exactly how to use them. Not denying that. But I can't return any feelings he may have developed. Heck, I don't even know him like that.

Damn. Like, I really don't. All that time stuck together, and all I know is that his name is Arrio. Not even a last name. I know he's an elf and not the north pole kind. He's blind *or not anymore*. And… and… that's about it. Oh, and apparently, he's a hundred and twenty-nine years old. Man, that's old. But he looks so young it's wild. Must be an elf thing. Would that make him a cradle robber? I inwardly shake my head. We're not together. So, no. I put a pin in that thought pronto.

"What feelings would that be?" I ask. The arrogant part of me already ready to let him down easy, like the handful of suitors from my past.

"I need to know if you've placed any kind of compulsion over me."

"A what?"

"A compulsion."

"Like urges?" I questioned. Because yeah, I know I've got my own kind of charm, but it's not like I ever turned it on for him. Not knowingly at least.

"It's far more intense than mere urges. It's like some kind of impulse compelling me to you. Or more specifically, to your wellbeing."

"Huh? I don't follow."

"Meaning every time, I deem an immediate threat to your safety, I have this compulsion to aid you. That's why things played out the way they did last night. When I learned how dire the situation was, I fully intended to seek a healer for you, but that didn't happen." He paused, eyes darkening. "I did try to resist it. But the more I pulled away when you cried out in pain, the worse *my* own body suffered. I truly believe that if I had managed to leave you there without aid, I might have lost my life as well."

Holy shit. I wasn't expecting that. "Seriously?" I blink a few times "I had no idea. Is this the reason you've been sticking around, because of this compulsion?"

He's says nothing. Just looks at me. His silence feels different to me now. He feels even more like a stranger. Like I'm seeing this man for the first time and he's not happy about it.

"So…" I swallowed hard, eyes flicking away from his gaze, "how long have you been having these feelings?"

"It first happened to me on our last day in the dungeon cell. When I heard the guard draw his sword and started his approach, my body reacted instinctively to protect you. It was shockingly unexpected, to say the least."

It was for me as well. One minute that predator guard was telling me what he was planning to do to me and the next thing I know both guards were dead. Weapon in Arrio's hand.

"So... is that the only reason why you've been helping me? Because something's been forcing you to keep me safe?"

He opened his mouth to speak, but I beat him to it.

"I think I know what's happening to you."

"You do?"

"Yeah, you're right. I think I am the reason for this compulsion of yours. But just know, I didn't do it intentionally. I mean I did, but not exactly. Honestly, I didn't know it would work like that."

"What are you talking about?" He now seemingly confused.

"Don't you remember our deal. The conditions we laid out." I let out a soft chuckle, still avoiding his eyes.

"Deal? What deal?"

"You know. The one where I promised to share the meals I received, and in exchange you agreed no harm would come to me." Why do I feel like I did something wrong, when he agreed to it? I see now things didn't go the way either of us expected. Guessing because I wasn't specific enough with my wording, the deal interpreted in a general sense. But I was clear about the terms of the deal and mister *use your words* over here, didn't seem to have a problem with mine back then. Hell, I don't get why he's acting surprised. Isn't this Therion, the world of magic? He's an elf, an old ass man that's been around for some time. Shouldn't he know way more about this kind of stuff than me. He is acting like it's the first time he's ever heard of a deal.

"I see now I wasn't specific enough," I said, indifferent. Not like I would have done things differently. I've still alive because of that mistake.

"I still don't understand. A simple promise would not do this."

"Promise? What are you talking about? It wasn't a simple promise. It was one of those *magic binding deals*. I was told if I ever make a deal with someone it should be magic binding. So that's what I did. Since I don't have any magic, I had to use the mana crystal someone gave me. I didn't think it would work at first. But it totally did." I studied the puzzled look on his face. "Did you not understand what we were agreeing to? Or do you not know what a deal is?" Maybe elves don't make deals the same way everyone else does.

"I know what a magic binding deal is. I just didn't know I was entering into one when I agreed to the terms."

"Oh." I paused. "I thought I was clear."

"You definitely were." He closed his eyes for a moment. "Its just humans don't possess magic and I never expected that the guards would allow you to hold on to a crystal containing magic. Nor at the time was I capable of seeing your actions."

"Uh, yeah. I didn't even realize I had it on me at first either. I don't think they ever checked my pock—"

He sighed as he cut me off. "Had I'd known, I would *never* have agreed." He said in a bitter tone.

Okay, he's upset. I can kind of see why, but I'm not sorry. If anything, I'm kind of annoyed myself. This was the best possible outcome for the both of us. Is he saying he would have rather slowly starved with the occasional rotten food tossed his way, than to have the urge to protect a lowly defenseless human? If that's all any of this ever was, then fine.

"Okay. So..." I give him my full attention. The air has been cleared. All the cards have been laid out. I understand that every time he came to my rescue over the last week was because of the deal. We are not friends. We *were* just two people locked away together. Nothing more than cell mates. He didn't save my life because he wanted to. He *had* to. He's not sitting across from me because he enjoys my company, he's forced to watch over me. From the very start, he made it clear I was just a dumb human to him, and I don't think that's changed now that I know the truth. Weirdly enough, I don't know why the idea of him feeling that way about me kind of bothers me. And that in itself makes me more annoyed with the situation. "...now that we know what's really going on, how do we undo it. Clearly, it's not needed anymore, right?" I gesture to the room around us. "You're a free man-elf, capable of getting your own food, and I'm a free woman who shouldn't have to worry about harm coming my way." As the words leave my mouth I know better, if this world's taught me anything else. But that's not his problem.

"So, how does this work? How does one end a deal?"

"Since you initiated it and set the conditions, the power lies with you. If the terms are simple enough, most deals can be broken by your verbal command. Similar to how you created it."

"Okay, so. It's that easy, huh? Then let's get this done with." I begin to project my voice louder. "The deal between Arrio and me…"

"Hold on, you don't have—"

I cut him off before he can finish. At this point, what else is there left to say? "…I would like to end it. Effective immediately." A red X materializes in midair between us. Then it begins to burn away. "I guess that means it's done." My tone turning sour. "You're finally free of me." A bitter thought crosses my mind. If it weren't for the deal, would he have let the guard have his way with me? I remember when I looked to him for help, he turned away from me.

"Kaliyah." He called out.

"Arrio. I do hope you make it back home safely." I say sincerely.

He opens his mouth to say something. Just as he does, there's a quick knock on the door, right afterwards Jemma walks in.

JEMMA

It's been four days since Kaliyah first collapsed, and they're only telling me *now* that she woke up. *Bitches.* I've been checking on her whenever I can. I should have been there the moment she opened her eyes, but no. Because of these stupid-ass obligations I'm forced to participate in. Like, really. None of this political crap makes a difference. That's why I've always hated politics. It's all fake. All I've ever wanted to do was teach, not this bullshit. I take a deep breath. I've only been touring all these cities and towns because I was told it is necessary for the Champion to maintain what little peace we have with the kingdoms and lords over the smaller territories.

With the rulers of Yurakora yet again refusing me passage at the borders and now I have yet to see King La'Claw, how am I supposed to complete my tasks. The princess seems hellbent on staying on my good side. She's under this notion that if she shows me the vastness of Palloria and all they have to offer, I'll favor her kingdom during the next calamity. And maybe I would have considered it. Palloria's larger, with way better resources. But I never liked this monarch bullshit, and Razakar doesn't have any of that. And now, after finding out what she did to Kaliyah, I just can't. It would be Ryan all over again. I really can't believe she's back. I want to hear it straight from her, what really happened. But if what the princess told me is true, then Galldric has some explaining to do. Why wouldn't he have told me what the Empress ordered him to do? Or maybe she never did. She's been gone so long, and yet he never mentioned any of it. Or maybe he doesn't even know.

How was she sent to this time? I don't know Galldric to have that kind of power. And if he did, I can't imagine he'd have let things play out the way they have. There has to be something we don't know, another explanation. I just can't wrap my head around it. All this time, we believed she made it home, that she reached our families and told them what happened to us. But she never did. None of our people know what really happened to us, to Ryan, to Darrius. I don't want to be the one to tell her. But who else is there but me? I never used to keep things from her.

Her... my girl, my longtime bestie, Kali, aka Sizzle. This has to be the craziest thing I've ever seen and I've seen a lot of wild stuff. She looks and sounds exactly like I remember her. Though there's something just a little different. Then again, it's been so long that maybe my memory's a little fuzzy. After seventeen years, I'm bound to forget some details. I remember her as my strong, spitfire best friend. The one I could always count on to have my back. But now, she looks so delicate. Kind of like I used to be. Not like the me now. After all the horrific shit I've seen, I'm not the same girl Kaliyah once knew. And this isn't the same world she left. Now that she's back, everything might change. I tap on the door a few times before stepping inside. There, at the breakfast table, sits Kaliyah and the elf who refuses to give me his elven name. If he was a prisoner here too, maybe he's someone important and that could give me a connection to Yurakora. For a moment, Kaliyah looks upset until she sees me. Then that all too familiar smile spreads across her face.

"Jemma, my spontaneous dilemma," she says with playful teasing.

"Oh danggggg," I chuckle. "Haven't heard that in forever."

"Which is wild, because it hasn't been that long for me, but I'm happy it still fits you." She looks me up and down. "Look at you, all bad-ass and shit."

"You can tell?"

"Hell yeah. The way you handled Miss Foxie with your ice powers." she says, wiggling her fingers in the air toward me.

I mimic her motion as we come in for a hug. Yeah, this is the Kaliyah I remember. It's incredible, how just being around her I almost instantly feel the old me wanting to come out. I fought so hard to keep that side of me alive, but this world has a way of cutting it out of you. Kaliyah used to be a big part of my life and it almost feels like a piece of me was preserved in her. This is such a strange feeling, seeing that this is only the second time I've gotten to speak with her since she's been back. But she's always had this warm, comforting feeling about her. That's why I gravitated to her even in college. I can't get this comfortable with anyone else here in Therion. Everything is just too different here. On top of that, I always have to be *the Champion*. Always on. Always showing strength, grace, and decorum. The exact opposite of who I am. It's fucking exhausting. It was only ever in the classroom or around my friends that I could truly relax. My friends were better suited to take the lead, especially Ryan and Kaliyah. It was because of them I was able to be so carefree and silly when we hung out. A side of me so easy to forget ever existed.

"I missed you guys."

"Same," I say, already knowing the question she's about to ask.

"So where are the other two pains in my ass?"

I should tell her. I'm going to tell her. Just... not right now. "They're not in Palloria. But when we get back to Razakar—"

"Razakar? What is Razakar?" She cuts in.

"It's a small nation off the west coast. I live in one of the cities there."

"So you left Sebbarus?"

"Sebbarus fell during the first war. It still exist, but it ended up—"

"First war? Hold up. Run that back. There was a war that took out Sebbarus? When? Why? And what happened to that Empress chick?"

My eyes flick to the elf. He was looking attentively at us, no doubt ease dropping. I'm still not sure who he is and considering the role his people played in the war, I don't want to say too much in front of him.

"Come on, walk with me." I say as I hold out my hands. She takes it and we leave the room.

We move through the castle halls as I fill her in. Empress Mirella's death, our being summoned being one of the factors that triggered the war. I explained to her how the empress didn't tell us the whole truth about the nature of the summoning and how the elder stones actually work. She lied about a lot of things actually. Nor did she explain the real reason there has never been more than one champion at the summoning. It is because only one champion is supposed to be summoned to each of the four nations and not all of them to the same one.

That somehow, Empress Mirella cheated the nations in order to horde more power for her empire. Her actions is what started the whole domino effect. War, famine, and disease. The Empress was killed in retaliation by her own subjects a year later. And that things have only just started to get better over the last seven years. But it won't last, because the Great Vireth-Kai vowed to bring calamity once more, and this time it'll be twice as bad.

I'm surprised she doesn't ask more questions. She just kind of accepts it. Now *that's* not the Kaliyah I knew. She was always one to question everything, wanting to know all the facts. *Now* I really want to know what happened to her while she was away. By the time I finish explaining the state of Therion, we've reached Palloria's Champion Summoning Hall. Princess Sarianna already granted Kaliyah and I access to the Elder Stones.

"Jemma, that is all the more reason for us to get the fuck out of here," she whispers through clenched teeth. "I'm trying to get my ass home ASAP. All our asses need to go while we still have access to their Elder Stones. You need to call Ryan and Darrius in whatever way its done here and tell them to get here now. Are they in that Raza place too? Is it far? There are Namma stones they can use. They will be here in no time. They'll just need a few things first. Then again... damn. This may take a while."

I say nothing to Kaliyah. The mention of their names again and the fact she doesn't know they're dead pulls at my heart so much. It's been years. I thought I had finally healed from the losses. But now, it all floods back. Before tears have a chance to come, I push open the two large steel doors leading to the summoning room. She can tell I'm keeping something from her. Back in our younger days... or *my* younger days, I could never hold anything in. I ruined Kaliyah's surprise birthday party two years in a row. Her grandad eventually stopped telling me about them. I lift my head and gesture for her to go inside.

"What's in there?" she asks.

"The reason why we never went home." I respond.

Kaliyah looks at me nervously before turning toward the room and walking inside. This summoning room doesn't look much different from the one that used to be in Sebbarus, minus the vines, the flowers and the fact it's indoors. Her eyes land on what was once Palloria's Elder Stones of Cosmara. Four large boulders with sigils carved deep into their surfaces, each cracked down the center. They are all split in two. I can see the expression on her face darken.

"And is it like this everywhere?" Her voice cold.

"Yes." I give her a moment to let her come to terms with what that means. I can hear the sadness in her voice. Not unlike how ours were when we realized we were stuck here.

"*I see...* And when did it happen?"

"Three weeks after you left. Lightning bolts rained down from the sky, striking the stones one after another, in all the nations at the same time, severing the magical connection to home. Many mages tried, but they couldn't get the stones to activate."

"So that's why you guys never went home. Why I'm also stuck here." A grin tugs at the corner of Kaliyah's mouth, but there's no humor behind it. "If I'd only known this a month ago, I could have saved myself a lot of trouble and headache trying to get here."

"But if you had never come, we might never have found each other. It's fucked up what the princess did, and I promise I'll find a way to get back at her. I will."

Her eyes finally tore from the stones, her gaze landing on me. "Is that my bag?" she asked, gesturing to the satchel clasped around me.

"Oh, yeah. I forgot. Princess Sarianna wanted me to give it back to you. She said she had confiscated it until her guards finished doing *some* crap. I really didn't care about what she had to say." I handed Kaliyah the blue strap bag with gold ribbon. I watched as she opened it and pulled out some kind of old, leather-looking belt. She looked at it longingly as her fingers traced along the edge.

"Hey, I have something that belongs to you." She dug deeper into the bag and pulled out a small clear ziplock filled with pink-looking candy.

"No." I gasped. "Is that what I think it is?"

"Um-hum."

I grabbed one of the candies and popped it in my mouth. A burst of watermelon hit me first, a flavor you can't find in Therion. I definitely tried. I let out a delighted moan. "Mmmm." Then popped another. "You have no idea how much I needed something like this."

"I knew I was saving them for a reason." Kaliyah reached in, grabbed one for herself, popped it into her mouth, and began to chew. "Yup, just like I remember... sweet, a slight tang, and the faint hint of THC."

I chuckled as the familiar flavor brought back so many memories. "How about the time you ate half a bag of these during Dr. Patel's ethics class before you even knew what they were?"

She burst out laughing. "Girl, I thought they were just regular gummies you keep in your backpack that were a little stale."

I snorted. "You thought they were stale but you ate them anyway?"

"You know I missed lunch that day. On top of that I was craving something sweet."

"You also missed your presentation for public speaking 101."

"How was I supposed to keep track of time when all the clocks kept melting?" We both dissolved into giggles, the edibles kicking in, and the years slipping away like they never happened... if only for a moment.

Kaliyah's tone shifted. "So..." She paused briefly. "You ready to tell me what happened to Darrius and Ryan now?"

My heart skipped a beat. I knew she'd figured something was up. I just wasn't ready to open that wound again.

"I noticed you said 'I' live in the city, not 'we'. And I've never known you to beat around the bush, especially with me. Every time I mention their names, you change the subject. Just tell me, are they alive?"

My bottom lip began to tremble, and my vision blurred with tears.

"Okay." Kaliyah understood without me saying a word. "When?"

"Not even a year after you left."

"Darrius?" she questioned.

I shook my head.

"So, Ryan." She whispered. "Then Darrius?"

"Six years ago. When things were really bad. Crops were dead, people were starving. So a group of soldiers traveled to Bloodthorn looking for some power source that could be used to jump-start the land. To feed magic into the soil to get things growing again. Darrius went along for support. But at some point, he got separated from the rest of them. He never came back." I sucked in a shaky breath. "But that doesn't mean anything. You've been gone way longer, and look at you now. Here in the flesh like nothing ever happened. So, it's possible... he... he..." My ragged breath made it harder to get the words out.

Kaliyah pulled me into a tight embrace as I melted into her, my words muffled against her shoulder. "He could still be out there."

I couldn't read Kaliyah's face. She was still. Not tense or relaxed, just still. In a soft, soothing tone, she said, "Did he ever finally tell you how he felt about you?"

My chest tensed. "You knew?"

"Jemma, the whole graduating class knew."

Barely able to get it out I say, "We got married."

Whatever restraint I'd been holding on to, I let it go. And I *bawled*.

CHAPTER 27
TOY WITH HER

MITUS

Hours turned into days, then days into weeks. I *refuse* to let weeks turn into months or deities forbid, years, before I find her. *That* day. I was so close. I *almost* had her. I can still hear the last word she spoke echoing in my mind. "Palloria." It was my fault. I never should've left her alone. Not when I didn't know where her mind was. Not when I knew she hadn't accepted me as her mated soul yet. But the moment she was gone, I knew my Kaliyah didn't do that all by herself. The *Namma stones* are fueled by magic. In that moment, I learned her true intentions for the crystal she kept in her pocket. I should have crushed it to dust when I had the chance. I had many opportunities, but I knew she'd be upset with me if I did.

Fucking *magic bleeders*. The moment she vanished before my eyes, I wasted no time hunting down that wench and her mage. I wanted them to pay for what they plotted. Unfortunately for me, it couldn't be physical punishment. Not yet. And even more unfortunately, they knew it. Kaliyah had told the tavern wench about our deal at some point. No matter. There were plenty other ways I can make them suffer. I would destroy every tangible thing they value. I couldn't take their lives, but I would take their livelihoods. I'd burn down the wench's tavern and the mage's precious little item shop. I would level the town just after I set flame to the crop fields, and every townsfolk's home. I would take every ounce of their peace. Once they understood the stakes, they were all too willing to help me locate her. My motives for dragging the wench and the mage along goes beyond punishment. I'm worried that if I go to Kaliyah alone, she'll run again. She seems to have grown fond of that wench. So maybe If she sees them with me, she might be more inclined to stay, at least long enough for me to talk to her.

Talk to her? Have I forgotten who I am. If I want her to stay by my side, then I should tie a damn rope around her waist keeping her from ever escaping from me again. I scoff. As if that could hold her. She's so feisty. She's just as likely to try to strangle me with it. The thought only fills me with thrill. Once she's finally back at my side, I'll need to figure out how I can convince her to amend our deal. Just one change. Exclude mages. Once that protection's gone, that magic-bleeder's ass is mine. Mine to bend and break. Until this ache in my core finally feels satisfied.

Fuck. The longer I'm away from her, the more I *ache* for her. She has no idea what her absence does to me. I want to go berserk. To kill. To maim. To burn everything to ash. I am just *beast* without her. With her not around, I want to lose myself to the chaos and become the orc I used to be. The dark demon Overlord that all feared. It would be *so* easy. I'm right on the edge. What little effort it would take to just tip over and *fall*. Fall into the wake of blood and carnage. *But...* I won't, because I want her so much more.

I know she's close. But where? Is she safe? She's strong, yes, but she's also so fragile in a way she won't admit. And if she's in danger, I want... *no need* to be there. I need to protect her. To love her with every fucking fiber of my being. *And I will.* I'll bury myself so deep inside her that she won't know where she ends and I begin. I *crave* the sound of her body purring undermine. I *know* she's as wild in bed as she is with her mouth, no matter how shy she pretends to be with me. And when she touches me... I can *feel* it. The beast inside her. The sensual, dangerous force she tries to keep locked away. Is she afraid of what she might do? Afraid of what *she* might awaken? But I'm just the kind of monster she needs to *tame* her. *Her... Her...* I *need* to find her.

These humans are slowing me down. We've been in Palloria for three days now and yet the wench, mage nor Carmello haven't been any help.

Carmello. Out of all the fairies of Therion, of *course* we'd run into the most insufferable one. I'm a little surprised he's still alive after all these years. We fought in a few battles together and now he acts like we're comrades, as if we're *equals*. The old me would've run him off by now. But my current power isn't what it used to be and it will be sometime before I'm back to my former self. Back then when we fought, although Carmello could never best me, he could make me break a sweat. So, I guess for now, I'll just have to put up with his nonsense.

"Mitus, *please*. Tell your fairy friend to give it a rest already," Sapphire groaned.

"He's not my friend."

"He's *right*. I'm more like his *best* friend." Carmello grinned.

"Well then *tell* your *not-best friend*, I'm not interested. And while you're at it you need to—"

"Are *you* giving me orders, human wench?" I turned to her with a growl in my throat. "You forget why we're here."

"I wasn't, but—" Her tone lowered.

"But *nothing*. The only reason I haven't killed you already is because you will help me convince her to come back."

"I thought it was because of the deal you made with Kaliyah."

My eyes narrowed. "Don't think I won't still make good on my promise. Your tavern, your crops, the whole damn town. Everyone that calls that shit-hole home, will know they lost everything because of you two. That the tavern wench and magic bleeder are the reasons their little town doesn't exist anymore. Nothing but ash will be left behind. How does *that* sound?"

"For deities sake, why are you so serious all the time? We've been together long enough to know that blue orcs are just as bad as the legends say. So you don't have to threaten us anymore. We get it."

"Do you really?" Apparently, she doesn't. Legend should have told her that I don't make empty threats. The next time I pass that shithole, it's going up in flames regardless.

Carmello chuckled. "You know, Sapphire, Carmitus used to be much worse. The old Overlord wouldn't have been caught traveling with a human or a mage. Unless *they* were actually dead. This woman of his must be *something* special, if she's got him chasing her across territories instead of reclaiming his territory." His tone turned mockingly slick. "Or maybe... he's just gone *soft*."

My blood boils. Before I knew it, I was on my feet, hand around his throat, ready to *rip* it out. The bastard didn't even flinch. He wasn't afraid of me. Not in the slightest. And that... That only made me angrier. "Say it again," I growled, teeth clenched. "I *dare* you."

He looked at me with hooded eyes and that smug curve on his lips. I never had any real issue with the fairy folk before. But I swear to the deities, if it'll wipe that look off his face—

"Hey! Let's all just... I mean *can we* just take a breather?" Sapphire stepping cautiously toward us. I growled again. She froze immediately, backing away with her hands raised. "Alright. I'll just... stay over here."

"Don't test me, dark fairy. I'm not in the mood. And fairy blood might be just what I need to get me out of it."

Carmello lifted his hands in mock surrender. "I apologize, *Carmitus*. I meant no disrespect. I actually *like* this version of you much better."

"Noiz, do *something*," Sapphire hissed.

The mage merely shrugged. "What exactly would you have me do, Sapphire? These two are some of the highest-level mythical beast-folk that exist today. If they fought here, they could wipe out the entire surrounding district."

"Exactly," she snapped. "If you two go at it here, the entire city will know a dark fairy and a blue orc are loose in Palloria. The king will have us hunted and put out. And then how exactly will we find Kaliyah?"

I released Carmello and turned to her, still fuming. "If you think this kingdom's army is enough to keep *me*—"

"Maybe not them," she interrupted. "But chatter around the city is that the Champion, Madam Noelle arrived here a few days ago. And being what you two are, it's best not to end up on *her* radar."

Carmello scoffed. "Don't you worry your pretty little tailbone about her. If she even thinks about making a move, I'll make *quick work* of her."

"You *can't* just stop a Champion!" Sapphire protested.

"And why not? I've ended the lives of a few in my time."

She gawked at him. "You *what*? But... they're Champions. Heroes blessed by the *deities*!"

"And what of it?" Carmello sneered. "One thing you should learn is that the Champions aren't as strong as everyone thinks. The blessings of the deities are just *parlor tricks*. Basic magic for small minds who eat up the spectacle."

I take another look at Carmello. I don't even know why the creep is still hanging around. He says it's because there aren't many of us left from the old days. That we should *catch up*. But I know it's bullshit. We were never close before, and nothing's changed. He's sticking around because of the annoying little wench with the even *more* annoying accent, for some twisted reason. If he wants to toy with her, I don't care. He's just not allowed to kill her. *Not yet*. Not until we find *my* woman. I did attempt to ask him to kill the mage for me, even if that meant owing him a favor. But the deal wouldn't even let me utter the words. It seems I can't have a hand in the death at all. If only there were a way I could incite him to do it on his own. But he's too focused on the wench. I turn my back to them and head for the door.

"Is this okay?" a voice whispers. I freeze. Slowly, I glance over my shoulder. Carmello is tugging playfully at the wench's sleeve. She jerks away from him, while the magic-bleeder sits at the table, fiddling with some trinket.

"What did you just say?" I ask.

"What?" Carmello blinks.

"*One of you* just asked me if it was okay. Is what okay?"

"I didn't say anything," Sapphire says, narrowing her eyes.

"Neither did I," Carmello replies.

The mage shakes his head. "Wasn't me."

My eyes narrow.

"It's late," Carmello says, stretching lazily. "Morning's just a few hours away. You should rest, if we're going to resume our search soon."

I don't answer. I hiss under my breath and storm out, slamming the door behind me. I head towards the bar tired of their bickering and the fact that they still breathe. But then I hear it again.

"Come to me…" The voice. Her voice.

My eyes snap wide. I scan the dim tavern crowded with drunks and whores. I shove past them, knocking over tables and people alike. "Kaliyah!"

"Please... come to me." It's softer now, but clearer. She sounds like she's in distress. I move faster, my heart pounding. The room falls away, noise becomes a dull throb behind my ears.

"Kaliyah, where are you?!" My chest tightens. I can *feel* her pulling me, like a thread tugging at the center of my soul. She's reaching out. Beaconing me.

"Mitussssssss!" She screams my name, and something inside me *snaps*. Something I don't know if I've ever experienced before. Fear. Real, bone-deep fear twists in my gut. Is she hurt? Bleeding? Dying?

"KALIYAH!" I crash through the tavern doors, into the cold night, chasing the pull of her voice, desperate and wild. I *will* find her. And when I do, nothing in this realm or the next will keep us apart.

KALIYAH

I didn't cry. Not while I held Jemma, my best friend who was now old enough to be my mother. Not after she was called away and I walked myself back to my room. I'm not crying now, standing on the balcony, staring out at this world of monsters and magic I know I'll be trapped in for the rest of my life. I'm not crying after learning that two of my best friends are dead. Not at the thought that, after seventeen years, Grampa who may or may not still be alive, has long since mourned me, buried an empty box, and moved on. Convinced, like most would be, that we all died. I should be crying. Someone in my position *should* be crying. But no. Nothing comes. *Not a single tear.*

Weird. But I don't feel sad. Not even a flicker of hurt. Because I feel *nothing.* I've turned it off. Chosen to shut down. This is not a reality I chose to be in, so I rather not acknowledge it all together. Why should I feel anything about it? But it's wrong not to. What I'm choosing is wrong. I should be crying. I should mourn them. They were my friends, my people... my family. It feels wrong not to grieve for them, not to acknowledge their lives. How they lived, how they died. But I can't take in anymore. I just *can't.* Darrius would probably be upset with me, think me cold. But Ryan, Ryan would understand. He was always that kind of guy. Those two. My Beavis and Butthead.

No. I won't go there. Ryan's back at his family's pawn shop, gushing over some collector's item. Darrius is home watching the game, yelling at the screen with a beer in hand. And Grampa... Grampa is on his honeymoon with his new wife in Vegas, probably wasting his money on slots. That idea feels right. It feels better. I say it again as my knuckles pale against the grip of the railing. Then again until my voice becomes more steady. Then again. And again and again. And just as the truth threatens to rear is devilish head back up, I shove it back down with the lie. *No.* The lie is the truth.

"Ryan is at his pawn shop. Darrius is at home. Grampa is on his honeymoon." I repeat it again. "Ryan is at his pawn shop. Darrius is at home. Grampa is on his honeymoon." I don't stop saying it. I keep going until my throat is soar. Until I start to convince myself. Until I start to believe the lie. *No.* The truth. Yeah, that's right. Everyone's okay. Everyone is fine. "Ryan is at his pawn shop. Darrius is at home. Grampa is on his honeymoon."

It's not even noon, but it feels like I've been awake for days. I should sleep. It's always been easier to tune the world out when I'm curled under the covers, safe beneath the weight of a blanket. *Yes, that's what I'll do.* I'll crawl into bed and stay there for as long as this world will allow me. I let go of the balcony railing and head toward the glass French doors. My hand hovers just above the handle when something strange flickers in my chest. A sensation. It feels like... relief? That can't be right. I shouldn't be feeling easiness like this. Not now. But if the lie is the truth, then maybe... just maybe, this feeling is right. I lift my gaze, fingers brushing the handle again. Then I see it. A faint reflection of someone standing behind me. I don't flinch. Part of me is curious. The rest of me doesn't care. The only thing I want is the soft silence of my sheets. I reach for the door, halfway through stepping inside.

"Little breakfast."

I freeze. My heart picking up speed. There is only one person that has ever called me that.

"Did you really think you could escape me. I will always find you."

Slowly, I turn around and my eyes go wide with recognition.

He's here. Tinted blue skin, streaked with dirt. Pale locs fall over his bare shoulders. Mud clinging to the leather shorts he still wears. The only thing new is a deep green belt slung across his waist. Mitus. The blue orc of a man stands at the edge of the balcony. For a moment, I wonder if I'm hallucinating again. But then I step closer. Slowly. Carefully. One foot at a time. He doesn't move. Doesn't even blink. When I'm close enough to feel his heat, I stop. I tilt my head up and study his face. Searching for a glitch. A crack. A shimmer that would tell me this is all in my head. But all I find is fire in his eyes and breath that smells like sweat and the earth and something wild. He's real, isn't he?

"Why did you run from me?" He's calmer than I'd expect him to be. His breath brushes my face. Familiar and... missed.

I smile. Just a little. "Are you mad?" I ask softly.

His brows furrow. "What do you think?"

"Are you going to punish me?"

"Do you believe I should?"

I nod my head.

"And what should I do to the one, who tricked me, plotted behind my back with that wench and magic bleeder, and then ran from me."

I pause for a moment, then shrug my shoulders. "If you want to punish me, then *eat me*."

His eyes narrow and his lips straighten.

"You can gobble me up as much as you like. But I have one request first."

His jaw clenches. "And what would that be?"

I lean forward, pressing my cheek to his collarbone. My arms wrapping around his waist. My body flush against his, as tight as I can make it.

"Let me stay like this for a little while. Please." From the moment my eyes landed on his, I wanted nothing more than to do this. His arms wrapped around my body as if I were a fragile flame seeking shelter, and it felt like curling under a hundred blankets. I felt safe, a shield so strong this world couldn't touch me. I didn't want to let go. I needed this. I needed... *him*.

"You still don't get it, Kaliyah. But even if I have to say it a thousand times, I'd sooner rip out my own throat than ever hurt you."

"I get it."

He let out a deep sigh. "You don't. I love you Kaliyah. I'm in love with you. There is nothing in this world I would not do for you. If you asked me to burn this world to ash I'd do it in a heartbeat. If you ask me to resurrect it. I'd find a way to do that too. You are my beginning and end."

"I don't know what to say to that."

"You don't have to say anything. Just continue as you are."

"Then if you really feel that way about me, does that mean no punishment?"

"No. You will be punished." he says gripping me tighter. "The only punishment that will do, is taking you back to my fortress, chaining you to my bed and making love to you over and over and over again until our bodies become one. And once you yearn for more... *yearn for me*, I will sink my teeth into you and make you mine, the same way I am yours."

I wasn't shocked by his response. He left no room for doubt. He definitely wasn't teasing. There was nothing but seriousness in his tone. Maybe it was the fact that the dull ache in my chest finally... *finally* went away, but without hesitation, I said "Okay."

I feel a slight vibration hum from his chest, almost like a kitten's purr. I forgot he could do that. I don't even think he realizes he is right now.

"That wench and magic bleeder slowed me down, but thanks to Carmello's magic, we got here sooner than I'd hoped. If I promise him a favor or two we could get back to—"

"Do you mean Sapphire and Noiz? They're here too? How are they?"

"I haven't killed them, if that's what you're wondering."

"Oh, I'm sure you haven't. We had a deal, remember?"

"Mmmm. About that... I've been thinking. I want to make some changes. Actually, just one."

"And what would that be?" I said skeptically.

"I want mages excluded."

"Let me guess. You found out Noiz gave me the crystal and now you want to like kill him or something. He was just helping me. I can't let you hurt him. So no, I don't think so, my guy."

"*My guy*? Are you finally claiming me?"

"It's just an expression from back home. But... yeah, I guess that too," I say slyly. "You're mine." It feels so embarrassing coming out of my mouth because I know deep down its true. I know he belongs to me. There's just no getting around that fact anymore. When my eyes finally meet his again, a nervous flutter hits my chest. His gaze is wild with hunger. I feel his hand slide down to caress my lower back, his touch sending a shiver through me.

He looks ready to lay into me right now. I don't know if I'm ready for that. Not yet. There's so much my mind still needs to sort out. I mean, this *man* is a beast. Not in the obvious monstrous way, but *between the legs*. And with all the strength I've seen in him... what if in the heat of the moment, he literally rips me apart? Mmmm. That would be a way to go. Taken out of this world in total bliss.

"You'll never fully understand what you do to me. With just one glance my body pulses for you. Say the word and I'll take you right here, right now."

My mouth waters as that thirsty horny desire returns. It has to be because of him. If his soul is tied to mine, then maybe this whole time I've been picking up on the feelings he has for me. My eyes catch the glint of the balcony railing. My mind flashes back to last night with Arrio, and I cringe. No way am I doing anything sexual here with Mitus. It would feel just plain wrong for some reason. Reluctantly, I pull back from him.

"We should wait. Sounds like what you have planned you don't want interrupted. So, I'll wait until we get to the place you want to take me."

"Then let's not waste any more time." He pulls me in and lifts me off the ground.

"What? You mean now?"

"Of course, my beautiful goddess."

Beautiful goddess. That's a new one for him. I liked the way it sounded leaving his lips. It's way better than little breakfast. *Little breakfast*... I feel my cheeks getting warm. I guess little breakfast doesn't sound too bad either. I rain my thoughts back in.

"No. I can't leave now. I have to say goodbye to my friend and let her know where I'm going. I can't just disappear on her."

He shoots me an incredulous look.

"I promise you, I'm not using this as a way to get away from you again. Actually, I want you to meet her. She's my closest friend in the world."

"If she is that important to you, then I will happily."

I comb my fingers through his dirt-smeared locs, his skin still covered in earth.

"You will, just not like this."

I shimmy out of his arms and pull him toward the tub in my bathroom. I turn my back only for a moment to start drawing the water, then I turn around to find he's already dropped his pants.

He stares at me with that same smirking smile, daring me to look at it. I know exactly what he wants, so I don't. Instead, I return the same mischievous grin and slowly circle around him, just before pushing him back. The back of his leg hits the lip of the tub, and he falls into the water with a splash.

346

"Wash yourself, and I'll go find you some real clothes."

"Kaliyah." He calls out.

I stop and give him a reassuring look. "I'll be right back. I promise. I've claimed you, remember." With that last remark, I quickly closed the door behind me, because I know full well, he was ready to leap out that tub and pounce on me like a cheetah in heat. I took a deep breath, knowing I mean it when I say I don't plan to leave him. Not when everything inside me says he is where I'm supposed to be. I'm still not sure how I feel about him exactly. Which are my feelings, and which are his own inside of me that are being projected. But I know one thing for sure. I'm ready to explore whatever this is between us. For now, I can honestly say at the very least, he's grown on me.

I managed to get one of the attendants roaming the hall to deliver clothes to my door, making sure to tell her not to enter under any circumstances. While she went off to do that, I found Jemma and had her request an audience with the fox princess. The one whose name I still don't give two shits to remember. I told them about Mitus, the blue orc I was trapped with in the mountains. I realized I never actually told Jemma the story, but when she didn't seem completely lost, I figured the princess must have filled her in on some details.

I made sure to leave out the part about him trying to eat me and the fact that his soul is tied to mine. Jemma definitely would *not* be okay with that. I'm already planning to leave her. I don't need to add more stress for her on top of that. The princess was hella nervous about meeting him, never mind that he managed to slip into the castle unnoticed. She seemed fully aware of how dangerous he was and hell yeah, she should be. I even considered voiding my deal with him, just so he could get at her. Hell, I don't need him. I would have beat her ass long time ago if she didn't hide behind all her guards. But *Oooow*, if I ever catch her alone, I'm going to have a new fur coat. Jemma suggested we invite him to tonight's dinner, so we can all talk and get to know each other better. I'm totally cool with that. It'll give me a chance to figure out what to say to her before I leave with Mitus. Me choosing to leave will definitely make her feel some kind of way. But it's not like we'll never see each other again, at least I hope we do.

It's just… I can't stay with her. There's still this small part of me that hasn't accepted that she *is* Jemma. The Jemma I remember was clumsy, silly, and always getting into some kind of trouble. But this version of her is more focused, edgy, hardened. The old Jemma, my Jemma, I would have never left her. The thought wouldn't have even crossed my mind. But the forty-four-year-old ice warrior and champion of the world has lived more of this hell than me. The Jemma who's spent seventeen years seeing and being around nothing but chaos and misery. She talked about the wars, the deaths, the pure unfiltered crazy. It didn't take long for me to understand that it changed her. She's not my Jemma anymore. She's Madam Noelle, and I don't think I vibe with her. The memories are there, but the connection, at least for me isn't. It's crazy to say, and even harder to believe, but the only person in the world I feel any kind of real connection to is Mitus.

I got back to the room to find a very naked man sitting at the edge of the bed. I hurried back to the room as fast as I could, and good thing too. His elbows were buried in his knees, and his fist was at his mouth, brows pinched deep. I could tell if I'd taken any longer, he would have raced through the castle's halls with his balls out and penis swinging, looking for me. This man has no shame in that regard. And with the package he sports, he absolutely has nothing to be ashamed of.

"Here." I handed him the clothes.

He grabs on to my hand, closes his eyes as he uses his thumb to trace circles around my wrist. I give a slight tug and he releases me.

"I told you I'd be back." I say as I made my way to the sofa. I watched as he got dressed, because lord knows he'd of done the same to me. He looked nice... suave, dare I say civilized even. *Although* the high-collar tunic, belt, and free flowing pants were not his style. I think I prefer the fantasy Tarzan look.

I took the time to explain the plan about dinner, and then afterwards we could leave. I requested he be on his best behavior, and he said he would. But I know better than to get my hopes up. He sat next to me with a smile playing at his lips, his usually cheeky one, replaced by something sweeter. Something that made me antsy. At that moment, the reality hit me. I was planning to run away with this man, and really, just like with Arrio, I didn't know much about who he *was*. I mean, I knew his personality, his mannerisms, and a few small details of his past. So maybe I knew a little more about him than Arrio, but I still didn't *know* him. Where was he really from? Who was he before all of this? What are his likes? His dislikes? We had several hours before dinner, so now was as good a time as any to learn.

I started. "So, if this is going to work between us, I need to know more about you. Get to know you better. It can't be all playful banter and lustful passes all the time."

"I agree," he said quicker than I expected. "I don't want you to think I'm just a horny orc. I'm in love with you, after all. And I have no problem showing that however you want."

His confession caught me off guard a second time. A flutter stirring through me just as hard as the first. I did my best to cover it up, clearing my throat. "Right, okay. So that means I can ask you things about yourself, and you'll have no problem answering?"

"Mmmmm. I like this."

"What?"

"*You* taking an interest in me. It feels... *good*. Go ahead. Ask me all the questions you want."

"Okay. Umm, I guess I'll start with... how old are you?"

His grin widened even more. "I can't quite say. I never really keep track of those things. If I had to estimate, I'm around four hundred and thirty, give or take a decade."

My mouth widened. Yep. Cradle robber. "And how long do you live for?"

"Don't know. I haven't lived it all yet."

That's actually pretty cool. Not so much for me, though. I wonder if he'll feel the same way about me, after I start developing crow's feet and grey hair. I'm talking as if I plan to marry the guy. I wonder... has he ever been married before. Nope. I don't think I want to know the answer to that one.

"Okay, makes sense. What about your family? Do you have any?"

I asked him question after question. He answered each one without hesitation. No silent stares or questions of his own. Unlike Arrio, who kept a mouthful of secrets, Mitus was an open book. And he let me read every single page.

CHAPTER 28
EVERY LITTLE DETAIL

ARRIO

Tonight, I will leave. I should leave now. I should have never been in Palloria in the first place. I don't know where King La'Claw is, but it's possible that at any moment he could make his presence known. And if that were to happen, it would make my departure all the more cumbersome. That is, after the princess discovers that I murdered her father. Pardon be damned. Every soldier in this kingdom would be hunting for me. Even if that were to happen, now that the curse that bound my magic has lifted, it would not hinder me from returning home. It was only because of that curse that I was captured in the first place. I must find out who placed it on me. Find out who betrayed me. That will be the first thing I will do before claiming my seat in the Elven Triad. The moment I do, that person will suffer, their punishment will be cruel. I will make Korrak's treatment of me look like child's play.

Making my way to the dining hall, I find myself becoming anxious to see her again. I think of how I will convince her to leave with me. It's already decided. She's coming with me. Even though the compulsion no longer remains, this growing desire for her to be by my side hasn't faltered. It is unusual, to say the least, for an elf to harbor such feelings toward a human. Let alone me. *Me.* I've tried so many times to rid my thoughts of her. But ever since last night, I've felt a pull to her. Not like the compulsion. This is much, much stronger. Unlike anything I've ever felt before. Whatever this is, it's not magic. It doesn't tug at my body like the enchantment once did. It pulls at my core. I need to understand how she affects me like this, making me feel for her, making me want to be with her. Touch her. Lay with her. Make passionate love to her.

Tsss. Leave. I should just leave. I am an enemy to many, and many are enemies to me. Though it has been several years, surely someone will recognize my face and then my quick easy exit from this kingdom will no longer be guaranteed. I've already gathered food and supplies, enough to last the first month of my journey and then some. I should grab them now and head out through the palace gates. The princess was even foolish enough to offer me an ironhoof and a small carriage for my travels. Although, I have the sneaking suspicion there's another reason behind her generosity.

Perhaps this is her version of a peace offering. But if she knew who I really was, she'd sooner offer a blade to my neck than transportation home. Then perhaps this is all a front and the moment the carriage crosses city limits, an ambush will be waiting. That seems far more likely. After all, she may not know why her father kept me locked away apart from all the other prisoners for all those years, but she knows he had good reason. Either way, her incompetence will only bring devastation to Palloria's doorstep that much sooner. Fifteen years of my life gone. For an elf, that would mean little. But when trapped and kept under those conditions, even fifteen years felt like fifty. I've dreamed of this moment. The moment I would walk free again and plot my revenge.

Idiot. I should leave now. Sooner rather than later. My jaw tightens as I struggle with the illogical thoughts that replays over and over in my mind. *Not without her. I will go nowhere without her. She is mine and they can't keep her.* We should skip dinner altogether. I should take her and leave now.

Tsss. If I did that, I would have to deal with the Champion. They seem to be close, and the protective watch the Champion keeps over Kaliyah suggests she means a great deal to her. She's far stronger than most Champions I've seen or even heard of. Probably because she's lived longer than any Champion I've known. I once read in my research that a deity's blessing strengthens over time. I never interacted with a Champion long enough to see if it was true. And now I see, it just might be.

Still, even in my current state, her blessing is no match for my magic. Her ice would be annoying at best. I should leave now. I highly doubt Kaliyah would appreciate me hurting or, if necessary, killing her companion. But it very well may come to that. How long would it take her to forgive me? Maybe not long. She has such a kind spirit, and she doesn't seem to hold grudges. The number of times I called her out of her name when we were locked away together and after only a few sharp words and an hour or so of silence, she'd be right back to talking as if nothing happened. *Don't be an idiot.* Murdering someone close to her is bound to place a wedge between us. I regret the thought as soon as it crosses my mind. I also regret every harsh word I've ever spoken to her.

She didn't deserve them. Once we've left Palloria and returned to my home, I will spend my days finding ways to make it up to her. I want to learn so much more about her. I want to help her discover herself. She is so much more than she believes she is. We'll talk, explore ideas, learn every little detail about one another. Never again will our conversations be one-sided. I will share everything with her. My mind, my home and my body. I'll share secrets I've never told another. And in exchange, all I'll ask is that she remain by my side.

Tsss. Again, I catch myself, unsure where my head is at. Why do I feel like some foolish, love-struck youngling? I pause at the thought. *Love?* I place my hand to my chest, trying to categorize the feeling. Is that what this is? Ridiculous. Elves don't fall in love with humans. Still, I can't deny the way my heart hammers in my chest, how my ears twitch at the sound of her voice, and how my body tightens at the sight of her. The very sight I only still have because of her. Whatever these feelings are, one thing is certain. She will be leaving with me. Even if that means we skip the suspicious dinner invitation altogether and I steal her away in the night before anyone notices.

I slowly approach Kaliyah's chamber door, giving the idea a second thought. Yes, that could work. By the time we reach Yurakora, there'll be nothing the Champion can do about it. Just as I raise my hand to knock, I hear another voice inside. A male's. A guard? If any man dares to lay a hand on her, there isn't enough steel or spell work in the world that could keep me from shattering every bone in his body. They would live only to experience the agony of living each day unable to walk or speak. Let alone ever sire children. I lean in closer. The voice is unfamiliar. But it can't be a guard. The tone is too casual. Whoever he is, she knows him well. Well, enough to sound relaxed. Cheerful, even.

Then the man's voice says, "Are you expecting someone?"

Interesting. Even while I'm cloaked in stealth, he knows I'm here.

"Ummm, why?" Kaliyah responds.

"Because there's someone prowling outside your door."

"Really? Let me check."

"No. I'll go."

"No. You sit. It's probably one of the attendants. I told them not to come in. I don't want you scaring them."

I lightly tap on the door. It would be awkward if I just stood here, doing nothing. She might think my lurking is deliberate and strange, especially after the way our last conversation ended.

"One second!" she calls out, then mutters softly, "I mean it. *You stay.*"

KALIYAH

I open the door, and my eyes widen slightly in surprise.

"Arrio. You're still here."

"Yes, I am," he replies, trying to tilt his gaze past me and into the room.

I narrow the door's opening. "I thought you would've left already. Now that I... you know—"

"I'm just about ready to depart. There's something I wish to discuss with you before I go."

"*Okayyy.* What's up? Is it the compul—"

He stops me, clearly knowing where I was going with it. If it has nothing to do with the compulsion, then I don't understand why Arrio is still here. He opens his mouth, then closes it again.

"Did you come here just to give me the silent treatment? I swear, it's like you have a kink for making me wait to hear you say anything."

"I apologize. I don't mean to make you feel that way," He says, eyes again trying to sneak a glance into the room.

I squeeze the door tighter. "Okay, then spit it out. Otherwise, you can say what you've got to say to the door."

"Do you have company?" he asks.

I let out a deep sigh. "More questions for me. Well, I'm not in the mood. If you ever decide you'd rather be the one doing the talking instead of me, then you can speak to me during dinner. Bye, Arrio." I move to shut the door.

But he places a hand on it. "No, wait. I—" He freezes midsentence. His face shifts into an expression I've never seen on him before. I glance over my shoulder to see what or who he's looking at.

As I should've expected, Mitus didn't remain seated. He stands behind me, wearing a dubious scowl.

My head snaps back to Arrio. "Like I said... we can talk at dinner." I use my full body weight to push the door closed and lean my back against it.

"Who was the elf?"

"Oh, him. That was Arrio."

His eyes narrow. Then they rise from me and pierce the door I'm pressed against. "What's wrong?" I ask.

"What did he want?"

"I honestly don't know."

"And how do you know him?"

"Does it matter?"

"You don't usually see elves in a place like Palloria. Demi-humans are too low-level a species for their taste. And he's a Falorian elf."

"Falorian elf?"

"Falorian elves are the only ones with skin as dark and hair as white as his. They also tend to hold high-ranking positions in Yurakora, but not always. Most elves don't play well with other species. But Falorian elves are the strictest of them all. They'd sooner toss you into the Castdor deserts than keep company with humans."

"Oh, really?" I was shook. In the last fifteen seconds, I'd just learned more about Arrio from Mitus than I ever had from Arrio himself.

Mitus continued, his voice a little quieter now. "Then there was his scent. It was faint... but familiar."

Ooh, now this, I was curious about. The time Arrio let me sniff him, he didn't smell like anything. Like nothing at all. But if anyone could pick up on his body odor, it would be the blue demon with a super sniffer.

"Yeah? And what did he smell like?" I asked, maybe a little too intrigued.

"You." His eyes slowly lowered to meet mine.

My spirited expression dropped. *Oh... shit.* I was sure he could see the color drain from my face. The sound of my gulp was so cartoonishly loud, it would've been funny if I didn't feel like I was one wrong move away from triggering a full-blown rampage. This man had traveled all this way to find me, confessed his love for me multiple times, and promised to take me away and do so many things for me and *to* me. There was no way in hell I was about to tell him what happened between me and Arrio last night. Because it's not like we were ever together. So, I don't owe him an explanation.

What happened between me and Arrio was out of necessity. It didn't mean anything. And even if it did... I'm a free woman. I can do what I want, with who I want, whenever I damn well please. I held onto that thought like a shield, fully prepared to hit him with a, *'Oh really? Huh. That's weird'*. But then I saw the serious look on his face. And in that moment, I knew there was absolutely no way I could get away with that.

"Kaliyah." The way he said my name in a tone lower than low, told me he was going to make me tell him why, one way or another. He leaned in toward me, but his eyes didn't meet mine. Because mine focused just beneath the curl of his lips. But I knew that look. That wasn't one of his usual cheeky grins. No, this one was different. This one smelled like murderous intent. And I knew it wasn't directed at me. If I tell him the truth about what happened between Arrio and I, he *is* going to kill him.

No wait. He can't. Our deal. He can't hurt or kill anyone as long as I don't break our deal. But the way he's looking at me right now. He might just force me to break it, just so he can break Arrio's neck. A second obnoxiously loud gulp hit the air. *Okay. I got this.*

"If I tell you, you have to be chill about it. No getting angry. No breaking things or going full blue devil on me. Promise me that, and... I'll tell you."

He doesn't look happy in the slightest. He pauses for a moment. Longer than a moment, actually. So long I start to get nervous. I have no idea what's going through his mind right now. But I can guess. Just when I think he's about to object, his body relaxes as he leans away from me and gives me a smile.

"Okay. I can do that."

"Really? You can?"

"Yes."

"You sure? Because the way you're looking at me now—"

"Kaliyah. I promised you I would behave, so I will behave."

I hesitate for a moment. I can't read him. He looks calm and sensible, but that's the problem. He's almost never those things. I give it one final thought before opening my mouth.

"Okay, the day I... ran away." Saying the words out loud felt strange.

"The Namma stones brought me here. Like, directly to the palace. Right in front of the fox princess. And the first thing she did was lock me in a dungeon cell."

His brow twitched. He was totally trying to hide whatever he was thinking. I hadn't even gotten to the next part yet. Maybe I shouldn't. I watch him for a few more seconds. When he seems to keep his cool, I continue.

"The cell she placed me in was with him."

A second twitch.

"While I was there, we made a deal. He would basically protect me, in exchange for food. After he saved me from that rapist wolf guard, I thought we became friends. But Arrio made it abundantly clear that it was just the deal compelling him and... and that we definitely weren't friends.

"So earlier today, I ended our deal so he could return home. We were trapped together so long, it would be weird if he didn't smell a little like me." My tone fluttered slightly at the end, hoping he wouldn't make such a big deal about Arrio. But based on how wide his eyes had become, maybe that was just a pipedream.

"Rapist wolf guard?" Mitus growled, his chest rising with anger. I shouldn't have said that part. I thought it might make Mitus see Arrio in a better light, but now I'm not so sure.

"Yeah, but don't worry. Nothing happened. Like I said, Arrio saved me. Killed the guards."

"Guards? More than one?"

No matter what I say, he's not going to like it. "Yes, there were two of them. But I think the other was just the lookout." A chill travels through me as the words escape, and I picture that moment in my mind. Arms crossed over my body, trying to shake the cold.

His eyes follow my movements. "How long? How long were you locked in this dungeon for?"

"Too long," I whisper. "I was trapped in that tiny, hot cell for nearly the entire time I was away from you." I chuckle bitterly. "It was really no different than the time I spent in the mountain with you. Only there was little light, and it was so hot, and I had panic attacks almost every day." The emotions well up inside me at last. "There was never any fresh air, not even a glimpse of the outside." Tears begin to run down my cheeks, tears I thought I'd long been empty of. "Every single day, I couldn't breathe, and no matter how much I begged and pleaded, no one came. I thought I was going to die so many times." My voice breaks. "I should have never ran. I should have never left you. Then I could have at least pretended my friends and family were okay. That I could one day go home. But now... now everything is fucked and I— and I—" My breaths shorten, and the familiar panic starts to take over, only knowing it's coming makes it worse. "I— I—"

In one swift motion, Mitus pulls me into him, his arms wrapping around me so tight you'd think I'd have an even harder time breathing. But the opposite happens. It's like oxygen is blown directly into my lungs as I float weightless in the sky. In his arms, I feel like everything will be okay. That somehow, by some miracle, things will work themselves out. But I know it's not true, because just as my body relaxes into his, he leans in close, his lips brushing the curve of my ear as he whispers, "I wasn't lying when I promised I'd behave. I thought I could. But not after this. For what she did, for what she's done to you. The fox princess will die. Slowly, agonizingly. She will suffer... and then she will die."

My eyes snap wide open.

"I won't be keeping my promise. She will see the full heat of the Blue Demon. And she will die. The guards that run to her aid will die. The servants that call out for help on her behalf will die."

"You can't. She's the princess." I say nervously.

"She will die."

A twist of dread tightens in my chest. I was so focused on Arrio, that I didn't expect his fury and madness to spill over to her. She's one of three beings I despise most in this world. But what would that mean for him? For me? For Jemma? She was the one that helped free me. The king might go after her too. A champion believed to be involved in the death of a royal, it might even start another one of those wars.

"Mitus." I whisper.

"She will die."

I tilt my head back to catch a glimpse of his face. Ever calm, ever relaxed, with not a hint of anger or aggression in his tone. It sends chills down my spine.

I squint at him. "As long as our deal is in place, you can't."

A slow, crooked smile curls his lips. "Kaliyah," he says, voice thick with promise and peril. "*She will die.*"

ARRIO

There's an actual Ordu'kai orc sitting across the table from me. The ancient text say the Great Vireth-Kai, the only one to hold authority over the deities, is the reason why the blue orc exist. A living omen that the world is set to begin again, that balance must return when peace and prosperity choke the world dry. But the texts can also be interpreted another way. When an Ordu'kai steps into the light, it is to serve the Great Vireth-Kai's wrath to sow chaos, destruction, and punish those favored more by the deities than himself. What does he want? Why is he here? And what is his connection to Kaliyah?

The Princess shifts in her seat, nerves taut. Her eyes dart to the orc, her behavior suggesting there's no sign of alliance forming between them. Instead, I'm able to sense the bloodlust that radiates off him and its directed at her. What has happened between them? What is restraining him from acting? I must get Kaliyah out of here before things get serious. A server enters the room, pouring drinks. Kaliyah gestures, that she doesn't want a drink, and the server skips over her cup and moves on to the orc's. Without a second thought, he growls, "Leave it." With malice in his tone, he ordered her to leave the pitcher and she does.

"Mitus," Kaliyah whispers.

How do they know each other? Once, she mentioned escaping a blue demon. Did she mean him? If she's afraid of him, she certainly doesn't show it.

She keeps calling him Mitus. Could it really be him?

I remember a lesson from my youth about the origins of the first Ordu'kai orc. The text was brief. There wasn't much research since the species is so rare. The most recent information I could find was about the last sighted Ordu'kai. I believe his name was Carmitus Delmorr, a complete tyrant. He became the reigning Overlord of Bloodthorn and quickly began claiming territory beyond his region. I wasn't born when it happened, but my uncle was. He carried the story like a wound. He had serious concerns that the Ordu'kai threatened to unleash his monstrous army on Yurakora after his demands for resources found only in our lands were flatly denied. When he brought his worries to the Elven Triad, they ignored his warnings and dismissed the orc's threats. Thus, is generally the case when it comes to any matters occurring in the world outside our walls.

So my uncle took matters into his own hands. Teaming up with the champion of Palloria as well as the rejected champion of Yurakora, the great mage and the Ogre King. On his return my uncle told everyone that him and his party managed to defeat the orc. Still, he was met not with gratitude. Instead, the three ruling bodies of Yurakora, his brother among them, condemned his defiance. His sentence, exile. My father's decree was clear. If he ever returned, he'd face trial for treason, and the shadow of death would loom.

Kaliyah reaches for the pitcher, trying to pull it away from him. The orc only smirks before taking one gulp, then another before stopping abruptly. He cups the rim of the mug with his fingers, frowning as he stares at it intently. In the next moment, the metal frame is crushed between his fingers like it's made of paper.

"What's wrong?" Kaliyah says, looking nervous, scared even. I tense as well. The orc rises, his eyes fixed on the pitcher. He lifts it with both hands, then spits a spark of blue flame into it. I brace myself, expecting the alcoholic wine to burst into roaring fire. But that doesn't happen. A thick, black smoke coils up from the pitcher, curling like a living thing, swallowing the space above it in a choking fog.

"What is that? What's going on, Kaliyah?" The champion questions, next to me.

The orc snarls in reply, eyes darkening. "This is old magic. Magic I've met before, courtesy of that accursed mage. I knew the fucker was still alive. Thinks he can poison me. Didn't kill me last time, won't kill me now."

"Poison?" The words ripple through the room.

"The wine is poisoned?" Princess Sarianna's gaze sharpens. "Elania, I want to know who prepared this wine."

"Um... I-I'm not sure, your Highness." the serving attendant stammers.

"Princess Sarianna, you drank the wine."

"I know, Lymon. As quickly as you can, retrieve the royal healers."

"Of course." Lymon says.

The Princess gives her attention back to the orc, "Sir Mitus, do you know the root origin of the magic? Our healers will have an easier time if they knew what—"

"No one leaves this room." The orc yells, with a vicious tone.

The princess's guard ignored the orc entirely and made for the doors, urgency in every step. But he never reached them. In a blur of motion, a blade hurls across the room and buried itself in the back of Lymon's skull. His body crumpled. Lifeless. The echo of his fall swallowed by stunned silence.

"Lymon!" The princess gasp.

The three remaining guards reacted instantly, swords drawn, eyes locked on the orc. Mitus didn't hesitate. He reached toward the table, grabbing a fork and two spoons and with a flick of his wrist three more bodies dropped. The clang of steel falling from dead hands. I froze. My eyes snapped to Kaliyah. I had to reach her *before* his fury turned toward her next.

I was just about to act when his voice cut through, "Move Falorian and you will die."

I ignored him and stood. Then *something* flew toward me. He was fast. So fast I hadn't seen him move. One moment his hands were still, the next, death was sailing through the air. Fortunately, I was fast too. My shield of magic materialized just in time. Steel rang against it with a sharp crack, sending sparks tumbling across the floor.

"Mitus, don't. Stop. I don't understand. How are you doing this? You're breaking our deal."

He looks down at her. "Rest assured, I haven't broken anything. I haven't harmed or killed a single *human*."

Kaliyah blinks, the word catching in her throat. "Human... Human?" she repeated, confused, as if hearing it for the first time.

He gave a single nod, "Besides you and the one across from you, everyone else is either demi or elf." His eyes flick toward me.

The princess addresses Kaliyah "Madam Kaliyah, please convey to him—"

"Don't you fucking speak to her. You will soon be nothing but a tangled mess of fur and hogswine scraps. I had plan to kill you out of my Kaliyah's sight..."

My Kaliyah? Has he claimed her in some way?

"...after how you made her suffer. But then you try to poison me? You've only given me an excuse. She needs to see you bleed as much as I do. You must think yourself a clever fox, seeing that this specific magic is tuned to me alone. Everyone here could drink a thousand cups and it would have no effect on them."

Kaliyah steps in. "Mitus, if you've been poisoned, let the princess call her doctors or healers, so they can help you."

He lowered his view to her. Eyes glowing an unnatural blue. Pupils thin and sharp as a predator. "You have nothing to worry about, Kaliyah. This magic won't kill me. It was designed to first attack the root of my essence, then spread through my body like venom. But one thing that cretin doesn't seem to remember is that my core runs hot. So hot, it'll burn through the magic before it has the chance to take hold. It'll take time. And it'll hurt like hell. But I'll survive."

As if to prove it, a flicker of pain tightens his jaw as dark veins began to rise beneath his skin, spidering across the sides of his neck. They pulsed like a second heartbeat, writhed for a moment, then slowly began to retreat. Sinking back under his skin as something inside him had already begun to consume the poisonous magic. The cycle repeats as his body battles the effects.

Eyes locking onto me as he tilts his body in my direction. He's studying me. "You know, this reminds me of that little tactic the hooded mage and the Elven knight pulled all those years ago."

I hold back a twitch at the mention of my uncle. The orc bared his teeth between something of a grimace and a grin.

"Come to think of it... your elf magic is strikingly similar to his. You help Kaliyah and for that I will give you an option. Tell me where the mage hides and I will consider sparing you. Or die now."

So he really is who I believe him to be. How the hell is he still alive? I reinforced my shield, bracing for his next strike. Then, out of nowhere ice began to crawl across the table, thin and creeping like a living frost.

Mitus snapped, eyes locking onto the champion, but pointing at Kaliyah. "Mortal woman. Your life will be spared only for her sake, but my patience runs thin. Don't make me test the limits of our agreement."

The champion's gaze flickered to Kaliyah. She gave the faintest shake of her head. *No. A silent warning. Don't provoke him.* I don't know what agreement he's referring to, but Kaliyah is right. If the texts hold any truth, he's a high-class mythical beast with strength and speed nearly unmatched. She may have just saved the champion's life. Mine on the other hand is in danger.

I've never faced a beast like this before, and in my current state, I don't know how I'll fare. If it comes down to it, I might last long enough to land some damage, but not untouched. However, that's not even considering getting Kaliyah out of here alive. I can't protect her *and* fend him off at the same time. My only other choice is to kill the blue orc. I suck in a deep breath, steadying myself to unlock my magic. The orc's claws elongate, as he shifts into an attack stance. We both lower our bodies, eyes locked, muscles coiled for the strike.

"Kaliyah, what's wrong?" The champion calls out heavy with concern.

"Ahhhh." Kaliyah's hands clutch at her chest, her body folding forward onto the table. Instantly, all eyes snap away from me and Mitus, to her. Mitus steps back, eyes narrowing. He spins her chair gently around and kneels down, bringing himself level with her.

"Kaliyah." He whispers.

"It hurts... Mitus," she chokes out, clutching her chest tighter. "It hurts so bad."

Without hesitation, he reaches forward, ripping at the fabric of her top. I move slowly around the side of the table, watching his eyes go wide, scanning her chest. "What's wrong with her? Is she okay?" I ask, my voice tense.

His gaze shifts sharply to the princess. "Undo the magic. Now." His guttural growl vibrates through the air.

"Magic? I... This wasn't me," the princess stammers, eyes darting nervously.

Mitus doesn't wait. Rising to his full, towering height, he strides over to one of the trembling servants nearby. With a rough grip, he grabs her arm and hauls her forward until she's directly in the princess's line of sight. With a furious scowl and without hesitation, he snaps the servant's arm like a twig. The sickening crack reverberates through the room as her scream pierces the intense silence. Every eye locked on him. The orc's eyes darken.

"Elania no. Please, Sir Mitus."

SNAP.

"Stop, she has nothing to do—"

SNAP.

"She's just a servant girl, you monster."

SNAP.

"I— I don't… wait just wait. We can figure this out." The Princess tries to reason with the orc. The servant's agonizing screams engulf the space until…

SNAP.

Her cries falter and quiet once again sweeps over the room. Her body goes limp, her broken limbs hanging uselessly by her side. Not a single breath stirs the air. Everyone but me is caught between shock and horror. I would take this chance to go for Kaliyah, but I know for not one moment he has taken his attention away from her. I don't understand. How has this happened? How was Kaliyah affected with the same poison. She never even drunk the wine and even if she did… this doesn't make sense.

When the orc spoke of his core, was he referring to *his* soul. I closed my eyes and peered into the orc's essence. His core was larger than most. That much, I expected. But its color, a pale, dark blue wasn't what caught me off guard, it was the fire. A bright blue flame wrapped around it, alive and devouring. The sight struck me with almost as much disbelief as when I first looked upon Kaliyah's true spirit. I looked closer. The black veins were trying to stretch around his core. The flaming energy burned them away slowly. He was right.

I turned my gaze towards Kaliyah concerned. My jaw clenches as I witness the same black veins wrapping around her core much faster than his. And unlike his, hers wasn't fighting back. The magical venom isn't burning away. It twisted around her in a strange way as if it was not directly connected to her, but like something that is roped around her. No, not a rope. A binding…? *A tie.*

"You." Mitus's finger pointed at the trembling male attendant.

"No, please… please. I have a wife. A child." The man's voice cracked under the weight of his terror. "Please, I don't want to die." He turned his gaze toward the princess, eyes wide and glossy with tears. "Princess, please he—" He stopped. Breath caught. Body frozen. Mitus was behind him in an instant. The servant's body locked in place. And then fear soaked through his pants, a wet trail down his leg.

"Please…" he whimpered.

Mitus didn't speak. Only reached out slowly and curled his claws around the back of the man's neck.

"Undo it. Now."

The princess's body shakes. Tears spilled down her face, unchecked, and through clenched teeth as she mutters, "*I can't* because it wasn't me. Kill every remaining person in this room and that fact will not change."

A second goes by. Only a second.

"Your highness. Tell my wife—"

SNAP. He is dead before he could finish. Then out of nowhere, pain lances through me sudden and not of my own. It cuts deep from within and it is unmistakable. It's Kaliyah. I can feel her. I can feel her pain. I can feel the unraveling thread of her life.

She's dying. And I know I'm not the only one who feels it. Mitus goes still. His grip loosens. His attention, once razor sharp on the princess, snaps away. The man in his grip crumples to the floor. Forgotten like he was nothing. Because *he is nothing*. The only person in this room that matters to me is…

"Kaliyah."

EPILOGUE

KALIYAH

I can't move. I can't scream. The pain is everywhere, and I'm trapped inside it. It crawls through my veins, burning and corroding every nerve, every fiber, every breath I try to take.

It hurts, it hurts, *it hurts~!*

My insides feel like they want to liquefy and scorch at the same time, as if I'm melting from the inside out. The agony tightly squeezing and twisting around me in waves of unbearable torment. It's like I've been dropped into the heart of a wildfire, and at the same time, drowning in a vat of acid. The smoke coils down my throat, thick and choking, eating away at me. What the fuck is happening to me? It hurts. It fucking hurts. This is the worse pain I have ever felt in my life. Please.

Please~ I can't take this. It hurts so much. I want to scream. To shout until my lungs burst. But when I try, no sound comes out. Nothing but a silent cry trapped inside me.

"Orc!" Arrio calls out, now fully in my line of sight. "You have a soul tie with her, don't you?"

Mitus ignores him, as if he's not even there. "Kaliyah, my love. Just hold on. The magic will burn out soon. You're strong. I know you can handle it."

"You're wrong," Arrio says urgently. "Because of your connection, the venom of the magic has spread to *her*. It's eating her alive. Unlike you, she can't burn it away. And her body is mortal, so it's working faster through her. She won't last long enough."

Mitus hissed, baring his tusks fully. His breath came heavy with fury and fear. His tone lethal. "If you know this Falorian, then tell me how to help her. I know you have a connection to the elven knight. Which means you're probably responsible for this as well. I swear to you, if she dies, *so will your people*. Every last fucking one. I will make sure your species goes extinct."

"Threaten me all you want Ordu'kai, but I would never allow you to bring harm to my people. And as for Kaliyah, I would never endanger her because she is my—"

Mitus's gaze sharpens tightly. "She is your *what*?"

They need to stop. Everyone just needs to shut the fuck up and get me to a doctor, a healer, a fucking mending mistress. I don't give a shit. Just please make the pain go away. *Jemma help me.*

"The only way to stop the venom from claiming her life is by severing the connection from you. And there's only one way to break a soul tie. One of you must die."

My body doesn't flinch, it can't. The pain has hollowed me out too deep for that. *One of us has to die?* Shit. I don't care anymore. The pain... it's too much. I'd rather die than suffer through anymore of this. I need to turn off the agony.

"Kill me." The words are just a lite tremor on my lips.

"No," Jemma's and Arrio's voices overlap.

Kaliyah, please," Jemma begs, eyes wild, thick tears streaking her cheeks. "Just hang in there. I'll go. I'll find help. Just... just *wait*."

"Je— Jemma. I'm... sorry I left you guys."

"Don't Kaliyah. Please don't." Tears spilled freely. "I can't go through this again."

I wanted to flinch. To move. To do anything. But all I could manage was a twisted grimace, pain locking my body in place. Arrio stepped forward and raised his arms, positioning them like he was drawing an invisible bow. Light bloomed at his fingertips, a bright, purplish-pink. A number of glowing magical arrows formed mid-air around him. Their sharp points all aimed at Mitus.

"Carmitus Delmorr." Arrio says the name like a curse. "For her to live, you must die."

I didn't know he could do something like that. Mitus might actually be in trouble. But he still pays Arrio no mind. His only focus is on me.

"Arrio..." I gasped, barely able to speak through the burn crawling up my ribs. "Please. Don't."

"I must Kaliyah."

"No." I forced in a ragged breath. My every word scraped from the bottom of my lungs. "If you do it... I will *never* forgive you." I did my best to give him an expression that meant I was serious, but I doubt I was able.

Silence stretched. Arrio's arms faltered. Slowly, almost reluctantly, he lowered them. The glowing arrows dissolved, fading into the air like they'd never existed. Mitus clamp my chin between his fingers bringing my face back to his direction.

"I'm r—ready," I whispered, wincing. I hoped he understood what I meant because I don't think I can manage to choke out anything else.

Mitus kisses me. I know his lips must be warm and tender against mine. But I can't feel them. Not really. Not through the torture that drowns out everything else. I want to melt into them, to forget the pain. But my body barely registers his touch. All I feel is burning.

"See." he murmured against my mouth. His voice was rough with something I couldn't name. "I knew you didn't understand. The only thing left is to prove it to you."

I don't know what he's talking about, and frankly, I don't care. *Just end it already.* I've been ready for something like this to happened for a while now. I knew with my luck, this was always how my story would end. The signs were always there. And now, I'm ready. If heaven exist in this place then maybe I'll get to see those two knuckleheads again. It can be like old times. I wonder if grampa has made it there yet. It's not like I'm hoping the old man has kicked the bucket, but if I could see him again, I would *really... really* love that. Mitus stands. I close my eyes, bracing for the inevitable blow. A moment passes. Then, the shadow that lingers behind my closed lids moves away, pulling my gaze open once more.

Mitus stands several feet away, back turned to me. But his eyes flick over his shoulder. "For sure in the next life, because you'll always be *my Little Breakfast.*" He straightens his gaze, and his body begins to shift into his second form. His claws elongate as he lifts a hand toward his neck. A difficult sound to describe follows behind. Then, in one swift motion, he swings his arm to the side, sending a spray of blood splattering through the air before him. I gasp, the world blurring at the edges as every ounce of my focus sharpens on the man before me.

Don't tell me. Please, don't tell me. He collapses to one knee, a guttural choking sound ripping through the air and drilling into my ears. I want to yell at him, to reach out, but my body resists. The same hand moves to the area of his chest while the other clenches at his side. His movements are much slower. My eyes felt as if they were about to pop their sockets. With every ounce of strength I had left, I pushed myself off the chair, collapsing to the floor. My vision blurring as I crawl desperately to reach him.

Stop it. Mitus stop. The words wouldn't come out. Arrio didn't need to be fast to catch my slow, stumbling body. He grabbed me firmly, holding me back from the insanity unfolding before us. The princess crouched nearby, ears pinned back, her body trembling uncontrollably. Jemma's hands were clasped tightly over her mouth, watching me, unsure of what to do. The crack of his bones stings my ears as his claws sink into his chest. I heard the painful swishing of blood gushing. His body pulses, once, then twice. His tattoos begin to fade and the frame of his muscular body morphs back into his previous form.

THUD.

He falls flat to his chest. That's when I feel it. That's when I feel him disappearing, fading away from me. The venom's grip loosens, retreating fast, but in its place, a new kind of pain takes hold. I put my hand to my chest. *Something is missing.* I don't... *feel him anymore.* All of a sudden there is a coldness that feels like it surrounding me from the inside out and it's freezing.

"No. No no no no no no no no no no no~"

I shove Arrio aside, panic clawing through me as I crawl toward Mitus. My hands tremble, hovering just above his back. I *know* that the moment I touch him, the truth I'm too scared to face will become real. I barely control my shaking palms as they land on his still-warm skin. I take a deep, shuddering breath.

"Mitus. Mitus."

Tears spill uncontrollably as I bury my face into his back, fingers clutching the fabric of his shirt like a lifeline. I sob raggedly as my mind races. I'm desperate to make sense of the unbearable. This isn't real. This isn't happening. Mitus can't be dead. He's not dead. Maybe... Maybe this is another one of his jokes. What if he's being petty, trying to get back at me for what I did? The thought is incredibly ridiculous. Yet I cling to it, desperate for even the tiniest shred of hope. I slowly lift my head, eyes tracing the stillness at the nape of his neck. I search for the barest flicker of breath... of pulse... of heartbeat. And in the briefest moment, I truly believe I see one. I let out a shaky breath of relief.

"I knew it." I choke a bitter laugh, brushing the tears from my cheeks. "You're such a bastard. This wasn't funny."

"Kali... Um, I think—"

"No, Jemma. Don't. You don't know him like I do. This is what he does. He teases and taunts, just to get a reaction out of me. He's just that kind of asshole."

"Kaliyah," Arrio says softly from behind me, "he did what he had to do to save your life."

Like Mitus, I don't acknowledge him. I don't even understand why he's still here. I press my forehead to Mitus's back, my hands shaking as they rest against his unmoving form. "I already told you, I get it. You didn't have to do all this to prove anything. I was wrong, okay. Is that what you wanted to hear?" I pull in a breath so deep it hurts. "I'm sorry I ran. I'm sorry I denied the soul tie. And I'm sorry I didn't return your feelings." I blink hard, trying to focus. "But I'm here now. I'm ready now. So let's be done with this punishment. Okay?" I nod, even though he can't see it. "Okay." Another tear slips free. I swipe it away roughly. "Now get up already." I wait. One second. Two. I stare at his back, willing it to rise. Waiting for that familiar vibration of his chuckle, the sarcastic mutter under his breath. But nothing comes. And the silence begins to scream. "Fuck you, Mitus. First you love bomb me into caring about you and then you pull this shit. You don't always have to act like an actual fucking demon, tormenting me and shit. Get up, damn it. I mean it."

The princess opens her mouth. "Madam Kaliyah, maybe we should—"

"Shut the fuck up!" I snap, the hatred burning in my throat as I cut her off. "You stay the fuck out of this, you fox bitch. I'm sick of all this Empress and Princess bullshit." I hiss through clenched teeth. "This is all your fault. When I came to you for help, you locked me away and trapped me here." My voice drops into a guttural growl, a visceral passion digging into my being. "And I hate you for it. I hate everything about you, about people like you. I will never forgive you. I am not one of your damn subjects, so you have no right to tell me shit. Utter another mother fucking word to me and I will gut you where you stand." I feel movement at my knees. "Mitus." I call as my head swivels back to him. My eyes spots the pool of wet thick blood form around me, soaking into my pants.

Blood.

My heart began to beat erratically. My vision shaky and not knowing where to focus. I comb the space to see more of his blood scatter across the walls and floor.

So much blood. It could be fake. I want to convince myself, like those staged pranks you see on TV all the time. I grip his arm to turn him over, the weight of him was heavy, almost unmovably so. I struggled at first, but then Arrio stepped in to help. Just before we flipped him, I pictured his face. The stupid smirk I hated and somehow had grown to want to see all the time. But it wasn't there. Instead, all I saw was a deep jagged gash across his neck and a gaping hole in his chest. His face was pale... so pale. And there was no life behind his grey eyes, even though they were still open. He *isn't* faking. My blue orc, my mated soul, my Mitus...

"*He's* dead."

Summoned to a Fantasy World and Left to Die

To Be Continued...

EMPIRE OF SEBBARUS
LUNARIS
TITHMAR FOREST
RAZAKAR
YEN
BLOODTHORN REGION
V
THE L

The Yurakora Kingdom
Castdor
Magdara
Glendara
Kingdom of Palloria
SCA
N
E
ORLD OF THERION

WORLD GUIDE

The Four Great Nations:

SEBBARUS – A vast human empire known for its powerful armies and sprawling cities.

PALLORIA – A diverse kingdom where various races coexist, dominated by demi-humans.

YURAKORA – A kingdom of elves, governed by the Elven Triad.

BLOODTHORN – Realm of the Monsters & Mythical Beast *(not recognized)*

Figures:

CHAMPIONS – Chosen heroes summoned from Earth by the deities, gifted divine blessings to alter the fate of the world.

DEITIES – Powerful, god-like beings who govern natural forces, realms, and aspects of existence.

THE GREAT VIRETH-KAI – The supreme ruler of all deities, wielding unmatched divine power and authority over them.

YORKA – A mystical dryad who dwells within the ancient sacred tree of the elves, serving as its guardian spirit and a link to the natural and magical essence of Yurakora.

ELVEN TRIAD – Three individuals, the head of each distinct elven species working together as one collective.

THE COUNSEL – A group of advisers to the King of Palloria.

Beings:

DEMI-HUMAN – Beings with both human and non-human traits, often possessing animal features and enhanced physical abilities.

ORCS – Fierce, tusked warriors known for their brute strength and combatants.

ELVES – High class beings with long lifespans, pointed ears, and a deep affinity for magic and nature.

GOBLINS – Small, crafty creatures known for their evil violent cruelty.

HOBGOBLIN – An evolve version of a goblin. Higher in intelligence but just as deplorable as their smaller counterparts.

MAGES – Humans who channel power through enchanted crystals, using their focus and affinity to cast spells.

WITCHES – Arcane beings that craft curses and hexes. Unlike mages, their power flows from pacts, rituals, and emotion rather than crystals.

ADVENTURERS – Brave individuals, who take on quests for glory or silver. They travel the world facing monsters and mysteries.

SUCCUBUS – Alluring demons with charm-based magic.

VAMPIRES – low-level fae with a taste for blood and shadow magic.

OGRE KING – Towering ruler of ogre clans, wielding immense strength.

LAMIA – Mythical half-man, half-serpent.

KOBOLDS – Lizard-like creatures often found in tunnels or ruins; known for their traps and scavenging skills.

Animals:

HOGSWINE – A large, wild boar-like creature with thick fur and sharp tusks.

HOGLETTES – The small, piglet-like offspring of hogswine.

FOGTURP – Massive, slimy, and brightly colored frogs known for their low intelligence, but dangerous due to their size, unpredictability, and tendency to swallow anything.

IRONHOOFS – Sleek, scaled-skinned horses with long, whip-like antennaes and metallic hooves, renowned for their incredible speed and endurance.

JAGGER WOLVES – Ferocious wolf creatures with razor-sharp spiked fur and glowing eyes, known for their pack hunting tactics and ability to shred armor with a single charge.

RUTOKKI – A small, agile rabbit-like creature with a single unicorn-like horn, known for skittish nature, and surprising bursts of speed.

GLITZERS – A breed of dragons that exhale glittering flame with a magical shimmer that can nourish plant life.

Terms:

ADVENTURER'S GUILD – A central hub for wanderers, warriors, and mages. A location where quests are posted, ranks are earned, and legends are traded.

HOLY LIGHT CHURCH – A sprawling religious order devoted to the deities, commanding immense power through countless followers across the lands, often seen as a cult.

WHAT'S NEXT?

Fate isn't done playing her games. Kaliyah has a lot more crazy to face in Therion.

I mean, what's really going on with being a "Champion"? What's the deal with Kaliyah and Star? There are so many ideas I'm contemplating, straight up *hood* isekai vibes going on here. (for those who don't know, that's a genre of anime and for those who do, *let's go!)*

I'm not necessarily the type of writer who comes up with ideas on the fly. I like to plan and map out my story down to its core bones. Every once in a while, though, I'll throw in something random. Like Kaliyah being deathly afraid of frogs. I really want to have fun with that in book two.

Speaking of which, I've already come up with the title and it's a banger. I have a bunch of funny, chaotic, and spicy scenes in mind, but I also want to do something you guys don't see coming.

I considered giving you guys a teaser of the first chapter in book two, but I don't want to be locked into what I've written so far.

Oh! Audio book in the works, so stay tune for that as well.

HELLA GRATEFUL!

To every one of you who picked up this book, *thank you!*

Whether you read it cover to cover or reached for it during one of those "life is lifing" moments, just know I see you, and I appreciate you. Your time, your attention, your support. It all means the world.

To my village: thank you for the love, the prayers, and the push when I needed it. This book is for us.

THE AUTHOR

Shauna Sagaji is a black fantasy writer dedicated to crafting vivid worlds and exploring the intricate relationships of characters that reflect the rich tapestry of melanin voices often overlooked.

Her creative journey began at the age of ten when she discovered the power of her imagination, creating stories that felt just out of reach. A battle with cancer illuminated her true calling, igniting a deep passion for storytelling that she now shares with the world.

In addition to her writing, she excels in voice acting, and content creation, blending her talents to engage and uplift her audience. Fueled by faith and resilience, she is poised to make her mark on the literary world, one captivating story at a time.

To learn more visit:
SHAUNASAGAJI.COM

youtube.com/@sagajitv
tiktok.com/@sagajitv
instagram.com/shaunasagaj

Connect with the Author
and Publisher on Soical Media.

OTHER WORKS